The Path Of The King

The Path Of The King

I.M. Solomon

Kravitz & Sons
INNOVATORS IN PUBLISHING, MARKETING AND ADVERTISING

Kravitz and Sons LLC
1301 Farmville Blvd, Suite 104
Greenville, NC 27834

Published by Kravitz and Sons LLC.

ISBN: 979-8-89639-098-5 (sc)
ISBN: 979-8-89639-097-8 (e)

Library of Congress Control Number: 2025903720

Dedication

To my family and friends, thank you for keeping me on my correct path.

Disclaimer

This story will contain mild to graphic violence, harsh language, and reflect views and opinions that some readers may not agree with.

Contents

Chapter One

West

"…Fuuu—"

"Westley!"

Sophia gasps as I realize what just happened. I am completely freaking out, using more profanity in one sentence than I have ever used in my life. I may have overdone it, but in my defense, I believe I maintained my composure better than most would have in the last two days of enduring this tournament. Rhodain was supposed to walk into the castle and take the crown easily, but he was betrayed by the Queen, who wanted power for herself. His dying act stopped her from fulfilling this desire but thrust the responsibilities of the kingdom on me. *Me?* Of *all* people, I am barely thirteen! How am I supposed to run a kingdom? I can barely run a block! I have been thrown around, beaten, shot at, grabbed, scared for my life, and now *this*.

"I'm sorry, Sophia. It won't happen again…"

I inhale deeply and close my eyes, feeling myself relax. As I exhale and let go of that momentary peace, I see all of Baronune and it all comes flooding back.

"I'm sorry… I lied, just one more. *What the fuck!*"

In a fit of kicking, screaming, and flailing, I completely forget that Sophia is not the only one watching me. The knights in their plate armor and lizard-shaped helms surround her and Inspector Roxette with readied weapons. The private investigator pats down his long brown coat exhaustedly as his sunken eyes drag over the scene before him.

They all wait in the doorway leading to the roof, the final test to anyone who is foolish enough to seek kingship. Which describes me. I didn't want or ask for this. I *asked* Rhodain to keep us safe from thugs and the other contenders while he fought his way to the throne. I want to go home and take a shower. We slept in sewage last night; I *want* a shower! That will be my first royal decree …my first…royal…

"Oh, Gods damn it… I'm the king now."

As if on cue, the roof rumbles. The knights quickly shuffle Roxette and Sophia into the ring, which marks entry for the final battle royale participants. If that line is crossed, they must fight for the throne. Something I foolishly did when Rhodain fell off the castle after being stabbed. I have a bad tendency to react without thinking in tense situations, which led to me claiming the title of king once I was thrown onto the throne. If Rhodain wasn't dead right now, I'd kick him. If… Rhodain…wasn't…He's dead. Rhodain, the once Triumphant Knight of Fire, and I never got to thank him for protecting my cousin and I. I never got to say goodbye.

"You weren't supposed to die… You were supposed to be king."

Slumping forward, I bury my face into my hands that are still soaked in Rhodain's blood. My elbows rest on my knees as I block out the world, failing to notice that we are leaving the world behind. We sink back through the tower's shaft into the castle. The opening above closes as we lower into the throne room whose walls are decorated in sapphire and gold. A cerulean rug spills out across the floor from the base of my feet. I glance up. Sophia has moved to my side and places her hand on my shoulder. She examines the cut on my cheek and the nip in my ear. The clang of armor grabs my attention as all the knights kneel before me.

"Please, correct my understanding," Roxette keeps his same exhausted expression as he fixes his gaping jaw. "How have you become our king?"

"Yes, West. Please explain what happened."

Sophia pleas in conjunction with Roxette. I mouth out everything that happened from the moment I reached the rooftop, yet failed to apply sound to my muted voice.

Minutes pass and I remain fastened to the throne, not because it's the softest thing I have ever sat on, which it is, but because I can't find the strength to stand. Sophia's hand is welded to my shoulder while Roxette leans against a wall behind the kneeling knights. During the minutes I took explaining everything, a tall, slender man in a gold and emerald robe had entered. He's Terrence Sollace, the Grand Advisor to the late King, and now, me.

We could be mistaken as brothers, both sharing dark brown hair, hazel eyes, dusty tan skin, long legs, and gangly arms. He's quite more sophisticated, taller, and older than me. Possibly in his mid-twenties. He wears thin rimmed spectacles across the bridge of his nose and makes me by comparison look like rolled up garbage in my sweat-soaked and sandcovered blouse.

His presence strangely makes me feel self-conscious towards the scars etched across my arms and face from being thrown around in the tournament. He adjusts his spectacles as his hazel eyes run between Sophia and I.

"Is she your queen?"

"***Ew***..." Sophia and I answer in unison.

"No, we're cousins." I answer.

"Forgive me," Terrence apologizes. "This is quite... *unexpected*."

"Tell me about it."

"Well..."

Terrence pauses, seemingly having as much difficulty accepting this situation as me.

"That is my role, to fill you in and educate you on... your duties."

"I'm sorry," Sophia chimes in. "But...Is this allowed? He's a kid! Can a kid be a king?"

Everyone has been wanting to ask such a question since the alarm marking the end of the tournament.

"Unfortunately, the late King Augustus never specified such details when making the tournament's rules. I'm sure he never considered that a child would be foolish enough to remain on the streets, let alone, make it to the throne."

"I didn't do anything."

"Yes, as you stated," Terrence fidgets with his spectacles. "Rhodain pushed you into the throne shortly before his death. Still, the rules as stated proclaim that now that the tournament is over, you, Westley..."
"West," I correct.

"*Westley*... are the new King of Baronune."

Silence falls heavily across the room. No one cheers, but everyone exudes an air of concern. I can't tell if it is for me, the kingdom, or both.

"Am I allowed to resign?" I ask and Sophia smacks my shoulder.

"Don't be foolish! You can't step down as king. You'll send us right into another tournament... *probably*. I don't know how this works."

Like I do? All I can do is glance to the knights, to Roxette, and then Terrence.

"Considering that Arcasia has only had three kings since the Hellsfire days, this has never come up. As King Augustus' death was an assassination rather than a timely demise, we never saw fit to contemplate the lesser details of who would be most qualified to next take the throne."

As Terrence walks me through this, a long agonizing groan stretches from behind the knights.

"It's in writing," Roxette says, muffled through a hand used to stifle a yawn. "The boy is the new king. It was unorthodox but he found his way through the changing streets, to the top of the castle, and sat on the throne. He can't step down. That would leave the kingdom vulnerable as the only others who could be considered *'runner ups'* to the tournament are the girl and myself. She's no better than the boy, and I simply don't give a damn. I was here to solve the case of the murdered King. The boy says the Queen is guilty, I'm left to take his word for it. After all, he is the King, and the King's word is law."

"Wait, otherwise my testimony wouldn't have held up?"

Roxette studies me. "In your word against the Queen? No. Especially if she had taken the throne. If your statement had been true then you'd probably had been executed for witnessing her crimes, because…" "The King is law," I repeat and Roxette shrugs.

I glance between him, Terrence, and Sophia. No one refutes my claim.

I let out my own groan. "Then as law, I am doing away with this ridiculous tournament."

"That…would be wise, my King," Terrence begins, and I feel my body shrink into the throne. "Seeing how it can only be initiated in the death of the current King. And currently…"

"Our King can barely make his bed, let alone defend himself from an attack."

"Sophia!"

She shrugs as if to imitate Roxette. "What? It's true. I've seen your room."

I leer at her, taking my attention off the current turmoil, if only for a moment. My mind then continues to race as her voice echoes in my head. My room. Her home. Our families. With everything I've witnessed during the span of this tournament, there's been so much chaos, so much pain. Families will return home and be forced to rebuild their lives from the damages inflicted by the thugs and fighting. The King's tournament to find his replacement brought carnage upon the people of Baronune.

"We…" my mouth is dry as I turn to Terrence and the knights.

I struggle to form words and swallow repeatedly.

"W-we need to do something about restoring the kingdom… a lot of families lost their homes in this tournament. It is our responsibility to fix them."

A long pause follows this, and while I can't see the knights' faces from under their helmets, I can feel all their eyes on me.

Terrence holds his hands behind his back. "Yes, my King, we'll make a list of all your orders and demands to be announced to the kingdom tomorrow when the citizens come to witness the public crowning of their new King."

My breath escapes me again. I have to face the citizens of Baronune? All of them?! There's over a thousand of them. That's a lot of people to disappoint even if they do accept me as their new King. Besides our teachings, I rarely ventured out to my classmates in Old Country and they had a population of under fifty.

Both Sophia and Terrence rush to my side as I struggle to breathe. I explain that I'm gripping my chest where a thug's foot pressed into it, but they seem unconvinced. I can't help but recall the light that seeped through Rhodain's chest as he slowly turned to ashes. Sophia begins to shake me and even Terrence has real concern in his eye, most likely because he wishes to avoid immediately having another tournament.

"I'm okay, just… Tomorrow? That's so soon."

"Would you have us hide you away in the kingdom?" Terrence asks.

"Yes! I can agree to those terms."

"King Westley…" Terrence forces through his lips.

That title sounds like screeching metal to my ears. "You don't have to call me that."

"You're going to have to get used to it… my King." Terrence frowns as if coercing himself to remain professional against his will.

"Everyone is going to be calling you that and you must face your people. You cannot show cowardice, you cannot falter. If you show weakness, people will question the tournament and revolt, and then we'll be right back where we started. More carnage too, only this time the whole kingdom will have their sights on *your* head, and unlike our former King, you are not untouchable."

Terrence pokes me to prove his point. It's been explained to me that King Sorenson used unbreakable barriers of light with his own protection Divinity, making him impervious to outside attacks. Which is why Susan poisoned him, as he couldn't protect himself from internal hazards. Unlike Sorenson, I don't have any Divinity. The only reason I was able to make it this far was because of Rhodain. He should be the King. Not me.

"We'll give you the rest of the day to get used to your title and come up with all your demands for tomorrow," Terrence instructs.

"Not too many though, my King. You wouldn't want to spread your forces too thin on your first day. Some may come for your life on the spot. Ceasing the King of the Round Table Tournament is a good start. It might cause hesitation in their attempts to kill you if they know that they will not immediately be able to take your throne afterwards. And if we're stuck with you as our king, then it's best to let the kingdom know that from the start."

I extend my leer to my advisor. "I love how you say, *stuck* with."

"Might want to get used to that too," I hear Roxette contribute with another yawn.

"Don't you have criminals to arrest?"

"As a matter of fact," Roxette shifts his attention as if looking out a window. "There are a few scattered outside your royal lawn...your majesty."

"Wait..."

I think back to everyone that Rhodain faced. I see all of their faces in my head. The three knights and the former Queen.

My blood boils. "They're... *alive?*"

My fears and worries have shifted. With clenched fists I rise from my throne so abruptly that Sophia gasps. Even Terrence is taken aback as I order the knights to escort me to the courtyard.

I am surrounded as twelve knights with their weapons resting against their shoulder march us through the castle. Sophia is on my right, Terrence at my left. She tries to take my hand, but I haven't opened my white tight fists since leaving the throne room. I walk with an urge to bury them into Susan's annoying face, those emerald eyes burn into me. The sight of her ready to strike me down, ready to kill me because I stood in the way of her ambitions.

The very thought of her scheme to execute the former King and frame it all on Rhodain ignites so much anger within me that I feel I could cast flames just like the once Triumphant Knight. We stride through the now lit castle. There is not much to look at among the corridors, merely bricks upon bricks. As we enter the main hall, I'm reminded of how everything was such a blur when we first arrived. Too busy running for our lives as we raced to clear the Queen and Rhodain's names. These memories make my rage boil over. Two knights approach opposing sides of the massive castle doors. It takes two of them to operate the mechanisms that open the cast iron doors. The light pours in from outside and I'm reminded of the last shimmering glimpse of Rhodain before he pierced Susan with one of his fiery scythes and tossed her from the castle's edge.

He was truly magnificent. A great and radiant warrior that had risen once more to right the Queen's wrongs. She had killed his friend, and with the last of his strength, he had enacted his revenge at the cost of his life. Though he would have died either way, stabbed through the chest by her shining blade. It left a wound he wasn't able to heal with his own Divinity, tearing away his dreams and promises to be king and make the kingdom a home again for his sister to return to. If I knew anything more about her, I would find her and tell of her brother's final moments. How he jeopardized his path of redemption to make sure Sophia and I were safe. He even aided the Queen, who betrayed him as she had done to her King.

Finally reaching the courtyard, I find four groups of nurses, the medical personnel that was sent to assist the fallen knights and former Queen. They wear silky white gowns that reflect the sun and radiate health. To my amazement their silver sashes avoid being bloodied as they tend to the casualties.

"Terrence, how did they survive the drop?"

"How well are you educated in the magical arts?"

"Are you referring to the Arts of Divinity?" I ask and Terrence looks to me impressed and intrigued. "...Rhodain mentioned it."

"Yes, he did believe that magic came from the Gods, thus calling it Divinity. If you ask me, magic is magic, still, the arts remain the same. All the knights are trained under the Martial Arts to improve their strength, durability, and endurance to protect their king. The more they train and better they become at the arts, the higher they are ranked. From basic knights, to lieutenants, captains, commanders, and finally... Grandier Knights."

"Like what Rhodain was... and that's how he managed to surpass the others?"

"In a way. Rhodain and his two followers were quite young. Too young to be a part of the King's court, but they all possess great magical skills which aided them as they took on the ranks and surpassed all tiers of knights."

"How young were they?"

"Rhodain was hardly able to call himself an adult... while Nova and Avery were actually around your age," Terrence admits.

My age, and they became the strongest knights in the kingdom? Rhodain's actions throughout the tournament spoke for itself. He was truly skilled and very powerful with the Mystic Arts. So how powerful are Nova and Avery?

"That being said, the other knights are no pushovers. When Rhodain and the others fled for their crimes against the King..." "False crimes," I interject.

"Yes. The next commanders: Lawrence, Matthews, and Greg, took their place—due to their enchanted weapons. They were unable to advance into the Mystic Arts themselves, so they acquired weapons that could. With those weapons and their Martial training, they were able to withstand most magical spells and offenses. The catch is, that they must hold their weapons at all times, or become on par with any other knight."

"Where'd they get their weapons?"

"No idea. Items, artifacts, and runes in the Mystic Arts are scattered throughout the lands. You just have to know where and how to find them."

"And…" I struggle through a wave of emotions and curiosity to find my words.

"The Queen?"

Terrence glances back at me from under his spectacles. I wonder if he can sense my hatred for her or if he can see that I still haven't released my fists.

"Former Queen Susan must have studied elder magic with our King. He studied the Sacred Arts of Protection, to be our shield. My guess is that she studied the Sacred Arts to be our sword."

The moment the words leave his lips, I recall the radiant blade she had used to pierce Rhodain.

"Those that study the Sacred Arts who don't lose themselves to the light are gifted with great magic. They are blessed with protection beyond that of the Martial Arts leaving all other magic to seem like child's play. That's why the King was untouchable for so long. It takes a higher tier of magic-user to harm them."

"What's higher than the Sacred Arts?"

"There is nothing on this mortal plane higher than the Sacred Arts. Even the Corrupted Arts sit on an even scale to maintain balance."

If there are only four arts, Martial, Mystic, Sacred and Corrupt; how was Rhodain able to pierce Susan if she was protected by the Sacred Arts?

"Nothing on this plane…" Terrence's words echo in my mind. Nothing on this mortal plane. The Four Arts of Divinity.

"Divinity… *Gods*."

"You catch on fast, my King."

Rhodain had somehow acquired Divinity from Gods that was meant… for Gods? The sheer thought of this leaves my head spinning. I'm reminded of something else Rhodain had mentioned. How the concept of Divinity was not meant for the weak-minded. I now see why, and it's not until one of the nurses calls out for assistance that I'm brought back from my thoughts.

As one of the nurses stands to call for someone in the other group, I see Susan Sorenson, the Killer of Kings and former Queen who started this all. She lies motionless on the stone brick courtyard. There's a small crater from her impact. I imagine the Sacred Arts must have shielded her when she hit the ground. I nearly thought her lucky, but the river of red streaming out of her makes me reconsider such a position. The wound from where Rhodain pierced her continues to bleed.

He did break through her magical blessing, leaving her in a state of shock. She remains fixed on the sky, where Rhodain hovered with his blazing light in the form of a bird. She must be unable to comprehend how he managed to not only survive but wound her. Unfortunately, the wound was not fatal. I feel rage pouring out of me as every muscle in my body grows tense. I want to make her pay, make her miserable. Her eyes fall onto me. Those demonic emeralds. I am about to snap when Sophia rests her hands on my shoulders.

"West…"

Her voice is so soft, and full of concern and sorrow that I break. Tears rush from my eyes and I lose my grip, turning away to make sure no one sees me cry.

"You…"

Susan's voice creaks, broken and shattered. Reminding me of someone well beyond her age. An elderly woman unable to comprehend exactly who I am but ridden with familiarity. At first I question if the fall gave her brain damage, but I glance back and her eyes fix a glare that cuts through all befuddlement. She knows.

"You."

"Bitch."

I break from Sophia and Terrence to approach the fallen Queen. My surrounding knights open a gap for me to walk through. I stop only a few feet before Susan, glaring down at her weak and broken body.

"You have caused so much pain. To me, my cousin, and this kingdom!"

"*My* kingdom!"

She cries and I almost back away from her shout. Almost. I stand my ground and stare her down.

"No, you are no queen. You are a traitor, a murderer, and you deserve to die,"

A wicked smile weakly crawls across her face. "You can't kill me. I am protected."

Terrence breaks away from amongst the knights. "My King, we have restraints in the dungeon that have runes to weaken her magical abilities. It should be enough for the executioner to enact the death penalty upon her." Susan follows the sounds of his voice, but before she can usher a retort, his words hit her. He called me king. She studies me and I do not falter. I stand before her infused with a strength I never had before. Especially from when she last shed her sights on me on the rooftop.

"King?"

"You killed Rhodain…" I remind her.

"…But not before he tossed your royal ass from the castle, leaving him and I on top of the roof. He's gone, and I became king."

"You… the King?"

"Yes."

I answer and she gradually breaks into a painful laugh. She tries to hold her side, to cover her wound, but she cannot move. She's paralyzed, but her body is glowing as if her sacred Divinity is trying to heal her but can't. This doesn't keep her from laughing however, and she becomes hysterical as her cackles carry up towards the sky.

My glare grows as hot as the summer sun above. "Well, I'm glad this amuses you."

She continues to laugh. "Oh, you're going to die! The whole kingdom will die. You are no king. You are a child. You will not be accepted. The people will either laugh or cry because you'll lead Baronune to its doom. You have no power, no strength. Just a boy, pretending to be a man."

I feel my sudden vigor shrink to a whimper. I thought there was nothing worse than what had already happened today. I thought that my own doubts were bad enough. I thought that if I could rub Susan's failure in her face, that I could feel the slightest bit better. I don't, and the fort around my heart comes crumbling down. I am a kid, I have no power, and I have no idea what I am doing. This is clearly a mistake, and Susan is taking full glee in rubbing this in my face. Just like she had done to Rhodain, she has pierced me right where it already hurt.

I pivot and return to the knights and Sophia. I care not if she makes an attempt on my life. Honestly, if she did, she'd relieve some of the weight from my shoulders. Instead, she continues to laugh until she starts coughing up blood. The nurses return to her aid and I meet Sophia's worried eyes. Terrence interrupts my view, and approaches to address me.

"My King, what are your instructions until the execution of the criminals?"

I glance back to the fallen Queen and she peers at me through the wall of nurses.

"Do not kill them," I say in a whimper.

Terrence leans in as if he didn't understand me.

"Don't kill them." I repeat. "Infuse the dungeon cells with those runes and strip the former Queen of her Divinity. By then you should be able to properly treat her."

Terrence seems to struggle with my requests. "Uh… okay, but my King, that is not how we do things here."

"It is now. Killing her would be too easy. She will suffer from the consequences of her actions just like how I must accept the responsibilities of my title. As King, I am law, and I say there will no longer be executions."

I announce loud enough for the entire court to hear me. They do, and their silence is broken by whispers among the nurses.

"Rid the fallen knights of their weapons and lock up all those that followed the Queen's rule. They are traitors and not welcome in my court."

"Yes, my King. Is there anything else?" Terrence asks as I have one last glance on Susan.

"Yes, add ridding the banishment of magic on my list of commands."

I conclude and walk past Terrence, who now resembles a statue in his stillness. The knights escort Sophia and I back into the castle. I figure if I'm stripping the Queen of her Divinity, I can return the use of Divinity to the rest of the kingdom. How's that for a slap to your precious face Susan?

⬦◦⟡⟡◦⬦

Sophia and I return to the throne room. It is the only place I am familiar with in the castle that doesn't bring back memories of Rhodain or the Queen. Back on the throne, my hands clasp my head as my fingers dig into my hair. I can feel the sand and grime crawl under my nails. Sophia stands below me with one foot on the steps leading up to the throne's platform. She seems to want to approach, but I get the impression that she also wants to give me some space.

"West, how are you…?"

"Yesterday was bad, but today…it's been Hellsfire."

"I'm just glad you're alive. When the Queen…When Susan had the knights that were loyal to her release her. I thought… I didn't know what to think."

"Well, now they're going to rot in a cell for like, *ever*. I have no intent on releasing them in this century."

"I'm glad you didn't have them killed but…"

"But?"

"You're a king now, you can't let all that power go to your head."

"I made a couple commands on the spot, so what? I won't get power hungry, I don't even want to be a king. Rhodain did this to me."

"I mean, since you're technically from Old Country maybe they'll relinquish your title?"

That's right, only people from the Royal District can become king. This might be my way out of this. My hopeful considerations are interrupted as the throne room doors open and Terrence enters.

"My King, the traitors are being rounded up and Roxette is personally interrogating the knights to determine who still swears fealty to the Queen. *Former* Queen, excuse me."

"Thanks, Terrence. May I call you Terry?"

"In all due respect my King, I'd rather you wouldn't."

"That's fine. I understand what it's like to be called something you don't approve of," I reply, and we exchange a meaningful look.

"Anyways, we've come across the realization that since I am not from the Royal Districts of Baronune then I don't exactly fit the requirements to be king."

"We've already looked into that. Well, Roxette did. As you lived in Old Country, you require signed permission to enter Baronune."

"Oh…"

I knew that was going to come back to bite me.

"However, your birth documents state that you originate from within Baronune, Royal District, Commoner District, it makes you an official citizen, thus qualifying you to be king."

"I was born here?"

I look to Sophia and she looks as surprised as I am.

Given that she couldn't remember where the safe houses were, how am I to expect her to remember something like where I was born? My uncle left out many details whenever he talked about my mother. The realization hits me.

"Oh man, Uncle Lester is not going to like this."

Sophia shrugs. "I mean, he doesn't really have much of a say…"

"Can that be a part of my list? I'd like for my uncle to be escorted here. I feel he's owed an explanation, and I'd rather do that in person."

"That can be done, my King. We'll have some of the best remaining loyal knights retrieve him for you. Would you like him here before the ceremony?"

"If possible, though I know how difficult it is to catch the train from Baronune to Old Country."

"I'll see what I can do, my King. Until then, would you like me to show you to your chambers? We can also escort your cousin home so that her family doesn't worry once they've been released from the safe houses."

I glance to Sophia and she looks to me unsure. She was so disheartened when we didn't make it to the safe houses yesterday that I thought the mention of her going home would make her ecstatic. Yet their home is completely in shambles, there isn't much to return to.

"Actually, Terrence. If possible, can we make room for Sophia's family to be housed within the castle? At least until the restoration of their home is complete?"

Terrence squints at me through his spectacles, regarding me with such uncertainty as if this is so against the rules that I shouldn't have even bothered.

"With many knights being ushered into the dungeons, I'm sure we can make room. How many will be staying?"

I glance to Sophia, she smiles awkwardly, and I let out a sigh.

"Uh, do we have room for like… twenty?"

Terrence runs his hazel eyes between Sophia and I.

"I'll see what I can do… Follow me, my King… and erm, the King's cousin."

"Sophia, you may call me, Sophia."

Terrence nods and I remove myself from the throne. *My* throne. That's going to take some getting used to. I take Sophia by the hand, and we follow Terrence to our chambers.

Chapter Two

My Kingdom

The King's chamber is huge, with floors and walls made of jade and a bed of scarlet blankets, and gold sheets, is large enough to fit four people comfortably. A large painting of the late King hangs over the bed, staring down at me.

"So that's what he looked like!"

Sophia gasps, it has been years since anyone in Baronune last saw the King. August Sorenson was a man of radiance, his skin was brilliant, and his blonde hair feathered down to his shoulders. His beard was thick and heavy to the degree that it concealed his neck while rose-red cheeks sat on his gleeful face. His eyes were dark jewels of green. Fierce, yet welcoming, and by looking at his picture I can sense his strength, and his kindness.

Terrence stands behind us. "Late King Augustus was a man who only cared about protecting his kingdom. Since the Days of Hellsfire he was determined to make sure that no harm befell Baronune."

"The Days of Hellsfire," I think back to what little my uncle mentioned of it.

"That was when a wildfire burned through the continents and nearly Arcasia…?"

"In part…" Terrence gazes over his spectacles at me.

"Is that all you recall?"

I feel like I'm missing something. Even Sophia looks at me questionably.

"Is there more?" I ask, causing her to smack her forehead.

"You're unaware of the..." Terrence pauses. "...Dragon of Hellsfire?"

"The folktale?"

"Our history."

"It's a story! Dragons aren't real. That was just a way to describe the fire's destructiveness."

"Oh, my dear boy." Terrence lifts a hand to his forehead.

"In his defense... West just found out about magic, yesterday," Sophia interjects.

I feel a few sizes smaller. I grew up telling myself that magic wasn't real, and I now know it to be called Divinity and a gift from the Gods. Did I also convince myself that our history was a fairytale because it involved a dragon that wiped out the western regions formally known as Eurosia?

The story says that's why they called it the Days of Hellsfire, because a dragon blacker than night with flames that burned you for eternity scorched the lands of Eurosia into Arcasia. It forced the people to flee their homes and retreat to the East. It was said that you would still burn in the life after if licked by those flames. That's probably why I believed it to be a fairytale. How could anyone ever know such a thing?

I always imagined that the real story was that we settled here from across the sea, and one day a massive fire erupted that took the combined efforts of our people led by those who are now our kings to put out the flames before both continents were lost. How they accomplished such a feat is still unclear. Even the fairytales simply said that the three kings banded together to stop the dragon, but how it was defeated was never mentioned.

"I never considered that the tale could be true, what happened to the dragon? Did it just fly off and go to sleep?"

"It is unclear," Terrence admits, and I roll my eyes.

"I was still young. I just know that the three kings of Baronune, Woodsforge, and Dragon's Guard defeated the Dragon of Hellsfire, and with its defeat the flames eternally burning Arcasia dispersed, allowing our people to build the kingdoms we have today."

"There are holes in that story."

"Holes exist in every story," Terrence sighs. "But this is our history."

"Told by who?"

"The kings."

"And they were the only ones present to witness the dragon's defeat?"

"Yes, King Augustus and King Bruno of Dragon's Guard wanted to ensure the safety of the people. King Bruno led the people to safety while King Augustus held off the dragon with his shields of light. He had the only magic that could withstand the dragon's flames, but he couldn't defeat the dragon. So, King Ivan of Woodsforge searched the ruined lands for a means to silence the beast, and when he returned the dragon was defeated."

"That means the only one who truly knows the end to the tale is King Ivan then?"

"It's not a tale…"

"Well, unless I see a dragon's head on someone's mantle, I'm sticking with the wildfire explanation."

Terrence digs his fingers between his brows. "But that's…"

Sophia interjects again. "Just let him have this one. West is quite stubborn despite how smart he is."

Terrence looks ready to pull his hair out. I stare up at the picture of the late King. If the stories were true, he must have been as powerful as they say to be able to hold off a whole dragon by himself. How could I possibly measure up to that? My greatest feat was throwing a brick at someone's face. I am no knight, I have no Divinity, I am just West—and I am tired.

I sigh, "Can you have someone take that down? I'd rather not sleep with the late King hovering over my head. I have enough on my shoulders as it is."

"There will be someone in shortly to remove it. We will have an artist tomorrow to begin work on your portrait."

"That won't be necessary, I don't need a giant picture of myself. Instead, I'll take a full night's sleep, but first... Where can I take a shower?" I look around the room, searching.

Terrence leads me to my own personal washroom, it's absurdly large, about half the size of my sleeping chamber. For what purpose? It was just the King and Queen. The thought of Susan sends shivers up my spine. Hopefully the King had her sleep elsewhere, I don't want to be sleeping in the bed of a murderer. Terrence leads Sophia to her chambers and I take a well-awaited shower. When maids come to take the painting, I also have them take those golden bedsheets too so that I'll be able to sleep much easier.

The next morning, I awake feeling as if I had slept on a cloud. My body feels completely rejuvenated, as if the tournament never happened. Climbing out of bed almost proves to be its own journey with how big it is. I look frantically for something to wear, my clothes from yesterday are out of the question, but everything that the King's chamber provides is far too big.

I eventually decide to take a large red and furry robe that looked big even for the former King and wrap myself up in it until I look like a caterpillar within a cocoon. I shuffle to the door to where I'm met by the same maids in beige and white dresses. They look me over once and giggle. I blush as I sink into the fabric. To make matters worse, Terrence enters. "My King...what are you wearing?"

"I have no clothes here," I reply, my words muffled through the robe.

"Yes, well these are your maids. They will tend to your every need throughout the castle while I get everything in order for your ceremony today."

Terrence takes a second glance at me.

"Ladies let's get him fitted so that we can dress our King in appropriate attire. We can't reveal him to the public like this."

"Thank you."

I murmur and Terrence takes his leave. I find myself wondering how long it will take for him to retrieve my uncle. I also wonder if Sophia is getting the same pampered treatment as I am. I haven't been dressed since I was a small child, and that was Uncle Lester, not five women tasked to make me presentable. Their hands are so soft that they tickle me, making me squirm and get poked with needles as they fit fabric to my actual measurements.

This goes on for about an hour before one of the maids return with a satin set for me to wear until they can put together a whole wardrobe. While the maids busily work, I venture out into the hall of cold adobe stone to get some air. On my walk I run into Sophia, she's wearing a long dress that hangs off her shoulders. Her skin is so clean that I'm reminded of pearls, though she seems to be having trouble walking in her dress as even after she harks it up it still trails a few feet behind her.

"Well, that looks fit for a queen."

"Shut up," Sophia blushes. "I don't like it. The maids said to wear it until they can find something I'd be more comfortable in."

"It's better than the sewers," I tease and Sophia's faces fills with disgust from the reminder. "Well, while I was getting poked, I had an idea about the kingdom. How maybe we should turn the safe houses into homes for those that live on the streets. If one night was unpleasant for us, imagine living like that every day."

Just a few days spent in that tournament changed my entire perspective of the kingdom.

"I agree. Especially since you did away with the tournament. Might want to run it by Terrence first."

"The next time we see him." I say and the maids return, separating us to continue preparing us for the ceremony.

Before I'm properly dressed, Sophia and I have a lunch of beef stew and bread rolls. We skipped breakfast since it was all Rhodain could talk about during the tournament, and we didn't see fit to have it without him. "…We should honor him somehow."

"Rhodain?" Sophia asks between bites. "What about all the other lives that were lost? Many people died because of that executioner alone." "Yeah…can't forget about them either." I know those lives probably would have been spared had Susan not flooded Hunter's mind with bloodlust against Rhodain.

Sophia stirs her food. "Have Terrence include a tribute to the casualties of the tournament too. Susan's crimes should be revealed too. The people should know who's responsible for the king's death."

"I will," I glance up at her. "And you were worried about me making too many demands."

"Oh, hush and eat your stew." Her cheeks puff and I laugh at this.

As I stare into the chunks of beef on my plate, I think I should demote the executioner to being a butcher. That's not too different than what he was already doing. There's so much to address after all that's happened. It takes us some time to get our ideas sorted before Terrence returns in formal robes.

"The maids are ready for you, my King."

"Is my uncle here?"

"He's waiting at the Grand Hall where the ceremony will be held. You will see him once it is over and the kingdom tour concludes. We'll also arrange to have the rest of your family move into the castle as well." "Did you say kingdom tour?" I say with cheeks full of bread.

"Yes, once the ceremony concludes you'll be escorted around the kingdom to meet your people and have them greet you."

"Isn't that dangerous?" Sophia asks with a concern I share.

"If no one likes the idea of West as the King, won't they attack?"

"He will be protected," Terrence answers. "Roxette has finished sorting the knights that are loyal to the kingdom from the ones loyal to Susan." "That was fast," Sophia admits.

"Roxette knows his ways around an interrogation."

That's good to keep in mind in case someone else threatens my life.

We finish eating and I run Terrence through the list of changes we have for the kingdom.

"Maybe you should write it down and rehearse it before the ceremony?" He suggests, then escorts us back to our chambers to change.

The maids have me change into my ceremonial attire, explaining that they took the old King's bedsheets and turned them into something I can wear. I hope they deep washed them over, and over, and over again.

I am in brilliant gold from head to toe. Pointed shoes with steel tips, and a miniature version of the robes I cocooned myself in earlier drapes over my shoulders. I wear jeweled rings on each of my fingers, and my trousers and blouse are a heavy silk. My vest might as well be a mirror with how the light bounces off of it, and I hold a three-foot golden scepter with a ruby jewel at its head.

"That's called a Boisterous Stone, it will carry your voice across crowds." Terrence explains and is quick to stop me before I speak directly into it. "It is not for close quarters my King…"

I can hardly move in any of these clothes, while Terrence approaches holding a glass case with the crown that will be placed on my head at the ceremony. The final induction into the kingdom to tell the people, *"Yeah this is no joke, your new King is a child."*

As Terrence and I slowly make our way down the main hall, I wish I had even an ounce of the strength that Rhodain had. I can hardly breathe in this getup. I see Sophia also waiting for me in a light silk dress that matching Terrence with lines of silver that crown her head like a moonlit halo. She's surrounded by knights with her hands innocently placed at her lower abdomen with golden bracelets crawling up her arms.

"It is too bad that she is your cousin," say Terrence as we walk, and I look at him peculiarly.

He elaborates, "She would make for an excellent queen."

I don't dignify that with a response. She definitely looks great, pearls decorate her neck making her face and skin glitter as we grow near, and I catch a whiff of a floral aroma, but I wouldn't curse her too with the responsibilities of a whole kingdom.

We exit through the main doors of the castle and waiting for us are more of those steam-powered carriages. These are bigger, made of steel, and have passenger compartments that are cushioned with soft seats. Much unlike the ones Sophia's family used that had hardwood which made my back ache. We climb in while knights pile into the other carriages. Several remain outside on horseback and we ride through the streets. The homes I see as we head away from the castle are still in shambles. Former shells of warmth and protection left abandoned after the tournament. Terrence tells me that everyone present came from the safe houses to the Grand Hall for the ceremony. I prefer it this way as I want the kingdom to know that their homes will be restored as an apology to the chaos the King's tournament brought.

It doesn't take us too long to reach the upper east side of Baronune. A mass of people cheer and yell upon our arrival. Just like with the safe house, knights keep the citizens in line. I also see angry thugs balling their fists and throwing glass objects. Did they already find out that I was the King? Or is this how they naturally react knowing that their fun and games of mayhem is over? As one of the thugs prepares to throw another item our way, a knight on horseback with a forest green cape takes a double-edged sword and slices the thugs' hand off. There are screams and yells of agony as people rally around the one-handed man, but are pushed back and silenced by more knights.

"That was not necessary!"

"The lower class will learn to respect your authority," Terrence assures. "Knights will be patrolling the streets for weeks to make sure they get back in line. They may have gotten too accustomed to the tournament rules too quickly. For some, it was the day they were waiting for; if only to cause chaos."

I glance to Sophia. A beautiful frown meets my gaze and I understand that she doesn't like it either, but it seems some punishment must be enforced to maintain order.

Our carriages and knights round the back of the Grand Hall, a large iron forged cathedral with brilliantly stained-glass windows, standing as tall and formidable as the dome structure of the train station. "I am surprised to see that this went untouched."

"Certain buildings are protected under the kingdom's law that if damaged or defaced, the perpetrator would face the death penalty."

Terrence admits to me and I make sure to keep that in mind. I would hate to see anything befall these structures after I make my announcements.

The time grows near, our vehicles park, and the knights dismount as we exit the carriages. We enter through the Grand Hall's rear and I stand in a small, decorated room of bright lights. My heart races as the ceremony begins on the other side of a wooden door. I hear loud and bolstering horns echo through the cathedral and rattle through the halls. I can hear the citizens being ushered into the front doors. Is there enough room for all of Baronune out there? I hope not.

Less is more, and I would feel better facing less. Two people would be pushing it at this point. I'm still breathing heavy as Sophia glides in front of me. The dress trails like the one from earlier, but this one is a better fit for her to walk in. She takes my hands and I try to steady my breathing. She assures me that it will be fine. I want to agree with her, but my nerves won't let me.

"My King," Terrence walks up beside me. "It's time."

"Oh…"

I begin and Sophia quickly covers my mouth before I say anything unpleasant. I stave off hyperventilation and finally calm down. Sophia lowers her hand and leads me to the door. This familiarity is enough to ease my nerves so that I follow her without question.

Terrence steps before us and opens the door leading into darkness. I expected a long hallway of some sort, but I see nothing. Terrence steps in first accompanied by four knights. Finally, Sophia and I step through the door into the blackness, and I feel something move. The door closes behind us and we lift through a shaft much like at the tower of the castle. We rise and light opens up ahead. Voices grow louder, and louder until we breach the surface. We continue to rise above the people, a mass of blending faces that have all eyes on me. We sit high enough to where I can't determine any defining features, I can't make out any faces, but as the lift comes to a halt so do the voices. I feel their eyes on me, and a sense of astonishment washes through me. I try to swallow a lump in my throat.

"Ladies and gentlemen of Baronune," Terrence begins with a loud and boasting voice that vibrates through my scepter and carries through the cathedral.

Hundreds of people stand below me. I can feel my knees shaking. My grip on Sophia's hand tightens and I feel like I could faint.

"*Keep steady.*" She whispers to me.

Terrence continues as he extends his hand out over the crowd.

"Two days ago, a great tragedy befell our kingdom. Our King, Augustus Sorenson, came to Life's end and began his journey into Death's grace. As we know here in the Royal District that once our King has fallen, a new King must be crowned, and the only way that king is determined is by winning the King of the Round Table Tournament. Many fought, and many died. All in the search for our newfound King. It is within my pleasure that I announce the winner of the King of the Round Table Tournament..."

Terrence pauses as he turns to me. He shatters the glass case around the crown with an unseen force, *Divinity?* My eyes go wide as he steps aside, allowing for me to move forward in his place. To be recognized by the whole kingdom, it is no surprise that my legs do not move.

"*West,*" Sophia whispers as she ushers me forward. "*Move.*"

I forgot that she can out muscle me. I stagger forward, the silence is unsettling. Terrence stands behind me and nods for Sophia to stand where he was previously. She hops to the side, and I would have found it adorable if I weren't petrified.

Terrence continues. "People and Citizens of Baronune, I hereby introduce you to Westley Jameson, your new King of Baronune."

Terrence places the crown on my head. It's a bit big and he has to slide it back so that it sits right. No one cheers and my worst fears begin to echo outside my thoughts.

"He's a child!"

"This is a joke!"

"How could he win?"

"Where are your parents?"

"Where's the real King?!"

Outrage breaks the silence. More and more voice their opinions, until it all turns into a muffled rage. Terrence steps around to my side. Sophia's face is unsettled, and I am covered with cold sweat. I feel a nudge and see out of the corner of my eye that Terrence is edging me forward. He's nodding me to the angry crowd as if to say, *"Do something. You're the King now."* It's not comforting, yet I dig through every ounce of me to find my voice, and I raise my scepter.

"E-Excuse… Excuse me." I struggle. The anger and rage of the people are like a barrier I can't break.

I raise the scepter higher. "***Hey!***"

The scepter vibrates and my voice becomes a sharp knife that cuts through hundreds of collaborated voices, leaving me as the only sound in the room.

"Now that I have your attention, it's true. I am now the King…"

Voices begin to protest but Terrence raises his hand and the knights on the outskirts of the cathedral unsheathe their weapons to silence the crowd. Why couldn't he have led with that?

"Thank you, Terrence. Now, as I was saying…" I try adding strength, confidence, and authority into my voice.

I manage one out of three. "I am your King now. If you don't like it, well… neither do I."

"West!" Sophia snaps and Terrence groans.

"Let me finish."

There will be no winning over the people in a matter of seconds. There will be no way I can convince them to trust me after I have done nothing to earn their respect. The only thing I have to offer them is the truth.

"I made my way to the top of the castle, but not to become King. I only wanted to survive and protect my cousin. The King of the Round Table Tournament was unkind and awfully stupid. Many families have lost loved ones, and many families have lost their homes. That is why my first order is to ban the King of the Round Table Tournament and avoid any of this nonsense from happening again."

There is no uproar. I feel that there's a conflict as if the people are torn on the matter.

"My second order as King is that your homes be restored after all the damages received from the tournament." There's a hint of glee from that one as I hear a few cheers.

"Without the tournament, there will be no need for the safe houses. So, they will become shelters for those who don't have homes."

Silence again. I guess the homeless are outside the Grand Hall. Not everyone made it inside for my glorious ceremony. I hit my main demands for what I want to do to change the kingdom.

"…There will be more regular trains out into Old Country for rations, and that permission slips will no longer be needed for entry…" Since that did little help to me in this whole ordeal. I guess it's my own little vendetta.

"Now, allow me to admit what became of King Sorenson, he was betrayed, not by the once banished knight known as Rhodain Kayden. The once Triumphant Knight of Fire was busy enduring the tournament on the streets and seeing that my cousin and I survived. We discovered the truth, that the Former Queen, Susan Sorenson, had poisoned the King and kicked off the tournament herself to become the new King."

There is a stir in the crowd. People are not too welcoming to my claim that the Queen was behind everything. I hear a loud and exhausted voice speak out amongst the people.

"What the King says is true," Roxette announces far below me.

"I interrogated the knights myself. A handful admitted to helping the Queen in her conquest to take the crown for herself."

"Thank you, Inspector Roxette. Her plan was simple, kill the King, fake her abduction so that she would be outside the castle at the start of the tournament and rig it so that she could easily walk back in and take the crown. If it weren't for the fact that Rhodain was using the tournament to re-enter the castle and clear his name, she would have succeeded. Because she also orchestrated the hit on the King that got Rhodain, and magic banished from the kingdom. Therefore, I am reinstating magic to Baronune, as if it were not for Rhodain Kayden and his skills, my cousin and I wouldn't be here today."

There's another conflicted silence at the mention of the return of magic. I can only guess that it's because the people had gotten so used to hating Rhodain, that seeing him as a hero again is challenging.

"Rhodain Kayden would have been king. I was there every step of the way. He fought valiantly but never took another's life on his way to the crown. He was strong and merciful and would have been a great king if not betrayed for a second time by the Former Queen Susan. She took his life, but not before he took away her chance at taking the crown and knocking her off the edge of the castle. She survived," I add to a gathered gasp. So that gets a response?

"But with Rhodain and I the only ones left at the top of the castle. With his fleeting strength, he cast me into the throne and faded into ashes. Rhodain, while banished and wrongfully accused, fought for the name of the former King and defended the purity of this kingdom. The hopes of the future he saw in two children left on their own to survive. His sacrifice will not be in vain. In his memory, and in the memory of the King and everyone else who fought for the safety and lives of others. The death penalty will also be banned. Former Queen Susan and her followers will be sentenced to a life of solitude, locked away in the dungeons where they will remain to dwell on their crimes. There will be no need for trial, and I conclude this with more rules and instructions to come in the name of your King, Westley Jameson, and your King is law."

"All hail, King Westley," Terrence announces, but no one contributes. He orders this time and voices join in a forced cheer. I don't feel their hearts aligned with mine. I don't feel the trust of the kingdom. I step back and Sophia places her hand on my shoulder.

"Give them time."

"I have no choice, do I?"

I am their King. They are my people. They are forced into having to accept this change, just like I was forced into that throne. We have to move forward together.

We exit the way we came. Probably for the best. We climb into our carriages and begin my tour through the kingdom. We roll through the streets of the Royal District. This is a little easier than my last stroll through the kingdom, running for my life to race the clock and see that Rhodain made it to the top of the castle. Now I wished I had reconsidered that option. I would say the sights were rather repetitive with the same building looking like the last, but that would be a lie. The kingdom is a mess. Homes have broken doors, shattered windows, and walls decorated with blood. The civilians that return home glare at us as we pass and I don't blame them.

Every so often we stop to greet the people of the kingdom. My kingdom. I remain well guarded as most people don't welcome me with open arms. We go from neighborhood to neighborhood so that I may greet the few hundreds that didn't get a chance to share their aggression with me at the ceremony. We manage to return to the bazaar, and all I can see is Rhodain. I'm reminded of our first encounter and how he single-handedly took out a dozen thugs without batting an eye. I'm stuck looking at the splintered wood from the demolished shops and stands. Expensive fruits and trinkets lay sprayed across the road and merchants try to clean up the mess, to little effect.

I recall the terror Sophia and I endured evading the thugs throughout the bazaar. Sophia's hand touches my arm and I'm brought from my daze. She gives me a look of understanding.

"We'll begin the restoration as soon as possible," says Terrence.

Before we leave, I remember something and take a few knights as I leave Terrence and Sophia with the carriage. After a few minutes, I'm quick to return. Sophia's eyes are in shock. In my hands lies the green scarf she longed for at the start of the tournament. She wanted it for me, but now it's my gift to her.

"For being such a great tour guide," I say softly. "For keeping me safe too. For being my strength—as proof that I will never forget all you've done."

She's without words, lurching out and hugging me. I accept this, being the first glimpse of positive reassurance today. Our embrace is kept to a minimum as Terrence clears his throat, and ushers us back into the carriage. I understand that we have a schedule to maintain.

We swerve through the Royal District to the Docking District. Baronune trades between Dragon's Guard, Imica, the continent across the vast Imicc Ocean, and Chariot, the desert kingdom of Heliosand; the southern continent across the Baron Sea. I know very little of these areas. Terrence explains that a lot of the merchants from the bazaar originate from Heliosand. When it comes to deserts, I always assumed that they were all the same.

I meet with a few of the captains and sailors as Terrence expresses the importance in maintaining relations with the sea trade, as they control a lot of our exports and passages that trains and carriages cannot reach. Then we return to our carriages to make a final lap around Baronune.

Families are reluctant to speak with me, and I'm about to climb back into my carriage when someone tugs on my robes. I'm reminded of how much Rhodain hated when I'd grab his cloak, but I choose not to replicate his reactions. I turn to see a small child, a little girl maybe half my age holding a stuffed animal that's missing some appendages. Another home torn to shreds. I kneel to meet the girl's eyes and she hugs me. I am taken back by this. It is unexpected and the second bit of acceptance I've received all day.

"What was that for?"

"For promising to make my family happy again."

She is shy and still learning to form sentences. I smile at her, and she returns to her parents. I return to my carriage, and think about how Rhodain made a promise to his sister to return the kingdom to the way it was before Susan framed him. I sit in my carriage with Sophia and Terrence. Glancing back at the little girl and her family I share my second smile since the ceremony.

"If I can keep true to my promises, maybe I *can* be the King."
"You'll grow used to it," Terrence replies.

I hope he's right. Our carriage stirs as we ride back off to the castle.

As the evening rolls in, Sophia and I are grateful to be off the streets. It reminding us too much of the tournament. I even recognized a few of the scorch marks etched into the sand. We enter the castle and there in the main hall is Sophia's family. Aunt Janis and Uncle Marcus, her siblings Charles, Rich, Janet, Marilyn, and Grace. Her Uncle Mathis and Aunt Silvana and their seven children. They're all here as requested. Aunt Janis rushes to hug us.

"Thank goodness you're alright!"

We hug her back, and Sophia begins to weep. I pull away and let them embrace each other. The rest of the family walks over. Uncle Marcus slaps his hand on my shoulder, proud that I am King, but mostly thanking me for keeping his little girl safe.

I wish I could say *"It was nothing,"* or that it was all in a day's work, but these last few days have been the most stressful in my entire life.

All twelve, nearly thirteen of them. Aunt Janis pulls from Sophia and turns to me.

"Westley… what happened? I was so worried. The whole time I-I…"

"It's a long story, Aunt Janis, but rest assure we're alright."

"Alright?" She regards me from head to toe. "West, you're the King now."

"Well, it wasn't on my list of things to do. I literally stumbled into the position."

"The knights are saying that we can live here until our home is restored?"

"My orders," I respond, and she falls speechless.

I understand, this is a lot and a bit much to handle suddenly.

"Like I said, it's a long story. Let's just be happy that we all survived the tournament."

"We can agree to that."

Terrence has the knights escort Sophia and her family to their chambers. "My King, I have been informed that you uncle is waiting in the throne room. It seems he and his sister did not have a quaint reunion and were separated."

Terrence shows me the way as I am still unfamiliar with the layout of the castle, and the second I enter the throne room, my uncle rushes me. He's tall with reddish-brown curly hair, wearing old dusty attire, and old spectacles that hang off his face with small cracks in the lens. He wraps his arms around me, and I can finally allow myself relief.

My body sinks into him. My arms latch on to him and I bury my face into his shoulder. Tears flood from my eyes, my face redder than my robes. I am just happy that I am can see him again. Terrence excuses himself, leaving me to have some privacy with my uncle.

"West, oh my God…I could hear the alarms way out in Old Country. I was so worried. All my fears and concerns came in at once. This idea of a tournament for the King was the reason I never wanted you in Baronune. I couldn't risk it. After losing my sister… your mother… I just couldn't risk something happening to you, and *now*…" He pulls away and takes me in his sights.

"This isn't the kind of responsibility I meant when I agreed that you could stay with Janis this summer. You're the King? How?"

I tell him everything. It's not a spectacle or grand story to be passed down through the ages. I just weep my way through the story and it leaves him speechless. He is flustered, but most of all distressed. I am the King now. He has every right to be worried.

"Uncle Lester, I'm scared. I don't know what I'm doing. I don't want to be King. I want to go home."

"I know," he looks deep in my eyes.

I can see my reflection in his broken spectacles as he holds me close.

"This is the path you must lead. You are the King so the people will look to you for their answers. They will question your rule, but as King you must remember that you are still a boy. You are still young and learning everything as you walk the very same path that you now lead. So, as much as I am against this and concerned for you, you must remember that you are not doing this alone, you have your family, and many resources. More than I could ever offer you in Old Country. Most importantly, you have the support of the kingdom to back you in your time of need. Never forget that. As King, you are held responsible, and I know it's scary. I'm scared for you too, but as you did in the tournament, you must be brave. You must be strong, and you must promise me that nothing will happen to you." "I-I…" I pause as his grip fastens on my arms.

I see the very weight of fear on his face. I shudder and sniffle as I find my words, thinking back through everything that has occurred.

"I can't make that promise, Uncle Lester."

"I know…" He embraces me again, holding me so close that our heartbeats become one rhythm.

"Just promise me you'll do your best."

I hold on to him. My tears still running down my face as my fingers dig into his sandy blouse. I shift my head and whisper back to him.

"That's a promise I can keep."

Chapter Three

The King's Men

Everyone retires for the night. It was a rather long and eventful day and even Terrence seemed happy to return to his chambers. I lay in bed staring at the ceiling. Over the day the maids filled my wardrobe with night blouses and pajamas to sleep in. I guess they are still fashioning my day wear. I have to look presentable as a king and I wonder what tomorrow holds for me until I finally drift off to sleep.

The next day I wake to a knocking at the door. I crawl out of bed and answer to find Terrence standing in his formal robes and attire.

"Greetings, my King. I hope you slept well." "I *was*…" I glance out the glass balcony door.

The sun is hardly awake, so why am I up?

"What's going on?"

"I'm here to tell you that the maids will soon be in with your training attire."

"Training?" I'm awake now and no, I am not excited about this.

"What kind of training?"

"You're king now. People are going to look to you to defend them from any outside force. It would be best if you also knew how to defend yourself in the process—seeing as how that you *stumbled* into the position."

I am not *fit* enough to be a king. He doesn't look all that tough either, but he carries himself with more confidence than I do, and he doesn't have to look ready for a fight. A king should be strong, confident and intimidating, yet I am none of those things.

"So, what? I go outside and do some drills or something?"

"I'll gather the personnel that will oversee your training. I just wanted to let you know so that you wouldn't be alarmed in any way."

"Uh…thank you…*Terrence*." I would much rather call him Terry.

"I'll be off."

He bows to me. I stand confused, do I bow back? Do I pat him on the head and say, *"Good boy?"* or *"Well done advisor?"* He rises back up and makes his way down the hall. I close the door and wait for the maids to bring me my training attire.

I don't know what exactly I was expecting but I wasn't expecting tights. "Am I supposed to dance in this or something?"

"No, my King. That's to wear under your armor as an extra layer of protection. The blacksmith is still forging your armor." "This is for protection?" I lift the single outfit.

It's lighter than my bedsheets. The maid laughs at my ignorance.

"It's made from the silk threads of the Dragon's Guard Eel Worm. It's light but durable, and the stronger your Martial Arts become the less you'll have to rely on it. All the knights wear it under their clothes and battle gear as an extra layer of defense."

"So, a type of armor under my armor?"

"If that idea makes you comfortable then yes, my King."

"Interesting."

I admire it and poke the fabric. It really doesn't feel like something that will save my life, but I take her word. The other maids roll in a cart with my actual armor. Thick leather for my upper torso. Shin and wrist guards, and lastly, a waist guard that protects my groin. I am given a leather cap that covers my ears, and a wooden broad sword that I swing around. I resemble a kid waving around a toy.

The maids escort me to the Martial Court, a large courtyard hidden somewhere within the castle with high walls that block out the outside world, leaving the sky above visible. There is cool air cycling through the confined space and blades of green grass cake over the white and gray sand that surrounds a large boulder formation at the back.

Several people are standing in the courtyard and I only recognize a few of them. There's Terrence who is waiting for me, and a nurse I saw the other day who was treating Susan. She's taller than Terrence and slender with fair skin. She reminds me of the moon on a starry night, and her eyes are a misty gray.

Next to her, a boy, maybe in his mid-teens from eastern Dragon's Guard descent. His hair is the night to her moonlit appearance. His skin a few shades tanner with peering eyes that make him seem like he's contemplating something. He has small pondering lips that puff up like he's about to say something but never does. He's my height, maybe shorter. Where she is wearing a white nursing gown with silver sashes draping over her shoulders, he is wearing a white blouse under a slick silver vest with large comfy trousers.

There are also three hooded figures and three knights. The maids walk me to Terrence, bow, and take their leave back into the castle. I compare the knights' armor to my practice guard, and I feel greatly outclassed, they have *actual* plate armor.

"Good morning, Terrence, and company."

"Good morning, my King," Terrence responds with a bow.

Everyone but one of the knights and one of the hooded figures bow as well.

"Here is where you'll come for all your Martial and Mystic Arts training. Since you have allowed for magic to be reinstated, you can train in that as well if you have any interest in it."

"I can learn Divinity?"

"Perhaps," one of the knights says.

He sounds old like my uncle but as if he's endured years of combat. "Depends on if you have a talent for it. Magic, or Divinity as you call it, must be approached in steps. The Martial Arts are a baseline for mastering Divinity. It will strengthen the body to handle the Arts still to come. It will quicken your reflexes, and most importantly, make you strong enough to defend our kingdom."

The knight beside him chuckles and the knight with the dark forest green cape silences him with a swift strike.

"Some people are born of magic, so for them it is easier to tap into, while others have to study it through artifacts and other mystical means," Terrence explains.

I immediately doubt my capability of learning the Mystic Arts. I have a hard time running, so learning Divinity seems outlandishly out of reach.

"If you prove to have no hand in the Mystic Arts it is nothing to fret. You can train to master the Martial Arts as many knights end up doing."

That doesn't sound too comforting either as I'm reminded how displeased Terrence regarded my physical physique. I shift my attention to the three knights.

"Why do they always wear their helmets?"

"Late King Sorensen preferred it that way."

"Yeah, and that made it easy for assassins to infiltrate the kingdom and lead us to where we are now. Have them take them off."

I will admit, I was not expecting one of them to be a girl. A woman to be more exact. Her hair trimmed at her ears and fans out in a way that reminds me of a feather sweeper used to dust sand off the counters. She has dark, nearly bronze skin, and a hint of freckles dance across her nose. The corner of her mouth tugs into a disapproving frown as she folds her arms before her chest and looks impatiently.

She's the knight with the dark green cape, and a long thin sword is sheathed at her waist. I wonder how many other knights are women and I never realized? Of the other knights, the one that chuckled, has long black hair tied into a ponytail at the base of his head. His skin fair and his eyes black. A goatee frames his mouth as he drops his helmet completely and leans against a long bronze staff. His cape is navy blue. He looks bored and uninterested in me.

The last knight is the one that spoke about the Martial Arts. He stands as a man with honor and pride, but his undertone brown skin makes him seem like a man withered in sorrow and regret. He's an older gentleman with a long protruding nose, dark scruff along his chin with sprinkles of gray. His eyes are baggy and his curly dark hair falls short at his ears. He has no weapon. His cape is the midnight blue.

"These three, my King, are your *Grandier Knights*: Thalia Ivorys, Alan Soul, and Marshall Colt."

"Greetings," I raise my hand to be proper.

"Whatever," Alan continues to lean on his staff. "So, we've been promoted to babysitting?"

"Alan," Terrence demands with a deep tone. "Show some respect to your King."

"I said I show loyalty to my kingdom when I went through that interrogation," Alan glares at me. "But I will not regard this kid as my King."

At least he's honest. It wasn't at all necessary as he's literally just meeting me, but he is honest. Thalia seems to disapprove as well and nudges him in the ribs.

"Show some respect."

"Why?" Alan grunts. "What has he done for me?" "Got you this position for starts," she reminds.

"That's only because the last three *Grandiers* were corrupt and the original three are criminals. Well two, Rhodain's dead now, I suppose, if we take **his** word for it," Alan points at me.

His face returns to resting against his staff.

"Just makes me hate Rhodain even more. He betrays the King, becomes a fugitive, gets killed and leaves us with a toddler for a king.

Thanks, you fiery cock."

"**Hey!**" I snap. "Show *him* some respect."

Alan stares at me and I glare back at him.

"Make me," he says unenthusiastically.

I take a step forward and Terrence pulls me back.

"Not what we're here for. Well not exactly," Terrence corrects. "We'll get to the physical part of training after the introductions are met." "*Hooray…*"

"Shut it, Alan." Thalia scolds.

"Moving on," Terrence walks me over to the nurses. "Here are your nurses. They're here to treat your wounds in case things get a little… out of hand."

He says this and I watch his eyes fall on Alan. He remains fastened to his staff as he smiles sarcastically and waves his fingers. Terrence disregards him for the moment and then focuses my attention back on the nurses.

The tall one is named Nessa, she's the head nurse in the castle. The boy at her hip is her assistant, Junah, and he apparently doesn't talk. Terrence then walks me over to the hooded figures. These were new nurses in training. Since my command to reconstruct the kingdom went into order, a lot of the other knights and nurses are dispatched throughout the kingdom to keep the peace around Baronune and treat the injured from the tournament. These three were the only ones left for my training this morning.

I step forward to greet them, and what happens next is so quick that it's definitely missed with a blink. The hooded figure who was hesitant to bow upon my arrival, lunges at me. From the figure's sleeve, a small knife appears in their hand. The figure reaches for my neck with one swift swipe, and would have cut my throat if the Grandier Knights did not have significantly faster reflexes. The second the hooded figure went for the attack, Alan twirled his staff and halted the figure with a straight jab to the chest. All I caught was the figure flying back, the hood dropping off their head, and Thalia standing over them with her double-edged sword drawn.

"Holy…" My eyes are wide as time catches up to me.

Someone made an attempt on my life, within the castle.

"What in Hellsfire?"

"My King, are you alright?" Terrence assesses me along with Nessa and Junah.

"Are you harmed?"

"I-I'm okay."

"Yeah, thanks to me," Alan lowers his staff, resting it to his side. "Nice reaction, kid."

His sarcastic tone brings me from my shock and daze. I shoot him a glare and move around Thalia to get a better glimpse of my attacker.

"Are you serious? Ollie?"

"Do you know this kid?" Thalia asks, her sword still keeping my attacker at bay.

"Barely."

I've only had the one encounter from the night we spent in the sewer. Brilliant teal colored hair with bangs draping down to his eyebrows. Light pale skin. This seems to be an unnatural skin tone for people living in the desert. Ollie's soft and feminine face is scrunched into a fit of rage with eyes glaring between Thalia and me. "What in Hellsfire are you doing here?" "What do you think?" Ollie growls.

"If he knew, he wouldn't have asked," Alan speaks up from behind us.

"I was at the ceremony yesterday," Ollie explains. "I had to be sure that the new King was anyone but Rhodain…"

"Were you as disappointed as the rest of us?" Alan interrupts.

Maybe I shouldn't have had them remove their helmets.

"Oh, I was," Ollie looks to attack me again, but reconsiders at the sight of Thalia.

"The little boy hiding behind the criminal is our King? It was so ridiculous I became furious. So, when you announced that the restoration of the kingdom would begin immediately, I knew you'd be vulnerable. No one would dare attack the new King soon after the conclusion of the tournament. Especially with there being no promise of someone else taking your place after your demise. But I'd rather have no king, than a child sitting on the throne."

"You're barely older than I am!"

"And that makes what difference?" Alan asks and I roll my eyes.

"Regardless of whether that's true or not," Thalia begins, and I let out a groan.

Thanks for the support, guys.

"Attempts against the King's life are against the Royal Law. You face the death penalty."

"Or you would," Alan interrupts. "If that was still a thing." "You face incarceration," she corrects.

"Fine," Ollie bites back. "I'd rather look at the inside of a cell than watch him act as King."

"I'm not acting!" I bark.

I may not have asked for this, but I demand some sort of respect.

"I am the King, and as King your fate lies in my hands. So, you will not face the death penalty, you will not rot away in a cell either. If you despise looking at me so much, then I will make that your punishment. You will be second to my Grand Advisor, Terrence, regarding me with information whenever and however I see fit!"

The Martial Court falls silent. All eyes are on me. Only the whistle of the wind above makes a sound. At least until Alan chimes in.

"That was either the dumbest and most childish thing I've ever seen or actually a well thought out punishment. If only I had a coin."

"Silence, Alan," Terrence barks. "My King, are you sure? As your Grand Advisor, I would advise—"

"I am sure, I am King, I am *law*, and it's about time people start getting used to it."

I glare down at Ollie, who bites his lip.

Terrence sighs. "Very well then, Thalia, help and have the kid join my side. Marshall, make sure nothing else reckless happens."

"From which one?"

Terrence growls and Thalia withdraws her sword to pull Ollie up by the collar of his hooded robes. She pauses for a moment as she studies Ollie, who looks ready to draw another knife from… somewhere. Where are those things hidden? She passes Ollie to Marshall who catches my new advisor with the use of his left hand while his right cradles his helmet. He takes the teal haired nurse off to the side and stands with Terrence as they overlook my training.

With Nessa's assistance, Thalia directs the other two hooded nurses back into the castle. To keep from any more surprises, only the main personnel of my court remain on the training grounds.

Alan taps the bottom of his staff on the ground a few times. The soft sand leaves no sound from contact. I take up my fake sword and widen my footing. I have no idea what I'm doing and my knees and hands shake, making my wooden sword appear as though it was made from rubber instead.

"On my mark," Thalia instructs me. "Make an attempt at Grandier Alan. This is to test your current skills so that we can grasp where to start your training…Attack!"

I go to lunge, and I don't know what tripped me up, my nerves or the sand. My foot slips out from under me and I fall forward. Alan barely needs to move. His staff meets my face, and in one fluid motion, he taps me on the head before I'm back on my feet.

It looks light, but feels harder than any thug's kick. Could it be the bronze, or something else? I drop to the ground and scream out in pain. My whole face is throbbing. Any ounce of presented authority I might have had is gone.

"All hail our King everybody." Alan jokes.

Ollie laughs hysterically and I can feel Alan's disappointment shift to both Thalia, and Terrence as I roll in pain. Nessa and Junah rush to my aid.

This training is going to be brutal.

Chapter Four

Beneath My Rule

My training continues for about a week and I don't get any better. Every morning I return to the Martial Court to get pummeled by Alan, then in the evenings before dinner, Thalia takes me for strength training which consists of running, pushups, pullups, and sit-ups—all of which suck. Thalia doesn't make the experience any better, she constantly barks instructions at me, forcing me to train whether I want to or not because I can't out power her.

She's really strong, stronger than any woman I've ever met. Of course, I've never met any knights before, so between her, Alan, and Rhodain, I'm starting to recognize the difference from my normal physical activities back in Old Country to what it takes to master the Martial Arts.

"Keep it up my King," Marshall watches from the sides. "The Days of Hellsfire were only dark because we as people over time began to rely less on the magic you call, Divinity. We left the arts to knights and mages, and that, left everyone else vulnerable."

After my training, I go to bed reminding myself that they all started where I am, then I wake up to have it shoved in my face how much stronger my knights are by Alan bashing me with his staff. Marshall oversees everything but does nothing, he often sits with Sophia who has started to come watch my progress, and to make sure my newly appointed Second Grand Advisor doesn't try to kill me again.

Normally, Ollie shadows Terrence, but whenever Terrence has to attend to matters concerning the kingdom while I'm busy getting my face beat into the ground, Ollie is my secondhand supervisor. One that never gives me any advice, but sits amused at witnessing how terrible I am.

I get a few minutes to recollect myself, as Nessa and Junah see to my recovery. She hands me a vile of some strange, possibly magic liquid that tastes like honey. It dampens my pain, and restores my strength. If only she could give me a potion to make me stronger. Sophia is beside me but still hasn't forgiven me for making Ollie my Second Grand Advisor.

"He tried to kill you, and your immediate thought process is to make him your advisor? What sense does that make?"

She had said when I told her what had happened. So, she now keeps a tight eye on Ollie's every move. Almost on cue, Ollie approaches us. Not looking happy, of course, Ollie never looks happy around me. Then again, if that wasn't the case, it wouldn't be much of a punishment. My arms are bruised, my left eye is blackened, and I can still taste the blood swishing in my mouth. Junah gives me a sack of ice to help the swelling in my face.

"Gods you're pathetic," Ollie says in greeting.

Hello to you too.

"If that's the best advice you have as my advisor then *you're* pathetic."

Ollie's arms fold at the chest. "I didn't ask to be your advisor."

"No. You tried to kill me. I showed you mercy."

"Yeah, well you're a moron."

"And you're a terrible assassin."

I'm not making things better but something is tugging at him. I can see Ollie's pale face change to a shade of red as his well-manicured nails dig into his sleeves.

"You're not pushing yourself enough."

Ollie seems just as surprised as Sophia and I were that he said such a thing.

"What do you mean?"

Reluctant to answer, Sophia begins staring too.

Ollie puffs out hot air. "Your doubt is holding you back. You're thinking too much about getting better and creating a wall that you'll never overcome."

"How can you tell?"

"Even an infant could muster *some* strength after the beating you've gone through this past week. The Martial Arts are about understanding your body's limits and pushing past them."

"You're some expert on the matter now?"

"Trust me, I know a thing or two about not understanding one's body. Also, I trained in the Assassin's Guild.

The way he stomps and yells at me is almost adorable. I can't help but chortle.

"You told me to fulfill my duty so that's what I'm doing!" Ollie snaps. "If you're not going to take me seriously…"

"No, it's just, I doubt you have the Martial Arts knowledge to help me with this, Alan beat you without even trying."

"He wasn't my target that day."

"He still beat you."

"Fine," Ollie growls. "You're so thick-headed that you need a demonstration."

He huffs at me and strolls off.

"You don't think he's…"

"I hope not," I respond, watching Ollie approach Alan and Thalia.

"Then he'll be the moron and *that* will look bad on me since he's my Second Grand Advisor."

Marshall remains quiet by a nearby boulder, watching but choosing not to intervene. Ollie challenges Alan, who at first looks at him as if he's joking, but then sees that Ollie is all too serious about this. What does he have to prove?

In the court Ollie and Alan take their respective sides. Unlike with me, Alan seems slightly on guard with one foot forward, and his staff firmly in hand as Ollie's at an angle, facing Alan sideways in a wide stance. Thalia steps up to oversee them.

"Are you both ready?" she asks.

"Sure," says Alan .

"Ready," says Ollie .

As soon as Thalia shouts, "Attack!" Ollie glides forward as swift as the wind.

I didn't even catch his first step and he's already on Alan, who seemingly hasn't yet budged. I am barely able to keep up with their movements. Ollie swipes at Alan with one of those medical knife things, it was so quick that I didn't even catch Ollie draw the blade, only the swipe.

Alan ducks and rams his staff below Ollie's ribs, batting him away as the Grandier Knight moves back to a proper stance. Ollie rolls through the sand but catches himself. He's squatting as I catch a flash of silver. Alan uses his staff to easily deflect the projectiles and as they spray across the ground I notice that they're thin and sturdy silver needles.

Back on his feet, Ollie attacks again. Alan uses his staff to kick up a whirling shield of sand, and at first I believe it to be Divinity, but on closer inspection it is clear that is just how skilled he is with his weapon. Between the sand and the staff, Ollie is forced to stop his pursuit. Alan switches to offense and thrusts his staff forward. Ollie dodges but Alan repeats with several quick jabs. Managing to again dodge them all, Ollie catches the staff but doesn't hold onto it for long, using it to propel himself forward and stabs at Alan's face.

He almost gets him too, but not before Alan catches Ollie's wrist. With the knife only an inch from his eye, Alan delivers a powerful kick to my Second Advisor's gut. Ollie slides back several feet, and splutters a pained noise as he holds his stomach then falls on his hands and knees. His knife glitters in the sand as he tries to catch his breath. All that flash and he can't take a hit any better than me.

With a sharp cry, Ollie swallows his pain and grabs the knife. He slices at the air and a thin soft green light follows the motion of Ollie's swipe. It cuts at Alan, but he doesn't defend. Thalia intercepts it and slices through the light as if it were made of glass.

"This was a Martial Match," Thalia barks. "No magic allowed!"

The crazed bloodlust leaves Ollie's eyes. "…I'm sorry, I don't know what came over me."

"W-what kind of Divinity was that?"

I stand up, forgetting about my own pain as the sack of ice falls to my feet. Ollie can fight, but it doesn't look like he's too great at taking hits.

"I…" He glances at Alan and Thalia.

She has returned her sword to its sheathe and waits impatiently for Ollie's response.

"Answer your King."

"As I was trying to say, I trained in the Assassin's Guild in Dragon's Guard," Ollie begins between breaths.

"That spell was called, Extend… You have to learn to push past your limits to learn the Martial Arts. I… *struggled* with this too. But I found other means to get around my… disadvantages. Spells being one of them, to use what little I knew of the Mystic Arts to enhance my moves. It is frowned upon, but I needed it to keep up with the rest."

Alan kicks at the sand as he walks. "So, you used magic to sharpen and extend the reach of your blade? That's advanced stuff, kid. You're not ready for it."

Thalia speaks with a softer tone. "Focus on mastering the Martial Arts first before you start cutting corners."

Ollie nods, bows to the Grandier Knights, then glances over to me. I'm unclear at what he's searching for. Acknowledgment? Congratulations? I learned so much from their bout. Ollie's speed. Alan's steady and swift confidence. Ollie's Divinity. Alan's trust in Thalia. He didn't even try to dodge that attack because he *knew* she'd intercept it.

Terrence appears and we call the training to a close.

"My King, go clean up. We'll be meeting with the blacksmith in his forge beyond the dungeon."

Sophia walks beside me as I take one last look at Ollie who dusts off his robes and winces.

"Nessa, can you see about his wounds?"

"I can see to my own wounds," Ollie says sharply.

I forget that he also studied as a nurse. He keeps a lot more than knives up those sleeves.

"If you wish."

Nessa and Junah follow us inside the castle. I glance back from entry. Last to leave the court before Ollie is Marshall. His eyes shift between us with an intrigued glimmer to them. He says nothing.

I head back to my chambers to change and find that the maids have worked overtime to fill my wardrobe. I change into a silk blue blouse that caresses my skin at the touch with smooth brown trousers that are almost black. I slide my feet into some loafers that give me the impression of what clouds feel like, and I drape a long furry cape over my shoulders. I rest a small golden crown on my head. I have many different crowns to wear like someone changes their hat to match the occasion. This one is my *at home* crown.

I find my way through the castle's corridors. I've learned a few of the halls, but I'm still mapping out the layout of my new home. Uncle Lester stayed a few nights as I settled in but had to return to Old Country to manage the shops. I told him that we'll be making improvements to the old district once done restoring the kingdom.

I turn a corner and meet with Terrence and a couple of knights. Hoover and Cooper. They are rather loud and boisterous until they notice me. Hoover is heavier, thick with a dark tan, and a receding hairline. A red mane crowns his scalp and ties into a bun. It matches his long beard as it sticks out like the leaves on a King's Fruit from the Imicc Islands. Cooper is taller with dark skin, of Heliosand descent, and a forehead that gives the former executioner a run for his treasure. It looks from another realm, nearly balding with black and curly hair. The way he speaks is fast, each word bleeding into the other. It's so distracting that I almost don't catch what Terrence is asking me.

"No Ollie?"

"Hmm? Oh, Ollie is still recovering from this morning. I don't know why he went so hard against Alan."

"The two were holding back."

"What?"

Terrence says as we walk, "Thalia and Alan caught me up on the events while you were getting ready, Alan is far better in actual combat. He only accepted Ollie's challenge to entertain the two of you. Still, Ollie claims to have trained in the Assassin's Guild. Their Martial Arts is meant to be quick and fit to kill. Perfect for someone trying to end a fight before it starts. So, to shift to a longer, drawn out spar goes against the Assassin Guild's style."

"Interesting…"

"Do you have other thoughts, my King?"

"I always have thoughts, but nothing to concern you with, we're to meet the blacksmith you said?"

"Yes," Terrence turns his attention ahead as we follow the corridor.

"I came to the conclusion from your lack of progress that it might be best to have you specially equipped with armor and weaponry that can make up for your disadvantages."

"Oh…"

"Ollie suggested it, said you'll never learn to believe in yourself if you keep fighting in basic training gear. I just didn't want our King poking his eye out on the first day. Ollie laughed at that."

"Even better…"

My shoulders slump, nice to know I'm regarded in such a manner.

We venture down a stairwell that takes us into the dungeons.

"Stay clear of the cells. The knights you've had placed here may not hesitate to make an attempt at you. Regardless of the runes."

There were about twenty and I didn't recognize any of them, but they knew of me, the kid King that had sentenced them to a fate worse than death. This is good enough for me. Let them rot down here under my kingdom, under my rule. As I walk by, ignoring their glares and curses, the last three prisoners catch my eye. Lawrence, Matthews, and Greg.

"Hi," Greg waves at me the moment I walk by.

Lawrence growls. "Don't greet him, Greg. He's the reason we're down here."

"You put yourselves in this position. Not me." "You gave the order," Matthews chimes in.

"I didn't order you to align with the Queen, you should have really weighed the consequence of your actions before you betrayed the King."

"We will follow Queen Susan until the end of days."

Lawrence hisses as she squeezes her face between the cell bars that glow with ancient writing which nullifies all Divinity. She reminds me of a snake. The dirty brown sacks for clothes they're given doesn't compliment them either. Lawrence's stormy gray hair looks wild and staticky. Matthews looks like he's gone far too long from regarding himself in a mirror and is about to break. Greg has his same neutral expression. He stands in the middle of his cell, blinking repeatedly.

"Don't waste your breath on him. He's still just a child."

A familiar voice echoes from the next cell. I walk over and find Susan sitting on an old soggy bed wearing the same potato sack prisoner attire. Her face is exhausted and drained, but her emerald eyes cut through the dread. Her hair remains in her formal braided bun.

"Hello, your majesty… junior edition."

"Hello, traitor."

I wish my stare could light her on fire. My fists are tight, and my heart beats heavily.

"Comfy?"

"Very."

Her voice quivers when she speaks, and I can see a slight twitch in her clasped fingers.

"You deserve much worse for what you've done. The lives you've taken and ruined in your conquest. I don't understand why you did it."

"You will… once you're older. This kingdom will shun you just like it shunned me, then you'll know. After years of no respect and being sidelined by those three buffoons who, merely because they slew a dragon, believed it made them qualified to rule. I have done so much to be recognized for so little… You'll see, and you'll understand. Without power, you are nothing to this kingdom, and when you finally realize that…" She tilts her head to shine a crazed look.

"You'll snap, and then this kingdom will come crumbling down." I can feel her pain and hate with every word.

"And that makes it okay to kill the King? The man you claimed to have loved? Have you no shame or regrets for what you've done? A great man should be wearing this crown, and now, because of you it's me instead."

She studies me and her vigor seems to waver. What little remained from her former glory has dimmed in her eyes. She removes me from her sights, and her hands continue twitching.

"Maybe you're not completely heartless. I'll leave you to those thoughts."

I turn to Terrence who is studying us both. "Hey, what became of the King's portrait?"

"It resides in the treasure chamber until I can think of what else to be done with it."

"Put it in her cell," I demand, and Terrence looks at me questionably. "I want her to see his face. I want her to be haunted by her crimes. I want her to suffer from her regret. I can't hurt her, so I'll let her do it to herself."

I conclude and bypass Terrence. He stands studying the former Queen and her cell.

"Very well, my King."

We proceed to the end of the dungeons where another set of stairs descend into darkness. I stand in the doorway and hesitate to go further. I can't see anything below me, and question if the blacksmith is even here. Terrence gestures me forward, and I find the steps, cautiously until I'm in what I believe to be the blacksmith's forge. It's still dark and cold and only the light from the entrance illuminates the area.

"Is anyone here?"

"Perhaps," A voice responds from within the darkness.

"Are you the new king?"

"I am King West, yes," I say reluctantly.

An icy blue stare pierces the darkness, are his eyes glowing? The fires begins to dance, flickering between smoldering orange and red across his face. He is an older gentleman with a scruffy black and gray beard that matches what's left on his balding head. I can't make out his skin from under the soot, ash, and grease that seems to cover every inch of him. The blacksmith walks over to a wall behind him and ignites more flames. The heat fills the room, chasing away the cold.

I can hear Terrence following me in as the knights stand at the entrance. "Sassarus, the Blacksmith. He will make you the finest armor and sharpest blades, truly fit for a king."

"Are you sure? Perhaps I should make one fit for a child," Sassarus responds, and Terrence scolds him.

"I know it's your name, but do not sass him. He is our king now, and it's our duty to make sure he's prepared for battle."

"Yeah? Tell me, King West. How did you arrive victoriously upon the throne?"

"You haven't heard?"

"I haven't heard from you."

His stare gives me chills despite how warm it is in here.

"I was not victorious. I did nothing to earn my title," His eyes fix on me upon the word, *nothing,* but he holds his tongue.

"I had no interest in the tournament to claim the crown. I was only trying to find the best means for my cousin and I to survive. When we came across Rhodain Kayden, I saw our best chance of survival."

"So, you tagged along."

Sassarus walks between piles of coal and fire pits then fiddles with something as more and more flames fill his workplace. Covering a nearby table are misshapen weapons. Are they unfinished? He stops mid step and shifts those cold blue eyes at Terrence then waves for him and the others to leave the forge, to which they do.

"You tagged along with a banished knight and deemed him safer than the tournament you were caught in. That's either perfect insight or sheer dumb luck."

He wipes his brow and tosses a cloth into one of the flames. I hear his heavy feet sink into the gravel as he grabs me by my shoulders and shakes me. I squeak, a sound not fit for a king.

"It was a bit of both, to be honest," I say to lift the awkward silence.

"I hadn't heard too much of his crimes within the Royal District so anything Rhodain had done was news to me."

"Still, you continued to follow him after hearing what he'd done."

"*Allegedly* done."

"You didn't believe what was said about him?"

"No one was able to provide concrete evidence, so I saw no difference in following him."

"And your cousin, the girl. She was okay with this?"

"No, she hated the idea. She usually hates all my ideas, but she trusts me."

"That's a lot of faith. Why is that?"

"Well," I hadn't really asked her about why.

"I guess it has something to do with how close we are. We're practically brother and sister; our mothers had us at the same time."

"So, you share a link. I see," he says and pokes me with a needle that makes me yelp.

"I'll try to be more careful. Not used to making armor for someone your size. Even dwarfs have been simpler."

"Dwarfs? *Ow!*"

He pokes me again, and I'm sure it was on purpose. He proceeds to size me up and gets my measurements then returns to the fire.

"Couldn't you have gotten the measurements from the maids?"

"I fashion my armor differently from how the maids fashion clothes. I have to understand the wearer and recognize the purpose of their movements. You, my boy, lack confidence."

Tell me something I haven't heard all day.

"You blindly followed a man you didn't know because you knew you lacked the ability to protect your cousin, thus putting you both in graver danger. That lack of confidence will be your doom. You'll need armor that is strong and loyal, much like your cousin. One you can bond with and form an unbreakable link. Once I craft that, it will boost your confidence, and then maybe you can believe it when you introduce yourself as king."

"You gathered all that from a few pokes?"

"I listen, my boy, if there is nothing else I do. I always listen."

"Susan should have visited you more." I hiss as he walks over to his tools.

"You speak of the former Queen?"

"I speak of the traitor."

"Interesting. Is it because of your claim that she killed the king?"

"She *did* kill the king. All for this stupid title."

"And that angers you? The unjust treatment of a man you never knew, a man you never met. How do you know he didn't deserve it?"

"No one deserves to have their life taken by someone else. There are rules and punishments for a reason."

"And what reason is that?"

"To learn."

"What if their crimes are so foul that death is the only answer?"

"Death is never the only answer."

"Is that why you did away with the death penalty? And have left those prisoners with no end in sight? To sit with their thoughts?"

"To learn from their crimes. For however long it takes."

"And if they never learn? If they shall die before such thoughts bear fruit?"

"Then a natural death will become their final punishment."

Sassarus goes back to the fires. "Hmm."

He grabs another cloth to wipe his hands then begins to roll up his sleeves. Revealing his strong, sturdy, and hairy arms.

"It seems you have much to learn yourself, Little Sparrow. Until then, I will fashion your armor and craft your blade. You are no knight, no killer, so, you'll need a weapon for distance and a swift response, but not quite to exact justice on your foes. A sword that will grow and form a will to match your own. I will get started tomorrow."

"Tomorrow?"

"I have to fetch supplies. Such works of art can't be forged with what little metals I have lying around here. I have obtained all I needed of you, you may leave.

"Why did you call me a sparrow?"

"First thing I thought of when you walked in here." He admits as he ruffles my hair.

"A lost little sparrow, learning to fly."

"If I am a sparrow, then what are you?"

He leads me to the top of the stairs. "Me?"

I block out most of the light and my shadow falls upon him as his piercing blue eyes regard me with kindness.

"I am nothing. There is nothing of me, therefore, I am. Now get going, little sparrow. You have wings to strengthen."

This reminds me of a thought I had earlier and I leave Sassarus to his forge and rejoin the others.

"All is in order, my king?" Terrence asks.

"I suppose so, he said he'll start tomorrow."

"Then it shouldn't be long before you'll have your own sword and armor to fight with."

The mention of fighting leaves me doubtful.

"Do you really think I'll be in combat?"

"You're the king, you tell me."

We exit the dungeon and I don't bother the former Queen or her followers this time. Between her and Sassarus' forge, I have had enough heated encounters for today.

As Terrence leads me back to my chambers, I ask him to take me to Ollie. We head down a hall and pass Nessa who smiles at me warmly, and Junah who nods at me hesitantly. Terrence takes me to Ollie's chambers where I forget to knock and enter immediately.

"*Who is that?*" Ollie asks in a panic, throwing back on his robes.

"What is wrong with you? Have you never heard of knocking?"

"I'm sorry, I just didn't think—"

"You know for someone who claims to be so smart, you are such a child!"

"Okay, calm down. I'm sorry. I'll remember to knock next time."

"What do you want?"

"Is that how you talk to your king?"

"What do you want, *sir?*"

I allow his rude tone as a funny little smirk tugs at the corner of my mouth.

"I have a proposition for you."

"Seriously, couldn't this have waited until later?"

"Well for one, I wanted to make sure you were doing better after your bout this morning, and no, it couldn't have waited."

I walk in and close the door behind me, which is probably not smart, since Ollie tried to kill me a week ago.

"You really are dumb," he's right behind me.

The wind couldn't have been quieter. There were about ten feet between us, Ollie was on the other side of the chamber.

"I could kill you right now if I wanted to."

"Yeah, but then you won't get to watch me make a fool of myself trying to be king, and I know how much you enjoy that."

I feel the pressure of my approaching death ease away.

"You're too trusting," Ollie backs away from me. "It will get you killed one day."

"Maybe, but that's why I'm here. I want you to train me, in secret."

"Excuse me, Thickhead? Why in Hellsfire would I do that?"

"Because I asked and it's a part of your duties. If you're not loyal to me, you're at least loyal to your duties."

"Okay…" Ollie steps off to the side and folds his arms at his chest, looking uncomfortable.

"Maybe you're not so dumb, but why me? I still hate you."

"Yeah, but this way you can personally watch me fail over and over again. I need to lower that wall of doubt I have if I am to succeed at this, and after watching you today. I know you are able to overcome shortcomings."

"So, you *were* paying attention."

"Terry said your style of fighting specializes in quick kills and catching your opponent by surprise. I feel I can adapt to that much easier than to whatever Alan and Thalia are trying to teach me."

"So, you just want to take the easy way out?" Ollie judges me. "Well, I have to tell you that there is nothing easy when it comes…"

"I want to raise my skill level faster so that I can earn their respect. Unlike with me, Alan recognized your skill, and I need for them to do the same with me if I am to be the king."

"You care what they think of you?"

I step away from the door and look through the window and at the kingdom.

"It's a start. If I can earn the respect of the people that are supposed to follow me, then I can eventually earn the respect of my kingdom. Only when they acknowledge me can I truly accept that I am their king."

I feel a shift in Ollie's mood. I feel a sense of sympathy. Or pity, it's probably pity.

"You can't win over everyone," Ollie says.

His head hangs as his eyes find something interesting. They seem heavy and dishearten.

"Trust me, they'll judge you regardless."

"I don't need everyone, just enough," I turn to him.

"Enough would be plenty."

There's a pause and Ollie thoughtfully brushes his hand along his shoulder then turns to me with a smirk.

"Okay, I'll do it. Only because you look so pitiful right now. Called it.

"You have to listen to me. I don't want to be wasting my time for nothing."

I smile. "What were you wasting your time with before?"

"Don't make me change my mind."

I laugh, and I can see a slight smile tug at his glossy lips. "Thank you, Ollie. We'll start tomorrow?"

"Well yeah, you idiot," he gestures dramatically as his hands swish through the air.

"I can't form a lesson plan on the fly. Give me some time to think things over."

"Okay."

"And get out of my chambers! I don't want people thinking I've changed my mind about trying to kill you or anything."

"Whatever you say," I chuckle and head towards the door.

Before I exit Ollie stops me.

"You do realize you called Terrence, *Terry*, right?"

"Yeah, but he didn't hear me."

"These walls aren't that thick, my king." Terrence answers from the other side of the door.

Ollie and I share a laugh, then I exit to meet Terrence in the hall.

"Sorry Terrence."

He pardons my slip up and we proceed back to my chambers.

Chapter Five

Choosing My Path

"Sprint!" Ollie orders.

"Faster!"

He has me running back and forth within the Martial Court to increase my speed, something I have lacked my whole life. I wish I could say that under Ollie's supervision my training got easier, but it didn't.

"Let the Divinity move through you!"

Adding Ollie's training on top of the training I am already receiving from Alan in the morning and Thalia in the evening is nearly breaking me. I still had royal duties between sessions and I wake every morning for weapon training. I still look like a kid flailing his toy. Alan never hides his disappointment when I fail to block his weakest attacks.

At the end of our sessions, I wind up back in the care of Nessa and Junah, while he's sipping water and complaining about me with Thalia. In the middle of the day I meet with Ollie, normally after my morning briefings on the status of Baronune. I wonder if I have so many of these meetings because Terrence thinks my memory is poor or that I often fall asleep during them.

This makes training in the evenings harder as Thalia continues to push me until I can't even move. We've gone from simple drills to exhausting my body trying to crawl from one end of the court to the other, reorganizing the boulders, and jump squat drills, along with the occasional *Thalia Surprise.*

"*RANDOM ATTACK!!!*" She shouts while I'm in the middle of a jump. "*Oh Gods!*"

I respond by flinching and being tackled to the ground. This is how she initiates my ground training and grapple drills, when I'm too tired to fully lift my legs off the ground, let alone react. Terrence usually has to carry me back to my chambers.

Today I meet Ollie in the castle's library, a large room with walls of books which stretch into an almost nonexistent ceiling. Today we spend time researching and studying ancient Divinity and spells.

"How is this going to better me?"

"For someone who is always trying to make sense of what's happening around him. Don't you think understanding the Arcasian history will further your capability of understanding certain situations?"

"…Maybe?"

"Just keep reading, West."

I do as I'm told, and we spend most of the day in the library until Sophia finds me. She's been like a *third* Grand Advisor in training, always around Terrence and I, giving her suggestions when she can. The rest of her family has been busy too. Aunt Janis and Cousin Silvana take turns in the kitchen while Uncle Marcus and Cousin Mathis have trouble maintaining their tiny kids of chaos. The rest of Sophia's siblings help out with the maids though the girls try to fancy themselves as princesses, while the boys are restrained from being anything like knights as Aunt Janis doesn't want to risk anyone being enlisted into my court.

"West," Sophia calls.

I look up from a book on the Days of Hellsfire.

"Terrence told me to come get you. He wants to do another tour of Baronune so that everyone can get used to seeing your face. You know, because King Sorenson was nearly forgotten during his rule."
"Thanks…"

Ollie chuckles behind a book he's reading.

"Also, so you can see the developments of the kingdom from when you made your demands."

"Has anything changed from the last tour?" "No," Ollie coughs.

"Not much," Sophia glares at him. "And what is it that you're doing? You're his advisor, aren't you supposed to be...*advising?*" This gets Ollie's attention.

"For your information," Ollie claps his book shut. "I am doing what I can, your cousin has the learning curve of a rock with its edges unsoften.."

 "I'm literally right here."

"Could have fooled me, you've been on that same page for thirty minutes."

"How could you possibly know that?"

Ollie crosses his arms. "Because I'm observant, and you were snoring just before your cousin walked in here."

"It's Sophia! We've been living in this castle for weeks, and you can't remember my name?"

"It's not that I can't," Ollie scans her up and down.

"It's just you're not worth remembering."

Sophia gasps, I gasp. That was uncalled for. I'm awake now as I prepare to defend my cousin.

"You listen here, you...you..."

"I'm listening," Ollie gloats as he stands, and Sophia shoves her finger in his face. He doesn't flinch.

"I have had it up to here with you," She raises her hand and jumps to sell her point.

"West may be king, but you're his Grand Advisor..." "Second—" I begin but Sophia hushes me.

"Not now, West," she points at me and turns back to Ollie.

He follows her finger and nearly goes cross-eyed.

"You tried to kill my cousin, twice! You sit here while I watch him day after day push and try to become a good king for this kingdom. What are you doing? How are you advising?"

"As I said—"

"*Nope*, it's my turn to talk," Sophia hushes him too and Ollie actually listens.

"My cousin did everything in his power to get us through that tournament. Was it the best or most logical course to take? No, but he tried, and that's more than you're doing right now. Some *advisor.* If anything, I'd say you're jealous…"

I can see Ollie restrain himself by the grip on his sleeves.

"I don't care what you have against my cousin," Sophia continues.

"I don't care what reasons you have for thinking you're better than him or me. All I care about is that you do whatever it takes to keep him safe! Stop treating him like he's the boy you tried to kill in the sewers, and do your duty! Or so help me, if something happens to him, the flames of Rhodain Kayden will look like specks in comparison to my wrath if I get my *hands – on – you!*"

Sophia huffs and settles back down.

"So West," Sophia pats down her gown as if trying to unruffle it from her outburst.

"Whenever you're done here, Terrence will be waiting."

She struts out of the library. Ollie and I regard each other. If I didn't know better, I'd actually believe him to be intimidated by my cousin.

"I think we're done here. Go find Terrence."

I say nothing. I don't have any words to follow Sophia's display. I nod and scamper off to locate my First Grand Advisor.

Days, weeks, months. I see little progress. Alan still knocks me aside without trying, and I figure that if I can't get the upper hand his way, then I'll do things my way. I make mistakes on purpose to test how he reacts. I still end each session with Nessa and Junah treating my wounds, but I'm playing a different game now. As we move from morning training to the first of many briefings, Terrence updates me of the kingdom's status.

The bazaar has been up and running for over a month now as the merchants have finally returned. The Round Table Tournament seemed to have had them extra cautious about returning to our kingdom. Their return signals that the Baronooners have started their rebuilding, but the full restoration of the kingdom remains a drawn-out process. I've had to call back the knights from Old Country to add more hands to rebuilding the kingdom. The crimes have quieted down for the moment, but that could be because I have most of the criminals in my dungeons, and we're almost full. I investigated what it will take to make a containment area for only the criminals, and we don't have the resources for such a confine. My day stretches into my training with Ollie. It's been off and on from training in the Martial Arts, to lessons in anatomy, to studying in the library. Today, we meet in the library. Ollie's reading something on mythical artifacts from the burnt lands of Eurosia. I plop in a seat across from him.

"*Gods*, I miss the days when it was just you trying to kill me and not the stress of being the king."

"Don't get your hopes up," Ollie says without looking up from his book. "I can be very fluid in my decisions."

"Don't toy with me right now," I say as I send an exhausted leer his way.

It seems to have no effect.

"What's this one you're reading?"

"*The Unlikely Myths of Eurosia*. Since no one dares return to those ashes, this is the only knowledge we have."

"Why do you bother? Even if they were real, those artifacts would have surely burned in the chaos."

Ollie peeks up at me. "I'm supposed to take the word of the king who a few months ago didn't believe in such things as magic? I'll stick to the facts that I can decrypt from these scribes of fiction."

"Well, my word *is* law."

"Yeah, and how are those laws going for you?" Ollie closes his book and studies me.

"Your dungeons can only hold so many criminals since you removed the death penalty. Your knights can barely keep order in the kingdom because, let's face it, the Baronooners still haven't accepted you as king. Along with this, the restoration is taking a little longer than anticipated with the safe houses being used for the lesser ones to get off the streets and making something out of the nothingness. You should have kept the kingdom the way it was. At least then it was manageable."

"Well, I'm no King Sorenson. I didn't ask for this, but if I am to be the King of Baronune then I need to make it a kingdom of my vision. A kingdom I see fit to rule," I let out a yawn.

"I'm tired and the changes I put into place are taking some time to get used to, but that's just it. It's going to take time to get used to them. I'm trying to get used to being the king. The kingdom will take time to get used to its changes as well."

"True, while I more than understand the challenges that come with changes, time is limited. Eventually, we're going to have to try something else," Ollie rises from his seat. "Until then, we have more training to do."

"Can I have like, five more minutes?"

"Sure," Ollie smiles, and I don't like this smile.

"We can take the long way around to the Martial Court."

Not the answer I was looking for. Ollie returns his book and grabs me by my robes.

Ollie permits me some time to meditate. He says my *Internal Space* will help me understand my limits by listening to what my body is telling me. I hear nothing. I can hear Ollie breathing. I can hear the desert winds whistling overhead, but I can't hear anything my body is telling me. What am I supposed to listen for? Are we supposed to have a conversation? "Stop thinking so much."

I smirk. "Is... that my body?"

Ollie growls as he sits beside me. He has a kind of calm rage radiating from him.

"No wonder you never discovered Divinity growing up."

"What's that supposed to mean?"

"The Martial Arts is the lowest level of Divinity because everyone has access to it. Only those willing to accept the changes that come with Divinity can grow."

"I think…" I say as my eyes tighten.

"I think you're full of it."

Ollie hits me upside my temple. I unfold from my crossed leg position and rub the side of my head as I lay in the sand.

"What was that for?"

"What's your body telling you now?"

"That that fucking hurt."

"Watch your tongue. I don't need your cousin rushing out to clean your mouth out again."

"You're over-exaggerating."

"Maybe, but I wouldn't be surprised if she was around the corner with a brush and soap ready."

Ollie stands over me with his arms folded at his chest. The thought of Sophia being near isn't that surprising, but I'm the king, I should be able to get away with a few unpleasant words.

"Now, what's your body saying?" Ollie asks as I lay in the sand.

"Pain? That's what you're experiencing. What is it *saying*?" I think about it, and then I stop thinking about it. I get up.

"Good. Bounce back. A natural reaction is to counter. Your body took a hit, now it wants to know why and by whom. After that, you'll have only seconds to properly counter," Ollie throws a couple of jabs at me, and I manage to dodge a few before he catches me in the face.

I stumble but wipe the pain away and take up a guard.

"Good. Now your body is learning and adapting. It got caught off guard, and the next thing it wants to do is defend. This is what your body is naturally telling you to do, but you're so wrapped up in your own thoughts that you're not listening."

Ollie comes at me again. His actions are slow but readable. Which is perfect because it allows me to follow and block his every move until he ups his speed. He comes at me harder, his actions less readable as my vision blurs. He rams his palm up into my chin and thrusts my chest with his other palm. I fly back several feet and land face first in the sand. The world is still swirling and my body is ringing, but not from Ollie's attack, but from my gathered exhaustion. I try to pull myself up but my body is stiff. "I used to struggle with this concept too," Ollie explains as I groan.

"My mind and body were not aligned, I couldn't comprehend what my body was telling me I was capable of because I wasn't accepting the truth about myself. Never fear to be who you truly are. I found other means and procedures to free myself of those restrictions. Now tell me, what is your body saying?"

"Nothing…"

"Tell me the truth or I'll strike you again," Ollie threatens.

I'm struggling to breathe as I can't pull myself up.

"I got nothing!"

"Not acceptable. A king with nothing to fight for is no king of mine."

Ollie moves faster and I try to coerce my body to defend. It refuses and Ollie kicks me back up, grabs my blouse, and holds me close.

He punches me in the gut between words. "Tell me—what it's—saying!"

I grunt and groan until my vision becomes so blurry that I think I've gone numb. I no longer feel his fist lodged in my stomach. "Good. Now, what is it saying."

"W-what…?"

I struggle as blood leaks through my lips. Ollie's angelic skin and face become clear. His emerald eyes and teal hair seem to glow as stars dance around him. Stars dance around everywhere.

"S-stop."

"Good. Now, are you able to see?" Ollie stands perfectly clear in my sights.

I am holding his wrist, keeping him from punching me again. The world is numb. There is no sound outside of Ollie's voice. I still see stars, but are they stars? Speckles of light that match Ollie's hair fill the square. "I see…Divinity?" I stumble away and remain on my feet.

My pain is nothing but a whisper. Still present, but not throbbing as before. I blink and I see the stars. I blink again and the world blurs back into what I'm used to seeing. No stars, just the open space of the square and Ollie who is coming at me with another punch. I deflect it almost as easily as I breathe, and he comes at me again. He shuffles together an arrangement of punches and kicks that I manage to block until the world's silence is unmuted. Whatever I was experiencing fades away and Ollie clocks me in the chin. These stars I see, I'm sure are from a mild concussion.

"That was an improvement. The first step of Divinity is being able to see it. Once you do and accept it, your body will welcome it as you take your first steps through the door of the Martial Arts."

"Why did it take so long?"

"You think too much. Sometimes it's a strength, sometimes it's a weakness. Right now, it's your weakness. You have so much going on that you're failing to listen to the changes within you. I had to occupy your mind long enough for your body to hit its limit."

"Its limit?"

"Yeah, for how much longer it was going to let you take a beating before finally responding; breaking that wall you hide behind when you're trying to make rational decisions."

"That's just who I am."

"That's fine, West, but free your mind and accept the Divinity around you. If you and your body don't agree, the Divinity won't work," Ollie dwells on that as if a memory inches up the back of his neck.

He shakes it off to regard me again. "It shouldn't be as complicated as you're making it. You're just a difficult person."

"So, I will clear my mind," I say as I hop on my toes and loosen my body.

"Listen to my body. See the Divinity. Accept the Divinity…"

Ollie punches me in the face again, and I fall back on my butt. I raise and feel the blood trickling from my nose.

"You were thinking again," Ollie stands over me with his fist still cocked.

"Get up and fight."

Ollie takes a stance as he waits for me to get back up. I rise back to my feet, wipe the blood from my face, and take up my guard again.

My training isn't as difficult as before. I guess my time with Ollie is paying off. Anytime my body feels spent and I don't think I have the strength to keep up with Thalia's rigorous exercises and drills, I just shut my brain off and push through.

"*Wow*. It's taken two months for you to show even the slightest progress," Thalia watches me inch a boulder across the sand.

I used to struggle with this completely, not budging the rock at all. Now when I see the speckles of Divinity fill the square, I accept them, allow them to fill me, and feel my strength increase.

"It's not much, but it's something."

"Thanks… Thalia." I grunt.

"Keep pushing!"

⋯⟞∘⟜⟝∘⟞⋯

Five months have passed since the end of the Round Table Tournament. I have been king for five months, and I have been thirteen little over one. The changes over time have been all but subtle.

"My king," a maid says as she opens my door to enter.

I quickly roll over, suffocating a pillow between my legs.

"Your training garbs for today."

"Thank you," I wave to the maid with my back facing her. "I'll get it in a second. Please leave it by the wardrobe."

"Yes, my king."

It takes a few minutes before I roll out of bed, I'm still not used to its immensity. As I change into my training gear, I think about my armor. Sassarus said it should be ready within the next few days.

I've gotten used to a lot of the layout of the castle, but not all of it. I pick up Sophia along the way to the Martial Court. She still likes to watch my training, I believe she still doesn't trust Ollie and I don't blame her. In those five months I've learned a lot, I've come so far, yet I have not landed one hit on Alan. I don't know which of us has more patience.

Aunt Janis refuses to watch such violence, and the rest of the family continue to have their hands full with Cousin Mathis and Silvana's kids, making sure they don't run amuck throughout the castle.

Alan leans against his staff. "Are you going to actually hit me today?" I take up my usual wobbly stance. "All I can do is my best."

"Bullshit. Thalia tells me you've gotten stronger, and don't think I don't know about your secret lessons with your Second Grand Advisor over there," Alan points his staff in the direction of Ollie.

He stands with Terrence, Sophia, and my favorite personal nurses, Nessa and Junah. He's blushing a little as he tries to wave off Alan's accusations.

"So why don't you stop wasting my time and show me something you've learned."

"Uh…" I stutter.

I was really hoping I could reveal my growth on my own terms, but if I've learned anything from becoming king, sometimes things don't go the way you want.

"Okay then. Again, I can only do my best."

"I swear you best do something because I'm about to—"

I don't let Alan finish. My stance shifts. In every session, I always mistakenly lunged in, but that was to test his reaction time. I'm trying something different. I release my sword and it hurtles hilt over tip at Alan's face. He deflects it, but the strength behind the toss raises his eye.

"Honestly, throwing your weapon isn't going to—"

I don't let him finish and launch forward using a technique I learned from Ollie that he calls the *Quick-Step*. An assassin's move to close the gap and catch my opponent in an opening so small that they don't have a chance to defend. It took me three months to figure out how to make the Divinity work for me to perform the move. The rest of the time I spent mastering it.

I didn't like the small window Ollie promised me. So, I used my own sword as a distraction to open the window slightly more. I feel like I am racing through the stars as Divinity flows through my every muscle. Alan's smug face is my target, and while he's in mid-sentence, I close the gap and deliver a punch to his cheek. Five months, and I finally got him. Though in those five months, I suppose I should have learnt how to throw a more effective punch.

My fist connects, but it's only strong enough to force Alan to take a single step back as he uses his staff to prevent me from budging any further. His turn. He pushes me off him, picks up his staff, and jabs it into me. Air escapes my lungs as pain ripples through my body.

"*Match him*," my body says.

I grip the staff and throw it behind me as I roll off it. Then I lunge with my elbow but miss as Alan side steps it. With quick footing, Alan twirls and swings his staff at me but I wasn't foolish enough to think I'd land that last attack.

I stay out of reach and find my dummy sword. I bring the sword down on Alan, he blocks it, and bats me away. I stumble back on my feet and ready a guard for an attack that doesn't come. Alan rests against his staff and my body collapses. Our bout was no more than a minute, but I feel like I've been fighting for hours.

"You need to breathe. Oxygen will limit how long your body can perform under the stress of the Martial Arts. You still have much to learn," Alan concludes as he begins walking towards Thalia and Marshall.

She looks surprised by my performance and Marshall continues studying me.

"He's still learning, but at least he's not crying anymore," Nessa admits as she approaches me with Junah at her side.

"That's an improvement in my book. June, add that to the notes."

Junah takes a book out of his pack and starts scribbling in her remarks. They assess me as I catch Sophia watching me with her hands covering her mouth. I can't tell if she's as taken back as Thalia is from my bout or if she's surprised I'm still alive. Ollie doesn't seem bothered at all.

Terrence is clapping. Thanks, *Terry*, I'm glad I got your approval.

"Well done, my king. Nice to know that you can somewhat defend yourself."

"For a few seconds at least," Alan takes a sip of water from a brown sack.

"He still got you good in the face. I believe the last time you got caught off guard like that, Nova launched you through that back wall," Terrence points to the wall behind the boulders.

I'm more taken by the mention of Rhodain's sister.

"Nova?"

"She cheated," Alan corrects. "She used magic."

"You provoked her, like you always do."

"You had that one coming," Thalia adds. "You called her small fry, and then she proceeded to fry your face."

Thalia and Terrence laugh. Alan looks at a loss of words. This is also a first for the past five months. Marshall remains as quiet as ever, but their combined laughter makes his expression soften.

After Nessa and Junah finish tending to my wounds, I walk with Sophia and Terrence to my chambers where I proceed to clean up and get ready for the rest of the day. As I stand in my shower, I can't help but grin. It still hurts, but I stare at my right hand and clench it into a tight fist.

"I got him."

I finish getting ready and meet in my throne room for the morning meeting. Terrence and Ollie stand by the throne in their formal attire. Today we have my three Grandier Knights, Marshall, Thalia, and Alan present. They all bow as I enter. Alan is still reluctant until Thalia jabs him with an elbow. I permit them to rise but I still feel the butterflies in my stomach when I issue a command. Sophia takes my hand as always and escorts me to my throne. She still sees herself as my guide.

I sit and Terrence opens the meeting. "Status update, the kingdom is still undergoing repairs. It appears the tournament was a little harsher on our resources than expected."

"We can afford it right?"

"That's not the issue, my king, we don't have enough resources..."
"Why not?"

Terrence nearly rubs his forehead raw. "If you don't know by now, I'll have to lecture you on the world later... Whenever I can find the time between all my...other duties. In the meantime, we'll just need to seek assistance from the other kings."

"Well, can we arrange for a..."

"Playdate?" Alan interrupts me as he rests against his staff.

Thalia elbows him again.

"...A meeting with the other kings," I grit my teeth.

"That's only part of it, my king," I turn my attention back on Terrence, leaving Alan to Thalia.

"The scouts report that the people still don't see you as fit to rule."

"It's been five months."

"Yeah, it's been five months and we're still not that much better off," Alan adds, and no one tries to hush him this time.

"All you've done is fill the dungeons. Your other promises remain empty."

"It takes time..."

Ollie chimes in, "Time is not something you have anymore, I knew this would come. If you don't start showing that you are a king worth following, the people are going to revolt against you."

"That's taking it a bit far, isn't it?"

"She's not wrong, my king," Terrence jumps back in. "I've tried to keep your face amongst the people so that they know you're not just hiding away in your chambers while your subjects see to your demands. It seemed to be only prolonging the inevitable."

"You need to be a man of action and not a child with a wish list," Alan says.

"Can you give me an ounce of respect?" "I can," Alan analyzes me.

"But will I? Who knows? Right now, you're still a child and I will not willingly bow down to a kid unless you prove such a feat worthwhile."

"I already punched you in the face, what more will it take?" "If you have to ask then that's the problem." I glare at him.

"*So*," Sophia speaks up. "What can we do to win the people over?"

"Put someone worthy of authority in charge."

Thalia rams her elbow into Alan's ribs this time and he winces. "He's not wrong," Ollie says.

"I thought we were past this."

"That's not entirely what I'm getting at," Ollie says.

I wait for more, he *is* my Second Grand Advisor after all. Wait, did Terrence call Ollie *she?*

"If you are seen working side by side with one of the other kings, it might be enough to convince the people that you might actually be worthy enough to sit on that throne. A true king respects another king."

No one argues this, not even Alan, but he could merely be recovering from Thalia's last jab.

"Which king should I work with then?"

Marshall speaks, "King Xi of Dragon's Guard is cooperative." Finally! I haven't heard a word from him in five months.

"He's been neutral between King Richards and King Sorenson since the Days of Hellsfire ended. You might seek an alliance with him."

"Yes, but the Garden of Dragons is difficult to enter these days," Terrence says.

"They rarely let merchants in, so getting approval might take more time than what it's worth."

"What it's worth? If it makes the kingdom accept me easier then I see it very much worth it."

"That's not what I'm getting at my king, please just listen. King Bruno would be the easy answer. If you truly want to win over the people and show that you have what it takes to be king, you must win over King Ivan.

He's the one people view as a hero. The one that defeated the…"

Terrence pauses. "Dragon of Hellsfire."

"Well, if you think that's best…"

Ollie perks up, "And if we can merge our two kingdoms, rather than be on edge with one another then you'll make the flow of resources that much easier. We'd practically be one kingdom. If you can do that… You might be worth that crown sitting on your head." This is a lot to take in. "West?"

I am failing at Alan's last instructions from our bout today. Breathing. It isn't until I heard Sophia's voice that I remember where I am.

"Am I allowed to think this over?"

"For what?" Alan asks. "Another five months? Some of us aren't as young as you."

"I just need to be alone to my thoughts for a moment."

Uniting two kingdoms is a big task. I'm barely capable of restoring one kingdom.

"West you're hyperventilating," Ollie observes.

"Everyone leave. The king will have his answer by this afternoon. He apparently took some internal damage from his training this morning."

Ollie buys me time to calm down, maybe he *is* being helpful. He asks for Terrence to seek out the nurses, and in doing so, Terrence closes the meeting to pick back up later today. Terrence and the knights leave while Sophia stays with Ollie.

"Okay, what's troubling you?" he asks, annoyed.

"I don't know about this," I struggle between breaths. "I don't know if I can handle managing two kingdoms."

Sophia puts her hand on my shoulder. "Well, you're not going to be doing it alone."

"I get that but you don't understand the pressure of having so many eyes looking to you for the right decision."

Ollie groans. "*Gods*, West, if you keep stressing over making the right decision, you'll never make a single one. I thought we were past this months ago. Stop thinking so much."

"*Rhodain was a man of action...*" I mutter.

I don't think Ollie caught what I said. Sophia did. She places her hand on top of mine.

"I'll have a decision by this afternoon. I just need to be by myself."

"Okay."

Sophia nods and looks to Ollie and there's a pause.

Ollie stops and turns to me. "Just know you can't run away from your responsibilities. Eventually, things are going to get worse, and you're going to have to stand your ground and make a decision. What kind of king will you be?"

I don't answer, and he doesn't wait for one. Ollie takes his leave with Sophia, leaving me alone to my throne.

Before the nurses can come to assess me, I make my way through the castle. I need to meet with someone that's been as good to me as my uncle. Down pass the dungeons where I pay Susan and her followers no mind, I enter Sassarus' forge.

He greets me without looking. "Little Sparrow, to what do I owe the pleasure today?"

"They want me to rule two kingdoms!" I blurt.

Sassarus regards me as he wipes his hands with a cloth.

"You are the king, why is this troubling?"

"I'm thirteen!"

He smiles. "Happy birthday."

"It was a month ago. You were away."

"That's why I am saying it now. This is hardly a crisis. I've seen many a crisis. This is nothing like them."

"Well, it is to me," I find a seat amongst his tools.

My arms are slump, hanging down to my knees.

"I don't know what I'm doing with one kingdom, how am I supposed to handle two?"

Sassarus tosses his cloth, glides over to me, and places his hands on my shoulders as if to give me an answer, and then walks away. He starts digging around his forge.

"I imagine you had something to say there?"

"I did, but if it was up for me to make your decisions for you, then *I* would be king."

"You want the task? I'm sure the kingdom will accept you over me." "That's not what I'm getting at, Little Sparrow. This is your decision just like this is your kingdom. It is up to you to forge your own path, just like it is up to me to forge the tools to get you there."

From a hidden shelf he pulls out a long cloth. He removes it as he approaches me, and a shiny new long sword glimmers in his hand. A silvery blade that lights the shadows of Sassarus' forge. He looks it over and then hands it to me. It's thin and lighter than my dummy sword. I could admire this silver all day then I notice the hilt, it's shaped like a bird with its wings spread.

"Spread your wings, Little Sparrow, and forge your own path. That steel is very rare. Mirrogold, a metal that becomes scarcer each year. Its strong, sturdy, light, and will allow resistance to certain attacks and spells of Divinity."

"Mirrogold," I let those words weigh heavier in my mouth than the sword does in my hand.

"Is that why it took so long for you to craft this?"

"Yes, I've only made one other weapon of this mineral, Thalia's sword. Even that was incomplete. I only had enough to make half the blade of Mirrogold. I wanted yours to be complete and then some. Your armor is crafted of the same metal too and I'll have it done before you set off to Woodsforge…"

He pauses. "That is, if that is what you decide to do. My king."

He smiles at me and retreats into the dark corners of his forge. I thank him for everything and am greeted by Terrence and several knights as I leave.

"My king, we have been looking everywhere for you. What were you…?" Terrence pauses at the sight of my new sword.

"I am fine, just needed to clear my head," I lower my sword to my side. "So how long will it take for us to reach Woodsforge?"

To this, I would have thought Susan would stir, but she remains sitting on the floor of her cell, fixated on the portrait of the former king.

Chapter Six

Welcome to Woodsforge

Standing before my very own private train I feel a sense of awe that had somewhat waned over the last few months. There is a secret track beneath the Baronune train station that only members of the king's court are granted access to. Terry, I'm calling him Terry now but not out loud, grants us entrance as we enter the station through the back. We all wear clothing to better fit in with Baronooners rather than armor or fancy fabrics.

We enter the station as a group but easily blend in with the crowd. No one recognizes me as the king. Probably for the best, I'd hate to start a riot in such a confined area.

Terry waves his hands across the gate, and it opens to his will. I am not yet able to unlock it myself, it's another entrance that's rune to my royal court. We proceed down a stairwell to an unused section that is covered in dust from lack of use.

My knights carry the chests down from the carriages as we wait for my train to pull in. Sand trickles down from all the passengers moving around to get to their destinations above. I watch as Alan dusts some off his unarmored shoulder. Everyone's personal items are in their trunks, including their weapons, armors, and other tools. Nessa looks stunning, as usual, in her regular clothing, trousers, and white blouse. Junah still wears his nurse's vest over his casuals.

Ollie stands beside me, very uncomfortable in baggy trousers and a hooded robe. I can barely see his eyes.

"Why couldn't I wear my usual hakama?" Ollie asks with his arms hugging his chest.

"Because we've been seen as the king's Grand Advisors, you stick out worse than anyone else in our court." Terry answers.

This doesn't make Ollie more accepting of the matter. As I stand amongst my court, I glance down at my hand. Being here reminds me of Sophia and how she was the first person to greet me upon arriving in the Royal District. I told her she should stay in the kingdom with her family until the restoration of their home is finished. It shouldn't be long now, yet she was adamant about wanting to come with me to Woodsforge.

"You're my guide here in Baronune. Not Woodsforge. I'll have my knights there to keep me out of trouble, so you don't need to worry."

After this past summer, I didn't want to take her too far away from home. She hugged me, and made me promise to return safely. Her promise reminded me of Rhodain, though he made a promise to his sister that he wasn't able to keep. It made me reluctant to make one to Sophia.

"Don't get in over your head this time."

My Aunt Janis said before I left. She too must have had flashbacks to the summer. Me being without our family, under the supervision of knights. At least these weren't banished and wanted for crimes against the kingdom. Still, I'd feel better if Rhodain was here. The sound of the train arriving fills the silent station.

Terry stands beside me. "My king, are you ready?"

"No," I answer honestly. "I'd feel better if you were coming along. You are much better at these kinds of arrangements than me."

"Yes, but Ollie is just as fit to be your Grand Advisor as I. She's brilliant, though your reasons for choosing her may have been questionable. It seems to have worked out."

"*She?* That's the second time you've referred to Ollie as a girl."

"Well, my king, Ollie has not strictly referred to their gender, but is that not how she identify herself?"

"I… haven't considered that Ollie would have a preference, I just thought he was—"

The conductor's whistle blows, and Terry cuts me off. "Regardless, Ollie is still your Second Grand Advisor. Find clarity on the matter when you get a chance, off you go."

"Okay, sure you have to stay?"

"Someone has to stay behind and make sure the kingdom is still running in your absence. You have your knights in case anything goes south. Just remain confident and follow your heart."

"My heart?"

"It's the only strength that you've demonstrated that truly separates you from King Augustus."

"Oh…"

I feel my chin sink into my chest. I would have thought five months of hard work and training would highlight other aspects of my character.

Terry places his hand on my shoulder. "It's fine, my king. Sometimes a strong heart is exactly what you need to be a good king."

He pats me a few times on the back. He's got some strength to him as well. With parting smiles, I thank him and hop on to the train. I find a seat in my section that has Alan, Thalia, and Marshall acting as my personal guard. Ollie is sitting alone at the center of the passenger compartment. I slide in beside h—*her* and study what little of Ollie's features I can see through the small opening of her hood.

"What are you looking at?"

"Oh," I blush. "Nothing. Just something Terry said."

"Well don't be weird, we have a long trip ahead of us."

"Right."

Too nervous to ask for myself, I continue to sit awkwardly as Ollie looks out the window. The train begins to move, and we roll into the darkness of a long tunnel.

————>o∞o<————

Let it be known, traveling alone sucks. When I first came to the Royal District, I hated my trip on the train. We were delayed and there was nothing to look at for hours. I had to find ways to keep myself entertained. This time around, everything is different.

"What do you mean I deserved it?"

Thalia's outraged. I have not been paying attention to her or Alan as they sit across from me next to their own window.

Alan replies are casual. "I'm saying Leo was a jerk, but you left me for him, so, you got what was coming to you."

"That's uncalled for and you know it!" Thalia gasps as she turns a different shade of pink. "No wonder why I left you. You're just as big he is!"

"Really?" Alan looks to the ceiling as if pondering a thought. "I'm pretty sure that I'm *bigger*."

He smiles at her and she slaps him. I have no idea what they're talking about, but Ollie snickers. I look past my Second Advisor to observe the changing scenery. No Baron Yaks to ruin the trip this time. We leave them and the desert behind as we pass through dunes and into lavishing green plains. It's so refreshing to no longer look at sand, sand, and more sand. The morning sun caresses the resting dew, making the grass sparkle as we pass.

I've always wished for Old Country to look more like, well, country. Cattle, sheep, and dogs run around the herds to keep them in line and it makes me smile. Ollie removes his hood and his hair sparkles just like the grass under the morning sun's kiss. I find myself again ogling him. Her. Terry's words whisper in my head. "You're doing it again."

It still feels invasive to ask. "Sorry."

I hear Marshall sneeze as he sits in the corner of the compartment. I glance back, he looks miserable with swollen red cheeks and saggy drained eyes.

"Are you okay, Marshall?"

He sneezes. "I'm fine, my king, I often catch a whiff of the old allergies whenever I return north."

"You go to Woodsforge often?"

"…I guess you can say that."

He coughs as if to clear his throat. I decide not to press as he's already dealing with enough as it is.

"Shall I have Nessa – "

"It shall pass." He kindly denies.

Since we still have some time before arriving in Woodsforge, I take this opportunity to stretch my legs and move throughout the train. Marshall keeps to himself, suffering through his allergies. Nessa and Junah appear to be the mirror opposite of Alan and Thalia, while Nessa shines her beautiful smile, she and Junah joke to themselves. Thalia sits in a silent rage while Alan chooses to keep his attention out the window. I think he's still feeling that slap.

I exit our compartment and enter the next part of the train holding the rest of my knights. I've only gotten to know a handful of my hundred warriors. They regard me as they do to the other knights and continue about their business. I shift my attention over to one of my lieutenants who is reciting poetry to some of the women.

He's tall with golden skin and rich blonde hair. The younger female knights seem to be eating it up but I don't get it. Poetry bores me, but they find something interesting about it. All but one at least, the bored lieutenant, Dawn.

"Excuse me, my king," Thalia huffs as she passes me. "Dawn, a word?" "Ah, the lovely Thalia…" the golden knight begins.

"Save it, Hayden. I'm not in the mood."

She growls and shoots him a cold *Arturnic* stare. Dawn doesn't hesitate to take this opportunity to leave Hayden's *thrilling* poetry. Thalia and Dawn have such an intense conversation that the few knights sitting near feel awkward and move closer to the front. One of which is as tall as the compartment itself. Kaleb, he has his head full of a tangled black mess for hair, nearly hitting the ceiling. I don't blame him, I don't like how upset Thalia looks all of a sudden, but I leave her to Dawn and return to my compartment. As I walk past Alan, he seems content with himself but lacks the smile he was boasting before.

"What are you looking at?" He asks as I study him.

"I don't know…" I answer honestly and return to Ollie.

Ollie sighs. "You're hopeless."

The train enters a very wooded terrain. A forest apparently, I've only read of them. Ollie pokes fun at me. "You also need to get out more."

I argue. "The last time I left home I got caught up in a battle royale blood tournament and ended up being king."

This causes Ollie to stop teasing and flashes a glare at me that makes me glad his scalpels and drying needles were in a different compartment.

There's not much to look at as we zoom through the trees. One blurry trunk after another. As we round a lush mountain's face, I notice a massive lake below us with waters so clean and undisturbed that I wish I could fall through the window and swim in it right now. Though it is something I've never had the chance to learn so I should probably reconsider.

Two large districts border the east and west sides of the giant lake, and together could make up two parts of Baronune. A third district known as the Stone Capital resides at the top of the lake is where the rest of the kingdom is. Large mountain ridges cover the backs of the three districts, on the largest of these a castle appears to be built into its rocky cliffside. Everything is stone gray, the buildings, the sky, even the mist that drifts across the lake.

If it weren't for the greenery sprouting out through the gathered kingdom and the crystal blue waters, I'd think this place to be dull. The sun sits behind one of the taller mountains, and we snake through the hills as we make our way to our final destination. We pull into a station nearly as empty as the one we left.

Alan whistles. "Now *there's* the beautiful sights of Woodsforge I admire."

He peers out the window into the abandoned station. I don't know what he's referring to. Stone gray walls and floors, it's exactly the same as the one we left.

"Calm down boy, we haven't even gotten to the castle yet."

Thalia pulls Alan back by his long ponytail, making him resemble an excited dog. We gather our things and exit the train, and maidens approach us in lovely, jeweled dresses that leave their shoulders exposed. Oh, they must have been what Alan was referring to. I guess I get it.

"Our king will be waiting for you in our Stone Capital at the base of the King's Crown," says one of the maidens.

I appear confused. "King's Crown?"

"The mountain ridge that surrounds Woodsforge," Marshall answers as he oversees the unloading of the chests and trunks.

"King Richards says the mountains are his crown. That's why his castle is submerged into its base."

"It's also easier for him to oversee the mining," answers the other maiden.

"Welcome, Sir Marshall," she says with a bow.

Marshall pays her no mind.

I lean to Ollie. "What's that about?"

He shrugs. Some advisor, what am I paying him for? Her. I keep avoiding the question.

We load into the stagecoaches while Thalia, Alan, and Marshall ride with the maidens on the horses. Alan and Lieutenant Hayden ride closer to them than any of the other knights. Normally, one lieutenant is necessary to oversee ten knights. There's fifteen in total outside my grandiers that came along to include my two lieutenants. Terry said this would be enough for security, but not enough to look too imposing in case someone gets the wrong idea that we're here to invade.

Along with this, as many of my knights are busy patrolling and overseeing the reconstruction of Baronune, this was all we could spare. In my stagecoach, Nessa, Junah, and Ollie join me. Ollie pulls off her hood to reveal teal hair. It's well kept, unlike mine, and makes Ollie's eyes more mesmerizing. I look away before I'm caught staring, but I'm hardly smooth.

Nessa giggles at me and as I turn red, she puts a finger to her lips.

To my surprise, our stagecoaches are pulled by horses. I know that the steam-powered carriages are more popular here, but it's strange that I get the more traditional treatment. Most likely it is to lower suspicion of our sudden arrival, the last thing I want is to announce my presence as the new King of Baronune and have even more people against me.

We exit what appears to be the mouth of a cave and are greeted by the pale light of Woodsforge's Eastern District, the people here are not as dressed up as the people of Baronune. Everyone wears dirty brown robes and gloomy faces.

"Why do they look so miserable?"

"I don't know," Ollie answers. "All of the stone gems and riches of Arcasia originate from the mines here, I would expect the citizens to be more, *lively.*"

They remind me of the thugs and less fortunate people of Baronune. As we proceed into the Stone Capital there's a noticeable difference as the people here are more fashionable. I catch a hooded man fall into the road, he looks tired, weak, and unable to get back up as the stagecoaches close in on him.

I slap my hand on the wood to alert the coachman. "Hey, stop! Stop the stagecoach!"

The horse whinnies as we come to a halt. I hop out with Ollie at my heels, I crouch down to the man while others try to calm the horse.

"Can you get that thing under control, please?" I ask the other maidens as they approach.

They take notice of the man in the road and frown.

"Get that peasant out of the way and it will be easier."

Hearing the word, *peasant* makes me think of Susan, and my face burns with rage.

"Have some respect!"

"No, no," the old man says. "This is my fault. I am just too clumsy." "No sir, this isn't your fault."

He trembles and I make out the wrinkled and spotty skin beneath his hood, protruding nose, and a mouth with few remaining teeth.

My rage lifts. "You look hungry, let's get you out of the road and feed you."

I help him up and walk him back into the crowd.

"Oh, thank you, young man. You are so kind."

Ollie rushes to a nearby shop and fetches stew and a cup of water. The old man takes it in his weak hands and attempts at a gummy smile.

Marshall approaches with his horse. "Westley…" He pauses at the sight of the old man. They lock eyes.

"We have to keep going."

" I just wanted to make sure this guy was okay."

"I'm sure he's fine now," he refrains from setting sights on him again. "Thanks to you."

Marshall turns his horse and heads back to the stagecoaches. I say goodbye to the old man and return to my stagecoach with Ollie, who shuts the door behind us.

"Was that necessary?"

"To be kind?" I stare at Ollie. "Always."

The day becomes grayer as we roll-up. The sun completely blocked by mountains as we sit at the base of the King's Crown. The distant smell of fresh water and fish swirl with the scent of the surrounding pine. The castle is rather unimpressive, another stone-gray structure like the rest of the kingdom. Rows of torches lead to the main entrance while rails and minecarts are pushed by burly men in and out of higher passages and shafts.

"I feel like I should be grabbing a pickaxe rather than a sword." "Don't judge everything by its appearance, my king," says Nessa.

Ollie and I peer out the window to the towering structure. We come to a halt and the maidens and knights dismount their horses.

The maidens gesture inside. "We will show you to your chambers. Feel free to don your armors and crowns. The Banquet of Kings will be this evening."

"That sounds fancy."

Feeling a draft from the northern airs, I'm reminded that we're not in Baronune anymore. Dare I say I miss the heat?

"Our king only dines in fancy," one of the maidens answers, unfazed by the chill.

"Uh, okay."

They lead us into the castle through massive wooden doors. No magic runes? Is Divinity banished here as well? We're greeted by more lovely ladies that only make Alan more excited and take us to our respective chambers. As I walk down the cold and long halls, splats of water drip through the cracks in the ceiling, and gives me more respect for Baronune. I am shown to my chambers that are decorated in crimson sheets and drapes behind golden dressers and wardrobes. This is more like a room fit for a kingdom.

A giant man carries in my trunk and chests. "Thank you."

"The door in the back is where you'll find the path to the king's courtyard," explains a maiden.

"You'll meet with the rest of your party from Baronune there."

"Okay."

She bows and leave with the giant man. Alone, I inspect my chamber and realize that the torch lighting the corner is not a torch at all. It's some sort of quartz, odd. I've never seen anything like it.

As the evening approaches, I don my newly crafted armor. A stainlesssteel silvery suit of plate armor made of the same mineral as my sword, Mirrogold. I sheath my blade to my waist and drape my cape over my shoulders. It's a beautiful teal, much like Ollie's hair. Why do I fawn over this? Ever since Terry mentioned that he might be a girl, I have had this strange fascination with him now. Her. Gah! The very thought leaves me scratching my head. I don't know what to make of it, but I know it's a weird feeling I've never had before.

I finish gearing up as I place my silver jeweled crown on my head. This is my *outgoing and professional* crown. I then take a few breaths to steady my anxiousness, and head for the door.

"Okay," I say as I grasp the knob. "Here I go."

I open the door and follow a brightly lit hall to the courtyard. I notice that quartz lines the wall and guide me to my knights who all wait for me in the darken court. With the sun setting, the courtyard is practically already under nightfall within the shadows of the mountains.

"Whoa."

This side of the castle is astonishing. The quartz gives it a heavenly glow, as the mountain coolness wafts over my skin. I turn to my knights; Alan, Thalia, and Marshall stand waiting for me in their armor. Ollie is beside them in a lovely ivory hakama, why doesn't she wear armor? Her cheeks seem to sparkle with the stars, even though she looks without patience as Ollie doesn't bother to regard me.

"Am I late?"

"No." Ollie answers.

"Then what's the matter?"

"Not the question here," Alan interrupts. "What's that armor?"

"Sassarus made this for me. It's Mirrogold."

"Oh geez," Alan groans. "And you get a whole suit made out of it?" "*Alan*," Thalia warns.

"What?" He gestures at me. "What's the point of us then? He seems well guarded on his own to me."

"Don't mind him," Thalia steps in front of Alan. "He's just sour that he didn't get any Mirrogold armor."

Marshall steps forward. "Shall we proceed? We don't want to keep the king waiting."

We enter the dining hall which is just as large as the one in my castle yet is filled with far more colors, people, and furniture. Maybe we are late? As we wait to be seated, more well-dressed maidens strut in from corresponding doorways. Alan claps his hands excitedly while I notice two lines of sackbut players enter.

They play loudly as a man decorated in a bright pin-striped suit dances and flips around us. Bells hanging from his shoes and hat ring with every movement. His lips are redder than the carpet, and his face is white as a cake with dark markings lining his eyes.

"What is he?" I whisper to Ollie.

"A jester, I suppose?"

He's so distracting that I almost miss another group enter. Two maidens, one in a violet dress, the other in maroon. The one in violet looks around my age. She has long dark black hair with eyelashes weighed in diamonds along with other gems and jewels imbedded in her dress and arms. The other woman is older, maybe the same age as Thalia and Nessa, but much more alluring. Far more alluring as her smile makes me dizzy. Her hair wraps in a crimson brunette bun, and her skin is so fair that I think she was born out of pearls. She's far prettier than any of the other maidens in the hall. So much so that I think Alan is broken as he doesn't ogle over her like he's done to the others. She regards us, unamused.

"Are you okay?"

Ollie glares at her. "I don't like her for some reason."

"Why?"

"I don't know," Ollie studies her as her finger trails the rim of a glass. "She's just giving me bad vibes."

Beside the woman stands the only knight I've seen from this kingdom, with a presence that leaves the room mute. Decorated in a bulky obsidian suit of armor, they put the *knight* in nightmare. Finally, a man with shaggy black hair enters and panic creeps into my throat. His scarred skin is sickly pale. He stands in front of the table with hands lined with rings. He scans my knights like a hawk overlooking his prey. No one seems at ease in his presence either.

"Which of you is the King of Baronune?" says the man.

He looks more prepared to attack than greet. I swallow my concerns and take one step. Ollie immediately grabs my wrist. He doesn't take his eyes off the man in black.

His right eye finds me. He wears a black patch over the other.

He frowns pointing a talon ring in my direction. *"You?"*

"...Yes. And you are the King of Woodsforge?"

"Am I?"

I swear his glare is burning through my heart. I feel uneasy, but I do not show it. My eyes leave the man in black and turn to survey the guests. "No…You are not."

So many purples, greens, blues. None of them seem right. Then I see him. Rhodain? No, but his presence is familiar. The hooded figure in a ragged cloak.

I point to him. "You. I know you."

"He's quite observant…"

The hooded figure speaks. His voice is at first familiar, then he moves through the crowd. The rest of my knights, except for Marshall, shift their hands to their weapons.

"…For a kind and generous, young man."

The Tricks of the Trade

He takes down his hood. Grayish white hair flows out wildly and he grins a gummy smile.

My eyes widen.

He removes something from his cloak and places a golden crown on his head.

"I am Ivan Richards, the King of Woodsforge." King Ivan approaches us. "You're the old man from before."

He doesn't seem as weak as he did earlier but stands upright with his toothless smile.

"You got me! I didn't think you'd spot me so quickly. I definitely thought you would have mistaken my associate to be the king. I mean look at him," King Ivan guides our attention to the man in black.

"He's far more intimidating."

The man in black watches us all with his one eye. I feel he's ready to swoop down and attack us at any moment.

"Intimidating he is, but we're here as guests for a specific purpose. I would not expect the king to look so willing to start a fight." "Yes, Eli is not a people person," King Ivan admits.

"You may relax, Eli. You did your duty."

Eli snarls as he takes his place in the back, opposite of the black knight. King Ivan glides past us, shedding his raggedy cloak as one of the many maidens places a royal robe upon his shoulders. Grabbing a challis from the table, Ivan gulps down the liquid and smiles at us again.

"May I interest you in King's Juice?"

"I think I might be too young for that," I state as I don't think it's just juice. "Your majesty."

"Yes, you are a curious one."

"I could say the same. Why the ruse?"

"Oh!" The king laughs. "I had to see you for myself. The new King of *Baro – non*, Baronune, is a child? Laughable! Hilarious! I thought that ole August was trying to pull a fast one on me for a change. I wanted to see just what kind of a king you were, and I found a *child* for a king."

King Ivan slams his challis on the table and nearly keels over laughing. His lovely escorts come to his aid, and he stands upright again. "Please introduce yourself, New King."

"I am King Westley Jameson of Baronune. This is my court."

I guide the king's attention to everyone around me. "My Second Grand Advisor, my knights in all, and my nurses."

"Interesting," his eyes fix on my knights. "It is always a surprise to see you in my presence, Marshall."

"Father..." Marshall addresses King Ivan with a disapproving tone.

Father? I glance between the two of them and the resemblance becomes clear. It's all in their faces. I could clearly imagine King Ivan looking identical to Marshall if he were roughly twenty years younger.

"I would not be here if not for my king's requirements."

"Given that you retired from my court for August's," King Ivan announces.

"Are you still a Commander? What happened to the others? The fire wielders and that fairy kid?"

He's referring to Rhodain, his sister Nova, and the one called Avery. I know little to nothing about them besides that they were the strongest knights in the kingdom.

"They were banished for being wrongfully accused of crimes against the former king," I admit with a little fire.

I don't like to recall the false crimes against Rhodain. It just reminds me of Susan and all that she did to become king.

"Those crimes have been dropped, but the whereabouts of the knights known as Nova and Avery are unknown."

"And the third?"

"Deceased," I struggle to admit.

The vision of Rhodain being stabbed and falling from the castle is still a vivid memory.

"In his efforts to become king, he was betrayed by the former Queen."

"How unfortunate, and what became of the ones with the weapons, those enchanted commanders?"

Lawrence, Matthews, and the ever-emotionless Greg. More rage boils within me. They wielded weapons that granted them control over the earth, the wind, and lightning. They were the final obstacles for the King of the Round Table Tournament placed purposely by Susan to ensure that no one else would take the throne besides her.

"They have been held accountable for conspiring against the late king. Being a part of Susan's crimes of killing King Sorenson and initiating the tournament so that she could take the title for herself."

King Ivan seems a little more invested in our presence. "You don't say? Fascinating. So, these are your knights now?"

"Yes...?"

I'm a little confused. He doesn't seem too torn about the death of King Sorenson or the crimes committed by Susan. Does he not care? Were they not colleagues of his? I know I read that the three kings stood against the Dragon of Hellsfire and saved what was left of Arcasia. Did they not keep in touch with each other? Were they not friends?

"Is there something bothering you about my court?"

"Well," King Ivan begins, looking about to say one thing and then reconsiders.

"No, it's just, the Kingdom of *Baro-none* was so heavily guarded between those powerful knights and the king himself. Now, you seem rather defenseless."

"*Excuse me?*" I hear Alan whisper under his breath.

"I can assure you my knights are still capable of defending the kingdom."

I'm not entirely confident about that. Those six knights alone packed far more power and abilities than anyone in my current court. Our defenses did take a hit, especially without Sorenson's Divinity of protection. What do we offer? I have no skills beyond what little I've learned in these past few months. My knights are formidable, but lack training in the Mystic Arts that Rhodain and the others had. I even remember how easily Rhodain was able to run through these very knights during the end of the tournament to avoid capture.

"That being said, there is a reason for us being here."

"True, but first where are my manners?"

The king raises his challis that has been recently filled by one of his maidens.

"I have not introduced you to my table."

He takes a sip from his drink or a gulp. King Ivan then swings his challis in the direction of the woman to his left and splashes red liquid across the table.

"My loyal black knight that I refer to as Kenny, and you may address this fine and beautiful maiden as, Madea Bansha."

The woman lifts her hand for all to admire her, and I can feel the discomfort radiating from Ollie again. The black knight gives a slight bow but remains silent. King Ivan then swings his challis to his right.

"You've already been introduced to my associate, Eli Jardock. And this is my greatest treasure, my prized gem and lovely daughter, Crystal Richards."

The girl takes a sip of what I hope is water, while Eli continues to look at us distastefully. Crystal doesn't look too thrilled either. The jester leaps around the room to no effect.

"Also, if you look amongst the crowd, you'll find my Grand Advisor enjoying himself," King Ivan points off to the side.

I find a man decorated in black and blue robes that mimic the sky as the colors move like clouds.

"He is my sorcerer, Longcaster Rose. He's wiser beyond his years, but a young spirit through and through."

"MORE KING'S JUICE!" Longcaster cries, then kisses one of the ladies surrounding him on the cheek.

I notice Alan regard the loud and bolstering sage with disapproval. *"Have some dignity and respect."*

Thalia stares at him as if she heard him wrong and Dawn rolls her eyes at them both.

"This is my court," King Ivan concludes.

"Are they your only two knights?" "Perhaps," King Ivan wipes his lips.

"There is a matter of concern I'd like to address, but first, why are you here King Westley?"

"West is fine."

Ollie elbows me. I glare at him. "Or not. The reason we have come all this way is to ask for your assistance. After the King of the Round Table Tournament, Baronune and its people have been left in shambles. We have done what we can to rebuild but the damages outweigh our resources." "That does seem to be a problem," King Ivan strokes his chin.

"I always admired the idea of August's tournament to find his replacement if he ever did meet his end, but that was because the man was blinded by his confidence. So sure that no one would get through his protective magic. As you can see, it kills to be that trusting in one's own abilities. The king with no weakness missed the greatest weakness to man. Overconfidence. If he had an heir… Still, he will be missed!"

King Ivan raises his challis, and everyone in the dining hall follows suit aside from Eli and the Black Knight.

"Yes, he will be missed," I say, thinking of Rhodain rather than King Sorenson.

"Thus, we have come here to ask for your assistance in rebuilding our kingdom."

"That's quite the request, and while I may have the resources to assist you. What's in it for me? I rule the north. Woodsforge is my one and only priority. August and Bruno agreed that we would look after our individual kingdoms, why should I break these rules for you?"

"I never made such an agreement. That was well before my time."

I admit, and Ollie keeps his voice low. *"We're here to ask for help and not further the divide between the kingdoms."*

Unite. That is our purpose. "That being said, we're here to alter the terms of that agreement. King Ivan, I come to you with the offer of uniting our kingdoms. To become one, stretching across the trees and the sands. Uniting the north and the south of Arcasia to share in wealth, strength and resources."

I kneel to King Ivan to offer my alliance and cooperation. He remains silent. I can feel his eyes looking me over, studying me. I peek up and see him regarding my court once again. His eyes gleam with concern.

"To be one kingdom would make for covering whatever we each may lack, but..." King Ivan pauses.

"But...?"

"You say strength," King Ivan strokes his chin again. "I just don't see it."

"I'm sorry?"

"Your knights lack the flair and pizzazz of those before them. If I saw any one of those warriors upon your ranks, I might have considered it, but now..."

King Ivan pauses again as he overlooks all of us.

"Now there's nothing here but some wimpy knights with tools."

"Hey!" I snap. "One of them is your son!"

"Yes, a bastard through and through, but that's not saying anything at all. He lost a duel with Eli and tainted his reputation here in Woodsforge so bad that he had to run to *Baro-noonoo*. Can he even lift his sword? Or does that scar still bury deep in his honor and pride?"

I have no response. Marshall hasn't done much with training me or demonstrating his abilities as a knight. He's a part of my court, but I was led to believe that he was truly spectacular in his day. I've seen nothing else and have barely heard a word from him since becoming king.

"The southern kingdom is led by a king that can't even defend his knights, let alone his people!"

He laughs and slams his fist on the table.

"No wonder you've come here to me."

"I don't know, Ivan," Bansha speaks as she swirls her glass in my direction.

"He's kind of cute. Maybe there's more to him than he appears. Tell me, King Westley, does your mother still tuck you in at night? Read you the old fables of the western lands?"

She laughs, and King Ivan joins her. No one in my court is amused.

"So, I take that as a no?" I ask through gritted teeth.

"Oh, don't be so quick to assume," King Ivan catches his breath.

"That's how I fooled you once already."

"I saw through your deception."

He winks, and I frown. "Only because I let you. Believe me, kid, I have more tricks up my sleeve. It's kind of my hobby. Now with the matter at hand. I would be a fool to deny the opportunity to add your kingdom to my treasures..."

"Treasures? It's still Baronune."

"You even talk down about your own kingdom?" King Ivan regards me having finally stopped laughing.

"Seriously kid, how did you become king?"

"I sort of fell into the role," I admit, and King Ivan breaks into laughter again.

"No seriously, how did it happen? I am aware of the rules of the Round Table Tournament, and you even say the Triumphant Knight, Rhodain, was a contender. How did you surpass the kingdom, the knights, and the obstacles put in place to test you, to break you, to make you king?"

I need to sell this. I need to fool King Ivan into believing my strength much like he tricked me earlier. "...I thought only of survival, and to do that meant ending the tournament as soon as possible," I swallow as my eyes flare with seriousness.

"By any means necessary."

These words leave my lips only halfheartedly. Withholding the truth hurts. King Ivan regards me with a stern gaze. There's no smile. No gums. For the first time, I see him as the king he is. Strong, sturdy, and weighing every ounce of my words on his personal scale to determine who am I.

"King Westly that was the first authentic thing you've said all day," King Ivan admits, and I feel myself and my court are all taken with astonishment.

He bought that?

"I can feel your struggles in every word you said."

"So, you'll consider uniting our kingdoms?"

"Oh, I'm considering it. The terms of this merging are what I must think about. How to go about uniting our kingdoms. I still don't see much in your defenses, which brings me to the matter of concerns." He drinks, and I don't like his change of tone.

"We of Woodsforge have stumbled upon a slight issue. Our mining proceeds have been constantly interrupted by a little... *problem*, and my forces have not been able to rid us of it."

"What's the problem?"

"You'll see soon enough. If you and your knights rid the northern mountain ridge of the pests that have been interfering with our mining procedures. I'll consider accepting the uniting of kingdoms and we can come to terms for the agreement moving forward.

"Great!"

This is a step in the direction I want.

"But what is this pest?"

"Trust me, you'll know it when you come across it." "What did you say about trust not too long ago?" He breaks out into laughter again.

"You have a mind in that young head of yours. I like that. It might get you somewhere in the future. You'll have to trust me when I say you'll recognize the situation when you greet it tomorrow, just like I trust that you'll have no problems getting rid of the problem at hand. That is, if you and your knights are worthy and up for the task."

He's challenging me and my court. I have to prove myself as a worthy king to not just my kingdom, my knights, but to King Ivan as well. It's like a real game of King's Men, and if there's one thing that I'm good at, it's King's Men.

"Okay. We'll see to your issues in the morning and rid you of your problems."

"Good! I'm glad that—"

"Because if we scratch your back, you will scratch ours, helping my people return to the lives they deserve."

I cut him off and the king stares down at me. "…Yes. Everything will be for the betterment of our kingdoms."

His eyes scroll down upon me. "That is why we're kings, to see to and serve the betterment of our people."

"We're already agreeing."

As we exchange gazes with one another, the sackbuts blare as the jester bounces about.

"Then tonight we'll drink to the start of an era," King Ivan boasts as he raises his challis.

"Tomorrow will begin the dawn of a new age for kings and queens!"

Everyone drinks to the cheers of their king. Ollie and I exchange looks of doubt. Tomorrow will be the dawn of something new, but to what?

Chapter Eight

The King of the Mountain

The festivities carry on late into the night. Ollie and I find ourselves in an awkward setting being the youngest here. Some of the maidens ask us to dance. I can't tell if this is out of kindness or pity. I kindly decline, not knowing what I would even do in this situation. I've never danced in my life, let alone with a girl, and especially not with a grown woman. The maidens do the same with my knights.

Alan leaps at the opportunity while Thalia protests. Her, Dawn, Nessa, and the other female knights are approached by men that look too tipsy to remember if they have two left feet or not. Junah tries to deny the courtship but since he can't verbally refuse, the maiden asking him thinks it's a cute gesture and leads him to the floor. Marshall is the only one to deny the maidens approaching him. He seems like a caged animal on the verge of attack as he remains fixated on King Ivan, his father, and the man in black, Eli. Seeing how this isn't the best place to speak, I'll have to ask him more about his relations with them later.

Marshall takes his place on the back wall, where he waits for the festivities to end. Ollie and I exchange glances and follow his lead. As elegant and captivating as Ollie may be, I don't feel the urge to impose upon us dancing. It rivals my embarrassment to ask Ollie's gender preference. I guess I could ask the king's daughter to dance, but she seems so bored with the occasion that I'd rather not.

Ivan proceeds to drink as his maidens feed him grapes, cheese and anything else that can slide down his throat. His queen… is Bansha his *queen*? Whether or not, she pays little attention to her king and watches the dancing. She gives a wicked smile as her fingertip rings the rim of her glass. She seems to approve of how the maidens treat my knights, while the black knight, Kenny, stands as stiff as a statue. Maybe King Ivan should offer his knight some King's Juice to loosen up.

As the night grows late, and the dancing ends and everyone in the dining hall is ushered out by the maidens. The king and his table exit, well he stumbles, out and I follow my court back to our chambers. Hoover and Cooper are even more loud and boisterous. They may have had too much King's Juice as they are escorted by a few maidens. Hayden is sloppily quoting poetry to his escorts as he sloshes through every word and rhyme, and Alan has a maiden under each arm while Marshall keeps Thalia from drawing her sword on a guy that got a little too handsy.

We enter the courtyard and all my knights and nurses part ways to their chambers. I enter my own and in haste to remove my armor and change into my satin pajamas. I lay staring at the quartz in the corner, wondering how to deactivate its light, and as I begin to drift in and out of sleep, the large gem follows my actions. My chamber goes black as I am welcomed by dreams.

Dreams. Is that what this is? I find myself waking up, but I have no idea what time it is. Is it morning? Is it still night? Where am I? The world around me is different. A realm of light, fuzzy, but warm. I glance down. I am standing, but there is nothing to stand on. Is this air? There is no breeze. This place, this void, is a pale yellow. I lift my hand to my mouth, trying to breathe. No breath. I pull my hand away and an image appears in the distance. It's unclear, out of focus, but recognizable. I lean forward to get a closer look and find myself gliding across the space between us. Closing in, the figure becomes clearer. A man in all white. He wears a large, hooded cloak, but his back is to me. His hair is dark and wild as if he had just rolled out of bed. He turns to me, slowly.

"Rhodain?"

He faces me. Clean. Healthy. Alive? No. I saw him… I saw him turn to ash and vanish before me. I stand before this image of Rhodain. He doesn't speak. He shakes his head in protest. His stare, his face, is blank. Empty like the space around us.

"Then who are you, and where am I?"

This false Rhodain tilts his head, studying me but doesn't answer. All he does is let out a yawn and stretch. He turns away from me as if rolling to face the opposite side of a bed. I reach out to grab his shoulder but can't. The space between us expands. I'm being pulled away by something yet nothing. There's no one else here to grab me. My vision turns into a vacuum as I'm sucked out of this existence and I wake in my bed. The reactive quartz springing to life. What was that? Where was that?

"What time is it?"

I can hear my voice again. I can breathe. Whatever just happened, I don't feel like I actually went anywhere. My body feels rested as if getting a full night's sleep.

There's a knock.

"My king, are you awake yet?" Nessa's voice asks through the door. "It's morning, we need to get ready soon." "Uh…" I respond groggily.

"Yeah, I'll be getting ready here soon."

"Okay, we've been told to meet in the courtyard. Our escort will pick us up there."

"Thanks, Nessa."

I stare at the ceiling. What just happened?

I don my armor again and attach my sword to my waist but wear no crown today. If I am to do combat with whatever is in these mountains, I don't want to lose it. Exiting my chamber I meet with everyone in the courtyard.

"My goodness, Alan… are you okay?"

He looks half asleep and half dead. As does Hoover, Cooper, and Hayden.

Thalia speaks up. "Some of us had a little too much fun last night." She leans into Alan with her hands on her hips.

"Last night… 'dis morning. You call it, I did it. Over, and over…" Alan answers groggily.

He leans all his body weight onto his staff.

"Get over yourself!" Thalia barks. "If you had even half the dignity and respect that you preached about last night, you wouldn't have this problem."

"Don't get hot with me now… your voice is so loud," he groans as he rubs his temple.

She wasn't even yelling. She's agitated but not yelling. "Besides, I offered you an invitation—"

"I wouldn't have come within ten feet of you last night!"

Her yell almost knocks Alan off his staff. She huffs as Dawn goes to comfort her.

"Whatever. Pull yourself together. We have a mission to do."

"Do we even know what or who we're looking for?"

I speak. "No, King Ivan seemed very sure whatever it is we can handle."

"Though his own men were having trouble," Ollie points out. "I don't like it."

"Ollie, you don't like *anything*."

"That's not true."

"Do you like me?" I ask and there's a long pause.

Ollie stares at me as if unrolling a scroll of comments to say but decides not to.

"…Which mountain are we climbing?"

Rude, then again that's Ollie. Nessa finishes chuckling to herself and then has Junah hand her a bottle from his medical pack.

"Here," she drips a light blue liquid into Alan's mouth.

"This will help the hangover pass faster."

"Do you have enough for everyone?" The other half of the knights in just as worse shape as Alan.

"Should be more than enough, my king," she promises with an enlightening smile.

I look to Junah. He nods and gives a thumbs up. I smile and turn back to Alan, Thalia, and Marshall. Now is as better time than ever to ask Marshall about his father, then I hear people approaching from one of the corridors up ahead. There are about seven maidens led by the sorcerer, Longcaster Rose. He's still drinking.

"What time is it?"

"Just after sunrise," Ollie answers stepping up beside me.

"And he's still drinking?"

"We have weird habits as we get older."

Ollie confirms as we watch Longcaster finish his small gourd and chucks it across the courtyard. He wipes his lips, hiccups, and approaches us. Well. He approaches Marshall.

"King Westley of Baronune..."

"That would be the boy, Longcaster," Marshall directs him to me.

"…You're not the king?" The sloppy sorcerer leans in to get a better look.

"I'm as much the king as you are sober."

"Funny," Longcaster glares. *"King Westley of Baronune!"* "That's me," I say reluctantly as he stumbles towards me.

Ollie looks disturbed.

"King Ivan has asked me to guide you to the mountain trail... *hic.* Where we'll, or no. You will venture and face the mountain. No. Climb the face of the mountain to face... faces?"

I sigh, rolling my eyes. "Just lead the way."

This will take all day if I let him stumble over his words. Instead, he stumbles over his own robes. How did he get dressed this morning? How did anyone that participated in the spirits of lasts night's festivities get dressed this morning? My knights all wear their respective armor as if it were any other day to them. It's either muscle memory or they've had a lot of practice in their morning-after routines. I try not to dwell on that idea too much. The maidens come to take Longcaster as he asks for another gourd. No one gives him one.

We sluggishly follow our escorts through a tunnel that empties us into the back of the castle. We're at the base of the mountain as the rest of the castle sits high above us. There are several horses in our wait. Not enough for everyone.

"Are there not enough horses?"

"The king didn't want to risk the safety of all of them on your outing," replies one of the maidens.

"I thought he was confident we could handle this task?"

"He said your knights should be capable," answers a different maiden.

"We also thought you still possessed knights with magic."

"Is that an issue?"

She shrugs, "that depends on your knights."

"You'll find that we are more than capable, even without, *magic*," Thalia butts in.

"We shall see."

The maiden snarks as she doesn't flinch and brushes past her. Thalia begins to draw her blade when Marshall catches her wrist with his left hand.

I lean over to Ollie. "What's got her goat?"

"That's one of the two maidens that escorted Alan to his chambers."

"So?" I stand back upright. "Why would Thalia be upset with that?"

"*Gods*, are you that young or just that naïve?" Ollie asks and I don't answer this.

"Both. Both it is."

Ollie decides as if dealing with an internal pain and walks off. I'm still confused but decide not to make anything of it.

Marshall lifts me up on my horse with a grimace.

"Are you okay?"

"Yes, my king."

"Your…" I catch myself, wanting to mention King Ivan, but decide better of it. "…Arm. Is it still bothering you?"

"From time to time, it doesn't hinder me from being your Grandier."

"Would you like Nessa to look at it?"

I ask pondering his remark as I've seen little evidence of this and look him over once more. I glance over to her. She looks eager yet restrained at the same time.

"When I'm ready, my king. Until then, I will wear my scar with pride."

I leave it at that and look at the reins in my hands. I have never ridden a horse before. Too much like camels, and I don't like them either. I look back to Marshall who lets out a sigh.

"Ollie," he calls. "You can ride, yes?"

"Yes, I can ride. Why are you…" He notices me and is stricken with disbelief. I must look pathetic.

"No…"

"The king could use your assistance."

"I can't teach him now, we're on a mountain!"

"That's not what I'm insinuating."

Marshall pauses. Ollie looks between me, him and the horse.

"No…"

"Yes." Marshall replies sternly.

"Seriously?"

"It's either that or he falls off and dies."

"Have we forgotten who we're talking to?" Alan interrupts as he rides up beside us.

"Tried to kill the kid once already." "That's in the past," I say.

A long and awkward silence stretches between us.

"Come, Ollie. Take the reins and I'll take your… waist." "…Just stop talking." Ollie urges and climbs up.

"Will do."

I agree and slide back, leaving room. I wrap my hands around Ollie's waist. It's thinner than I expected. In our months of training, Ollie made sure that I didn't lay a hand on him in our spars. If I ever did, I must have been struck so hard in the head that I didn't remember doing so. He seems to cringe at my touch. I admit this is awkward, but Nessa doesn't seem to mind Junah holding her.

"Ollie relax."

"Please stop talking. You said you'd stop talking." Ollie snaps, a little more antsy than usual.

"Just saying, Junah is doing the same with Nessa. I don't want to fall off."

"T-That's different."

"How?"

"I really need you to grow up!"

Ollie groans and the horse reacts as it rises and shuffles in place. Ollie's grip tightens on the reins, and I tighten my grip on Ollie's waist. I can almost see his blushing intensify as he gains control of the horse.

"You okay?"

Maybe now is the time to ask...

Ollie growls. *"You—say—nothing."*

Maybe not. I try to respond but am hushed immediately. Nessa giggles as she and Junah ride pass us.

We designate horses to most of the knights, but we still have to leave a few on foot. Longcaster strides in front with two maidens at his side. He seems to have recovered quickly. Maybe Nessa gave him some of her antidotes, or maybe he used Divinity to cure himself?

"You will follow this trail to the highest peak in the ridgeline," Longcaster takes the last horse by the reins and hands it off to the maidens.

"There you'll find the source to the king's issues. Only return once the problem has been solved."

"You're not coming with us?"

"Gods no," he gasps looking appalled.

"I don't want to die. This is your task from the king. If I get involved, he will have my head."

"Why *haven't* you gotten involved?" Alan asks.

"If you have magic, why don't you just magic this problem away? Better yet, what exactly…"

He stops when he sees Longcaster pull another gourd from his robes and begins to drink. Where did he get that? I thought the maiden's agreed he had enough? Longcaster finishes the gourd and chucks it over the mountainside. He hiccups and begins to sway.

Alan sighs. "…Never mind."

"Welcome to my world," Thalia says. "I have no idea what you're talking about." Alan looks on her smugly.

We take what little information we were able to grasp from the sorcerer and begin our climb up the mountain. It takes us a few hours to follow the trail, not wanting to leave the walking knights behind. King Ivan couldn't have risked a few more horses? I'm starting to wish I had enlisted Roxette for this, he would be able to inspect something off about the king.

The path begins to thin as midday glare sets in, leaving barely enough space for the horses. We stop for a bit of food and water before venturing forward in a single file line and I stare down into the chasm below. White rushes across the roaring river as rocks protrude from the water like the razor-sharp teeth of a monster. A pebble rolls down and hits me from above.

I look up and find mountain goats struggling to climb the jagged cliffsides. Are they the problem we seek? I don't see how a couple of goats could give King Ivan such issues. No one else seems to think this, so I keep my thoughts to myself, and we ride on. Another hour passes and the trails bends eventually stopping as it runs flush with a cliff edge. We've reached a dead end. There's just enough space for us to gather and gaze upon the towering mountain over us.

"Well, that's it," Alan says.

"Anyone else think this is a wild goose chase?" "More like goats," I say pointing upwards.

The goats bound across a separate path up ahead.

"There seems to be more of a trail up there."

"Well, that's it for the horses."

Alan sighs and dismounts his along with my other knights. Ollie and I remain on ours.

Marshall remains on his too. "Do you expect us to climb?"

"We have to keep going until we find whatever it is we're looking for," Alan slides his bo staff out from the saddle.

"Last time I checked horses can't climb."

"How about we send a scouting party?" Marshall suggests.

"No point wasting our energy climbing up if we don't need too."

"This isn't because of that injury of yours, is it old man?" Alan asks glancing back over his shoulder.

"I am more concerned for our king's safety," Marshall looks as if he's biting back a retort.

"Sure you are."

Alan leaves to gather Hoover, Cooper, and some other knights to climb the face of the mountain. I slide off my horse.

"Where are you going?" Ollie asks as I grab my gear.

"Up the mountain," I say, fastening my shoulder bag to my back.

"Why? You're safer down here."

"But our problem and task might be up there, and what kind of king would I be if I just sat around and let you guys have all the fun." "Scaling the side of a mountain is not my definition of fun."

I don't listen, my mind's set on doing this. The whole reason I'm in Woodsforge is to prove I am capable of fulfilling my duties as king. I've trained hard enough for the last couple of months. I should be able to do this.

Ollie lets out a groan and dismounts, grabbing a shoulder bag too.

"Okay, what are you doing?"

"I promised your cousin to keep you safe. If you want to be a moron and not listen to your advisor, I'm left no choice but to follow."

"See, you *do* care."

"Don't make me change my mind."

I chuckle. How hard is it to scale a mountain?

<hr>

I change my mind. I want to go back down. Only halfway up, it looked like a much shorter distance from below. Each grip, each outreach of my foot is almost my last. Rocks crumble, dust sprays into my eyes from my knights up above. Ollie is above me with Alan not too much farther ahead.

"Ah!" I scream as my foot slips out from under me.

I hold tight to the mountain.

"You okay down there?" Alan asks.

"Yeah…" I lie.

I should have stayed on the ground.

"*Okay*," Alan calls back as he proceeds to climb.

"The next time someone advises that you should stay on the ground. Perhaps listen to them? Especially if they are your Grand *Advisor*."

Don't need to tell me twice. Ollie shakes his head at me. He doesn't need to say anything at all. There are four more knights just above Alan.

The sun sinks back behind the mountain and a thick mist rolls in that makes it even harder to see above.

My knights vanish and I can barely see Alan. "Hey! Perhaps hold steady until we're all together! This mist is making it hard to see, I don't want to lose anyone."

"AH!"

A knight screams from up above. Ollie and I look up in a panic. I watch as one of my knights drops out of the mist and falls passed me into the chasm below.

"Like that," I respond with fright creeping into my throat. "I'd hate to lose someone like that."

"*What just happened?*" Alan calls asking for a response from above.

"Something bit him!" Cooper answers a bit too fast and murmured.

"What?" Alan asks back befuddled.

"The mountain!" Hoover says. "The mountain bit him!" "*What?*" Ollie, Alan, and I all ask in unison.

There's a rumbling from up above. There's a rumble from below. The mountain is shaking. *Please* don't tell me the mountain itself is the issue King Ivan was referring too. The rocks shake until I make out a rocky face looking me dead in the eyes. Wait. There's a rocky face looking me dead in the eyes. It roars, I scream, the mountain shakes again, and I lose my grip. Okay, I let go out of terror, but the mountain just roared at me.

"*West!*" Ollie yells, reaching for me.

A little late for that. Then he shrieks, a little more girly than me as he falls too.

"Damn it!"

I hear Alan yell as I lose sight of him. Ollie vanishes too. Oh, wait. Never mind, here comes Alan. He's diving towards me. As I'm falling to my death… How is this a great plan? He reaches out with one hand and grabs my cape. With his other hand, he wields his Bo staff and uses it to catch between the mountainside and a protruding rock pillar that I had completely missed in my descent.

"Are you okay?"

"Yeah, but what are we going to do now?"

"Hold on."

He tries to lift me up, but his effort causes his staff to slip, and we slide a few more feet down until it catches again.

"Well, that's not going to work…"

"Got a plan B?"

 "Nope, going to Plan Z."

"What?"

"It's do or die!"

Alan yells and before I can protest, he begins swinging back and forth, building momentum. He swings us around and around his staff until I become a projectile. He tosses me back up through the mist. My screams must have alerted the remaining knights of my incoming because I'm snatched out of the air before I can fall again.

My heart is trying to break through my armor and when I glance back Ollie is the first person I see. He's lying next to me with Marshall standing over us on his horse.

"Are you okay?" We ask simultaneously.

"Of course I'm okay," Ollie shakes free from the awkwardness.

"I slowed my fall to where Marshall could grab me. What about you?"

"Alan… Oh gods, Alan is still down there!"

Thalia grabs my attention. "We have other problems!"

The mist begins to thin as the sun passes from behind the mountain. I watch as Hoover and Cooper fall from above. There's something else clinging to the mountain.

"What are those?"

There were two, no three boulders like creatures clinging to the mountainside with two arms and legs. The terrain shakes again. Two more boulders fall from above and land before Ollie and me. They spin, revealing the same rocky face I saw before. Arms bust from their sides and they rise up on two stout and sturdy legs. They roar in unison and I flinch. Ollie comes to my aid and slashes the boulder across the face with his scalpel. It scrapes off the stone face and the boulder roars again.

"King West, Ollie, fall back!" Thalia demands as she draws her arming sword.

"Those are Mountain Golems!"

Oh, so that's what they're called. Great, I can scream better knowing that.

Ollie and I scurry to retreat, falling back to Thalia and Marshall. My remaining knights surround and guard us from the two Mountain Golems. The three boulders from above drop-down behind them and my last knight on the cliffside falls into the chasm below. Panicking, this makes five Mountain Golems. The ground beneath us shakes. Two more emerge from behind us. That makes seven.

"ROAR!"

Three more crawls over from the edge of the trail. Ten. We have ten Mountain Golems and ten remaining knights. Seems fair. The golems roar and my knights all take up their weapons. All except Marshall, he reaches for the claymore strapped to his back but winces in pain. If we make it through this, I'm ordering him to let Nessa take a look at that injury.

One golem approaches and Thalia slashes at it, leaving a deep scratch across the golem's face that it's unfazed by. It curls back into its boulder form and rolls toward us. One giant stone ball rolling towards ten knights. This would inspire something if I weren't terrified! Thalia dives out of the way, but my other knights do not. Three of them take the full force of the tumbling boulder and spray in different directions. The golem doesn't stop and strikes through Ollie, Nessa and I, sending me flying off the mountain. Again.

I fall but at least I can see the river below me this time. I look death in the eye screaming, until my cape snags on a jagged rock pillar and slams me into the rocks, winding me. I am really loving this Eel Worm silk. Ollie runs to the edge.

"Again? Seriously?"

I flail around furiously. "It's not like I'm doing this by choice!" The golem bellows and Ollie looks back in fear.

"Stay there!"

"Like I have a choice."

I can hear fighting and the golems' roars are like the worse choir I've ever sat through. Their bellows cause rubble to fall into the chasm, and I don't suppose they could roar each other off the mountain in the same manner?

"Hey!" I hear across from me.

It's Alan, he's alive and climbing back up to the trail followed by Hoover and Cooper.

"How many times are you going to fall off this mountain?"

"I'm trying to develop a new flying method, but gravity doesn't seem to be agreeing with me, can you get me off this thing?"

"Must I do everything?"

"To save my life?" I ask, glaring back at him.

"Yes, do everything that you can!"

Yes, that is an order. Alan orders the two knights to continue up as he takes his staff and tries to reach out for me.

"No, keep climbing and extend down from up top."

"Uh, in case you don't remember, there are monsters up there." "Mountain Golems," I correct.

"And it will do you no good trying to support both our weight with one arm."

"I did it before."

"You had more support with the mountain then."

Plus I do not want to be another projectile again. Alan scoffs at me but follows my instructions.

He manages to climb back to the trail and I watch as he deflects a Mountain Golem rolling at him. The stone creature falls into the river below and this gives me an idea.

"It won't work!" I hear and I'm immediately disappointed.

I didn't get to tell anyone my plan before it got rejected. I look up. Alan is trying to extend his Bo staff towards me, but it is a few feet short from my reach.

"We should have done it my way!"

"Hold on," I gulp in panic. I got a stupid idea.

"I've got a really dumb idea but given the situation, it's better than nothing!"

"…What?" Alan asks doubtfully and I don't blame him.

"Get some good footing… and prepare to swing."

He looks at me even more doubtfully. I take in a breath. This is not what this move is meant for, but I really have nothing left to lose. I get one chance.

"One."

In one motion I flip, unsnag my cape, plant my feet on the side of the rock pillar, and launch myself forward. Imitating the *Quick-Step* technique I learned from Ollie, the air around me glides off my skin, armor, and hand as I feel Divinity move through me and reach out to grab the staff. I make it. Without hesitation, Alan swings me back onto the trail with enough force that I collide with a Mountain Golem that was rolling on a crash course towards Ollie and the others. I knock it off its trajectory and the golem proceeds into smashing into another, shattering the two to pieces.

"Hey look at that," I pant. "It worked."

"Oh good, let me try flinging you at the other seven!" Ollie yells.

"I told you to stay down there!"

"Yes, but I am really bad at listening."

I smirk and another golem lets out a roar. It begins to roll towards us, but Alan swings his staff to trip the creature up. Thalia mimics my actions, ramming it with the Mirrogold side of her double-edged sword, and sends the golem careening into the chasm.

"See, now there's six," I point out and Ollie growls at me.

"If we can continue to deflect them off the trail, they'll fall into the river and sink like a—"

"Don't say it." Alan urges.

The Mountain Golems aren't using their rolling attacks as they close in on us. My knights surround me again. Ollie is still at my side holding his scalpel while the nurses wait behind me with the horses, protected by Marshall.

"We just need to repel these off the mountain," I say and catch Nessa out of the corner of my eye nod towards Junah.

"To heal and protect," Nessa declares and Junah hesitates at first, but then rushes forward, letting go of the horses.

"Everyone get in close!" Nessa cries as Junah rushes to confront the golem.

The look on her face is so urgent, so concerning, that it convinces me to trust her. I order my knights to fall back, and Nessa clamps her hands together. She closes her eyes and mutters something to herself. A chant? She begins to glow. Divinity? The light becomes brighter, and I get a literal flashback to when Susan killed Rhodain. This is different. There's no malice towards us. I feel safe. Her light omits a shield around everyone but Junah.

"What about—"

I don't get a chance to finish my sentence. My voice is ripped from me as everyone falls silent. Everyone, but Junah, who opens his mouth to unleash a haunting shriek. Initially, the golems don't react, but the longer Junah screams, the stronger his voice becomes. The ground trembles, the mountain shakes. It's as if the whole mountain is trying to escape. Rocks fall from above and around us yet Nessa's shield holds up; no rubble gets through as she continues chanting.

The force from Junah's voice pushes the golem back as pieces of the trail's edge break off. One golem falls and then another. Junah seems to be fading. His song coming to its end. I can see rockslides from the surrounding mountain faces occurring. Junah's voice gives out. There are still four golems left. He looks out of breath as the mountain continues to tremble. Finding their bearings, the golems regroup and approach Junah. Nessa keeps chanting.

"Nessa, stop," I plea. "Junah's in trouble!"

She doesn't stop, and as the golems close in and let out one final roar. Junah uses their own voices against them, clapping his hands as if gathering their collective bellows to throw it back at them. This is strong enough to shatter their faces, the shield's front, and the trail below. The golems are launched over the edge and Junah collapses from exhaustion, nearly falling with them. Nessa lets up her shield enough that Marshall leaps off his horse, dives, and grabs Junah by the collar of his vest.

Alan and Thalia fall on Marshall's feet to keep him from going over too, and with the combined strength of Ollie and I assisting, together we pull everyone back onto what's left of the trail. Rocks continue to fall, but the area around us appears to be safe. Nessa falls upon Junah and places her hands on his bleeding ears. After muttering another chant, her hands light up, when she pulls them away the bleeding has stopped.

"Okay…" Alan sits back panting.

"What in Hellsfire was that?"

"Perhaps," Nessa begins as a rock tumbles passed us into the river below.

"We can explain once we're out of direct danger?"

We agree and gather the horses very cautiously, and slowly make our way back down the mountain. When we manage to get to an opening in the trail, we take a moment to collect ourselves. Marshall and Thalia remain on their horses. I'm down two knights from the rest that has accompanied me. Nessa approaches while Junah takes his medical pack from the horse to assess the other knights for injuries they may have sustained during the encounter.

I wait as Alan and Ollie join me in curiosity. "Okay Nessa, explain."

"Which would you like to hear first, my story or Junah's?"

"Sound boy doesn't seem as complicated, and neither does your magic," Alan answers.

"I want to know why you never mentioned this before?"

I ask and Junah returns. Looks like the group isn't as banged up as expected. He stands beside Nessa, and she takes a breath before speaking.

"When King Sorenson banished Divinity from the kingdom, Junah and I had to rely on our other nursing skills. I wouldn't reveal my traits unless dire. I'm not really supposed to be in Baronune."

"What does that mean?"

With great apprehension, Nessa answers. "…I'm a fairy."

"What does *that* mean?"

I had grown up believing magic was a fairytale. Fairies were certainly part of that *fairy*tale.

"Bullshit!" Alan barks.

"Not bullshit," Nessa remarks and omits a radiant glow around her.

It's so peaceful and welcoming that I almost forget why we're questioning her.

"Fairies are kept away in a secret realm known as Bellshire. Our Divinity is the purest form of the Sacred Arts, almost on a tier of its own. Its use must be restricted or the secret to Bellshire is at risk."

"Okay…"

"Hold on," Thalia interrupts.

"What about Avery Verylight? The knight that was banished. He was supposed to be the Knight that Danced with Fairies or whatever?"

Alan chuckles. I know Avery is the knight that fled with Rhodain's sister, Nova, but not many details were shared about him.

"He's my brother," Nessa admits and there's some more details shared about him.

"He was raised in Bellshire until he wandered off, still at a young age. I went to search for him to keep our secret from being discovered, but it was too late. He had been found out, though he never revealed the whereabouts to Bellshire, he was never allowed to return." "So why are you still here?" Alan asks.

"With my brother exiled at a young age, I felt responsible for him. So, to be allowed to search for him I had to give up my wings and become mortal. Never would I imagine he'd become the powerful one that ended up one of the king's Grandier Knights and protecting me."

"And what about Junah?"

"June? He's cursed with a powerful Divinity over sound. He can release and warp it to his liking, but they can become a danger to him and those near him."

I glance back to the crumbling mountains behind us. "No kidding,"

"I found him while looking for my brother, and he shielded me from an attacker not knowing what I was. To return the favor I graced him with my light. We both went into medicine while my brother trained to return to Baronune to become a knight. As a fairy, I've sworn against violence, only to heal and protect. I must allow others to do my fighting for me, but I heal them in return."

"How do you if you gave up your wings, or whatever?" Alan asks.

"I still have access to my Divinity. You can't take that away, it's within everyone and everything. Mine's just not as potent as it used to be. Divinity is limited to how much your body can withstand, that's why it's advised for mortals to train in the Martial Arts first to strengthen their bodies and durability. I have to fully concentrate to access my abilities whereas if I had my wings, if I were still immortal, it would come as easy as breathing."

Ow. Trying to comprehend this with what Rhodain, Terry and Ollie have explained to me over the months give me a headache. A clear warning from Divinity itself that I am not ready for this much information yet.

I groan. "Nessa, thank you for everything."

"Hellsfire!" Alan barks. "Had we known she could do this the whole time we wouldn't…"

"That's precisely why I withheld this information," Nessa admits in an apologetic tone.

"People hear about us fairies and they immediately want to find ways to use our Divinity to their advantages. That's why the realm remains secret, among other reasons."

"Why didn't they try getting at Avery for his wings or whatever?" Alan scoffs as he folds his arms in front of his chest.

"He doesn't have them."

"Huh?" another collective gasp.

"Avery wasn't born a fairy. He stumbled into Bellshire and was raised amongst us. Due to his optimistic personality, he became accepted by our Fairy Light and grew to master it as his own Divinity."

"The Knight who Dances with Fairies…" I ponder. "Ow."

Perhaps I should stop thinking about this subject. I can see the rest of the knights struggling with the concept more than me, though Ollie seems fine.

"You understood every word of that?"

"For the most part," Ollie admits, sounding smug.

"I've trained in Dragon's Guard, I've seen this Avery of whom she speaks, and studied in the Mystic Arts. This isn't too hard to grasp, and I respect their not wanting to come out and reveal themselves until they were more comfortable with the group. Though fairies are in the same class as dragons. Their Divinity is so strong it nearly makes them Gods." My brain almost goes on fire trying to comprehend that.

"Okay, that's enough for now. Marshall," I turn to him as he's still upon his steed.

He's been listening intently to Nessa's story.

"Take some knights and follow this trail to the river."

"You want us to scout to see if we can find any survivors?"

"Yes please."

"As you wish my king."

Marshall agrees and calls for Hoover and Cooper to follow as he rides off down a trail we had recently passed.

"Are you sure you want to waste our resources doing this?" Ollie asks sounding legitimately concerned.

"We should get back to the kingdom to inform King Ivan of the situation."

"Yeah, I have a few words I'd like to share with the King of Woodsforge," Alan grasps his fist with his hand.

"I also want to see if I can knock out the rest of those teeth." "Alan!" Thalia barks.

"You know any direct offensive acts against the king will result in war between the kingdoms."

"Yeah, and?"

"That's not what we're here for."

"We're here to unite the kingdoms, but I agree with you, Alan," I admit and there's another collective gasp.

We are really coming together today.

"I have some words I'd like to share with the king."

Ollie looks to have chills, while Alan looks like he wants to give me a small round of applause. As we recover and wait for Marshall to return, the sun begins to sit closer to the horizon, the skies over the mountain match the fire in my soul. I am determined to return to Woodsforge to speak with the king.

Marshall returns but only with the knights he took with him. I have even more words to address with the king.

Chapter Nine

Hearts meet under the Moonlight

We arrive back at the castle as the sun sets. I would not want to try navigating that mountain trail at night. As we return to the tunnel, two large guards await us. Our return seems to surprise them and they take the horses back and guide us through the tunnel again.

As we approach the exit and spill back out into the courtyard, I hear the sounds of festivities and celebration much like the night before. Do these guys ever rest? Making it to the dining hall, maidens stand along the aisle as the guests in the stands drink, laugh, and enjoy the gift of life. A gift that was taken from two of my knights today.

King Ivan sits in his usual seat while Longcaster is lost among the crowd, but I can hear his boisterous voice guide me to his location. His daughter and who I assume to be his queen, sit at his sides again and his elite guards, Eli and the Black Knight, Kenny, are posted in their respective corners in the back.

"King Ivan!" I roar the moment I set foot in the dining hall.

My voice must be powerful because the music and laughter stops. I storm towards the king with fury in my eyes and heat coursing through my veins. Before I'm halfway down the main carpet, the jester leaps from beyond my view and startles me. I find him creepy, and he's in my way.

I step around him as he turns his gleeful attention on the rest of my court following me. I tell them to stand down, and they all kneel. They're tired from the haste we made back down the mountain but eager to have their turn at the king. Alan especially, Marshall maybe a bit more. I stand before King Ivan and not even Ollie stands by my side. The king regards me as he holds a challis in his hand.

"Your presence tells me that you handled the situation as I asked."

I glare and huff. "Yes, Mountain Golems? You couldn't have given us a heads up?"

"I requested your assistance when it was my understanding that you still had knights in your court that could wield magic. Mountain Golems wouldn't have been an issue for them."

"But you saw last night that his court did not contain the knights you mention," Ollie storms up beside me. King Ivan regards him peculiarly.

"Who is this?" King Ivan looks puzzled. "Your queen or something?

"*This* is Ollie, my Second Grand Advisor."

"And don't make accusations of me."

Ollie folds his arms. I glance at him. This probably isn't the best time to be taking offense to King Ivan's insensitivity. My minds gets wrapped around the queen comment and how I keep forgetting to ask Ollie's preference.

"Yeah, well what does it matter?" King Ivan pulls me from my thoughts as he takes a swing from his challis.

"The situation is handled, and the Mountain Golems are gone, yes?"

"Yes, but I lost two knights."

"Pish posh, it's been one day…"

King Ivan jokes but I don't laugh. No one in my court laughs.

"We lose people every day. That's the cruelty of Life and whatnot," The king takes another drink and wipes his mouth on his sleeve.

"Your knights knew the risks when they joined your ranks. Well, August's ranks. I doubt they expected that they'd be taking orders from a child."

"Excuse me, *your* majesty—" I begin but Ivan cuts me off.

He points his challis at me and King's Juice spills across the table. "No, you will not be excused or put in time out or whatever your parents do with you before bed!"

He sits back and his maidens refill his drink.

"You are a king now, and it's best you start acting like it. You want to come in here and point blame at me, but you agreed to the task, and you assured me that your knights could handle it. If you had any doubts, perhaps train your knights. Or even better, train yourself so you can lead *your* knights. Then maybe you won't lose two measly lives." I clench my fists and Ollie bites her lip.

"That being said, you did handle the situation. So, I thank you. To that, we will celebrate!" He stands and raises his challis. The guests all cheer and drink along with him.

"As to uniting our kingdoms. Your disrespect tonight leaves me worried that you are still unfit to rule. I will think it over. As to your reward for ridding us of those Mountain Golems, your knights will be companied tonight by any maiden of their choosing. You know. To heal their wounds and such."

He winks at me. I feel perplexed. Bansha smiles as she does that thing with her glass again. Circling it with her finger enticingly. I peer back to see the maidens all take one united step forward and approach my knights. They kindly lift them all from their kneeling positions with a gentle touch.

"We have our own nurses," I stutter. "Your maidens don't need to…" "He doesn't know what he's talking about!" Alan yelps from the back.

I look to see three maidens circling him. "We'll be just fine, King Richards. Thank you for your fine treasures."

"Very well, young knight. See, he gets it," King Ivan gestures to Alan as if this should be obvious to me.

"Enjoy life while you can, King Westley, you never know how long you've got."

I don't need a reminder. The thought of death sends shivers down my spine as my vision flashes between images of Susan and Rhodain. I relive Rhodain's murder. I'm haunted by the sadistic look on Susan's face. I don't need a reminder. My memory drains me every time I am called *king*.

"As for you King Westley," King Ivan grabs my attention and points to Ollie.

"If this… *individual* is not your queen, then I will grant you a night with my daughter to do whatever it is you wish." *"What?"* Ollie and I respond in unison.

We exchange uncomfortable glances and then quickly rip our sights away from one another. My eyes fall on the princess, Ivan's daughter, Crystal. She's beautiful, yes, but her darken stare from her ever lashes and the way her hair imitates the night sky leaves me speechless in a different way. I lose focus. Everything that angers me, and all my troubles is substituted by one thing. Nerves.

My body trembles beneath my armor. I never troubled with talking with girls because I never troubled with them at all. I never thought of myself as that intriguing and not too many girls back home could grasp the concept of King's Men so what else would there be to do?

As my eyes meet with Crystal's she seems uninterested. This is not surprising.

"As for you… Olive?" "Ollie," she corrects.

"Green hair!" The king decides with glee.

"What would you like? I'm sure my maidens can find you someone—" "I'm good."

Ollie rejects him as her eyes fall into an unsettling squint. She seems just as uninterested in this idea as Crystal appears with the idea of me. King Ivan frowns if only for a moment and then waves it off.

"To each their own. As for the rest of us," He raises his challis again. "Drink and be merry!"

"DRINK AND BE MERRY!"

The crowd cheers and the music picks up again.

The jester returns to leaping about, while my knights become quite friendly with their company. Alan's circle of maidens expands more and more like he dipped himself in an alluring pheromone before entering the dining hall. I expect to find Thalia mad at this again, but even she and Dawn are enjoying the company of men all of a sudden as they flood in from the crowd.

They laugh, giggle, and Thalia gets in a flexing match with one guy I would have mistaken to be an ogre. Hayden recites poetry that the maidens swoon over while Marshall and Nessa chat happily. Nessa looks far more interested in whatever Marshall is saying as she gives him an unsettling smile and looks like she's glowing faintly. Hoover and Cooper drown themselves in King's Juice as they wrap their arms around a pair of maidens and look as if they never want to let go. Even Kaleb with his lengthy body and gnarly smile is conversing with a maiden that only comes up to his thighs.

I notice Ollie turn to leave.

"Ollie—"

"King Westley."

A soft yet stern voice cuts through the festivities and freezes me in place. I look back to find Crystal. She stands atop the few steps leading up to the king's table. From her glittering dress, and the gems embedded into her arms, I find myself speechless in her presence.

"I would like a word with you if that's alright?"

I am caught up in her accent, it's strong enough to make me believe she could wrestle a bear.

Crystal cautiously makes her way down to me, and I swear she's flying. We are separated only by a few inches. Her eyes are a dark gray and her skin is stainless like my Mirrogold. Her hand reaches out to me and falls on my shoulder. She does a similar motion that I've seen the other maidens do to my knights and glides around me, studying my every muscle, my every breath. Am I breathing? The oxygen seems unable to reach my head. The world seems to stop and my heart beats to the sound of the song played by the sackbuts.

"A word, if you don't mind?" She asks.

Unable to form a sentence, I simply nod.

"Follow me."

Her hand trails across my chest as if painting the path for me to follow as she leads me away.

She walks past me, and I turn in pursuit. My image of the princess is disrupted by the sights of the jester once more. A false face of happiness and glee, yet his eyes. I stare deep into his eyes, deeper and deeper until I nearly feel like I'm falling into an abyss. Something pulls me. Someone. The world returns in a dizzy crawl. Crystal has taken me by the hand, but I can't tell if we are moving in haste or if I'm stuck standing in place. I'm removed from the jester's sights. I keep watching him as the world and sound gradually come back into play. The jester twitches and rolls his head in my direction. He follows me as the world returns to normal. I could not ask to be in a better place. Anywhere is better than being in the presence of that jester.

⚬⚬⚬

Maybe I spoke too soon. After a long and awkward silent stroll through the hall, Crystal leads me out into the courtyard. She seems to belong to the nightly scene as the lights and the stars above complement her beauty perfectly. She walks out to the center of the courtyard where I laggardly follow behind her. Crystal turns to face me, and I freeze from the night air. My hands clamp and rest at my waist. I'm having a hard time maintaining eye contact as I keep glancing between her and a pebble sitting at my toes.

"So," she begins. "I guess I'm your prize for the night. I've never been someone's prize before. How does it work?"

She's asking me? I'm still trying to get a grasp on being a king, I can't even begin to understand whatever is happening here.

"I-I don't know…"

"Do you want me?"

"*What?* I…uh…"

I hold that '*uh*' a lot longer than intended. She looks bored with me again. There's an unpleasant tug at her gray as granite lips.

"Do you have any other words or are they all saved for my father?"

"*Uh*," I think I'm broken. "Yes, no. This is all new to me."

"What is?"

"Everything!" That leaps from my lips almost like Junah's sound Divinity.

"I'm sorry. I don't mean to fright. I'm just…I'm under a lot of pressure."

"Really? You'd think someone that overcame the King of the Round Table Tournament would have a little more weight to his loins." I shift a little uncomfortably in my armor after that one.

"How much about the tournament do you know about?"

"Not much really. My father said it was a ruthless tournament to sort out the boys from men. To find a strong and mighty king if anything happened to King Sorenson."

"Yeah… it's a little different when you're looking at it from the outside."

"You said you did what was necessary to win."

"I did what was necessary to *survive.* So that meant hiding like a little child as Rhodain did all the fighting."

I walk towards one of the benches and gaze up to the mountain ridges, The King's Crown, comparing them to the Baronune Castle's towers, reimagining Rhodain's final battle.

"The Fire Knight?"

"You know him?"

"I've heard very little mentions," she admits looking disappointed. "I know he was the strongest in all the lands."

"I mean, he had a reputation that's for sure."

"My father feared him."

"Why…?"

The last person I knew to fear Rhodain was Susan, and that was because he was a threat to her claiming the title of king after her plans flew into motion. Why would King Ivan fear him? Crystal strolls away from me. Her demeanor shifts. The night breeze seems heavy as I turn to follow her. She seems to be walking further away from the entrance to the dining hall.

"Would you mind accompanying me on a stroll through the kingdom?" "A stroll?" My legs suddenly want to retreat in the opposite direction. "Through the whole kingdom?"

"We won't go too far. I don't know my way around without my escorts."

"Wouldn't your father worry?"

"My father already thinks you're doing as you wish with me."

What does she think her father thinks I intend to do exactly? It's headaches like this that leave me sticking with King's Men. Game pieces aren't this difficult.

I agree to follow her, and we step into a different hall that becomes a separate tunnel leaving the Woodsforge castle. We walk side by side. Her hands fold before her waist. Mine flail every which way because I have no idea what I'm supposed to do with them. I try holding them behind my back, but my armor makes it uncomfortable.

It's colder than Baronune. The chill from the mountains bouncing off the lake makes the night cooler than any desert night back home. Crystal strokes her arms. I can't imagine her gown is as insulated as my armor.

"Are you cold?"

"Yes. I didn't think—"

"Here," I extend out my cape for her to wrap herself in.

"It's better than nothing."

"You are considerate," she says as she slides in close, and I drape my arm and cape over her shoulder.

"I wish more men were like you."

If only she knew just how badly my heart was trying to leap out my chest and take off running at this moment. I'm not comfortable with this, but I'm also not comfortable with the idea of the king's daughter freezing under my watch. I don't imagine that was one of the king's intents when he offered her to me.

"I don't think of you as a prize, I don't like how that sounds."

"Neither do I, but that seems to be all I am around here."

"What do you mean?"

"Men come into our kingdom to appeal to my father for a glimpse of his treasures. I am my father's greatest treasure. So disgusting men of all ages would arrive to... *acquire* me. Thinking it would be a way into my father's court. Weak men!"

She spits and I get a sense of her vigor, but it hides behind something that's unsettling her. Her eyes wander off down the dark and empty cobblestone roads.

"He, my father, wouldn't part with me willingly, but..."

"But?"

"He has his own agenda."

"What does that mean?"

She shifts uncomfortably beneath my arm. We make a turn around a street corner and keep following the light of the moon as it guides our path.

"I don't know if I should say."

"Is that why you wanted to leave the castle?"

"Yes."

"Does your father...scare you?" I ask unsure of what word I want to say.

"...Yes," she says in hesitation. "But not in the way you think."

"I can think of many ways."

"He's under someone's watch."

"That would not have been something I thought of."

King Ivan doesn't seem like someone that would report to anyone else. A king shouldn't report to anyone else. I listen to my Grandier Knights and my Grand Advisors, sometimes. Mostly I listen to my people, my kingdom. Everything I do, I do for their sake. For Sophia, and for our family. For my Uncle Lester. Restoring Baronune is the sole reason I'm here.

"I don't know everything. Just that when I was a baby, during the Days of Hellsfire. He made a deal to save the people, but it cost him something."

"Something? Like what?"

"I said I don't know everything."

"That is fair," I glance away worryingly as she regards me with a stern look much like her father's.

"You did say that. I just have a very stubborn curiosity."

"Curiosity can lead to death." "Yeah…" I say uncomfortably.

"I am familiar."

"Rhodain," she shifts to look up at me.

"You feel that you are to blame?"

I do. Not a day goes by that I don't blame myself for the results of the king's tournament. If I had done things differently maybe Rhodain would still be alive. Maybe he'd be the king right now, and I would return to Old Country to continue living out my days as the reigning champ of King's Men.

"I don't know everything," she snuggles closer to me for… warmth?

"But you seem too good to be cruel."

"That's nice of you?"

I feel she's doubting my ability to be king, which isn't anything new, but not something I want to add to my thoughts tonight.

"Did you kill?" She asks as we stop. I'm at a pause.

"In the tournament. Did you kill anyone? That was the point, right? To kill off your competition to be the king?"

"Uh…" The idea of me being physically capable of killing someone back then is a fairytale of its own.

A dream, or even a nightmare.

"If you had seen my pitiful display in that tournament, you wouldn't ask that question."

"Then how could you be responsible for the death of one man?"

"…I may not have done it physically, but the results of my actions led to his demise. My decisions led to the loss of my knights today…"

"You need to not think like that," she snaps before my attention can waver.

"If one thing was true it was what my dad said. Your knights chose the life of the sword. They chose to be strong and loyal. They took responsibility for their own actions. We all choose our own paths to follow."

"Yeah, but I didn't choose this. I didn't want to be king; it was thrust upon me, and because of the rules, I'm stuck with this role."

I remove myself from her. I feel bad taking my cape with me after I offered it to her, but I need the space. I need to breathe. I can feel my emotions turning like the gears that rearrange Baronune and I don't know why, but her opinion of me matters. I don't want to share my tears. I don't want her to see my fears. I don't want her to view me as another *weak* man.

"…I don't know everything," I hear her step towards me.

She's at my back.

"But I know there are things in this world we do not control. Things we do not ask for. If my father should pass, fall ill, or worse. I will be forced to marry to keep our legacy alive. To carry forward. I do not wish it. I do not want to rule. The life of ruling is not the path I choose to follow but follow it I must."

"It shouldn't be this way."

"Then how should it be?" She asks with the lightest touch that comforts me, compels me to face her.

My eyes are watery, but no tears have fallen. Her hand rests on my chest and I wonder if she can feel how fast my heart is racing.

"I…I do not know."

"Even you don't know everything."

"You'll be surprised to find out how little I know."

"Then perhaps that is your path? Not to be a great ruler. Not to be the best leader…"

"Thanks," I frown.

She smiles a beautiful smile that would make the moon jealous as it watches over us.

"Perhaps your path is to find out what it takes to be all those things, and more. Or discover your own path," she regards me, placing her hand on my cheek.

"What sort of path is that?"

"The path of the king."

Her hand continues to rest upon my face. Mine has magically moved along her waist without realizing it. I was lost in the moment.

"You are a good man. Remember that. Remember what gives you strength, and you will be a strong man too."

Her eyes, her lips, her head tilts up at me slightly. I am hesitant. My mind is running laps in my own head. What is happening? She can't possibly be into me, right? Is she really wanting me to…wanting me to… kiss her? Should I do this? Is this how I am to unite our kingdoms? By uniting with Crystal and forging a…a…relationship? Was *this* the king's intent? There's movement. Her hand slips from my face as she pulls away.

She studies me looking as confused as the thoughts ricocheting in my head.

"What's wrong? Do you not like me? Do you not want to—" "No, no, it's not that!" I panic.

"It's just… It's just… Oh, you got to be kidding me."

I groan as I catch something out the corner of my eye. I glance up the road and spy a familiar figure appear at the top of the hill. The king's jester.

"Why is he here?"

"And how did he know where to find us?"

The jester continues to dance and hop about until he starts pretending to be pushing something. A wall? A boulder? He turns away from us and keeps up the same act. He turns around, still struggling against something. He raises his hands, makes it seem like there's something above him, but there's nothing. What's he doing? Confused, my instincts compel me to take a step forward to assist him. Crystal takes my wrist. An eerie dark fog-like vapor rolls across the cobblestone and forms around the jester's entrapped space.

"I don't like this…"

The darkness spills out and the sounds of cracking bones fill the air, coming from the jester as he compresses into the nonexistent confined space he's trapped in. It squeezes tighter, and tighter until… *POP!*

The jester becomes nothing but a small box of black liquid.

"I *really* don't like this…" I say with fright widening my eyes.

They are responding to the remains of the jester as his little black box rotates and expands. It expands until it shatters, and a hungry hiss fills the silence. Long slender arms reach out of the black vapors that form a large and robust body over thin legs that should not be able to support the weight. The once jester hunches over with the darkness drifting off his shoulders and spine. He's something maddening, and seemingly *hungry* as it bites and licks at the air.

"I definitely don't like this."

Chapter Ten

Dark Humor

The jester scuttles forward and is on us. His face is paler, and his skin is cracking from his chin to his cheeks. The once red lips are black drooling dark vapor. The dark markings under his eyes slither and fuse into the cracks on his face.

His presence makes it nearly impossible to breathe. My body trembles as I take a step back with Crystal at my side. The jester tilts his head and smiles. His teeth are jagged and I notice something struggles to emerge from the dark void behind his lips. His tongue? No, it's sharp, long and in a split second a silver tip spear shoots out to stab me, narrowly missing my face. The spear retracts back into the jester's mouth. The tip still visible.

"Well, that's enough of that," I say with terror in my eyes.

I take Crystal's hand.

"Run!"

"What?" She asks as we take off away from the monster.

"You're a king, you have your sword! Why don't you fight?"

"This *is* how I fight!"

"Is this truly how you won the Round Table Tournament?"

"Survived," I correct. "And yes!"

We take off down the street. The cobblestone echoing under our fleeting feet, until the kingdom around us fades away and we are engulfed in darkness leaving our bodies as the only source of color.

I examine my hands. "What's happening?"

"Where are we?" Crystal asks and her voice sounds distant and near all at once.

"Come on, let's keep moving."

"To where?"

"Anywhere, keep moving. Staying in place will make us an easy target."

"But…" she swallows her fear. "He's just a jester."

"I think you're the one joking because that was no jester."

I take her hand, like Sophia would take mine, and we press into the darkness.

I have no idea how long we've been walking. Minutes? Hours? There is no *"here"* or *"there"* in this space.

Crystal points and I turn back around. "What's that up ahead?"

I don't need her to point it out. There's another person up ahead. We advance on this body and stop. His back is toward us, but I don't need to see his face. Silver-plated armor, brown shaggy hair, and a long teal cape. This… is me.

"What?" I ask and Crystal tries to back away.

I immediately grab her wrist again.

"Don't. If you leave me and we get separated, this will only get more confusing."

"Leave me," my other self says as he turns around.

Almost as if looking into a mirror.

"I'm confusing."

Well, he's not wrong. Or I'm not wrong? See, already this is messing with my head. Crystal frees from my grasp and turns. She gasps. I peer back. There's another version of her too.

"Stay," her other self says.

"Die," mine concludes.

I don't like mine. He reaches for his sword. I *really* don't like mine. I take Crystal's hand again and we run. She doesn't seem to argue this time. She keeps in pace with me, hiking up her dress to move easier. We run and the vapor spits out another version of us. We don't bother with them this time. We just keep on running but get nowhere fast.

"What is this?" I ask as we stop.

The vapor spits out another version of me, but this time I'm sitting with my Uncle Lester. I recognize the small round table of rock. It's the one back home in Old Country where we'd sit at and play King's Men. In fact, that is exactly what we're doing. My Uncle Lester with his red curls and dark rim glasses looks as exhausted as ever.

"If you're tired, you don't have to play."

The image of me says. I feel like I'm there. I feel like that's truly me. My image moves and places a reflective pebble forward along the spaces on the board. There are different cards laid out and dice sitting within cups. How I miss a good game of King's Men.

"No, it's fine, West," Uncle Lester sighs.

"I'm just glad you're alright."

"Same," I say as I draw a card after my uncle's move.

"I never want to go back to the kingdom. Those last two days were the worse of my life. I almost died."

"Please don't speak of it. That's been my fear for years. After your mom passed that's why we left for Old Country. I never wanted to risk you being caught up in that tournament."

"You could have warned me about it. Especially since I was going to stay the summer."

"I couldn't bring myself to. I didn't want to tempt fate into making it a reality."

 "Well, it happened," I say, laying down a card and moving another piece.

"Luckily, Rhodain became king and ended it before things could have been worse."

"What is this?" Crystal asks and I'm pulled from the scene.

"I don't know," I say.

This appears to be what would have been had I not been named king at the end of the tournament. Had Rhodain claimed the crown instead, and I returned home.

"Just something better."

"Westley!"

My uncle gasps after a remark I made against Susan. This scene continues to play out. They don't even notice we're here.

"I thought… I thought I lost you."

"You didn't Uncle Lester. I'm still here. I survived, and most importantly, I made sure Sophia survived too."

"I am thankful, guess I'm not doing half a bad job of raising you am I?"

"No, just bad at playing King's Men."

I remove his last piece from the board. "I win."

"As you always do."

My Uncle Lester smiles. I want this to be true. I wish I were back in Old Country with my Uncle Lester, with my ordinary life. I don't want to be king.

Crystal pulls my arm this time. We move away from the scene and proceed deeper into the void. The vapors respond and we stop.

"What is this?"

It's Crystal's turn. I watch as her alternate self is in a kitchen. Everything is gray and made of stone. She wears a plain shroud over her head, and I can make out her face. She's standing over a sink washing a plate. This is not the life of a princess.

"Hey, dad," a familiar voice announces in the other room.

The layout is much like the homes in Baronune. The next rooms over are the dining and living rooms. Crystal walks in and her father,

King Ivan, sits in a chair reading a parchment. Marshall stands at the door. He's in his armor but it's different. It's an older style like my practice gear, and his sword is shorter than his claymore. He seems younger and healthier.

They converse much like Sophia's family did when I stayed with them. They talk about their day and what should they do for dinner that night. They mention something about a Lord Oriic, but the name isn't familiar to me.

"This is what I want," says the real Crystal.

"This?" I question stepping up to her. "This is…"

"Normal. A life without riches and royalty, where my family can be just that. A family,"

She's almost teary. "It's all I truly want. Not the jewels or the treasures. I don't want people's respect because they admire my father. I want my father. I want my brother back. I don't want to grow up to be a queen of anything."

"I…I…"

If I could give it all up and return to my normal life I would. This is what Crystal's life could have been had her father not became the king. Ivan smiles and he even has a full set of teeth.

"This isn't real," I say regretfully. "We have to keep going. We have to get out of here."

"I know but," she hesitates.

She takes a step forward. "Why can't we stay a little longer. What's the harm in watching these scenes?"

"They're not real. These are fantasies. Illusions. The jester is tricking us so that we don't try to escape."

"To what prevail?"

"I don't know. I can't figure out what game he's playing, but the longer we stay here the more vulnerable we are."

With another shuddered breath Crystal agrees and we move from her scene.

We keep together as we journey into the darkness. The void warps into a tunnel. This feels familiar. This *is* familiar. I know this passage. We're back in the castle, *my* castle. We're in Baronune. Did we travel this far? Did the darkness act as the absence of space and distance and somehow deliver us to my kingdom? We continue forward. We reach the doors to my throne room. Great, I can seek advice from Terry. If anyone can make sense of this, he can. We walk through the doors.

"Oh, gods damn it."

I admit this is not what I was expecting. Everything is lit and sunny, and there I am, another version of me, standing with Sophia at the base of the throne. Alan, Thalia, and Marshall are to our left in their armor. Marshall looks older and silent. Terry is standing next to Roxette and some other knights, a taller boy and smaller girl. They stand around a small cage meant for a pet, but that's not what is inside it. I smile, in the cage is Susan, looking far more miserable than in any cell I could have put her in. I shift my sights to the throne. There he is in Mirrogold armor and a cape as fiery as the Divinity he controls. Rhodain Kayden, the King of Baronune. Seeing him alive as king brings tears to my eyes. This is what should have been. He looks great as the king. "That's…"

"That's him," I say wiping away the tears before they can fall.

"That's Rhodain, the rightful King of Baronune."

"No," Crystal responds, pointing towards the cage. "In the cage."

"That's just Susan. She betrayed the kingdom and—"

"King Westley!"

She calls and my attention follows her frightful tone to the cage. Susan sits staring and smiling at us. Her smile widens as her face begins to crack like a porcelain doll. Her eyes turn black and soulless, which isn't saying much in my opinion. Then Susan begins to grow and expands to where the cage pops out from around her.

"And we're back to the original plan."

"Run?"

"Run."

We both tear back through the doors as the jester chases behind us. The hall turns to darkness and we're back in the void. I no longer hear the jester smashing through halls as the sound abandons us again. We keep running, something I used to hate but all those laps around the castle really paid off. Crystal, on the other hand, has come to a stop as she needs to catch her breath. I scan the void. There has to be a way out of here.

"King Westley?"

Crystal calls to me again and I turn back around. Another household manifests around us. Crystal is back in the kitchen. Is this the same scene from before? No. This is different. She's older and slightly taller. Her skin is fair again, but no jewels or gems are embedded in her arms. No diamonds hanging from her lashes, though she is absolutely stunning. This Crystal takes up a tray and is greeted by two children, one with dark hair and the other brunette. I'm not going to read too much into that. Older Crystal sets the tray on the dining table in the middle of the room and hugs and kisses her children. The real Crystal could not be happier watching this scene. She covers her mouth with one hand as I can see tears swelling in her eyes. "Another dream of yours?"

"A life away from the kingdom and royalties, yes. I am not queen. I am a loving mother instead."

"You are beautiful," I say, and she turns to me.

My face fumes in red. "I mean, your adult self. Not that you're not beautiful now. I just —"

BANG. A man pounds at the table. We hadn't noticed him before. Was he always sitting there? He has shaggy brown hair, and wears a collared blouse with a knife and fork in both hands. This guy has no face. It's blank.

"Uh…?"

"Honey I'm sorry, please be patient," both Crystals respond.

"*Uh…*" I hold longer as the man at the table bangs his fist impatiently. "I know you're hungry, your food is right here."

There is only one Crystal now. The real Crystal. She grabs the tray and passes through the children as she walks into them, and they turn to vapor. They retake their forms as Crystal stands beside the faceless man at the table. He tilts his head toward her in a familiar fashion to someone else. Something else.

"Crystal…"

"Honey, I know," she ignores me and responds to the faceless man as if he is me.

He is not, I haven't moved. "Please, eat."

The faceless man takes his knife and moves it to where his mouth should be. He digs the blade into his skin. There's a pop as black liquid squirts out. I am horrified but Crystal seems unaffected. She smiles at him just as endearingly as she did her children. The *children*. Illusions and reality seem to be merging and its messing with my mind.

The faceless man starts to carve into his face and black ooze sprays across the table and Crystal. The man's face cracks and peels. He carves open an empty mouth as he stands which opens wider as he takes Crystal by her arms. She seems in a daze as he leans in, to kiss her? No, the gaping darkness seems to be sucking an essence from her. Like Crystal's spirit is being drained from her body by this thing.

"Crystal!"

I yell and kick the dining table forward. I force the two apart as the table slams into the faceless man, pushing Crystal back and breaking her from the daze. The faceless man hisses. His skin turns pale as he grows larger. Crystal's eyes scream and she stumbles back. Her children vanish. *The.* The children vanish. I hurry to help her back to her feet. The faceless man tosses the table aside and we take off. We run until our legs are tired, but even then, we don't stop running. Everything around us is a void. No more scene changes. No more illusions. Then we see it, a hole where the darkness peels away into another gray hallway deprived of joy and warmth. As we continue forward dolls hang from the walls around us. They're all different kinds of puppets that dangle from hooks. Their eyes follow us as we proceed down this hall and the dolls grow larger as we move.

We try not to let them touch us as they begin to take up space and the hallway narrows. Their clothing touches me and sends chills through my spine. I don't trust these things. This could be another trap, another trick. Finally, we squeeze out of the hall and enter a small, rounded room. It's gray, cold, and covered in ash. Papers and parchments are sprayed across the floor and a pale blue light shines through a window. I walk towards it and peek outside. Nothing. All I see is light. I look back to Crystal, and she shifts her attention to the hole that used to be a fireplace.

"Do we try it?"

"It could be a trap."

"Everything in here can be a trap."

"You're not convincing me otherwise."

I motion towards the hole. I let her go first as I place my hand on my sword and stand guard.

"Let me know when you're through and I'll follow."

"You're *such* a gentleman."

"Do you want to stand out here in case that jester comes back?"

"Do you?"

I shake my head viciously. "No."

This makes her giggle if only for a moment. Crystal squats down and makes her way into the hole. I stand with my back to it as I watch the hall. The puppets look as if their feet are kicking as they sway in a nonexistent wind. The hall has returned to its normal size, but no sign of the jester. It's even quieter with Crystal somewhere deep in that hole.

"Hey, are you alright in there?" I ask, concerned.

The lapse of time sinking in. The quiet becoming bothersome.

"Crystal?" I ask again, this time peeking over my shoulder.

There's no response. Maybe she made it out? Hopefully, she made it out and she's free on the other side. I turn to face the hole and dust kicks out. Rubble scutters to the floor as Crystal's hands reach back out. She pulls herself from the hole with her hair in her face as she dusts off her gown.

"It loops back around. There's no exit."

"Damn," I say turning my attention back to the hall.

"Then it's a dead end."

"Emphasis on *dead*."

She hisses. Hisses? I don't like the sound of that. A cold sweat crawls down my face as I slowly turn back to face her. She stands still. Her arms hang at her side and her hair drapes over her face.

"Crystal…?"

"*Kiss me…*"

She drags out with a long hiss as she removes her hair from her face. Pale cracking skin, black lips, and dark markings under her eyes. Nope. I think I'm good on the kissing front.

The fake Crystal opens her mouth as the spear tip struggles to free itself from the depths of her throat. Black ooze drools from the corner of her mouth and I take off running down the hall. Another pale blue light reaches in from an exit ahead of me, and I run faster than ever to escape as this monster chases after me.

The light takes me outside. The world is sunny and covered in sand. The buildings around me are made out of adobe, and there is madness in the streets again. I'm back in Baronune. Back in the King of the Round Table Tournament. Thugs and civilians are fighting up and down the streets, breaking down doors, smashing windows.

Knights scurry about as if searching for someone. I turn to find one thug staring at me. He wears a mask of a rosy cheeked jester. He tilts his head at me, and I don't bother waiting to see him change. I rip and tear down alleyways, not sure if the jester is still behind me or not, but I've learned not to look back.

I enter an intersection in the shape of a square filled with large wooden crates, barrels, carts, and other miscellaneous items. This is where we fought Roxette. I glance down each alleyway, then finally the one across from me. The one I remember Roxette emerging from. I hear footsteps and draw my sword. I wait for the jester, but it's not him.

"You've got to be kidding me," A voice echoes from the dark of the alley.

"I try to take a shortcut, and I find myself here of all places. With you again."

"Rhodain?"

He emerges from the alley looking the way he did when I met him in the tournament, a brown shredded hooded cloak and gray trousers.

"What are you doing here kid?"

"Is this…you?"

"Who else would I be?"

"Another trick," I say as I raise my sword.

He scoffs at me.

"I don't have time for this," he says as he brushes past me.

He begins down the alley and then stops. "Aren't you coming?"

"Why?"

"That's what you wanted right? Protection?" "Yeah," I say confused.

My head goes fuzzy. "But the tournament is over. You…"

"What? Don't be messing with me, kid. The tournament isn't over, I have to become the king!" Rhodain roars as he turns back to face me.

"That's what you want, right?"

"For you to be the king?" I ask back.

The sun rays beam down harder. My head becomes hazy. "More than anything. You are the rightful king. You deserve the throne." "*Say it…*" he hisses. "*Tell me what you want.*" "I want…You to be king," I blink.

I feel myself begin to sway. "I want to protect…Sophia, protect… the kingdom. Protect…Crystal."

I snap back to reality. We're still in the square but Rhodain is not the same. His hair is a cloud of darkness. His eyes are soulless with dark markings. His mouth is a black abyss and I feel like part of me is being sucked into it. This is not real. He is not real. I swipe at him with my sword, and I'm freed from his vacuum-like grasp. Rhodain lets out a distant scream and I dart past him. I have to find Crystal and escape this world. This nightmare.

The world around me starts to fall apart, returning to the dark void again. I quickly spill into the streets and hurry in to one of the homes while everyone fighting turns to vapor. I fall to the floor. I managed to escape the void, but where am I now?

"Westley," a voice calls to me. "Get off the floor and sit at the table properly."

It's a familiar woman's voice. I haven't heard this voice in so long. I pull myself off the floor and return my sword to my sheath and sit at the table as instructed. I don't know why I'm being so obedient. This voice seems so nurturing, so welcoming. I glance around. The scene is familiar to the one Crystal saw with her false family. I find myself clutching a fork and knife much like the faceless man did before. A woman enters from the kitchen with light black hair that fluffs with curls under a red hairband. She has tanned skin and a beauty mark below her lip.

"Aunt Janis?"

"West, seriously after thirteen years, you'd stop mistaking me with my sister."

"Your sister…?" No way.

"Mom?"

She smiles at me, placing a plate full of food before me. It's her, my mother. She passed away when I was nearly five. I only vaguely know what she looks like because she's Aunt Janis' twin. She lifts her hand to my chin.

"Close your mouth, West. We'll eat in a minute," she giggles.

She's so beautiful. I can't believe this.

"Honey! Hurry down before the food gets cold!"

Honey? I turn and hear footsteps hurrying down the stairs to see a tall and slender man. He has a dirty blond ponytail and thin rim spectacles.

He kisses my mom on her cheek as he apologizes.

"My bad, I got caught up looking over the artifacts I uncovered last dig. They should be worth some gold once I clean them up."

It's my father, the man who loved his work more than he loved me. He spent so much time in the desert after my mother's passing that he just never came back one day. He might be alive, but no one knows, and I could care less if he was.

My mother huffs. "James, you need to find a healthy work-life balance or it is going to completely consume you."

"Maybe, but right now I'm ready to consume some food. As long as it's not Putt-Puk, right my boy?"

I frown at him. Don't patronize me, I don't know you, and I never will.

"What's biting him, Wynona?"

My mother looks at me peculiarly. "I don't know."

"What's wrong, West? Is this not what you want?"

"No, it's just…"

"I tell you what," says my father.

"The next time I have an expedition, I'll take you too."

"Really?"

"Seriously? You know how dangerous the desert can be. Scorpions, vipers… Sand Raptors."

My mother shivers at the mention of the raptors.

"Oh, it will be fine. Look at him, he's fit enough to be a king," My dad nudges me as he too takes up his fork and knife.

"He's thirteen now, strong enough to handle a little dune ride." "Okay," my mom hesitates.

"As long as it's what he wants. Right West? Is this what you want?"

"What I want… king?"

This doesn't feel right. I mean, it feels great, but it just doesn't fit. As I glance down at my knife, I can barely see my face in the reflection. I'm almost… *faceless.*

I drop the knife and jolt out of my seat. They stare blankly at me, suddenly unresponsive. When I wave my hands at them, they don't react or blink. On closer inspection, I notice something shimmering in the light. It's thin, barely noticeable, but it's there. A string?

"Mom?"

She doesn't answer, and her head tilts, then rolls off her shoulder and onto the ground. I shriek as they both fall limp. As I back away, the ceiling falls away and I notice that string again, it is holding my mother by her feet and reaches up into a void of darkness. The jester's face suddenly peers in from above.

I try to escape, but there is no door as everything turns to vapor and returns me to the void. The jester drops in behind me and I run. I hear him behind me, tumbling. The sound of something large is rolling after me. I keep running forward. Where do I go? How do I escape? Where is Crystal? The emptiness drops into a narrow hallway, and I find myself back in the room where I lost her. I ready my sword and hear something behind me. Dust kicks out of the hole as rubble scutters across the floor.

Crystal pulls herself out and brushes dust off her gown.

"I think it loops back around or something," she whips her hair out of her face.

"I lost track of time in there. Are you okay?"

I can't move, my body is trembling and I can't even lift my sword. She steps back from me in fear, then I feel the ground thump. A cold hand grasps the entire right side of my body as the jester's massive face pulls up beside me yet his focus is on Crystal.

"He can't protect you," the jester hisses.

The room grows with him.

"…He can't save you from your fate. He is a coward, a fraud. He's watched those he cared about burn!"

The jester barks and doubles in size and I am wrought by all the neardeath experiences I've faced. Every time my first instinct was to run. Never to fight. The jester is right, I can't protect anyone, I can't even find the strength to save Crystal. I am a coward, a fraud, and a failure.

"You will be no different," the jester continues as he looms over her.

"What are you to a king? A prize? A trophy? A tool with no respect to your name. He will sacrifice you like everyone else… To keep what's important. To keep pretending to be king…"

She's no prize. She is not something to be won, but a person, and like any person, she's to be respected. Gritting my teeth, I muster my strength and stab my sword through his back.

The jester hisses in rage as I dig my Mirrogold blade so deep into him that it pierces through to the other side. The room shatters and we are back on the cobble streets of Woodsforge.

I growl as I continue to force my sword through this fiend.

"The only one pretending here, *is you!*"

I hear a voice coming out of the jester that I'm not expecting.

"…What am I to you?"

It's not Rhodain. It's not my mother. It's Ollie's.

"What accusations do you continue to make?" the jester asks in Ollie's voice.

I know he's not him… her but I am paralyzed as I stare into the gaping darkness of his maw.

"Am I a boy? Am I a girl? Are we friends? Enemies? Or more…?"

I relive every moment I have shared with Ollie all at once. The night we first met, the day Ollie tried to kill me, all our days of training, our nights of studying…Then I am no longer looking at the jester but staring at Ollie at the end of my sword.

Ollie slides deeper on my blade. "What am I, West? What do you want from me? Do you even see me as your advisor? What do you want? Do you want… *me?*"

Ollie's voice hisses as her entrancing face turns into a hideous nightmare. I snap back to find the Jester hovering on top of me with his silvertip spear preparing to strike. There's no one to rescue me. I am trapped under this creature, looking death in the eye. I should have trained harder; I should have gotten stronger. I am left with only one thing to do, accept my fate.

Crystal finally comes out of her daze. "King Westley!"

It's too late, this is where it ends for me. I can already see the light. A bright light shining and reaching from above, no—ahead of me?

The jester looks just as confused. He looks up and a brilliant ball of light fires down his throat, then he explodes in a blast of blinding radiance. Black liquid and vapor spray throughout the road and leave me covered in ooze.

I let my arms fall as I lie spread out on the cobblestone. My sword scrapes and pings to my side, and I glance over to Crystal. She falls to her knees exhausted and dazed. I feel my strength leaving me as well. I glance up the road, everything is flipped upside down. At the top of the hill under the coat of night, I see two figures. Two suits of armor stand side by side. One tall, the other short, and both incredibly bulky. I'd roll to my feet to confront them, but my vision goes black.

Chapter Eleven

A Fateful Day

The darkness startles me awake. I survey the area in a panic. Everything is bright, and I feel something soft, warm, and cozy. A quilt? I move my hands and find that my armor has been removed. .

"Where am I? Crystal?"

"Shh," a familiar voice soothes me.

"Rest, my king. You've had quite a night."

"N-Nessa?" I ask looking for any figures through my blurry vision.

I see a tall silver haired woman sitting at the foot of my bed. She kindly caresses my head with a wet cloth.

"Nessa? Where—how?"

"My king, you're safe. You're back in King Richards' castle," she says, and I flinch.

My memory comes back strong. The king, the jester. I hardly feel safe.

"Where is he? Where's the jester?"

"Jester?"

"He followed me! He chased me and the princess. Crystal... Is she...?"

"She's safe. Whatever happened, you did well to protect her. King Richards is most grateful. He wants to see you first thing in the morning to understand what happened."

"His jester is what happened."

Nessa removes the cloth from my head. I nearly died, twice. Chased through the district or some dark illusion of that jester's twisted mind games. There was the whole Mountain Golems incident today too. I'm starting to suspect that the people of my kingdom aren't the only ones hoping I fall into an early retirement.

"My king, you can explain it all in the morning. For now, you need to rest. You were clinging to life when we found you."

"Who found us? Last I remember we were blocks away in the kingdom."

"Someone found you and left you at the front of the castle."

"You didn't see who?"

"No. They were long gone before anyone arrived to retrieve you. The guards said they saw a blinding light and there you were."

The two knights at the top of the hill had to be the ones that returned us to the castle. I didn't see their faces. Could they belong to King Ivan? That would go against my theory that he's secretly trying to eliminate me or scare me into relieving my duties as king, but why would he want that? There still remains the question of who were those knights? Two knights.

Maybe…?

"King Westley."

"Yes?"

"Save your worries for the morning. I am your head nurse. I have authority over you in this manner."

I let out a deep sigh and agree. My exhaustion creeps up on me as I lay back down. She wishes me goodnight and exits my chambers, but I don't fall asleep. I allow my body to rest but my mind, my eyes remain awake. I watch the darkness warily. I can still hear the jester's eerie hiss.

I watch the quartz wake with the dim morning light. I stagger once my feet hit the floor, feeling both awake and asleep. I hurry to grab my gear and move it into the wash. I then equip my armor, sword, crown, and cape then venture out of my chambers. I am ready to face the king, and as I stride down the halls, I run into Marshall. My confidence wavers as I realize that two of my knights will not be joining us today and never will be again, lost to the bottom of the mountain's chasm.

"My King," Marshall greets me with concern.

"Are you alright? What happened last night?"

"I was attacked. That funny not-so-funny jester changed into some monster that attacked me and the princess." Marshall looks more concerned. "Oh."

Then I remember that he's Crystal's older brother. Probably not the best way to start someone's morning.

"That explains where the jester went during the festivities. I didn't give it much thought, never liked that guy."

"For good reason, it had Divinity that messed with our heads. It showed us things, things I wouldn't have wanted to see in my nightmares."

"Sounds like the Corrupted Arts, my king. Dark magic, and no good can come from it. Those that try to study it lose themselves. They become twisted, sinister…"

"Corrupted? That makes sense."

"It would be best that you stay with your knights from here onwards."

Ollie interrupts as he storms out into the courtyard. "I could have told you that."

I hadn't seen him since before Crystal took me on that stroll. Before the attack. *Her*. I should finally clarify this.

"But he never listens to what I have to say, anyways. Makes me wonder what I'm even doing here."

"Ollie… I—"

Alan's voice booms across the courtyard. "What in Hellsfire did you do last night?"

He looks grumpier than usual, and with him stumbles the rest of my knights. Thalia also looks unpleased.

"Just because the king said you can do what you wish with his daughter, it doesn't mean you go and nearly get her killed. Are you even trying to unite our kingdoms?"

"Hey, we were attacked alright. Maybe spend less time flirting, and more time fulfilling your duty to protect me!" I bark back.

"If you were a half-decent knight, maybe you could protect yourself rather than cry and complain to me," Alan argues as he digs his Bo staff into the stone walkway.

"Unfortunately, all we have is a child pretending to be king!"

"Alan!" Thalia stomps as Marshall turns to face the out of line knight.

"Regardless of his age, he is our king, and you will show him some respect!"

"I'll give him my respect once he earns it," Alan growls as he backs off. "But until he grows up, I'm stuck babysitting." "He's not wrong," Ollie says.

"Seriously, West, with all your fears and troubles that came from the Round Table Tournament. You'd think you'd be the last person to go anywhere without your knights."

"Ollie," I'm still steaming, as she brushes past me to stand with Alan.

"You're supposed to be on my side."

"What can I say? I'm in a mood."

I feel like punching both of them, but unfortunately, I can't take either of them single-handedly. How could I expect to handle them together?

"Maybe take keen on your own advice since you don't like listening to mine, and fulfill your duty, King. Then you wouldn't have to worry about sides," Ollie begins walking away before stopping and turning back as if remembering something.

"Oh, wait that last bit was some of my own advice to you. Disregard it as you do best."

I watch Ollie walk off towards the tunnel leading to the dining hall. Alan follows, as well as the rest of my knights aside from Marshall and Thalia. My fist remains clenched.

"What's his problem?"

"Wow!" Thalia gasps. "You really are dense."

I blink, releasing my tension but my earlier exhaustion clouds my mind.

"What's that supposed to mean?"

"I'll tell you when you're older."

Thalia groans and then follows the other knights.

"What's *that* supposed to mean?"

"My young king perhaps ask Ollie about your concerns later," Marshall sighs and he places his hand on my shoulder. "And stroll a little closer to home."

He pats my armor and passes me to join the other knights. I'm even more confused.

We are eventually joined by Nessa and Junah. She looks me over and narrows her starry eyes on me, she can tell I didn't sleep like I was supposed to. I'll rest tonight, that is, if I'm still alive by the end of the day. If not, then I'll just sleep when I'm dead.

We travel down the corridor, having done this enough in the past few days we don't require the escorts. Which seems for the best. The mention of the maidens seems to make Thalia's hair stand on end.

We enter the dining hall, and it's just as quiet as the corridor. There are no loud and rambunctious guests. There's no drinking or festivities. The dining hall is empty aside from King Ivan, Queen Bansha, Princess Crystal, and his two guards. No jester. I approach the king's table with Ollie begrudgingly at my side and the silence is broken by a loud snore. It is from where the guests usually drink, laugh and give me a headache.

Everyone turns to fine Longcaster passed out with his gourd resting on his chest.

"Longcaster, either get on your feet or get out of my sight!"

King Ivan roars and I jump. He's not his usual carefree self but he's acting like an actual king. I wonder if he'll trade tips this time. With a loud snort, Longcaster rolls off the bench and vanishes in a puff of black smoke, taking the snoring with him.

I raise an eye. "A little harsh?"

"Last night my daughter came home nearly dead," King Ivan sneers at me.

"I'm in no mood to kid, I want answers. What happened?"

"Did Crystal not tell you?"

"The princess was left to rest and heal so I decided to save the story for this morning. Or would you have rather had my wrath upon you last night? You too seemed on your last leg."

"Nice of you to show your concerns. Where were these feelings last night when your jester came after us?" I narrow my eyes on King Ivan.

"Or did you not notice your lack of unsatisfying entertainment?"

Ivan glances around with his toothless frown. He *did* just notice his lack of a jester.

He peers over to Eli. "Where is he?" "Dead," Eli growls coldly.

"Vanquished last night. His soul is among the Abyss."

King Ivan turns back to me. "King Westley. Why is the jester dead?"

"Well, it was either him or us," I direct King Ivan's attention back to his daughter.

"I didn't see much good in trying to unite our kingdoms if something befell the princess."

"Crystal," King Ivan turns to his daughter. "Is this true? Was the jester the assailant last night?"

Crystal's eyes fall onto me. I stare at her, but her gaze seems distant. She clears her throat and takes a sip of water to assist.

"The assailant resembled the jester at first."

Resembled? Is she mad? She knows that it was that annoying fool of a man hopping around and chasing us last night.

"And then whatever that thing was, changed, becoming something else. Something evil."

"A shapeshifter?" Ollie speaks up, suddenly invested in the story.

"Those are rare. Not many of them survived the Days of Hellsfire."

King Ivan snaps. "Do *not* speak of such history in my court. In front of my child."

"Children," I correct.

"Just…!" King Ivan barks and then calms himself. "Don't."

"Fine," Ollie agrees with a smirk tugging at the corner of those glossy lips.

"So, the Days of Hellsfire were the last documented sightings of shapeshifters…"

I swear I saw a vein pop in King Ivan's head. Ollie seems smug, though I'm concerned.

"Ollie," I turn with my back to King Ivan and whisper into Ollie's ear.

"Let's not anger him any further."

"Like you weren't trying to rile him up with your accusations?"

"That's my business with the king."

"Whatever," Ollie's eyes roll as I turn back around to face King Ivan. "I apologize, King Ivan."

"King Westley, be sure to watch this one. It will be hard to watch your tongue if I have it removed. Or perhaps I can return it as a necklace?"

"I'll watch my court if you watch yours."

"Are you accusing me of something?" He snarls toothlessly at me.

"Be careful, King Westley."

"You should understand why I have a few *trust* issues when it comes to those wearing the crown."

"Yes," King Ivan says as his toothless snarl turns into a gummy grin.

"I know all about how you claimed your title, *King*. Your court becomes so free of speaking with a little liquor in their systems."

"Okay…"

Liquor, so that's what King's Juice is. I knew I was too young for it. My Uncle Lester hates the stuff but must sell it to customers occasionally to supposedly raise their spirits.

"You followed the knight, Rhodain, all the way to the throne, but when he bit the sandy dust. You claimed the throne for your own."

"That's not—"

"Spare me the unnecessary details," King Ivan waves away my attempt to speak.

"I know enough to know you are a terrible fighter and as good as a knight with no hands when it comes to wielding a sword. Your kingdom doesn't trust you, and by the looks of how your court regards you. You are a king without the respect of his followers."

His words weigh down on me as my knees shake. First the jester's dark words last night, then my own knights belittle me, now King Ivan looks down on me like the child I am. They're all right. Even with the training I received, I am still that scared little boy from the tournament. What kind of a king am I?

"I tell you what, King Westley."

The room's atmosphere becomes lighter and the pressure weighing me down lifts.

"Whatever happened in that tournament to get you here, I am grateful that you saved my daughter. I will look into this jester matter, but for now, you have my thanks, my gratitude, and the gift of my daughter."

"WHAT?!"

The dining room explodes from Ollie, Alan, Crystal and me. King Ivan holds up his hand to halt any further interruption.

"Your triumph last night has earned my respect as a father. So, when our kingdoms unite, I will allow you to marry my daughter so that she can rightfully take her place as queen. What is a king without a queen?"

If there is applause filling the room, it is a silent one. "But for my respect as a king, you couldn't be further."

"Again, what?" I'm alone on this one, and a little embarrassed.

"You have your trust issues, and I have mine. If you were Sorenson, I would have agreed in a heartbeat. In fact, I proposed such a union sometime before his untimely demise. Of course, he denied my request. For some reason, he was more on guard than he used to be."

This sounds like after Susan set up Rhodain for his crimes against the late king.

"Well, I assure you that once we unite, you can have control—"

Ollie elbows me in the ribs. "*Ow!*"

I scowl and Ollie turns away from King Ivan to hiss in my ear.

"What in Hellsfire are you doing?"

"I could ask you the same thing!"

"You're being foolish! You just had a spat with one of your knights in front of your court where he challenged your authority…"

I glare. "I'm pretty sure you had a hand in that too."

"You can't relinquish your command as king in front of your court. You'll lose all respect, or what little you have left."

"You're advising."

"And?"

"I thought you didn't want your duties after this morning?"

Ollie growls. "Don't make me cut you in your sleep."

"Glad to know we're on speaking terms again," I smile.

Ollie turns back to face King Ivan, and he looks at us with curiosity.

"As I was saying, King Ivan. Once we unite, you can have *shared* custody of my forces and resources, as I expect to gain from yours."
"Yes, I'm sure…"

King Ivan studies Ollie and I. "I still need more convincing that you're up for the task. I need you to prove that you are worthy to be called a king."

"So the Mountain Golems and the jester weren't enough evidence for you?"

"Well, there is no physical evidence of such feats…"

I see red. "I'm alive! I lost two men! I saved your daughter, how much more proof do you need?"

"Do you want to sit there and argue, or hear what I have to say?" He's treating me more and more like a child.

"Proceed."

King Ivan grins. "Good *boy*, now I've thought about it and while you have conquered the mountain, the road ahead is still bumpy."

"…Is that meant to be a metaphor?"

"On the opposite end of the lake, there is a trail that will cut over a mountain's pass into the thick woods. There you'll find my grandmother in a little house and her name is…"

He stops, unable to contain his laughter.

"Goodness, you took that so seriously. If you could only see your face. Okay, but seriously, follow the trail through the forest and you'll reach one of the old battlefields."

"From what war?" Ollie asks with a smile.

"The war and battles during the Days of…"

King Ivan threatens as he realizes Ollie's trick. "I will remove your tongue and feed it to Eli."

"Sorry, King Ivan," Ollie shines a clever smile.

"I thought we were being funny."

"Keep challenging me, and I'll have the last laugh," King Ivan glares and then returns to his less intimidating self.

"Now, as I was saying. On the old battlefield you'll find a pile of stones, and at the top resides a sword once used by King Bruno of Dragon's Guard, but in the heat of the battle, it became molded to the stone. It is now known as the Sword of Fate. If anyone can remove that sword from its cursed bindings, then Fate herself must deem them worthy to meet her hand. Bring the sword back, and I'll have enough trust in you to unite our kingdoms."

"So, he needs you to find some old sword before he'll believe you worthy of kingship…" Alan says.

King Ivan scans over Ollie and my head to locate my outspoken knight. "Precisely."

"But you already trust him enough to marry your daughter…?"

"My daughter is one person, and my greatest treasure. I deem what's best for her," King Ivan gestures to her and then raises his hands to the ceiling.

"I can't simply put the future of this kingdom and its people in anyone's hands. They look to me to protect them and I will do whatever it takes for my people."

Something from last night tugs at my memory, but all I see is darkness. I look to Crystal, yet she won't meet my eyes. If we do marry, I hope that changes.

"So, all I have to do is fetch this sword?"

"Yes."

"No tricks this time? No surprises?"

"Fetch the sword and bring it back. I'll even send Longcaster and Eli to accompany you."

"That…" I say, shifting my eyes from the man in black, to where I last saw the sleeping sorcerer.

"…Makes me feel *so* much better."

Eli's one eye peers through me, and as Ollie turns to say something, King Ivan snaps.

"Stop that! By the Gods, if you have something to say, let everyone hear!"

"It's fine Ollie," I say, then return my attention to King Ivan.

"If it's to unite our kingdoms, I'll find this sword and bring it back. I'll even have my Second Grand Advisor tie a ribbon to it for you." "Great!" King Ivan stands with his challis in his hand.

"Take your court and leave tomorrow. I'll have my maidens prepare the boats and escort you at noon, but for now, we drink!"

No one agrees to this. I feel my knights have had enough of their share of drinks for the remainder of our stay here.

We exit the dining hall and return to the courtyard, my knights forming a half-circle as Ollie and I approach.

"Tomorrow we search for this sword," I announce. "It's just one more day before we accomplish our task to unite the kingdoms."

Alan looks displeased. "It better be."

"Tired of me already?" I joke, but Alan doesn't protest.

He huffs. "As long as King Ivan doesn't think of another task to prolong our stay."

"Let's hope…"

"Hope?" Alan tightens his grip on his staff.

"No, you need to put your foot down."

"You know we can't do that, we need their resources to rebuild our kingdom. That's always been the task. I will jump and climb ten mountains full of those golems if it means the restoration of Baronune."

"What our kingdom needs is a stronger king," Alan admits, and I glare at him again.

"Marshall, with your permission, I'd like the rest of the knights to rest and prepare for tomorrow while I remain here to train our…I still can't say it."

I bite my lip, but agree that I could use more training after last night's attack. Marshall agrees and the knights move out. Nessa has Junah run back to his chambers to fetch medicine for when I inevitably get injured.

Ollie takes a step toward me, to stay but suddenly looks sick when Crystal emerges from the dining hall corridor, and storms off to his chambers.

"King Westley?" Crystal calls.

"Hold on." I tell Alan and he looks displeased.

I hurry to the princess.

"What happened in there? Why didn't you back me up?"

"I spoke the truth, King Westley. I'm not sure what we saw last night, but I also don't trust my father. He lies and I'm sure there's something he's not telling you."

"Is that why you're here? To warn me?"

"Yes, *no*... I don't know. I want to thank you for last night—for saving me."

"I did what I could, but I don't deserve much praise. There were other knights there, I don't know which ones but—"

"It makes no difference. You showed bravery when you needed it, and I... I remember what you said about me."

"Oh?"

What did I say again?

She gives a slight smile. "You have my respect... But I don't know if I am ready to be a queen."

"You're telling me, and I understand what you're saying. I'm not rushing to make anyone my queen, I'm only thirteen..."

"Really?"

"*Yeah*... why? Is that an issue?"

"No, it's just, I'm older."

"How much older?"

"Fifteen?"

"What?!" I shout, louder than intended.

Alan and Nessa look in my direction. I gesture that everything is fine, and Crystal laughs.

"*I'm* fifteen."

"Oh," I say and then it dawns on me. "Oh…"

"It's not that much of a difference but… You're still maturing and have so much to worry about."

"Yeah… No, yeah, I get it."

I think I get it. I'm suddenly stricken with confusion and an odd pain to my heart.

"Perhaps we will talk more when you return?"

"Perhaps…"

I can't bring myself to meet her eyes. She gives me a weak smile before kissing my cheek and running off. I turn laggardly and regroup with Alan and Nessa.

"Nessa…?" I say as Junah return to her side.

"Yes, my king?" She says softly.

"Do you have medicine for… this?"

I point to my heart, unable to explain exactly what's hurting.

"Oh," she pauses.

"No, my king. I'm afraid only Time can heal that wound."

Alan places his hand on my shoulder. "You didn't even get to the vows before ruining the marriage. I don't know if you're that naïve, or really becoming a man."

I can't tell if he's picking on me or trying to help.

"But don't go breaking your heart yet. I got to break your face a little first."

"Huh?"

"Draw your sword," Alan orders and twirls his staff.

He takes up a stance and points it at me. "Today, we train."

I find myself wishing the jester had finished me off as I draw my sword less enthusiastically than Alan had and we spend the rest of the day training.

I must really get under Alan's skin because he really drilled into me during our *training*, a term I use loosely. In a weary delirium, Junah carries me on his back to my chambers. Nessa uses her Fairy Light discreetly to mend my wounds while no one's around. Each step he struggles to carry me, and to refrain from making a sound. We don't want to bring the tunnel down on top of us. They return me to my chambers and apparently undress me as they did the night before.

"Maybe you would have better held your own if rested last night as I suggested."

Nessa pulls my chin down and pours a liquid into my mouth.

"Since our king stubbornly doesn't listen to what his court suggests. This potion will put you to sleep in minutes and allow your body to fully heal."

Nessa prepares to leave and I can already feel the effect taking hold. My eyelids grow heavy, and if I didn't have any strength before, I definitely don't anymore. My body feels like it's fusing with my bed.

"Nessa…" I yawn.

"Why does Ollie hate me?"

"That is still a question better suited for Ollie," Nessa smiles from the doorway.

"But since you're asking me. I believe it to be the inverse, my king."

I don't really catch that as my eyes shut, and I drift into unconsciousness and pray to avoid nightmares. I don't want to think about Crystal, I don't even want to think about Ollie. As I drift deeper into sleep, I recall the one good thing that's happened as I succumb to the world of dreams. I let the image of my mother be the thing to nurse my body back to health.

I wake up, finding myself in a realm of warm wavery light. I've been here before… I glance down. Nothing, but yet I am standing. I study the pale yellow to stain white void full of soundless pops.

"I'm here again? Where *is* here?"

An image appears in the distance again, and I glide across the endless space. The figure becomes clearer as I close in. It's not Rhodain, it's a woman. She looks as if waking up and rolling out of bed. She stretches, her back to me. She turns and if I had breath in this space I'd gasp.

She's dressed in white and her hair is navy blue. Her skin is a brilliant golden yellow, but she has the same beauty mark below her lip.

"Mom?"

She looks me over as if she's seeing a dream. She then looks down at herself. She looks at her body and then her hands.

"Is that the form that I'm in this time?" She asks to my bewilderment. I glide several feet away from her.

"Do not be alarmed. My form changes depending on the person. I just didn't think you'd see me as someone different. I didn't think you'd see me at all, let alone again."

"Who—*what* are you?"

"Well," she smiles as she stops studying her body, my mother's body.

"As you mortal beings like to call me, I'm a God. Or rather, in this form, Goddess."

My jaw drops and so do I. It feels like I'm falling for eternity and when I finally stop and look up to where my mother was, she is the size of an ant. Then suddenly, I zoom back to face her.

"You didn't let me finish."

"Sorry…I wasn't exactly prepared to be talking to a God today." I'd say my brain hurts but it just feels fuzzy.

"You can call me whatever you'd like. I'm just telling you what your kind normally calls me."

My eyes squeeze as I struggle with the idea of calling her mother. I can't bring myself to say it and I understand why Alan struggles with calling me king. I must look funny because my mother laughs at me. I accept this because I don't remember seeing my mother laugh.

"This calms you? Good. I'll keep that in mind."

"Where am I, and who exactly are you… Goddess?"

"I am known as Fate. You are somehow in my consciousness. This doesn't usually happen."

The world is spinning. I'm starting to wonder if this is a reaction to my confusion or to hers.

"Oh, calm down my dear, calm down. Stay with me," she urges as she goes to take me by the arms, but hesitates.

The world stops spinning, and my head feels normal again.

"Yes, that seems more accurate. Your kind has trouble comprehending our existence. It's like surfacing from a pond only to hit your head on glass that you don't know is there. You see the sky but hurt yourself trying to reach it."

I blink. "That… Makes sense."

"And with that, the pain is gone."

She laughs. I smile, and the fuzziness disappears. The world becomes a solid void of light though the soundless pops remain around us.

"So, you're the Goddess, Fate?"

"I am Fate, yes. I am not subjected to the label God or Goddess, but be this form is apparently female. I will accept Goddess today."

"Right, because you take the form of however or whoever I see you as?"

"Yes," she smiles. "You catch on fast."

"I'm known to be a fast learner, and I'm open to interpretation these days. Five months ago, I discovered the truth about Divinity and now my life has changed."

"Oh, has Divinity become less used in your time?" She asks looking confused.

"Whichever time that is?"

"I guess?" I respond unsurely and the realm shimmers.

"Oh, okay, okay, sorry. I'm just still learning so I may not have all the answers."

"Maybe I should give you more clarity. Divinity is not something that vanishes, it's everywhere. So, you're saying that you only recently discovered it means that from the last time I was around, the number of mortals that can withstand it must have plummeted."

"And when was that?"

"Hard to say. I am Fate. That's a question for Time."

"There's more of you?"

"Yes, at least there was. I've been taking a bit of a nap, so I don't know all the changes."

"I'm sorry to disturb your sleeping?"

"Oh no, I'm still asleep. If I weren't, we wouldn't be in my consciousness."

"So, this realm, this world… is inside your head?"

"To keep the matter light, yes."

She says this and I lift my foot as if I am stepping on her. She laughs again and the world, her consciousness turns to a solid light again.

"So why am I here?"

"I don't know. None have entered our consciousness before, normally we visit others if given the opportunity."

"Opportunity?"

"We span across multiple realms, worlds, and realities. To be able to pinpoint a single existence is rare and difficult. As such, it doesn't happen often. Had I known we could have you mortals delivered to us, that would have made things easier."

"What things?"

"Oh, right. You're saying that you only just discovered Divinity, so I'm left to believe that you have yet to learn of the Elemental War, Endless War, and the Hands."

I lift my hands up, questionably. She laughs again and gestures for me to put my hands back down to my side.

"No, not like that. Like I said we… *Gods*… are stretched thin. So, I came up with the brilliant idea, as I used to do, to create Hands to help and assist us. Mine, of course, were known as the Hands of Fate, and they kept order, and balanced the justices of the worlds so all I had to do was string together mortals' meetings and paths."

"Okay…"

Dare I ask this.

"What happened then? If there were Godly Law Enforcement running around, I think I'd notice that."

"You believe you'd *notice* that? You only just discovered Divinity."

"I am not up to date on my history, we were supposed to be studying that after the summer, but I wound up becoming king."

"Ah… what?"

The world seems to freeze and Fate looks at me so peculiarly that I feel uncomfortable. I try to hide my body, but she leans in to inspect me.

"Westley…Jameson. King. Thirteen. The Kingdom of Baronune… huh?"

"Fate saying '*huh*' is not comforting."

"No, it's just… Fascinating," she says and then she looks up to the nonexistent sky.

"Wow, just… you don't exist."

"Huh?"

Now she has me doing it.

"I mean, clearly you do, but… It would take me asking Time for assistance, but I'm asleep for a reason. I don't feel like being bothered with the others. Still, from what I can see. None of your roads were supposed to lead to this… interesting."

"So, I'm king by accident?"

I feel like I knew this already. The world seems to be jarring.

"Yes and no. Someone has been dipping their hands in fate, thus altering yours ever slightly."

She says this and the world begins to shake violently. I'd run for cover if there *was* cover.

"Intriguing."

"Can you stop star gazing or whatever, you're stirring yourself." I assume gazing around the unsettling void.

"Oh, sorry. As I said, I'm asleep, connecting your mortal paths is simple enough, but it appears I have been taken advantage of in my absence and someone has been playing around with your fates. Just enough to not raise suspicion, but it can be world-shattering if done right. Or wrong, depending on how you look at it."

"Someone's messing with Fate, does that means you're going to stop them?"

"No, darling. We're not permitted to get involved. We're allowed to exist and do what our existence provides. That's why we created the Hands so that they could do the dirty work we couldn't."

"So, what became of the other Hands of Fate?"

"After the Endless War, we agreed to suspend our Hands. All because the Hands of Life got too greedy and made a whole mess of existence. That's why we don't get involved anymore. When one of my Hands managed to defeat the nine Hands of Life, we decided to suspend the production of more and allowed the existing ones to die out and become Hands of Death which merely usher the souls of the dead."

"There's Life, Death, Time, and Fate..."

I'm managing to keep up so far. This is oddly easier to grasp than Divinity was.

"Who's messing with Fate? With *you*."

"Stop while you're ahead, dear." She suggests as the world turns fuzzy. "Don't worry about that now. Time will tell."

"...Are you saying that because in time I'll find out or because the god, Time, will eventually tell me."

"Well, both of those are the answer, aren't they?"

I apparently spoke too soon when I said I was grasping this.

"It's fine. Do what I do and let the others handle their existence. You just focus on you," she says placing her hand on my chest.

"In fact. To correct this down the line, as that is in my realm of ability. There."

She says and removes her hand from my chest. I look down though there's nothing there. I look to her and Fate smiles back.

"What did you do?"

"What I'm supposed to do. Now you go do what you're supposed to do."

"*Fate*, what did you do?"

"Evened the scale. Time will enjoy this," she smiles wider.

I'm concerned.

"Go now and let me sleep. Follow your path, King Westley Jameson. It's there to guide you."

Fate concludes as she rolls over and fall back asleep. I find myself floating backwards and looking down, I see a teal light extend into a road. To where, I can't discern, but as I travel it my vision becomes blurry and the world becomes bright.

⊶∘〇〰〇∘⊷

I wake again and roll out of bed. The quartz shines with a nightly glow and I stare at my hands. Hands…Was that real? Was anything I experienced real, or a dream? I feel fine and clear headed. My strength has returned and I stare down at myself, I'm wearing my silk bottoms, but Nessa and Junah failed to give me a blouse to sleep in.

I open my wardrobe and slip into a top to match my pajamas. I head towards the door. I'm unclear as to why I'm awake at the dead of night. The passage is lit by dim lanterns, but otherwise, it is dark and empty. I can hear the echoes of bats from both ends. I walk, my feet are bare, and my body feels different. I would say I'm sleepwalking but I'm not. I'm walking aimlessly, but I feel I as if I know where I'm going, or where I need to be next.

After a few minutes pass, I stop in front of a door. Whose door is it? I don't bother to knock and walk in. "Ollie…?"

I say knowing where I am now, but I wasn't expecting to see what I saw. Before the glow of the quartz, Ollie leaps out of bed, wrapping up in the sheets. Ollie's silhouette… is the silhouette of a girl's… I quickly shield my eyes.

"Oh, I'm sorry. I am so sorry! I forgot—"

"Gods, West!"

Ollie's voice flows from the corner where I saw the silhouette. I peek cautiously. The bedsheets are now wrapped around Ollie's shoulders, but I know what I saw.

"I-I'm sorry… I should go…"

"No," Ollie sighs, peeking back at me over the shoulder.

There's an air of exhaustion, but not because of suddenly being awoken from bed.

"No, West. Come in but close the door behind you."

I do as I am told, since I do listen, just don't remember to knock. I quietly close the door behind me and turn to face Ollie who approaches. The sheets drag from the bed. They're thin. So thin that the light from the quartz shines through it and confirms what I saw before. Ollie's body is that of a girls.

"Ollie…I, I'm sorry…Are you, you're a…Your…preference is… **She?**"

"It's taken you five months and that's how you ask? I swear if I didn't know you so well…"

Ollie eyes do exaggerated summersaults.

"I have never hidden who I am, I just haven't cared to correct people. I am whatever I choose to be, but since you finally asked, yes, I prefer to be referred to as *she*."

"A shapeshifter…?"

I think back to earlier today. Ollie stops and stares at me blankly. Her cheeks turn red with laughter.

"I suppose I asked for that after speaking about it today. No, West, I am not a shapeshifter. Not really. It's a more medical transition, not one that completely uses Divinity. Though I wish, that would have been easier. Less complicated."

"But... You... your body. I'm confused?"

Normally this would be weird for me, but oddly enough I feel used to this concept already. As if I just dealt with something similar only moments ago. Maybe it wasn't a dream. Ollie's left-hand cuffs my cheek while her other hand holds the bedsheet around her shoulders, and keeps it closed at her chest, which I can see a lot easier now without her usual hakama. My face turns hot as I immediately look up to the ceiling.

"Sorry, I wasn't staring."

"*Wow*, you are such a little boy."

"I mean, yeah. I've been pretty honest about that. Can you...can you help me understand?"

I ask and Ollie lowers her hand. She looks to be struggling with this as she takes in a breath.

"When I was born and proclaimed a boy, my parents named me Oliver, but I always felt... different. It wasn't until I was around your age that I started to make sense of it. I started listening to my body. I was training to join the assassin's guild, I was finally old enough and my parents allowed me. But things... things were *challenging*.

My body wasn't reacting the way I wanted it to. I couldn't maneuver right; my coordination was off. My mind, body and soul weren't aligned for Divinity to flow properly. That's when it all made sense to me, and I sought medical help. When I couldn't find it, I thought I could become a nurse and figure it out myself.

So, I stopped my training and started nursing. Though that wasn't the answer either. It wasn't until I heard rumors of someone with the skills and was bold enough to go through with the procedure was I able to fully embrace who I truly was. I was finally able to be, me, and I chose to present myself as Ollie. And kept up with nursing to further help others like me someday."

I'm in awe. "Wow. Around my age... wait, how old are you?"
"Fifteen."

"What is with that today?"

Ollie tilts her head and frowns at me as she usually does when I get distracted during her lessons.

"Focus, King," she snaps.

This is so familiar that it's like I'm trained to respond to it.

"Unfortunately, *you* do not change. Always distracted by your own thoughts."

"Sorry, I'm trying…"

"You've been trying all week. Don't think I haven't noticed. Assassin Guild, remember?" Ollie raises an eye. I feel a familiar shrinking feeling again. Ollie lifts my chin.

"West, it's me, okay? I'm no different than when you met me. Minus trying to kill you."

"I welcome that change."

"You welcome a lot of things."

"What's that supposed to mean?" I ask, slightly offended.

Ollie directs my attention to the chamber we're in. She's right, I have a terrible attention span because I don't grasp what she's getting at.

"That's why we're in this situation. You trusted Rhodain to protect you and look where it got you, king. You trust your court to guide you, and look where it's led you, Woodsforge and being joked around by a king that loves jokes and… follow me on this one… lying!"

"I trusted you and you haven't been that up front with me either."

"Did Alan hit you extra hard today or just from the start? Everyone else knew except you. Regardless, it's my decision to choose when to come out to people. Or at least it was."

"I said sorry!" I yell in defense as she glares.

I will not do this again today. I will not let someone else put me in my place.

I scream with a new vigor of strength surging within me.

"I've had a lot on my mind! The pressure to be king is hard! I must enforce, listen, and instruct all at the same time and I don't even know what I am doing! I must be able to fight and protect myself while being able to protect others! I've only recently learned how to fight let alone grasp Divinity. I've nearly died twice in one day mind you. Been called a liar, fraud, and outed out as weak and inexperienced. Most of all, I pissed off the one person that I want to call a friend and I don't even know why!"

Ollie puts her fingers to my lips, and suddenly the storm brewing within me is calmed.

"I get it. It's hard for me to watch somedays, but I get it. People making accusations of you because of who you are and how you look. People expecting more of you than you're ready for, but disappointed in whatever decision you make. Whoever you decide to be, I—get—it." Ollie sighs.

"But when it comes down to it. All you can be is *you*, and whoever you want to be. I may be cautious coming out to the public. Hellsfire, I only went to Baronune because I heard of a community led by that Matthews guy that I could fit in with, and then the Round Table Tournament happened. But... I'm comfortable knowing who I am. Being in Baronune has allowed me to truly be me, and no one can take that. I let those judgments and indifferences fuel my strength and push me forward as I follow the path I laid out for me. I follow my—" "Fate." I say as clarity flows through me.

I look at Ollie confidently and our eyes meet to share the same light. "Sure. Fate," Ollie agrees with a soft smile. "But I take control of it."

"Because that's what Fate does. Takes control of the roads we wander."

"You're starting to lose me, Westley."

"Yeah, I may have talked to a God and or Goddess tonight in my sleep, so none of this is new to me."

Ollie blinks repeatedly. It's nice to see that expression on someone else's face for a change.

I laugh. "I know, right? What a world."

"What a world indeed."

She laughs with me then drops her hand, and we stand in the midst of her chambers laughing amongst ourselves. I think this is the first time we've laughed together in months. It's nice. It's reassuring.

"Was that why you came in my room tonight?" Ollie shifts to a softer tone.

"To rub it in my face that not only are you a king, but you commune with Gods?"

"No, I found myself awake and it dawned on me that I just didn't want to go on this adventure tomorrow with you mad at me. I can make you mad at me for far other reasons with a new day." I joke, but Ollie doesn't laugh this time.

"It's not your fault. I was in a mood today. King Ivan really gets under my skin. I don't trust him, and neither should you. Still, hearing that you nearly died last night made me blame myself for not being by your side but hearing that you were out with that princess…"

"Crystal?" After everything that's transpired tonight, I had nearly forgotten about her and her, I guess, marriage rejection.

"No worries there. We agreed that this marriage idea is not right for us."

"Because you're too young for her?"

"Again, all day today!"

I shout and Ollie laughs loudly, it's a cute laugh this time. "It's a gift we have. You'll understand when you're –" *Now* I pout.

"Older? I've heard that one too."

"Well, you just turned thirteen, what do you expect? You were going to roll out of bed ready for adulthood? Take it from me, it doesn't get easier any time soon. We're all still learning, growing, and discovering more about ourselves every day. So, enjoy what you can and remember to live a little amongst all this chaos."

Ollie smiles at me as she places her hand on my cheek again. I smile back and we share this expression together for what seems like minutes.

I blush. "So… Do I have to kiss you now?"

"Oh, no. No, no, no, West. Too young," Ollie shakes her head and pats my shoulder.

Is today on a loop?

"I need my men a little more, manly. Though, Lieutenant Hayden is rather alluring."

I'm not going to say that hurt like what Crystal did to me earlier today, but my shoulders are weighed down with something heavy. Shame? Regret?

"You're still figuring yourself out. Don't rush these things," Ollie smiles and leaves me to my emotional paralysis.

"Go get some rest, West. We have a long day tomorrow to go fetch that king a bone."

"A sword," I correct, snapping out of my embarrassment.

"Good boy," Ollie smiles from across the room.

"You *do* know what you're chasing. Off to bed now."

Ollie waves me off. It's weird how that worked out, but I feel like we've come closer to being friends. Perhaps that's just the road we're supposed to travel.

"Good night." I open the door and step outside smiling then close the door behind me.

Chapter Twelve

Sinking the King

I wake fully rested, hearing a knock at my door and Nessa's sweet voice greets me.

"My king, are you awake?"

She cracks the door ever slightly, "Alan would wish for you to meet him in the courtyard while the rest of your knights are getting ready." "Okay," I answer as I continue putting on my gear.

"I'll be down shortly. I got up early."

"Were you able to rest properly this time?"

"Yes, Nessa. I got a full night's sleep."

I choose to leave out the part of creeping in on Ollie in the late of night. It was already embarrassing as it was to interrupt her privacy. As I enter the courtyard I find Alan waiting for me.

"More training? Don't you think we did enough yesterday?"

"Your performance hasn't been the best. If you're going to wear that crown, you need to be better in case the rest of your knights aren't present to babysit you."

I groan but I don't want to spark another argument with Alan again today, plus he's not wrong. We take our respective sides of the courtyard. Nessa and Junah already prepare their medical equipment. Since we discovered yesterday that Nessa is secretly a fairy, she refuses to use her Divinity in King Ivan's castle, not wanting to risk exposure and putting the hidden fairy realm, Bellshire, at risk.

"Ready?"

Alan asks taking up his Bo staff. This is different. He squats into a stance that I haven't seen him take before.

"Uh…?" I reply unsurely as I unsheathe my sword.

He normally waits for me to make my move first. He's done this for five months, showing very little interest in training me.

"…Ready?"

"Go!"

He barks and rushes me. Not what I was expecting at all. I'm on my guard. He's leaves enough distance to jab at me with his staff and I manage to parry a few of his attacks with my sword but lack the strength to keep this up. He lunges a sharp jab straight at my chest that I block, leaving me stumbling over my feet. Alan retracts his staff and swirls it overhead. I'm given only a moment to breathe before he swings at me. I forget how ridiculously fast Alan can be when he tries, only witnessing this once when he briefly sparred with Ollie.

Alan's staff collides with my shoulder, and I lose my footing. I stumble to the right. He whirls back around and bats me on the opposite side. I stumble back into my starting position only to catch another sharp jab to my chest. This time I'm not ready. I'm too befuddled by his swift movements and strikes to maintain my balance. He hits me dead in the chest, my Mirrogold armor giving me more resistance than my practice armor, but Alan is strong with the Martial Arts. I'm thrust off my feet and hit the ground hard.

I don't bounce as I make sure to keep my head from colliding with the cobblestone, but that doesn't keep Alan from pursuing me. He's already on me, raising his staff for another strike. I flinch at the sight of his staff slamming down towards me. I don't think to roll out of the way or try to counter. I throw up my hands in a pathetic attempt for a guard and close my eyes. Alan stops his attack, or so I thought.

I open my eyes. There's a brief flash of green and I catch Alan flying across the courtyard as the light fades. Nessa gasps. She is quick to cover

Junah's mouth before he does the same. I'm confused as I sit up. Alan rolls back to his feet enraged and befuddled as well.

"What was that?" He's breathing heavily.

He isn't the only voice I hear echoing in the courtyard.

"What was that?"

Ollie asks as she happens to walk out in the moment of that green flash. I almost thought that was her doing. The light was very similar to the light that emits from her use of Divinity.

"That… That wasn't you?" I ask turning to Ollie.

"No!"

Her eyes are wide and Alan storms towards me.

"Okay kid," he snatches me off the ground and holds me to my feet. "What was that? When did you learn to do that?" "That what?" I ask completely at a loss.

He yells and shakes me. "You emitted some light that blasted me away! You used magic!"

He has me lifted from under my arms. I feel like a cat that has committed some household crime.

"Alan!" Thalia cries from the other side of the courtyard. "Let him down! What are you doing?" "He…"

Alan drops me. I manage to land on my feet. Maybe I am a cat?

"He used magic and blasted me across the courtyard!"

Thalia stops mid-march. She has Dawn, Kaleb, and the other knights behind her. They look around the courtyard as if searching for evidence. There's nothing to support Alan's claim aside from Nessa, Junah, and Ollie being here to witness the phenomenon.

"My king," Thalia continues as she marches up to us. "Is this true?"

"I'm not sure what Alan saw, but I have not trained in the Mystic Arts, so I wouldn't know how to use it."

"That didn't stop you from springing that quick technique on me before," Alan argues.

"Thalia never taught you that and you showed no signs that your Martial Arts were even close to that level, so explain that one!" "That was me," Ollie closes in.

"It was during the time I was training King West in between your lessons."

"Yeah, took me months to get that move down. The rest of the time I was figuring out your fighting style just so I could catch you off guard once. Once! Five months to land one punch. Do you think I'd be able to master the Mystic Arts simultaneously?"

Alan looks dumbfounded. He struggles with what he saw and what Ollie and I are telling him.

"If there is no evidence of this, then we'll have to take the king's word as truth," Marshall announces as he strides up.

The court's all here.

"The king's word is law, after all," Marshall admits and Alan grinds his teeth.

He's having a hard time accepting this and he looks to Nessa and Junah for support.

"Hey," Alan points at Nessa. "Fairy, tell me what just happened. You saw it too."

"Uh, well..." Nessa ponders this.

"It's rather hard for me to explain. June, would you feel like explaining it better?"

She asks and Junah looks at her baffled. He shakes his head in resentment. None of us try to persuade him to speak knowing what emits when he opens his mouth. It's best for everyone if he remains silent.

"You know he can't risk speaking," Alan growls.

"That's true. Well then we'll have to accept the king's word then," Nessa shrugs adorably. "I can't explain it any better."

"You!" Alan shifts to Ollie. "What did you see?" "A bright light and you getting knocked on your ass.".

"What caused it?" Alan growls deeper, not taking too kindly to Ollie's tone. I chuckle. "What have you been teaching him?"

"What little I can. He's quite stubborn. You've seen him in combat," Ollie smiles as she crosses her arms.

"How many times have you had to save him now? And don't you think if King West could use the Mystic Arts, he'd used it to save him and our butts yesterday? He's not very keen at sacrificing other's lives for his own safety. He's naïve sure, but pure."

My court seems to agree with her and Alan backs off.

"Fine, but I want answers and I expect to get them later."

Alan shoves one finger in my face. I go cross-eyed looking down at it. He removes himself and goes to retrieve his staff. Ollie steps to my side

"I'd like answers too," she whispers. *"What are you hiding?"*

"If I was hiding anything," I whisper back. *"I would have revealed them to you last night. This open honesty thing works both ways."*

Ollie seems to pause at this. "Right."

Out of the corner of my eye, I see her pale cheeks turn a little redder. "I just had to be sure."

She tries to make herself out to be strict, but I can hear the appreciation in her voice. Only for a moment as the sound of Longcaster's loud and sluggish speech enters the courtyard. He's accompanied by a few maidens, mostly for support as he's struggling to walk on his own and is with the last person, I wanted to see this morning, Eli. I swear there's an aura of darkness emitting from him with each step, but after this morning I don't know what my eyes are telling me anymore.

Longcaster attempts counting us as his gourd is tightly in hand. "Good, good, you're all here. All one, two…"

He hiccups. "When did you bring an army, King Jameson?" "Uh…" I reply, unsure how to answer that in his current state.

"No—*hic*—bother. I'm sure we have enough boats for your men," he hiccups again.

"And women."

"Thanks," I say uncomfortably with Eli stepping forward dressed head to toe in his usual black garbs.

"Shall we?" He hisses, and I immediately feel like I'm being pulled back into that nightmare realm again.

I say nothing and let them lead the way. The rest of us grab our gear, sling our packs, and follow behind them down the tunnel that Crystal and I took to leave the castle.

Steam-powered stagecoaches await us, looks like this time King Ivan wants us to ride in a little more style. With the rumbling of the water container and the turning of the mechanism to operate the vehicles, we're off and riding down the road in a single-file line.

I stare out the window as new scenery passes us by. The *Forgers* of the Stone Capital are a little more active today, dressed in attire robbed of life. The miners' faces are covered in dirt and grime, but for the most part, everyone seems to be content with their lives in Woodsforge.

The sky is a cold gray. Pale cloud vapors linger across the tops of structures, and we seem to be heading downhill. The air chills and the smell of fish and fresh water fill my nostrils again. We must be getting close to the lake. I begin to ponder about the Sword of Fate and the uniting of the kingdoms when I spot something familiar. Two bulking suits of armor enter a building, and I'm immediately on my feet.

"Stop!" I yell to the coachman. "Stop!"

I let my voice carry to the rest of the carriages, but I'm not really yelling for them. I'm yelling to get the attention of those knights.

I leap from my carriage and take off. I hear Ollie and Nessa yelling after me. There's been an itch, an inkling, about the identity of the knights who saved Crystal and I since yesterday. I have to be sure.

I bust into the building they entered. It's dark, damp, and smells rather stale. There are only a few older gentlemen scattered throughout the floor. Fishermen and merchants sit in gloom at long wooden tables and benches. There's a large counter to my right that takes up most of the area, and a man in his late twenties walking around with mugs. He fills and disperses them to his paying customers.

I've never been in a tavern until now. Standing out in the middle of the room, as if I wouldn't notice their large less than splendid suits of armor, are the knights. Again, I can't make out features as their armor covers them from head to toe, which leaves me wondering why they'd enter a tavern fully suited if they didn't intend to drink?

I walk in. I approach them, but I can't tell if they are aware of who I am or even recognize me from the other night.

"Oh," says the smaller of the two suits of armor. "It's you."

"You remember me?"

"The idiot that almost died the other night?" the smaller knight responds.

"Yeah, we remember."

"…You're not much of a knight, are you?" asks the taller of the suits. "You seemed rather helpless and hardly put up much of a fight."

I sit across from them, "It was a troubling situation to say the least."

I feel their gaze on me now whereas before it felt they were trying to avoid eye contact.

"I wanted to say thank you."

"You're welcome," the smaller one is quick to respond. "Now leave."

"Rude. Do you know who I am?"

"Someone annoying?" Answers the smaller knight.

"A terrible knight?" Responds the taller one.

"I am the King of Baronune," I say more so to get a response or a reaction from them.

They remain perfectly still. "Does that mean anything to you?"

"Should it?"

The shorter one asks in return, and I look to them both peculiarly. They're cautious with their answers. Much like someone else I used to know.

"Are you…" the taller one speaks up. "Looking for someone?"

"Not particularly."

I hear my knights shuffling in through the main entrance. I don't look back to see which ones are there, but I hold up my hand to tell them to standby. I do notice that the two knights in front of me shift a little uncomfortably in the presence of my court.

"I just popped in as I saw you, recognizing you from the other night."

"Well," the smaller knight speaks more cautiously. "As I said, you're welcome, *King…*"

"Westley. You may call me, West."

"King West, you're welcome. Now if you don't mind, we'd like to be about our business now."

"Which is what exactly?" I ask, surveying the area.

I also take notice that it is Ollie, Marshall, Thalia, Dawn, Hoover, and Cooper standing in the doorway. I meet Ollie's eyes. We come to an understanding that I am okay.

"There's not that many people here, yet you have no drinks. Not thirsty?"

"We haven't ordered," the smaller one answers.

"Why? Too afraid to reveal your faces?"

"No, we're just too young for King's Juice," the taller one admits, and the smaller knight pounds the table with their fist.

"What? I was going to see if they had milk or any other juice instead."

"…Just stop talking."

Underage knights that are trying to conceal their identity. Their hostile replies shift to being more cautious at the mention of Baronune and the sight of my knights. Roxette himself would be proud of how well I'm solving this mystery.

"You're them, aren't you?" I whisper as I lean in with a smile.

"You're Nova and Avery?"

"Yes."

The taller knight leans in to meet me while the smaller one sighs. I can almost feel the chill retreat as the tavern heats up by a few degrees. Did I see smoke drift from the cracks of the smaller knight's visor?

"Calm down, Nova," Avery says.

"He knew who we were. It was pointless to lie."

"If he knew he wouldn't have asked." Nova replies as her hand squeezes tighter.

My eyes linger on her a little longer. Waiting for her to remove her helmet and reveal her face so that I can look Rhodain's sister in the eye. She doesn't, and I'm left a little disappointed.

"You've caught us, but I can assure you that if you attempt to arrest us it won't end pretty."

"Oh, trust me, I have no means to start a fight. I've heard of your reputation through Rhodain…"

The mention of his name generates a response. The heat in the room simmers down. It's nearly cool again.

"You know, Rhodain?"

"Your brother?" I answer carefully.

"I knew him. He helped me and my cousin survive the tournament. He didn't make it."

Nova remains motionless and Avery's shoulders sag. I lean back and tell my knights to wait outside. There's a bit of resistance and hesitation, but Ollie convinces them to listen to my plea and they step back out.

"Thank you," Nova admits but they still leave their helmets on. "So, there was a tournament? What became of Sorenson?"

"Killed by the former Queen."

"Susan?" Avery asked out of astonishment.

"I didn't think she had it in her."

I look at him peculiarly as if we're referring to the same heartless Queen.

Nova laughs. "Rhodain never trusted her. Guess he was right."

Nova laughter stops, "What happened? What became of my brother?"

This takes me a moment. I've been trying hard to not relive the last moments of the Round Table Tournament. The thoughts and actions of Rhodain were all because of me. I didn't want to fight his sister, but the topic of his death might spark her into a fury. To which I'll accept every bit of her outburst, I deserve it.

"Rhodain… he fought brilliantly. The tournament was his to win. That's why I saw fit for him to protect my cousin and me until the end. Until he could become king. We were not fighters…"

"You're still not much of a fighter." Avery admits and I don't argue with him.

Nova signals for him to silence and allows me to continue.

"This is true but… as a result of reaching the end of the tournament, we were being pursued by the knights of Sorenson's court as Rhodain was a wanted criminal and we came across the Queen, who at the time was acting like she was abducted against her will and trapped on the streets, but it was all a part of her plan. Inside the castle, we split up. Rhodain went to claim the crown, my cousin and I followed Susan to find out what happened to the king. In our attempts, we were captured. Susan and my cousin at least, I got away…"

I'm breathing heavily. This is the part I'm having difficulties with.

"…I found Rhodain atop the castle. The last obstacle in his way. A couple of knights with enchanted weapons…"

"Lawrence, Matthews and Greg?" Nova sounds appalled.

"He can make quick work of them. They're annoying but not that strong."

"I'd beg to differ," I object.

"And he barely survived a confrontation with the executioner with an axe that can apparently slay Gods."

I feel Nova's eyes burn into me through her helmet. "You should have mentioned that first."

"Well, I don't much like reliving these events let alone retell them."

"I'm just saying you're a terrible storyteller."

"It's easier in the moment," I agree, and she gestures for me to finish.

"After an epic showdown, and Rhodain pulling out all the stops to regain his strength and beat them. He was inches from becoming king when Susan interrupted."

"Wait, I remember the rules of the tournament," Avery admits. "If you enter some ring around the throne you have to duel or fight or…" "*Avery,*" Nova protests.

"What?" He pauses as if glancing at her. She remains still. I would make her out to be a statue if I weren't talking with her.

"*Oh…*"

Avery seems to catch on as he eases back into an upward position, and I swear I see a flash go off within his armor like someone quickly turned on the lights to their home.

"Yeah, Susan wanted the throne. She wanted to be king and took advantage of Rhodain's weakness to do it. She killed him with some sword of light, though he became some magnificent bird or something that burnt the last of his strength. I rushed to assist him, but there was nothing I could do. He turned to embers and ash and vanished, but not before throwing me into the throne… making me the new king."

My fist rests on the table tightly clutched. I can't bring myself to look at them, but I feel the heat in the tavern dissipate and the coolness from the nearing lake drifts back in.

"*He should have healed. Rhodain was a Warrior of the Phoenix,*" Nova whispers more so to herself and then exhales as if the whole story had her tense.

"Well thank you, new king, for the fabulous story. I think that will do for today."

"I'm sorry…"

"For what?"

"Had it not been for me and my cousin, Rhodain probably would have made it to the castle, and he probably would have been king. The rightful king."

"Oh, believe me when I say my brother would have made for a terrible king."

"What…?" I say, caught off guard.

"How can you say that? He's brave, courageous and stronger than anyone I know."

"Yeah, but he's arrogant, hotheaded and too passionate for his own good. Trust me, this isn't any of your fault. He would have protected you regardless. That's just who he is. He only ate that damn egg because he thought it was the only way for him to protect us."

She points between herself and Avery. "When we were fully capable of protecting ourselves."

"B-but…" I stutter. "Isn't that what makes for a good king?"

"In part, yes, but I know my brother. He didn't want to be king. He only wanted to prove his strength and protect the ones he loved. The kingdom shunned him when he was young, kicked him to the streets. He had no heart for Baronune, but he did have ambition. He wanted to make a name for himself and that's it. He gained respect and friendship from the king; he never wanted his title. I don't know why he bothered to win the tournament anyway."

"…He did it for you," I say hesitantly as I let everything Nova said sink in.

It all sounded so much like Rhodain, but I only knew him for a little over a day. She grew up with him. Of course, she'd know him better than me.

"His whole reasoning was so that he could return Baronune to the one you knew and so you both could return safely."

"…That," Nova begins after a long pause and sigh. "Does sound like my brother."

Her vigor that has been expelling all throughout the tavern has shrunk to a whimper of strength. Avery rests his hand on her shoulder and leans towards me.

"King Westley, I think that will be enough for today, but thank you for telling us what became of Rhodain."

I nod, "…You're welcome."

I remove myself from the table and turn to head for the door. As I reach for it, I remember something else. As my heart thumps heavily in my chest, I am reminded of Rhodain's parting words. I peer back over my shoulder to the only two people Rhodain called family.

"Just before I go, there's one last thing. The last thing Rhodain said before… before he passed."

I feel their eyes on me. I turn to face them once more. I close my eyes and take in a breath. I exhale and regard them again.

"Rhodain said to tell you, Nova… that he believes in you." "That was the last thing he said?" Nova asks, again not budging.

"That's the last thing he said to you before he passed?"

"Yes."

I say and there's another pause as if she's letting those words sink in. Avery has one hand on her shoulder and the other on her fist.

"Thank you, King West. That will be all," Nova replies, and I nod.

She doesn't sound like she's taking it to heart. She also doesn't sound as confident as when I first greeted them. I walk outside where Ollie waits for me with Hoover and Cooper as Marshall and Thalia watch from a distance.

"What was that about?" Ollie asks sounding strict but concerned.

"Who were those knights?"

"They were…" I say and shift my eyes over to Marshall and Thalia. It's quick but for me, my eyes linger on them for hours.

"They're no one. My mistake."

I say and head back to my stagecoach. Marshall and Thalia don't press for more details, and Ollie simply follows me.

We proceed down the road in our caravan until we reach the lake. There are a few fishing spots and men along the shore. The lake looks a little more ruffled from this angle. There are dozens of long slender wooden boats prepped and prepared for us and all our gear.

"King Jameson," Longcaster calls to us.

He seems to have recovered from earlier this morning. "Are your knights skilled at rowing?"

I look to Marshall and the rest of my knights. He nods assuring me that they are well capable to handle this task.

I turn back to Longcaster. "We can manage."

"Splendid. Then we'll load the boatmen with us so that they may properly see to the boats once we venture on away from the shore."

"Sounds good to me."

We grab our gear and march onto the outstretch dock that cuts across the lake. We switch up our seating arrangements a bit. Marshall joins Ollie and I while Thalia and Alan take a handful of knights with them. The rest ride with what gear we could carry on our individual boats. The boatmen make sure everything's situated with each boat while the maidens take the stagecoaches back to the castle.

We push off. I am told it should only take a couple of hours to make it across the lake. The bouncing and bobbing of the boat is a different feeling for me. I've been experiencing a lot of different things since becoming king. I let my hand glide across the lake's surface. It's icy cold, so my original ideas to take a dip are immediately gone.

Marshall watches the waves from the front while Ollie sits to herself in the back reading a small book. I decide to venture forward and join Marshall. I pass the two knights, Kaleb and Lieutenant Hayden, as they row. Ollie occasionally peaks over her book to take in Hayden if only for a few seconds and returns to reading while I sit at Marshall's feet.

"So," I begin not really thinking exactly how to address the subject.

"Your father. A piece of work, isn't he?"

"I was wondering how long you were going to wait before bringing him back up," Marshall replies without regarding me.

He keeps his eyes focused on the lake, acting as our lookout. "Too intimidated to address your future brother-in-law, my king?" "Not… exactly…" I say a little embarrassed.

I had nearly forgotten that King Ivan gave me his blessing to marry his daughter. A blessing I didn't really want, nor do I want to get married any time soon.

"I don't mean to sound rude, Marshall, but marriage isn't really in my plans right now."

"Correct me if I'm wrong my king, but neither was you becoming king," Marshall says and I feel like maybe I should dive overboard to escape this conversation.

"Do not worry, young Westley. I have distanced myself from my family heritage. I abandoned my title as prince. My father and I have different approaches when it comes to ruling."

"I was curious about that."

"You are a curious king," Marshall leers down upon me with a slight tug of a smile.

"Your curiosity should be handled wisely. If you poke your nose in the wrong thing, you could come out of it not wanting the answers you discover."

"That is very much true," I agree thinking back to all my curious thoughts in the Round Table Tournament.

Look what good that got me.

"It's just, I don't know what to make of King Ivan. He seems one way, acts another, but still holds the respect of his kingdom."

"You'll find that after the Days of Hellsfire, the people looked to their *heroes* of those days to rule and lead them to safety. What we needed were men, or women, to lead us to a better world and rebuild."

"The kingdoms seem well enough. Minus the results of the Round Table Tournament that is."

"That is only part of it, my king," Marshall replies with a grimace to his voice.

"Arcasia is a shell of its former self. Eurosia in the west continues to burn so it went on without us after those dark days, along with whatever became of the Imica in the east."

"The Days of Hellsfire…it affected other continents?" I ask and Marshall studies me peculiarly as if this has been made obvious.

"You are still behind on your history?"

"He's a horrible student," Ollie exclaims from the back of the boat.

"And a terrible reader."

Marshall seems to chuckle at this. How does she hear us from back there?

Marshall continues. "If you are to continue to be king, it would be best if you pick up on your history."

"I'll make a point of it when we return to Baronune."

"I'm *sure* that you will…" Ollie adds from the back, and I stick my tongue out at her in return.

I'm a very mature king.

"While we faced the Dragon of Hellsfire here, Imica faced their own battles. The once-great Phoenix used to protect those lands, but somewhere amid the chaos the Phoenix was lost, and some say so was the rest of the continent."

"Don't we still have trades from Imica?"

"Very few, my king. Truth is we need to send expeditions across the lands in means to rebuild from those dark days."

"What became of those native to Imica?"

"Some fled here, only to discover Arcasia had its own problems. Some say others sought refuge in lands beyond what we could reach on foot or by ship, but those tales were lost to time."

"Do you mean time or *Time*?"

"What's the difference?"

"There isn't one," I say as my mind momentarily flashed back to my vision with Fate.

"I guess."

"Getting back to what you asked of me. I wanted my father to unite with the other kings and allow me to lead those expeditions which I spoke of, but he said our numbers were best to be kept to Arcasia until we could repopulate to the point in which we'd be able to expand our borders once more."

"It doesn't sound too farfetched to me."

"That's because you weren't there to hear the tone of his voice when he said it. As if preserving our existence in Arcasia for some other purpose."

He stares out across the lake unsurely. I follow his gaze. There's a thick mist suddenly, but Marshall seems to be focusing on Eli and Longcaster. The sorcerer seems to be muttering something as he reads from a book, almost mimicking Hayden and performing some sort of poetry though I can't make out what he's saying.

He's moving around livelier, no one else seems bothered by this. Eli, on the other hand, seems to be watching us. His one eye's locked on Marshall and I.

"What's Eli's story. Who is he?"

"My king," Marshall's voice hangs heavy. "I have been asking my father that question years before I left the kingdom. The only answer I got, is the scar that resides under my once good arm."

The lake turns violent as waves rock us harder than before. The mist rolls in thicker and the visibility between the boats become harsh.

"King Westley, remain close."

"Where else am I to go?"

I am getting a familiar sense of dread. My mind flashes back to the night of the jester as the world becomes an eerie calm.

Screams break the silence and we turn to see that one boat has vanished. Only massive ripples in the water remain. I survey the area. Thalia, Alan, Nessa, and Junah are still with us. We lost the knights with our gear.

"What's happening?" I ask feeling my heart racing like I'm still running away from the jester in that nightmare realm.

"We need to get through this mist and quickly!" Marshall orders.

Kaleb and Hayden row faster. All my knights row faster. A sense of urgency stretches across the lake. Alan and Thalia take up their weapons as Ollie moves up to my side. None of this will do a thing if we can't see our enemy. I turn to Longcaster who is still performing his poetry.

"Longcaster!" I call. "Can you do something about this mist?"

"I think he is doing *something* with this mist."

Ollie points out and I look to her confused. She whips around and throws her silver drying needles in Longcaster's direction. They almost reach him when Eli deflects them out of the air. He snarls back at us.

"Ollie, what was that about?"

"Remember when I said you were naïve?"

"As if it was this morning."

"Well, I'm saying it again," Ollie scolds me. "Longcaster is summoning this mist."

I glance back across the lake. "What? Why?"

"That's what I plan to find out. Marshall, get down!" Ollie directs as she reaches into her sleeve again.

Marshall is about to do so when something bumps our boat from beneath. Something big. We're nearly all knocked into the water, but we remain secure in our vessel. We aren't the target this time.

"Mother—" Alan yells before a large splash and his boat is split in half.

He and his knights resurface, but they are in no better condition than they were moments ago in the boat.

"Alan!" I call out to him. "What was it?"

"Monster!"

He cries out in response, and this does nothing to settle my panicking heart. From Mountain Golems to dark jesters, to lake monsters. I'm starting to think someone has it out for me more and more.

"Nessa!"

I shuffle to the middle of our boat as if that will make communicating easier. "Can you or Junah do anything?" "NO!" Nessa cries in response.

Not what I wanted to hear. Nessa and Junah vanish under something large and blue.

"We're sitting ducks out here!" Thalia yells.

Nessa resurfaces with Junah in her arms. She looks as if she's struggling to stay afloat. Junah looks unconscious.

"Thalia!" I call out again. "Try to round up the survivors!"

I order and then tell Kaleb and Hayden to row us over in their direction. Ollie argues that we're better scattered than in one location, but my concern is to make sure my knights don't freeze to death or drown or worse.

"AH!" I hear from under the thickening mist.

Two more knights, Hoover and Cooper, vanish under the mass of blue. Thalia looks frozen by fear.

Nessa kicks to propel her and Junah to their boat while Alan and his few knights swim towards Longcaster and Eli. If Longcaster is behind this, then Alan will surely stop him. Then I see it. A large fanned out fin cutting through the surface of the lake. It's swimming in the direction of Alan and his knights.

"No…" I say under my breath.

I can't lose any more of my knights. "Ollie that way! Get its attention!"

"Are you kidding? Then it will come after us!"

"Yeah, better us than them. If Alan can reach Longcaster then he can stop this, but we have to keep that thing off them."

"I guess?"

Ollie looks like she's trying to come up with a better solution.

"I'm not trying to defy you here, but their safety is just as important as ours!"

"I—just—*GAH!* – I hate you sometimes!"

Well, at least it's been dropped to *sometimes*.

Ollie directs herself towards the creature in the lake.

She makes a fast-slashing motion with a scalpel she draws from within her sleeve.

"Extend!"

Much like when she attacked Alan all those months ago, a long teal blade of Divinity stretches out across the lake. Ollie swung in the direction of Longcaster, but Eli pulls him down into the boat to avoid the blade. Ollie's attack keeps going and slices the top of the fin. The remaining fin sinks underwater, and massive ripples cause waves to rock the remaining three boats.

"There, happy?" Ollie asks as she tries to keep from being flung from the boat.

"I got its attention."

"Would you believe me if I said I wasn't happy about any of this?"

The next thing I know, an explosion of water erupts beside me. I see a pair of demonic red eyes moments before our boat is destroyed.

I wish I knew how to swim, I wouldn't be sinking to the bottom of the lake right now if I did. My eyes flitter open and all I see is darkness. I don't know where anyone is. No chance of survival this time. I sink further into the abyss as what's left of my consciousness leaves my body along with the air bubbles that I wished still filled my lungs. I attempt to swim, but my arms and legs have grown too weak.

How long have I been down here? Did no one try to grab me? Did anyone care? I glance up. The light of the surface world seems so distant.

I glance back down. If I could scream I would. I see two bright red eyes. Is this a dragon? I notice its neck and body is long and snake-like. It's a serpent. It has a monstrously long snout with nostrils the size of caves, two tentacle-like whiskers, and webbed ears fluttering at the back of its reptilian head.

It opens its maw to swallow me and I react unconsciously. Much like with Alan, I close my eyes and throw up a pathetic guard. I can smell the stench of its breath as I prepare to die. Wait, I can smell? I open my eyes. The murkiness is parted by a teal light. Ollie? I survey around, there's no one in sight. I am floating in the lake, surrounded by a sphere of Divinity, keeping me from being swallowed.

The serpent speaks *"This…light. I know this power. You have been touched by the Gods."*

"I have?" I ask, looking at my hands. Its voice seems to ripple through the lake, through the edge of the abyss.

I remember my dream. My encounter with Fate. I peer down to my chest where she touched me and find a glowing teal mark in the shape of a hand.

"I have…"

"I was summoned to devour weak and meaningless knights," The serpent admits.

I will not oppose the Gods today. Tell that sorcerer to study his opponents better, or I will swallow him instead!"

The serpent snorts and as I am overtaken by bubbles, pushing and propelling me back to the surface as the serpent sinks into the darkness. It along with the blackness vanishes, and I emerge from the lake. I gasp for air and notice the mist is gone and that the water is calm again.

Ollie yells from the shore. "West!"

She's *alive*. Ollie dives into the cold waves and swims out to me, followed by Thalia. Where was this effort when I was drowning earlier? They reach me and their combined efforts return me to the sandy white shore.

I'm cold and dripping wet, but alive. I scan the rest of the shore. My remaining knights are barely alive, thirteen, I lost two more. Alan, Kaleb, and Lieutenant Dawn stand guard over the tied-up boatmen and Longcaster.

I shiver. "Where's… Eli?"

"Gone," Ollie answers between breaths.

"Took off some time after we went under."

"We have Longcaster," Thalia adds. "He was…"

"Summoning the serpent. Yeah, I'm aware."

"How did you…?"

"I had a brief conversation with it before it spat me up here."

I lock onto Longcaster. "Now, I have some words for the festive sorcerer."

He doesn't meet my eyes and I storm over to him and take him by his cloak.

"What gives? Why did you try to kill me?"

"I'm sorry young king, but whatever do you mean?"

"The golems, jester, and now this? What kind of a fool do you take me for?"

I sense my court prepare to answer, I jerk back.

"Not from you guys!"

"King Jameson you are deeply mistaken. I don't mean to kill you. These have all been tests by my king to push you, to make you stronger."

Thalia strolls up and places her arming sword beneath Longcaster's chin.

"You really are drunk off your ass if you expect our king to believe that."

I will not admit that I believed his story.

"Yeah, what she said!" I imitate her toughness.

"That's the third attempt on my life, and even your serpent said that if you try that again he'll swallow you instead."

"You lie."

"Do I? How about you try *my* test and find out for yourself!" "No!" Longcaster whimpers in protest.

That worked?

"Okay, we were meant to make your death look like a convenient accident. The golems were a test, more of a coin flip. If you died then, then problem solved. If you survived, then we got a glimpse of your capabilities. The jester acted on his own, taking the opportunity to be rid of you, but got a bit carried going after Crystal as well.

That wasn't a part of the plan, but it did provide the king with an out. He does care about his daughter, and he truly would never want her in danger… even if it meant ending you. I came up with the serpent idea, though it is a very difficult summoning. While you were out to fetch the Sword of Fate you happened to be eaten by a lake monster that we had no knowledge of. It would have been perfect, how did you survive?"

"Let's just say Fate is on my side today."

He sounds intrigued. "Really…? Well, then you wouldn't mind one more test then. See, I wasn't just babbling my majesty's evil plan. I was *stalling*."

Ollie's right, I am naïve. Longcaster slips from my grasp and vanishes into a void of darkness. I don't have time to process this as the boatmen vanish with him. The mist returning, Ollie and my knights surround me while Marshall stays back with Nessa. In the distance, I can make out two shapes. One tall, one short. Nova and Avery? *No*, it's not them. Someone else, something else.

Chapter Thirteen

Sins of the King

The mist around us begins to bleed with blackness, with *dark vapors*. My body tenses, two individuals that look nothing like humans. I'm getting bad vibes. The figures come more into view as the mist dies down around them. I wish it hadn't. I'd rather tremble from their silhouettes alone. Which one is worse? The enormous round mass of toad skin?

I don't even know how it moves those short and stubby limbs. They barely look long enough to scratch its grotesque saggy underboob. I'm curious if you slap its stomach hard enough if it will make the sounds of a banging drum. Luckily, it has clothing.

Its head is tiny, sitting on top of rows of chins with no neck. It's hard to tell if those are three horns sitting on its dome or if it has two long ears and one pointy horn up top. Its cheeks look rubbery and about to pop. Its eyes are tiny, much like its mouth that's slimy and watering with hunger.

The smaller creature is about as tall as Thalia with a human-like shape to it. If I wanted an image to go with the word, *demon*, I would use this creature. Two long protruding horns arch back from its forehead. A long white mane of hair spikes down its back. Its skin looks charcoal red and reptilian. Scales cover its upper body like armor, but the creature has on trousers with iron plates covering its knees and shins.

Its bird like feet has two long toes and its hands are also long with five black clawed ligaments. From beneath its hair lifts its back like the hide of a beetle to reveal its wings. Instead of wings, there are two long thin swords that I recognize as daito. I can feel their sharpness by looking at them. It's covered in scales as two fang-like spikes curve from the bottom of its cheeks along its jawline. It grins a smile of stained fangs, and its murky yellow eyes beam at me through the mist.

My hand hovers over the hilt of my sword, but my body is frozen with fear. Ollie stands beside me, while Alan and Thalia ready their weapons. I've never seen Ollie so scared.

"What in Hellsfire are you guys?"

Alan sounds tough but I can feel the tremors in his voice. The smaller demon grins intensely.

"I am Slyce, the *Gr'atest* Swordsman among all the *r'alms*. This—"

He nods towards the massive demon beside him. "—is Mongo *tuh Gobblr'r. 'Nough* said."

Mongo looks ravenous while I can't tell if Slyce has an accent, speech impediment, or if the fumes from Hellsfire burnt his tongue.

"Demons, why have you come?" Thalia asks.

Slyce hisses. "*W're ordr'r* by tuh king to kill tuh king. *'Nough* said." I manage to speak.

"I honestly would appreciate more details, like, why kill me? What's Ivan's play?"

"I *b'lieve* that's for you and tuh king to discuss," Slyce answers and reaches under his insect-like hide to draw his daito.

"*W're hr'r* for killing."

"And eating!" Mongo includes as he slaps his belly. It does sound like a drum.

"I'm hungry and starving for human flesh!" I feel my blood run cold.

Slyce steps aside. "Right, Mongo. Go ahead. Have *sum* fun."

"Yay!"

Mongo slaps his belly again.

Alan rushes in with howling speed. "Not a chance in Hellsfire!"

"Oh, have you *bin*? *B'cause will* save you a place. *Weeeee* have a *r'rputation thr're*," Slyce says with another toothy grin.

Alan pays the demon no mind and reaches Mongo, jabbing his staff into the monster's enormous gut. Mongo bellows in agony, Alan's staff presses deeper, almost sinking into Mongo's belly until… *BOING!!!* Alan is sent soaring overhead and landing in the lake.

"Alan!" Thalia and I yell in unison.

He surfaces looking all but pleased.

"King West, stay here."

"Wait, Thalia, I wouldn't…"

She's off without a second thought, leaving me with Ollie as Alan swims back to shore. She rushes in, as fast as Alan if not quicker then slashing Mongo across his gut. It leaves no blood, bouncing her blade away. Thalia slashes at it again and again. "What—is this thing—made of?" Mongo rocks forward. "*Stahp it!*"

He rocks back, and Thalia keeps side-stepping to his blind spot. She can't find a weak point. Alan dashes past Ollie and I.

"Thalia get back!"

Thalia leaps out of the way as Alan digs his staff into the ground, using it to launch him through the air and slams a mighty kick to Mongo's face. The force sends him tumbling backwards.

Mongo groans. "Mongo mad!"

He springs forward and rolls far faster than he was moving earlier, leaving Alan and Thalia barely any time to dodge.

Ollie screams as she grabs me. "West! Move!"

She snatches me like I'm lighter than air, and we dive out of the way, leaving Marshall, Nessa, Junah, and the other knights in Mongo's path.

Marshall reaches for his claymore but hesitates with a shaking hand. Mongo closes in. There isn't fear on Marshall's face, but agony as he grips his sword and tries to draw it.

"Marshall! NO!" Nessa calls as she sees the situation at hand.

She throws up a dim shield of light that has barely enough power to redirect Mongo. Nessa pants while Marshall lets out a sigh of relief. Mongo rolls back and stops, looking confused at where he is, then his eyes sees the knights clinging to life.

"Food."

Mongo rocks forward and falls upon the resting knights. Kaleb rushes in to protect the others, but with his unnecessary height, he is snatched along with one of the unconscious bodies. Alan and Thalia rush in to stop the demon. Despite their speed, they're too slow. Mongo's mouth grows three sizes and in one unsettling chomp, Mongo bites down on Kaleb's head and begins to chew.

The sound of crushing bone makes me gag as Thalia and Alan slam and slash their weapons against Mongo to no effect. He doesn't even seem to care as he continues to eat through armor and all.

"Alan, boost!" Thalia calls.

She leaps without hesitation. Alan readies his staff as she lands on its end and Alan launches her into the air. Thalia stabs down, and cuts the demon from neck to shoulder. This gets Mongo's attention as he bellows so loudly that he throws Kaleb's headless body a few feet from me and Ollie. She covers my eyes.

I hear Mongo yelling in pain, and I move Ollie's hand and witness the demon peer down on Thalia and Alan, rock forward, and spews out an eerie green gas. They leap out of the way and the gas continues to drift towards Ollie and I, melting anything in its way. I grab Ollie and pull us to our feet as she not looking in regard to Kaleb's body. She doesn't have to worry, his body withers away after the gas.

Ollie gasps. "Gods… What is this thing?"

"Heeee is Mongo *tuh Gobblr'r*!" Slyce reminds us, standing patiently.

"*Whatr'vr heeee eeeeeats b'comes tuh* source for his toxic fumes!" That seems unfair. Unsatisfying and unfair.

Thalia takes up her sword again. "Alan! What do we do here?"

"We slay the beast and make this his last meal!"

Alan whirls away the rest of the gas with his Bo staff and charges in.

Thalia calls after him as she follows in his pursuit. "I was more asking for how!"

Both on Mongo, they fight side by side, striking and slashing at the demon's exposed stomach. He winces in pain, looking to be taking little damage from the combined assault.

"Annoying… You're an annoying meal!"

Mongo swallows the remains of the knight still in his hand, rocks back but instead of spewing gas, he rolls forward. Alan plants his Bo staff underneath Mongo to launch him off course, but fails, vanishing under the demon. Thalia tries to slice at Mongo, but this also fails as he rolls on top of her. The demon comes to a halt and both my Grandiers are in his grasp.

I scream, knowing what Mongo intends to do with them next.

"Shit," Ollie mutters under her breath and rushes in.

"Ollie, no!"

She doesn't listen and throws needles into Mongo's rubbery skin.

"Puny insignificant snack." He groans as Ollie slides in front of him.

"Snack on this!"

Ollie flings quick silver at Mongo's face and more drying needles pierce into him, while one of her scalpels cut into his nose. He wails from this and wobbles. Thalia takes her sword while Alan raises his staff like a javelin and they both strike his eyes. The demon bellows in such pain that he flings them both towards the lake.

That did some damage. I go to draw my sword, but I'm stopped. Jagged steel meets my throat. Slyce is either super-fast or I was so transfixed on the others that I didn't notice him.

"Draw that sword, and I'll kill you."

"Noted."

I'm too frightened to swallow my spit at the risk of my Adam's apple scraping against his sword. Ollie notices this and hurries back to my aid. Slyce raises his other daito and points it at Ollie. She stops in her tracks, her right hand reaching for what I guess is more needles.

"Your blades are little but 'ffective," Slyce admits with a satisfying hiss.

"Once Mongo is dun with them, *your'r* my playtime."

"West…?"

"Hold your position, Ollie."

I don't feel like testing Slyce's reaction time. He must be skilled to wield two swords at once. The only other person I've seen capable of this was Rhodain and it helped him turn the tides in his fight with Hunter.

Mongo stops crying in pain and shifts to search for Thalia and Alan. One of his eyes is soaked in blood from Thalia's attack.

"Mongo not happy!"

Now he just sounds like a cranky baby, a cranky baby ready to crush my knights flat as he rocks back and forwards to build more momentum and rolls after them. Thalia slashes the demon and as he spins to chase after her, Alan beats him with his staff. The two continue alternating their attacks while Mongo remains on the defensive. "Stay still!"

"No!" Alan and Thalia respond.

Mongo growls and then rolls back in retreat. Did they win? Did he give up out of spite? No, he's putting distance between them.

"Thalia! Alan! You're cornered!"

They are standing in the wash of the lake meeting the gray sands of the beach and both directly in front of the demon.

Alan cries catching on. "Thalia, dive into the water!"

Mongo spews out gas and the pair jumps into the water, narrowly avoiding the green gas which fuses with the pale fog resting over the lake. Nessa had created her shield of light to protect everyone nearby. Thalia and Alan haven't resurfaced and Mongo waits, wiping away the vapors of his gas from his mouth. How long can Alan and Thalia hold their breath? Minutes pass, and as the gas fades away, Alan and Thalia float up to the surface face down and unmoving. "No!"

I knock away Slyce's sword and run forward. Ollie chases after me. I'm too focused on my knights until Mongo waddles to face us.

He points and we stop.

"You… are *next*."

"Not while I'm still here to oppose you," says Marshall.

Hayden, Dawn, and a few more of my knights join him wearily. Mongo waddles to face Marshall and my remaining knights.

"Fine, King last. You next."

"Knights of Baronune, steady yourselves."

Marshall's right hand reaches back for his sword.

"The demon's hide is tough, and your weapons will do little to harm it. Don't let it bend your will. Fight hard and work together to find a weakness. Now charge!"

The four knights take off, surrounding Mongo and to maneuver around him, making it impossible for him to grab them. I glance over to Nessa who is focused on healing Junah. Marshall keeps watch, still unable to draw his blade. Ollie nudges me in my ribs, and I glance at her. She directs me over to Alan and Thalia. They're still faced down in the lake. I nod and we hurry to fish them out of the water.

"We have to get them to Nessa," I say to Ollie.

"For once I agree with you."

We run to the water as hopelessness overcomes me. Marshall can't contend, and Nessa is our only healer. I am failing more and more as a king. We should have been prepared, but how do you prepare for this?

"Nessa!"

Ollie and I drag Alan and Thalia through the wet sand.

"Stand fast, my king!" Marshall yells as he and Nessa hurry to our side.

"Nessa are they…?"

Nessa assesses them. "Barely alive. Please, bring the others closer. I can't risk leaving them exposed to that monster."

I pant. "Right, Ollie. With me."

She doesn't protest and we hurry to the other knights. Mongo appears distracted by the lieutenants and others, but what's stopping

Slyce from jumping in? He remains where we left him, watching everything take place. Demons make no sense, but I'm not complaining.

Nessa heals Thalia and Alan though her light begins to flicker. We have to finish this quickly, but how do we get through Mongo's hide? Ollie and I manage to drag two knights over, then rush to grab two more. My training has made me stronger, but this is still exhausting.

"Mongo hungry!"

I glance back to find Mongo rocking to build momentum again.

"No!" I cry, dropping the knight in my arms.

"Get away!"

Too late. Mongo rolls through my knights then tumbles towards Nessa and Marshall. She throws up another shield, but it has grown so fragile that Mongo easily breaks it.

"Time to eat…"

He leans forward, reaching down for Marshall and Nessa. I prepare to rush in again, but Slyce intercepts. He *is* fast.

"Nuh-uh," he wags his talon-like finger in front of me.

"No *int'rfurance.*"

I grit my teeth. Ollie is at my side, I wonder if she's going to test her speed. When she takes a step forward, I grab her wrist and shake my head then watch Mongo close in on the others. He gets closer, opening his mouth so wide that drool pools out from it, then something pelts him in the head. He stops and looks to a small pebble in the sand. Junah stands, still soaked, with a handful of rocks. When the uninterested Mongo turns back to Nessa and Marshall, Junah pelts him again, successfully getting his attention.

"June, no! He's too tough. Your voice won't break his skin!" Nessa yells.

Mongo waddles around to face Junah, who approaches with weaponless outstretched arms. What's he up to? I glance back over to Nessa and Marshall, then to the unconscious pair. Junah is putting them at risk, either by the effects of his sound Divinity or by Mongo crushing them.

Mongo lurches forward. "You… Free meal."

He grabs Junah with no resistance, he glares at the demon while Nessa pleads for Marshall to let her go. Mongo opens his mouth again, he's going bite off Junah's head. Mongo moves my nurse closer, I turn away, not wanting to see him be eaten. Yet I don't hear a crunch.

When I return my gaze I find that the fiend never bit down. Instead, Junah's screams into Mongo's throat. The demon is unaffected by external attacks, but internal attacks sing a different song. Blood oozes out of Mongo's earholes as he staggers backwards and loosens his grip on Junah. My nurse removes his head from the demon's mouth and stands on his chins like an uneven hill. With an absent stare in his bloodshot eyes, Mongo turns on the rest of us. He rocks back and Marshall and Nessa flinch. He rocks forward, and Junah leaps and rolls. Mongo falls face first into the sand.

"Hmm," Slyce responds with a shrug. "Bit off more than heeee can ch'w."

"June!"

Nessa crawls over to him, he hasn't gotten up. She musters what left of her flittering light to heal him. Marshall stands, turns to us, and our eyes fall on Slyce as he brandishes his two swords. We have the numbers against him, but does that really mean we have the advantage?

Chapter Fourteen

Talk the Talk

Slyce turns his devilish face towards Ollie and me.

"So, you've *busted* Mongo. No *furs hr'r*. I'm the *Gr'atest* Swordsman in all *tuh r'alms*. You won't *bust may*."

This is bad. Thalia and Alan are still down. Nessa is using the last of her Divinity to heal Junah and keep the others alive, and Marshall… He stands with his right hand on his sword. He can't seem to muster the strength to regard us let alone draw his weapon.

"I *tail* you what," Slyce begins as he walks away from us.

"I'll *gift* you *itch* a chance to make *tuh* first move against *may*."

He puts a substantial distance between us. I glance at Ollie, we have one chance. She nods at me, knowing what I'm hinting at and shifts her gaze back on the demon, and then in an instant, she disappears. Ollie closes half the distance between us and Slyce, reaches into her sleeve and silver sprays across the misty terrain. The needles suddenly crashes to Slyce's feet, did he deflect them *all*? Before I get too overwhelmed, I take in a deep breath. One.

I feel the mist and wind brush across my skin. Divinity flows into my muscles. I dash towards the demon, draw my blade, and…*CLING!!!* My Mirrogold sword meets his demonic daito. He didn't even flinch.

"That makes two," he hisses before knocking me away with a spin kick. I roll across the rocks into the sand and meet Ollie's feet. She bends down to assess me, but I'm fine.

Slyce eyes Marshall and Nessa across the beach.

"*Thr're's* still two of you that can fight? Right? Make your moves *than*."

Marshall watches the demon and sighs regretfully. Nessa is sitting beside Junah as he clings to consciousness, his attack must have backfired onto him too.

"*Wail?*" Slyce asks keeping his attention on Marshall.

My last knight grips his claymore, wincing as he struggles to unsheathe it. The blade's indents remind me of an hourglass. Marshall tries to steady his blade to little effect.

"Come on *than*," Slyce urges.

Marshall goes to take a step, but a unanimous *"No"* echoes through the fog.

"*Wail…*" Slyce shifts his attention to Nessa.

"One more *than*."

"Two," Ollie demands but looks upon the demon unsurely.

"You two had your chance."

"We'll take their moves," Ollie barters.

"Two of them, two of us. We'll take their moves." "…Fine." Slyce agrees with his devilish grin.

"Makes no *diffr'nce* to *may*. I've blocked you *b'fore*, I'll do it again.

"Right, West…"

I'm unsure about what chance we stand. Slyce is right, he already blocked our attacks. How are we supposed to get through a second time? Ollie gets on my back for my irrational decisions, but this is dumber than anything I could have come up with. We're outmatched, and I am terrified. If only I had the time to figure out how to access that Divinity I used earlier in the lake.

"West!" Ollie calls and I'm snapped from my thoughts.

She lowers her voice. *"I need you to do that thing you do so annoyingly well."*

"What?"

"Talk to him, like you did when we first met. Remember? How you annoyed the living crap out of me and made me want to do nothing but kill you."

"I'm not sure I need to convince him to kill me."

"Get him talking, find his weakness that way and get him to lower his guard. Like you did with me which allowed Rhodain to get the jump on me."

"Are you sure you weren't just outclassed by Rhodain and that's why he got the jump on you?"

"*See...*" Ollie grits her teeth as she looks like she's struggling not to hit me.

"You're already doing it, now do that to him. That's your move. When I see the opportunity, I'll make mine."

"*Okay...*" I say shifting my attention back on the demon.

I raise my sword to look like I'm planning an attack. My blade protest as it shakes in my hands. Okay, that's all me. With great effort I steady my breathing and study him. His small thin body allows him to move swiftly, but if Alan and Thalia were up I bet they'd find a way to best this swordsman. My eyes widen on that thought.

"So," I begin, choosing my words carefully.

One wrong move and I'll waste my turn.

"Swordsman, huh?"

"The *Gr'atest* Swordsman in all tuh *r'alms!*"

"*Yeah*, got that. Had to hear it once more. You know you're like a demon, right?"

"Yeah, I am..."

"Doesn't that disqualify you from being a *Swords—man?*" Slyce doesn't respond and Ollie looks to hit me. "I..." Slyce begins but he hesitates.

"...I was once a man. Still counts."

"Are you sure? There might be a date in which the title expires by. When did you claim your title as being the *Greatest*?" "I…" The demon pauses again.

"It was so long ago. How long has it *bin*?"

"Hey, don't go taking the questions out of my mouth," I demand then I think about it.

"Actually, you're repeating it. Never mind, carry on."

He's actually putting some thought into this one. I look to Ollie, who is more shocked than me that the demon is considering my question rather than taking the opportunity to attack. Perhaps my talents are too good, I'm disabling *everyone's* ability to fight.

"I gain my title back… during *tuh* old war with *tuh*… Gods. No," he snaps.

"Immortals. *Th'm*, I *bust'd* all of *th'm*."

This befuddlement seems to go both ways. "Really? Care to tell me about it?"

"No," he glares. "Why *wud* eye?"

"Because I don't believe you're the *greatest*."

"You want to make your move and come *ov'r hr'r* and *tail may* that?" "No," I admit still smug as I mimic him.

"Why would I waste my time? If I'm going to die at the hands of the *Greatest Swordsman*, I'd want him to actually be the greatest."

In that moment I saw him twitch. I'm sure he wanted to rush in and slice my throat, but he didn't. Instead, he holds firm to his word and hurt pride.

"Do you know what it takes to *beeee* able to go blow for blow with an immortal? *Th'y* can fight *forev'r*. That's why *th'y* immortal."

"Yeah, but that doesn't prove anything."

He begins stomping his foot. "It proves *av'rything*! I am *tuh gr'atest*!" "Look, I'm just saying you're all talk."

"And I told you to come *ov'r hr'r* and say that. Watch how fast I'll slice you limb from limb."

"Okay, for one, I already told you I'm not coming over there, so again you're repeating yourself. Two, it would be a bit hard for me to watch you slice me up if I'm being sliced up in the process. Even a novice swordsman would know that, and I'm not even a novice. I'm a much lower tier."

If those words were punches they would have done some damage. I glance back at Marshall, he's smiling, Nessa is trying not to laugh, and Ollie seems to be holding in a giggle.

"So, you'd like a *d'monstration*?" Slyce grins fully as if adding more teeth will make him scarier.

I won't tell him that it does.

"I'll just slice up *sum* one *othr'r than* you and make you watch."

"Uh… I'm not saying you *can't* do that, but that's cheating," this makes him blink away his grin.

"You said we get to make the first move. Ollie hasn't moved yet. So, you'd be a cheater *and* a liar. How can you be the greatest if you can't even honor your word?"

He glares at me. "I—*em*—*ay*—*D'mon*! What honor is *thr're* in that?"

"So, you admit you're a demon and not a swordsman?"

"*Yus…NO!*"

"See, you can't even make up your mind. Who even thought to put the title of greatest in your name because it wasn't you, and clearly they were mistaken."

I thought this would push him over the edge, but it doesn't. He seems to calm down.

"My *mast'r* gave may *tuh* title back in *tuh* war." "Really?" I ask recovering from this setback.

"Was he as foolish about titles as you or just old and senile?"

It happened too fast for me to see, but at least he's a demon of his word since he didn't kill me. His sword struck mine and he guides me back. I'm just lucky my body responds better than I do at times.

With our swords pressed against each other, I realize he has far more strength than I do.

"*May mast'r is tuh gr'atest mast'rmind of all.*"

I struggle, I can't hold him off much longer. My arms are screaming. My legs are on the verge of buckling under this demon's strength.

"Is he King Ivan? Is this part of his plan to kill me? Demons aren't so inconspicuous as the other obstacles he's thrown at me."

He hisses. "Ivan is not *may mast'r. May mast'r is gr'atr'r* than Ivan. *Gr'atr'r* than you! *May mast'r is…*"

"Greater than you?"

Slyce's expression falls blank as his strength gives out. I take the opportunity to leap away.

"W-what?"

"I mean, he's your master, right? Which means you obey and listen to him. Making him better, superior…Making him greater than you. So you're not the *greatest* after all."

That got him. His face flashes with rage as he bites down so hard it draws blood. The demon's whole-body shakes as he screams through the mist to the heavens.

"Y-you *dare…*"

"Come on," I urge him with a smile.

"Get it *all* out of your system."

"I-I'll kill you!"

"Well, that was my move…" I say calmly as clearly Slyce is beyond reasoning.

He lets out a harsh battle cry as he raises his daito. His cry falls short as a flash of teal cuts not only Slyce's uproar of hate towards me but also his neck.

"And that was Ollie's."

She used her speed and Divinity to slice clean through the demon.

"Enough said."

Slyce drops to his knees. His swords slip from his hands and his head rolls off his shoulders.

We stand over the body. "You don't think he's like that bug that goes on living without its head, do you?"

"I hope not."

Ollie flings a scalpel at Slyce's body. There's no reaction.

Marshall walks up to us. "Good job, my king, splendid work."

"Well, you know, just doing what I do best. Pissing people off until they want to kill me, apparently." I say as I sheath my sword.

Ollie chuckles. "Your cousin would not approve of your language."

"My cousin doesn't have demons trying to kill her," I turn to Marshall.

"What's the deal with your dad?"

"Clearly, you possess something that the king wants."

A woman's voice reaches us through the mist before any of us can continue. We turn on our heels. Ollie and Marshall take defensive stances. I scan the pale fog and chills crawl down my spine as more of that dark vapor drift around the maroon gown of the Queen. Marshall's jaw drops. "Bansha...So, you've come too?" "Of course," she shrugs with a smug smile.

She sits on a boulder with her arms crossed and resting beneath her robust chest.

"As per the orders of the king in allegiance to my master."

I groan. "Oh great, another evil queen. That's nothing new."

"You poor little naïve child of a king. No wonder Ivan's taking this as an opportunity to strike against you," Bansha admits as she uncrosses her arms, hops off the boulder, and rests one hand on her curvy hip. "I am no queen. I'm one of the Hellsfire Generals of Chaos." I stand corrected. That is something new.

Chapter Fifteen

The King's Desires

"You're…what?"

She keeps her crooked smile fixed on me. I turn to Ollie. She's as baffled as I am. I glance between Marshall and Nessa. They seem awestruck. "What?" Bansha shrugs.

"You never heard of us?"

Between Divinity, the Gods, the God Slayers, and the demons… "…No," I reply blankly.

"I must have skipped that page in the history codices."

"Well, you *are* young, but to think that no one mentioned the Generals of Chaos?"

Bansha then ponders to herself. "No that makes sense. We killed anyone we encountered in the Days of Hellsfire, so I guess there was no one left to tell our tales."

"You have my curiosity," I admit.

Ollie looks like she wants to say something, but the mention of the Generals of Chaos seems to leave her speechless.

"Hmm… It seems our reputation has at least made it throughout the kingdoms."

I face her and redraw my sword. "Fine, who are the Generals of Chaos?"

"Oh good, I'm glad you asked."

She titters sadistically to herself then struts towards us and there's an odd presence to her. With every step, it's as if something in the air moves with her until she stands a few feet from Ollie and me. She carries no weapon nor armor unless that dress is made of steel.

"Where to begin?"

She pats her finger against her glossy bottom lip that looks as beautiful and deadly as a black rose. My curiosity wanders as I wonder how they would feel pressed against my own. Then, in that instant, my mind retracts back to the scene at hand. It felt like I was trapped in that daze for days.

"Do I start with the full history, how we've been around for over a thousand years?"

She lets her hand rest on her hip, and I'm caught ogling her curves as if watching the twists and turns of a river.

"Or do I keep it relevant to how we're working alongside the king to kill you?"

I don't know why my mind keeps getting sidetracked. I recognize that she's beautiful enough to make any man, or king, lucky to have her, but she's obviously evil.

"Young King, are you listening? Or are you distracted?"

She asks squeezing her arms tightly and raising her chest. I don't answer. All I can do is blush. I shake my head, but my eyes fall back to her... *distractions.*

"My, are you cute. No longer a boy, but not yet a man. My spell seems to be having trouble with you."

"...Spell?"

"Nuh-uh," she lifts her hand to her lustrous lips, and my mouth shuts immediately.

"I'm talking now."

It comes and goes. One moment I have my senses, and then the next I find myself drawn to her.

I struggle to keep focused. "What... are you..."

She flashes her evil grin. "General of Chaos, remember?"

Her skin is ghostly pale but vibrant and alluring at the same time. I wonder what she looks like with her hair down. Does she let it flow all the way to the back or allow it to drape over her shoulders and caress her...

"I take that as a no."

She breaks my concentration again. Or is she returning my mind to the topic? Either way, she's affecting me with this spell of hers, but I'm confused. I find myself more frustrated that she won't let me admire her fully, but I know she is the enemy. She's a threat to my knights and I. Fighting to take back control, I raise my sword once more and try to coerce my body to act, but for some reason, I can't convince myself to harm her. I don't want to harm her, I want to hold her.

"West!"

Ollie barks and I realize I nearly dropped my sword in my state of admiration. I quickly shake free the temptation and raise my blade again.

"Oh, you too?" Bansha raises an eye in response to Ollie's resistance.

"Young, but much older than your king it seems."

I struggle, "Not by much!"

This draws Bansha's attention away from Ollie and she curves back on me.

"How cute. I struck a nerve," she leans in to examine me.

I am lost in her deadly aroma. I am willing to be tortured with immense pain if it means I can stay close to her, next to her. I want to be with her... *ew*. This thought shakes me free, and I retreat from her attempt to stroke my cheek.

"You're still fighting me. Gods, I've forgotten how frustratingly inconsistent young boys can be."

I find every thought I just had about her sickening, and her scent now leaves a bad taste in my mouth. My face scrunches as I scrape my tongue against my teeth as if that will remove the disgusting flavor that remains.

"Wow," Bansha responds looking at me unpleased as she turns around.

"How immature."

"Why do I feel like I just kissed my grandmother?" I say, still attempting to clean my palate.

"I don't even remember my grandmother."

"Wow, rude. Don't you have any respect for your elders?"

"I do, but not when they're some sort of demon."

"Oh, come now, I'm nothing like the demons you've faced. I kept my good looks while the others became disfigured by their own Corrupted Arts."

"Wait..."

My mind snaps back to reality at the mention of the demons.

"You're saying that those demons were generals like you?"

Bansha gestures with her hand as if brushing my comment aside. "Lower tier, but yes. The Swordsman, the Gluttonous Oaf... the jester... All part of the Hellsfire Generals of Chaos, and all working with the king to kill you. While Jessie operated on his own, Slyce and Mongo at least waited until our master gave them permission."

"...Your master?"

"Yes," she answers smugly.

"But you're so beneath him, I won't even regard you with his name."

Not fair, now my mind is pondering whether she's referring to Ivan or the Dragon of Hellsfire I've heard so much about.

"What about Eli and Longcaster? Are they demons too, or like you?"

"Oh, child there's no one like me. I'm one of a kind," she winks, and I blush again.

"That lazy excuse of a wizard couldn't even summon a serpent properly to make our task easier. Seriously, how hard is it to kill a thirteen-year-old?"

"You don't seem to be doing much better."

"What can I say?" She moves in close and brushes her exposed shoulder against me.

"I enjoy the tease."

My heart thumps so hard it might explode. I don't like this feeling. It's making me as uncomfortable as whenever my maidens would come into my chambers in the morning and catch me rolling over and shifting my pillows beneath the sheets.

The touch of Bansha's skin against my armor nearly causes me to faint.

"Stay away from him you succubus!" Nessa cries.

She's still beside Junah, Thalia, and Alan.

"How dare you!" Bansha stomps her foot and glares. "While you're not wrong, you don't strike that tone with me." "Succubus?" I ask faintly as my senses slowly return to me.

"Is that what…"

"In a sense," Bansha finishes for me.

"You see, when you dabble in the Corrupted Arts, they tend to have more… *lasting* effects than you may desire. You see, we all wanted something. I wanted to be a Hand of Love but was denied. Slyce wanted the skills to match his pride as a swordsman. Mongo's hunger turned him into… well, *that*. And Jessie was so envious of our master's power that his soul became twisted by the flames of Hellsfire. We all were. Except me, I trained with my Divinity to remain beautiful. It's hard to lure your enemies to their doom when you look hideous."

"You're still ugly if you ask me."

Bansha immediately slaps Ollie across the face with enough force to launch her off her feet, but she doesn't budge. Her face swells in red.

"I'm slipping. I lost my grasp on you as I dealt with that woman."

"Your grasp?"

My body feels like it's swaying.

"Have you not figured it out?" She asks.

"No, I guess not because I'm not allowing you to. When I was denied by the God of Love to become my mistress' hand, I searched for other means to make the hearts of man bow to my whim."

She waves her hand and on response, my male knights begin to rise. Limp and dazed, the men return to their feet. Even Alan and Marshall respond to Bansha's gestures as she curls her finger inward, summoning them to her. My body wants to follow, but my mind protests. I don't know why I should listen to her.

"See, you're too young. You don't get it yet. I control the hearts of *men*." Bansha holds out her hand, instructing the men to stop. Mindless and acceptable to her every command, they hunch over awaiting their next order.

"And my Divinity doesn't stop there."

The men suddenly drop to their knees. Some fall over and return to their unconscious state. Marshal shakes his head from his daze while Alan coughs violently from nearly drowning and exposure to Mongo's gas.

Bansha waves her hand again, and this time the women respond.

Nessa struggles. "No…"

"Don't fight it, my dear," Bansha speaks in a seductive whisper that carries through the mist and across the cold sandy beach.

"Your Divinity is strong, but you're lacking a certain *vigor* it seems. Tell me. What are you?"

"I-I…" Nessa fights, but she loses.

She's on her feet along with Thalia. Their dead gaze lingers on Bansha as she smiles.

"I am a fairy that has given up her wings to serve as a mortal." "Oh, how wonderful!" Bansha claps.

"Stupid decision on your part. That much power in the Sacred Arts would have easily countered my Corrupted. But as you said, you are mortal. Come."

Nessa drags her feet through the sand as she marches forward. Thalia follows with the rest of my female knights.

Marshall is back on his feet. He's prepared to draw his sword but again he hesitates. His handshakes violently as it struggles with the hilt.

"See how much easier it is to obey? No need for senseless fighting… Unless…"

A dark gleam hits Bansha's eyes. She licks her lips as if lavishing them with poison and the women under her control draw their weapons.

"I tell them to."

The women rush the men. Marshall's hand falls upon his sword but he stops. He yells in pain but not from drawing his weapon. In a blink of an eye, Nessa is behind him, locking her arms under his bad arm to restrain him. She knew exactly where to attack him to eliminate him as a threat despite not having weapons of her own.

The other women pounce on the unconscious men.

"NO!"

I watch them raise their weapons and begin bashing and stabbing their comrades. Blood sprays through the air and soaks the sand. Only Alan and Hayden manages to put up a fight as Thalia and Dawn attack them. Alan sluggishly blocks Thalia's slow attacks, neither seemingly fully recovered from the previous fight with Mongo. Hayden makes weak attempts to fend off Dawn's weaker assault.

"Bansha stop!"

"Hmm…? Oh, you're right this isn't fair."

She snaps, and the women all drop their weapons.

"I should give the men a chance to counterattack, shouldn't I?"

She claps her hands and the men that can move grab their weapons. They make weak attempts to attack, unable to fully commit with their newfound injuries.

Nessa comes to her senses but doesn't release Marshall as he struggles to free himself despite the pain. Beside them, Hayden strikes Dawn and Thalia backs away from Alan in a daze.

He jabs at her and she deflects his staff away with her sword. Alan wheels around on his heels and attacks from the other side and Thalia's sluggish reflexes leave her taking the full brunt of his attack and falls to her knees. Alan raises his staff overhead and slams it down on her, forcing her deeper into the sand as she blocks.

Bansha gleams another sadistic smile. "Oh, there's some intensity there, a lover's quarrel? Interesting, let's switch again."

Bansha makes a loop with her finger and the men fall limp. The wounded collapse into the sand and the women begin kicking them. Nessa tightens her lock on Marshall, and he screams in agony. Dawn and Hayden's weapons are locked as he struggles to hold her at bay. He's still weak and he is buckling under her returned strength. Alan falls off Thalia, but she pounces on him. She tries to stab him with her sword, but Alan arches upward and throws her off. He rolls and picks up his bo staff. Thalia crawls to her feet and takes up her double-edged sword. She swings, he defends. The brutal song of their steel against steel sings through the mist.

All I can do is watch. My body feels drained after each time Bansha switches control. I'm left to watch my knights rip each other apart, ignoring my every order, and plea to stop. Junah is the only one not participating. The drawbacks from the use of his sound waves must leave even his body unable to respond to Bansha's desires. Wait. Junah's not the only one. My eyes peel back to see Ollie who's in a deep sweat and worse off than I am. "Ollie…"

"Don't!" she snaps, restraining herself.

She fights to resist the urge to attack me as her body lurches and pulls while remaining in place.

Bansha takes notice. "Okay, what gives? I know you're young but come on, even at this age your sexuality must be strong, what are you? Come on, spit it out."

Ollie fights as she glares back at the succubus before her. She looks ready to collapse but denies her body the opportunity.

"I-I am… Ollie."

There's a release. I suddenly fall to my knees and everyone around me collapses. What happened? I peer up, Ollie stands panting. Blood is splashed across her face and hakama. Her now red scalpel held tightly in hand. Bansha is left speechless by the large gash across her throat. She stumbles back with eyes wide with astonishment. Her body shakes as she collapses into shock.

"It's back to Hellsfire for you," Ollie falls to her knees and spits. "Bitch."

Bansha's eyes fill with fury but she lets out one last gasp and grows still, leaving the seductress dead before me. Ollie helps me up, then collapses into my arms.

"Let me help…"

"…Okay."

She allows me to take her arm and together we hobble over to Nessa and Marshall. He's soaked in sweat and his face is knotted by pain. "Marshall, I'll need to heal it."

"You've done enough!" He barks and stumbles away from her.

"I don't… I don't mean to be rude, but… the pain."

"I know, I know," Nessa's nearly in tears as her body quivers.

"I'm sorry, I would never…"

"It's not your fault…" Marshall interrupts.

"But you know my condition all too well. It gave you too much of an advantage, and I fear it has pushed back your means of recovering it." "What's all this about?" I ask, joining the commotion. "Marshall, your arm. What's been going on?" "It's…It's…" Nessa tries between whimpers.

"It's my existing injury that never healed," he struggles but with not just the pain.

"I didn't want to concern my king with an old man's traumas, but I fear I haven't been completely honest with you. This pain, this injury…"

I cut him off. "This can wait."

I see his pain, but this is not the time. I glance around the battlefield at the bodies. My men and women, and the demons.

"We need to focus on getting the survivors back to safety before more demons emerge."

"That's probably the smartest thing you've said all week," Alan groans as he and Thalia limp up.

"There's an entrance to the forest up the hill. We scouted ahead while you were supposedly sleeping with the fishes." "Alan…" Thalia groans weakly.

"Not here. Not now."

"I'll…" Nessa takes a moment to let her emotions settle.

"I'll need to revive June first. I'll need his assistance to tend to the others. My Divinity has grown weak."

"Thalia, Alan…" Marshall grits his teeth.

"Do what you can with your understanding of nursing. I'd help too but…"

"You can't really lend a hand when you only have one good hand left." Alan concludes and Marshall growls.

Ollie shifts from around me and struggles to stand on her own. "I have my nurse's training. I'll help too." "Are you sure?" I ask.

She looks even more shaken up than Nessa.

"Not much of a choice is there. I either die trying or we die sitting here in the open."

She makes a good point so I don't argue with her, but Alan does suggest for Ollie to wash the demon off her hands before tending to the wounded. With a unanimous agreement Ollie, Alan, and Thalia head down to the lakebed to wash up before assisting the weak and injured. Nessa uses what little Divinity she has to get Junah back on his feet, and they all work together to patch up as many survivors as possible.

Three more of my knights bled out, including Dawn. She passed with Hayden kneeling by her side, his head dripping in sweat and sorrow as his short sword sits pledged into her abdomen.

Chapter Sixteen

Talk Amongst the Trees

It takes Nessa some time to get my surviving knights back on their feet. Even with that, they have not fully recovered from the fight with the Hellsfire Generals of Chaos. They did a number to my knights. Alan and Thalia have stabilized, but are weary and using each other for support. Junah is fine and keeps an eye on Nessa mixing potions despite their exhaustion, helping us all tremendously.

I've lost nine knights since leaving Baronune. They knew and accepted the risks in serving their king, but this was supposed to be simple. Come to Woodsforge and unite the kingdoms… Instead, I must face challenge after challenge as if I am still in the King of the Round Table Tournament. I wish Terry had prepared me better.

Who would have known *King Richards* would take my inexperience as an opportunity to be rid of me and, what exactly? Take my kingdom? Why does he even want my kingdom? What's so special about Baronune? Woodsforge has so much more going for it. Why would Ivan want a desert kingdom? I'll ask him next time I see him. I will not stand there and let him talk down to me. I will not buckle under the pressure and weight of being king. He wants my kingdom, I want to know why, and if this was worth the sacrifice.

I sit on a boulder with my elbows resting on my knees and rest my chin on my hands. My knights scrounge up what little equipment survived the lake encounter. My eyes trail over to the mounds in the sand. The bodies of the fallen that we took the time to bury, mourn, and give our respects to. Hayden and Thalia remain silently among Dawn's grave.

I wish we could take them back with us, but that's more than we can currently carry and will only slow us down if we get attacked again. How many more demons has Ivan enlisted to kill me? How many more Hellsfire Generals of Chaos are working with him, and what did he offer them? What do they get in return? Crystal said her father made a deal, but what? Baronune? If he wants Baronune, why would he offer it to demons? I shake my head in protest as that makes no sense. Again, these are answers I will demand from the king when I face him.

"What's the plan?" Alan asks as he regroups with the rest of the knights around me.

I glance at Ollie, she's at the edge of the lake washing off the blood from tending to the injured. I return my attention to my knights. Thalia and Marshall stand beside Alan. Nessa leans on Junah while the rest appear to be in a state between moderately alright to worse for wear. Lieutenant Hayden seems to have lost that glowing blessing from the sun that women find so endearing. He's as gray as the rest of Woodsforge. No poems left in him, only sorrow and regret. "There's a forest up ahead" I remember.

"We'll use that for cover in case more of those demons show up. Our priority is to recover completely. If we push on as is…"

I can't bring myself to finish, but everyone recognizes my concerns. While the majority approve with my decision, Alan stands straighter.

"What about after? What's are plan for after we rest? You can't seriously be thinking of going after the sword?"

My eyes shoot up to meet his discouraging glare.

"In case you haven't noticed, we're being butchered out here. We don't know what else is waiting for us, and we don't know if we can handle the next demon around the corner."

"I am aware," I say without meeting his eyes.

It's not like we can turn back. I for one don't feel like taking another dip in the lake. I glare through my knights and through the mist, back towards the castle. I can't see it, but I know it's there and I want Ivan to feel my gaze.

"But we also have no safe means to return if Ivan's truly out to get me, the train is out. So, for the time being, until we get answers, we press on. We rest in the woods, and if I find that sword…"

I pause to meet the eyes of my knights. Ollie makes her way back to the group and her eyes share the same fury. Fury that was once pursuing my own life yet now she seeks the life of a different king.

"…Then I'll take that sword and shove it right up Ivan's ass," I turn sharply as my cape whips at the air behind me.

"Onward."

There is no protest nor cheers. My words must not carry the same assurance to my knights as they feel inside me. Ollie is at my side as we march up the slight slope which leads into the thick mist. My knights may not agree with me, but because I am king, they are forced to follow. I just hope we can have enough time to fully rest and heal.

The mist makes it difficult to navigate our surroundings, we march at a laggard pace. I hear my knights cough and groan with each step, leaving me to regret all that's happened to them. I wish I could bring back those we've lost, but that's not within my power. All we can do is push forward. The images of each demon, each Hellsfire General of Chaos, flash through my mind.

I can imagine Ivan sitting on his throne, laughing and goggling King's Juice as he finds hilarity in the fate of my struggling court. He's been all lies and tricks from the start, how could I trust him? Why hadn't I seen through his façade? Ollie was right, I'm too trusting. After Susan, I should be better at spotting betrayal, but Ivan was right in front of me, lying straight to my face. The thought of that toothless grin lingers in my brain. It pains me so much that I wince. Even Crystal warned me about her father, he's such a headache.

My eyes squeeze shut and I grit my teeth so hard they ache. Ollie nudges me and I open my eyes, the gravel path has begun to grow green and the scent of grass fills my nostrils. The mixing fragrance with the lake air is soothing and as I shift my gaze to Ollie. She directs me ahead.

Before us stands a massive creature, tall on four legs and covered in fur. On top of its extended neck rests a head with two protruding tree limbs.

"Is… is that a deer?"

I have only seen them in pictures while studying with Ollie. It's taller than how most deer have been depicted, and its majestic fur coat is a pale green. It lifts its head and makes a loud cry seemingly to nature itself. The mist thickens as vapors roll across my vision acting as a screen to cover the deer as it changes, shrinks. What's left in its place causes all of us to step back in defense. A man with long white hanfu robes and coat stands before us. His skin is pale and luminous through the fog, and his hair a shimmering lime green.

"Hello, travelers," he says with a wave.

Not the usual greeting for someone trying to kill us.

"I mean you no harm. Come, this way. You may seek shelter in the woods."

I know after everything that has transpired, I should not be seeking shelter with strangers as a king is trying to kill me, but this guy gives no sense of malice. I look to Ollie. She's unsure but not disapproving.

"If anything, we'd come across this guy anyway."

She's not wrong, our plan is to rest in the forest, so we're going to rest in the forest. I'll just keep an extra attentive eye on *Mr. Glowy Green*. I nod my knights forward and we follow the mysterious man.

We leave the mist and lake behind. The rocky terrain beneath our feet softens and turns into grass and soil. There's a whiff of relief in the air as the smell of pine is peaceful and the sound of the wild is tranquil. Even my knights ease up on their guard as we travel deeper and deeper. The passage of time seems far behind us as the brush overhead thickens to where we can't even see the sky.

Small birds of blue and gray fly by, tweeting a happy song. I spy other forest creatures like rabbits, squirrels and a horse with a man for a head in the distance… Did I just see a centaur? I do a double take to try and find it again but the creature is gone. The glowing man leads us further and I can hear a doubtful huff from Alan.

"Ease up," I hear Thalia whisper to him.

"Yeah, I'll ease up. Just like I did with the mountain and the lake. Does no one sense a trap? I sense a trap."

The glowing man speaks up, "There is no trap, Young Warrior, I am simply providing you some aid and the chance to regain your strength."

"Why? No sport in killing the weak?" Alan asks with his arms crossed.

"Oh, I have not sought battle in many, many years. I couldn't tell you the last time I dove into conflict," the glowing man says.

"I am Elkrin, by the way. Spirit to all that is nature. The land, the trees. It's all within my domain."

"A nature spirit?" Alan asks.

"*The* Nature Spirit," Elkrin answers, calmly but whimsical.

"I was once a warrior like you, but I guess you can say that I got quite the promotion. I have been one with the land ever since."

"So, a God?" I ask thinking back to my weird dream with Fate.

"I'd rather not compare myself to the Gods," Elkrin waves off my response as his attention keeps forward.

"My power is minuscule compared to them, but I was at one point in their service. A true warrior of justice back in my day."

He turns and looks directly at me as if sensing my next question to exactly how long back he was referring.

We stop, and Elkrin stretches. His body glows more brightly until he's difficult to look at. He exhales lightly and the ground rumbles, making Alan jump. Thalia and the rest of my knights along with him. Marshall, Ollie and I turn our attention to the forest floor and then the trees. This seems all too familiar, reminding me of when Baronune shifted and changed to reflect the difficulties of the tournament. The trees, the bushes, and the path before us all shift and open into a clearing. The thick brush overhead remains, providing us cover, and long logs emerge from the soil creating seats that form a circle.

Elkrin waves his hands around and stones, twigs, and leaves fly through the air from every which way, creating a funnel of nature around him. Elkrin then guides the forest debris to the center of the log formation to complete the makings of a campsite big enough for all of us.

"You can rest here," Elkrin turns to us with a smile. We're awestruck. "It will be night soon. Nessa will be able to use this time to fully heal those that are still injured.

Alan jabs his staff into the ground, "You did that, but you can't use your magic to heal us?"

"I can't," Elkrin begins with his smile fading despite his body glowing brighter than before.

"Though I may be a man of Fate, those days of service are history, as is my physical body. I must follow the Gods' rules and remain restricted to my realm of responsibility. I may tend to the land and only the land. It is not for me to intersect with the paths Fate has carved for you."
"*Great*," Alan groans.

"A follower of Fate. Fine, keep your tricks. If the fairy is up to it, then I'll put my allegiance with her."

Alan trucks off to find his place in the camp. Thalia apologizes for his rudeness, but Elkrin looks as if Alan's reaction is nothing new to him. She and the remaining knights make their way to the camp. We stay back to take in Elkrin and his use of Divinity, then his eyes fall on us. He nods. "King West." He knows who I am?

"Please take this time to regain your strength. You have many questions and I will answer them to the best of my ability, but not now."

I nod, a little taken aback by how easily he read me. Am I that transparent? I glance over to Ollie, who shrugs then we makes our way to the camp.

Nessa, seemingly replenished, makes quick work of healing half my knights to their full strength. Something about being here or being in the presence of Elkrin has lit a fire under her. Thalia takes a few knights with her to hunt for food while Junah and Alan travel together to gather ingredients for medicine. Alan almost asked Elkrin to summon the items Junah needs but decided not to bother the land spirit.

Ollie leaves me to keep an eye on them, believing Alan would take this time to vent about the overall journey than actually help Junah with his pickings. I decide to check in on Nessa and Marshall.

"As I feared," she examines him thoroughly.

I don't know how while he's wearing his armor. It's almost like she can sense his injuries through touch alone.

"You reopened the scar in that fight. This will take even longer for me to heal."

"What happened?"

Nessa glances at me and then goes back to examining Marshall's arm. "I fear I have been all but honest with you, my king," Marshall begins. "At least not completely."

"You have been injured in battle," I remember. "A lasting injury? What could have scarred so badly that you can't even draw your weapon?"

"So, you have noticed?"

I frown. "I am quite observant when I'm trying to find out why my knights can't fight."

"That's apparent," he sighs, and Nessa lets his arm down.

Marshall rolls his shoulder. He winces.

"Remember my father?"

"The King *Dick Hard* that's trying to kill me? Yeah, we've met."

"He wasn't always like this, there was a time where he was noble, a knight in his own right. Brave and strong, a man I admired. That's why I became a knight, to follow in his footsteps and fight alongside him." I sit beside him on a neighboring log. "What changed?" "The Days of Hellsfire," he says, and I sigh.

Of course, everything bad and evil seems to carry over from those days.

"The demons we faced weren't as bad as when the Beast of the Abyss emerged. You see, we came from Imica, fleeing our home when the battle with that beast destroyed our land.

"I thought it was a dragon?"

I try to remember my history lessons with Ollie. This would be easier had she not run off to pick berries.

"The Days of Hellsfire spread across to Imica?"

"As I was explaining back at the lake, the books of Baronune mostly cover the battles from Arcasia. How the three kings rose to face the Dragon of Hellsfire because that was the creature that awaited us when we arrived on these shores."

Ow, my head hurts trying to recall these history lessons. I know Dragon's Guard was the last line of defense against the Dragon of Hellsfire while King Sorenson, King Richards, and King Xi did the fighting. The kingdom was the last bit of salvation in case the dragon overcame the three kings here in Woodsforge and went after the survivors. I didn't know there was another creature just as savage on Imica.

"So, wait," I hold up my hand. "What became of the beast?"

"It was said to have been defeated by the Phoenix."

"That's right there's a Phoenix too."

"There *was* a Phoenix," Marshall corrects.

"It vanished soon after defeating the Beast of the Abyss, which is why we were left to fend for ourselves against the dragon."

"Oh."

I am actually managing to follow this.

"So, the battle with the dragon is what changed your father?"

Marshall corrects me again. "Fleeing our home changed my father, he abandoned his home and courage to see that Crystal and I were safe. She had only just been born so her survival was crucial though her mother was lost in the escape. We had no idea about the dragon until we arrived in Arcasia. It was then my father was left with a choice, to abandon us and fight, or abandon the fight for us."

"He chose the dragon?"

"No."

"He chose you?" I ask in awe.

"No."

Now I'm confused, Marshall didn't say there was a third option. I feel like I was passing this test and then thrown a trick question. Maybe he *is* like his father.

"My father remains a coward through and through," Marshall continues.

"Where I wanted to fight, he chose to run. He abandoned everyone and fled to the mountains."

A cloak of depression weighs heavy on Marshall's shoulders. Ivan gives me a hard time? This guy ran away from his family and the fight for his own safety. Who is he to judge me?

"We thought all was lost," Marshall continues. "King Sorenson did his best to fend off the dragon. King Xi rallied those brave enough to stand against the dragon's flames, but…"

"It sounds like it was a losing battle," I admit as Marshall takes a moment.

"It was. The dragon seemed impossible to overcome. We were forced to retreat. We were forced to try and make it back to Imica and abandon Arcasia. Leave it to the dragon. I was there when we were trying to pile as many citizens of Woodsforge into the carriages as possible. There were too many, there would be no way we'd evacuate the remaining survivors while Sorenson and Xi fought just beyond the wood line. Then, my father returned. It had been days of fighting and blood lost but he returned. It was hard to understand him, he had somehow lost all his teeth, but claimed he had found new strength to contend with the dragon, and so with his courage returned he rode off to join the fighting and after that…"

"The dragon was defeated?" I ask in shock. "Just like that?"

"That's how it seems," Marshall frowns. "Only my father was able to retell the story."

"The man that became a liar and a trickster?"

"You can see why the years that followed became challenging. My father retold the story of how the Dragon of Hellsfire was defeated, and the people named him, Sorenson, and Xi the new kings of Arcasia for their courage and triumph. There was no evidence to prove my father wrong but after that…"

"He changed?"

"He became the King of Woodsforge and in the following years he built his kingdom. Bansha, Eli, and that black knight all appeared around the same time. My father didn't remarry, but he didn't deny Bansha the option to sit by his side as he ruled. My father didn't feel the need to build up forces much like how Sorenson and Xi did, he had confidence being the man that ended the Days of Hellsfire that no one would challenge him. Then…"

Here it comes, the truth that Marshall has been reluctant to tell me. "What happened?"

"My father tried to unite the kingdoms, much like we are now. The only difference, he wanted to be the one and only ruler. King Xi said he would only be on board if Sorenson agreed. Our late king refused. It was odd. My father and August were friends, allies. I didn't understand the sudden change in heart, but something convinced King Sorenson that my father was not to be trusted. Shortly after, my enraged father threatened to take Baronune by force, but I argued that it would be foolish to challenge King Sorenson, he had the numbers, and he alone could hold off my father no matter how strong he thought he was. King Sorenson's Protective magic was unrivaled."

Marshall clutches his fist and it shakes violently as he struggles through his story.

"My father didn't want to listen to reason, so I told him that if he chose to oppose the King of Baronune then he'd have to oppose me too because I refused to ally myself with his thirst for power. Rather than fight me himself, he had Eli do his dirty work."

"Sounds about right," I admit carefully. "He doesn't seem like someone that's willing to get his hands dirty."

"Not if he knows it's a losing battle. A king in appearance but a coward at heart," Marshall admits with disappointment hanging from the corners of his mouth.

"So, I left Woodsforge to join King Sorenson, but I did not leave without a reminder of my betrayal to my father."

"Your injury…"

"A scar to not just me but my pride as a knight. Eli wields a wicked blade that is cursed with the Corrupted Arts. One gash to my arm and I haven't been able to lift my sword since, ridiculed to being a captain then commander after the banishment of Rhodain and the others who could only train recruits. Until recently…" "You're welcome?" I say.

Maybe I should be apologizing.

Marshall winces as he tries to move his arm. "I fear until my wound is healed, and the curse is lifted, I am dead weight to you, my king."

"Nessa," I glance up to her. "Are you able to cure him? To fix his arm?"

"I have been working on it since I revealed myself as a fairy. I never knew Marshall's story just like he never knew mine. Had I known sooner, if I had my full abilities…"

Marshall smiles as he muscles the strength to pat her on the shoulder. "You're doing your best, Nessa, that is all I can ask for."

"Perhaps Elkrin…" I begin but as if sprouting from the soil, he appears at my side.

"As I have already explained. I am not to mingle with the roads Fate has paved for you," Elkrin admits disappointingly.

I sense this hurts him to say, as if, under normal circumstances, he wouldn't hesitate to help us.

"That's why I have allowed you to seek refuge here in the forest. Here my Divinity flows through the soils and trees. This will allow you the strength to rebuild your forces for wherever your journey may lead you."

"I sensed his Divinity as soon as we entered the woods," Nessa admits. "It's the reason I had the strength to tend to the others, but I still have my limits. I will continue to heal the others and work on Marshall however it would take much more time than we have to rid him of this curse."

I frown then go to wait for the others. Marshall won't be returning to the fight any time soon. Some time passes and my knights return from their hunt. Elkrin seems unbothered by the rabbits, deer, and… is

Thalia hauling a bear? Does that bear have antlers? As Junah stumbles in with arms filled with assorted berries and herbs, Nessa rushes to his aid, helping him sort the edible food from the potion ingredients. Alan helps skin and chop up the bear... *thing*. This takes the remainder of the day. Ollie and the knights make a campfire strong enough to cook the meat, while Nessa uses her Divinity to purify the water.

After a full meal, my knights take this opportunity to rest, while I keep watch over everyone. I can't help thinking back to the ones we lost. The bodies that lie buried at the beach, eaten by the serpent, and lost on the mountain. Their memories haunt me. The looks on their faces before their deaths plague me. To add to my coming nightmares, the jester's face flashes between each of my knights' deaths and I can rule sleeping out of the plans for the remainder of the night.

I stare deep into the campfire and watch its brilliant orange dance. The fire reminds me of Rhodain, but the light makes me think of Fate and the dream I had last night. It seems so long ago since that dream, since I walked in on Ollie and discovered the secret she's been keeping. I look over to her, and my stare seemingly wakes her up. Noticing me with tired eyes, she pulls herself from the dirt and brushes the twigs from her hakama. Sitting next to me, her shoulder brushes against mine.

"Long day?" She asks and I shift my eyes. "Understatement, right. Look none of us knew what to expect on this journey. None of this is your fault..."

I continue to stare at her as she is holding back the urge to say, *"I told you so."*

She leans back with a sigh.

"Okay, not entirely your fault but what could you have done?"

"I should have been stronger," I return my attention to the flame. "I should have..."

"Well, you weren't and besides what difference would it have really made?" Ollie asks and I peer back at her.

"The Mountain Golems may have gone differently, but the rest? The lake monster, the demons..."

"They prefer to be called—"

"Oh, to Hellsfire with them all! That's not my point," Ollie sits forward.

"None of us were prepared for that. The fact that any of us survived is a blessing, and you helped me take down the swords guy."

"He could have easily killed us had he not been so arrogant."

"They all were strong, but they all had weaknesses. If any more come, we'll have to work together to figure out their weaknesses too, and for that we need our king to have a level head on his shoulders," Ollie nudges me.

"You are braver than you know, West. I remember a time when you would have run from those battles."

"If I could…"

Ollie glares at me. "No, don't lie to yourself. You didn't run from the Mountain Golems. You damn near sacrificed yourself, and you did the same to the lake monster just to buy Alan and the others time to subdue Longcaster…"

I think back to how he and the boatmen seem to vanish into nothing in place of Bansha and the other two demons.

"What happened to that guy? How were they able to appear like that, and what became of Eli?"

"We don't have those answers."

"Well then our ignorance is *our* weakness, and that's how Ivan has kept his advantage over us."

I become lost in my thoughts again as I gaze into the flames. Again, I see the treacherous king laughing and drinking as he mocks my inexperience. He had me from the beginning. I don't have anyone in my court that is strong enough with Divinity. Junah and Nessa can assist but their abilities are limited.

I let out a deep sigh. "We should turn back, head home, and…" "And what, wait for King Richards to bring the fight to Baronune?" I look at her in disbelief.

"He's after you, West. He's after the kingdom. We don't know why, but we know that much. I'm not against retrieving this Sword of Fate, if this will provide evidence to everyone back home that you are worthy to be named king, then all the sacrifices that got us here will not have been in vain. Then maybe we can win over the people of Woodsforge too and help them see who their king truly is."

Elkrin walks out of the darkness. "Sword of Fate?"

Has he been listening this whole time? I nearly forgot he was even here. "That's what you're all after?"

"That's my fetch quest from the king. If I retrieve the sword, Ivan was to agree to unite our kingdoms."

I admit but now I don't know if uniting with the *Trickster King* is a good idea. Elkrin stands before us, and the glow of his luminous pale body mirrors the dancing fire. His hair is still a brilliant lime green that glimmers like starlight.

"Oh," he follows as he stares down on us.

"I fear that sword is nothing but a story. There is no Sword of Fate." My eyes squeeze shut and I rub two fingers against my forehead.

"We cannot have gone through all of this for nothing."

"Why do you say the sword is a story?" Ollie asks, looking up at Elkrin.

"I mean, there's definitely a sword out beyond the woods, but it's no Sword of Fate. What would such a sword even be? A sword used by a Hand of Fate? There's no Divinity left over, if there was, it would be entirely too weak. The Hands of Fate that would have used it died somewhere over the last thousand years."

"You seem to know a lot."

I'm not happy with anything he's saying. Elkrin's aid seems to have been used up to allow us the time to rest and rest alone.

"I know because I was there," he says this, and I remember how old he's supposed to be.

But he looks no older than Alan?

"I was once a Hand of Fate before I became the Spirit of the Land. My Divinity was so strong with nature that Oni, the creator of earth, chose me to be the guardian of all the lands at the end of the Elemental War." "That's quite the promotion," I admit, and he smiles at me.

"So, your Hand of Fate powers...remind me, what exactly is a Hand of Fate?"

"You don't know?" Elkrin asks and my only reply is a blank stare.

"King West, *you're* a Hand of Fate."

Ollie matches my expression as our jaws drop so low that they would roll away across the camp if not attached.

"I'm a... *what?*"

"A Hand of Fate," Elkrin stares at me baffled. "You really had no idea? You met with Fate, didn't you?"

"Yeah..." I answer, unsure. "I was confused about whether that was a dream or not but then..."

"Was that the sudden Divinity burst you had against Alan today?" Ollie snaps back to the conversation.

"I guess?" I have no idea. "There was also that moment in the lake with the serpent... I'm sorry, how does being a Hand of Fate change me?" "Well," he pauses, as if to consider a catalog of explanations.

"It does and it doesn't. By being a Hand of Fate, Fate has chosen you to enact justice and serve as a warrior for the Gods. The Hands of Fate were the first heroes of legend. All the tales you were probably told as a young child of great warriors that fought monsters to protect all were the Hands of Fate."

"So, I'm some kind of hero of justice?"

"No," Elkrin answers and I slump back in disappointment.

"Those days are over. After some of the Hands of Fate grew too power-hungry the Gods realized their foley and stopped seeking the aid of mortals. Those that remained were left to live out their lives in servitude until Death came for them."

"So, there are no more Hands of Fate?" Ollie asks and Elkrin kind of nods. "Then why was West...?" Elkrin shrugs.

"For reasons unknown, I do not know the paths Fate paves, but something about West woke the God enough to choose him."

"Woke?" I say vaguely remember something about that interaction with Fate.

"Fate was sleeping? *Is* sleeping?"

"After the Hands failed, Fate turned away from the world and entered a deep slumber, believing that creating the roads for us to follow were easy enough. Yet you were chosen, West, the first in centuries. It must be for a greater purpose, did Fate truly tell you nothing?"

"Just that she was doing what she was supposed to do," I say trying to remember.

"No explanation or details on what you're supposed to do with this power?" Ollie asks, looking me over.

Then she turns to Elkrin. "What are his abilities?"

"Being a Hand of Fate allows you to connect with the paths of others and allows for an easier access to Divinity."

"Cool," I say in the middle of Elkrin's explanation.

"But you still have to train to control that access."

Not so cool, I slump back down.

"The Divinity that comes from being a Hand of Fate will increase any of your natural abilities tenfold."

"Oh…"

Sadly, my natural abilities are not that great. Despite my months of training, I'm not that skilled of a fighter. My swordsmanship is subpar, and though I have gotten stronger, I have barely scratched the surface of the Martial Arts.

Elkrin gets my attention. "King West, you seem discouraged." "He's not the best," Ollie answers.

I stare at my hands. Tenfold? Ten times nothing is still nothing.

"At?" Elkrin asks, leaning in.

Ollie sounds as disappointed as I feel. "Anything really, he *tries*, it's just…"

"I'm not good at anything I attempt, or it takes a lot of trial and error."

"Heavy on the error."

Elkrin squats down to study me, then picks up a rock.

"King West," he begins, and I lift my head.

"Do you see this rock? It's small but with the right amount of effort it is dangerous."

He demonstrates this by knocking me on the head with it. It's a light tap but I get the message.

Ollie giggles.

"Now here is a demonstration of the capabilities that come with the gifts of being a Hand of Fate," Elkrin lets the rock sit in his palm.

A fiery glow, much like his hair, shimmers around the rock giving it an intense aura. Elkrin stands and with a light flick of his wrist, throws the rock. It flies through several trees becoming lost in the woods. Ollie and my eyes grow large.

"Again, that's not the exact power that now flows inside you, but I believe you understand what I'm getting at. Just a moment ago, that rock was barely strong enough to give you a headache. Add more Divinity, and the possibilities are endless."

I stare through the hole in the nearest tree trunk. "So, you're saying that I could do… *that?*"

"Possibly," Elkrin shrugs.

"Maybe more. That power is yours to command, so do what you will with it. You're a Hand of Fate, it's only fitting that you use these gifts to pave your own way."

He leaves me with that, and in a whiff of leaves, he's gone. The rock sits back in my hand though I'm not sure what to do with it. Ollie places her hand over mine and closes the rock in my fist.

"It's a lot."

"Loads," I say, still contemplating all this information.

"How am I supposed to be a Hand of Fate on top of being king? It's just so much, and it's so confusing and…" "West," Ollie's voice is soft and comforting.

My attention is drawn to her.

"I understand one hundred percent how difficult and confusing this may be. You don't have to decide what to do with it now, you can sleep on it. But one day you will have to make decisions, decisions that you won't be proud to make in the moment or after. But they'll need to be made, and those choices will be how you pave your way."

"I just wish Fate had given me some kind of instruction. How to move forward."

"If the Gods gave us the answers then what would make us different from everyone else? Your decisions are what truly separate you from others, that's why Fate leaves us to follow our own paths," Ollie says, smiling.

"I chose mine and my family shunned me for it. As Oliver I never felt comfortable in my own body. That's why I chose this life for myself. The world views me differently, but I couldn't be happier. It's not easy, trust me, every day is a challenge, and I spent a lot of them not really hiding but not really being open about who I am because I fear the world's opinion of me.

The accusations of others. Then you bumbled into my life and opened the door for me. Rudely mind you, but because that's who you are. Your innocence, your lack of comprehending, is troubling at times, but it also gives you strengths and wonders that no one else expects or understands. Use your weakness to fuel your strength and open the door for who you truly are."

"What if I'm not strong enough?"

I ask thinking back to Ivan's words and how terrible of a fighter I am, as good as a knight with no hands as he put it. My kingdom doesn't trust me, and neither does my court. I don't have anyone's respect, why do I bother? "What if I can't be this great king that everyone expects me to be?"

"Then I'll continue to stand by your side as your Second Grand Advisor, your aid and support, and fight with you until your confidence is strong enough to support the king that I know exists."

"Well, you are the smart one, aren't you?"

"I am, but you gave me the chance to be."

We exchange smiles, the dancing flame reflecting in our faces. The fiery blare lighting up our eyes. It's in this moment that it becomes obvious to me. The teen that I met in that sewer all those months ago, that tried to kill me inside my own castle, she is no longer just my Second Grand Advisor. Ollie isn't merely fulfilling her duties to keep me alive, she's my best friend, and I want the world to truly see that too.

Chapter Seventeen

Knights Fall

I tried to sleep, knowing that we can be attacked at any moment makes rest important. This knowledge is also what *kept* me from sleeping. Every time I closed my eyes last night I either saw flashes of the jester's face as that spear in the back of his throat prepared to kill me, or I saw the faces of my knights that have died along the way. The two I lost against the Mountain Golems. I envisioned I was clung to the mountainside watching their faces as they fell into the river below.

They screamed in panic and fear as their fall was slow and gradual. The image lingered in my mind until they got closer to the water, and a monster broke the surface and ate them. Water sprayed across my face, that forced me to close my eyes. When they opened, I was back on the lake watching a lifeless scene of black and white as my knights, Hoover and Cooper swam for safety, they swam for me. I wish I could say I reached for them, cried for them. I did nothing. I only watched as the serpent's eyes glowed a bright red through the fog.

The only life or color to be seen as the beast ripped through the mist and swallowed my knights whole. The lake turned violent. The waves rocked the boat that I was sitting on. I was flung as it capsized, but I didn't fall into the lake as I had done before. I hit land. I rolled through the sands on the beach. I looked up and watched my knights fight the demon Mongo. Alan and Thalia to no prevail as they danced around the mound of evil and their attacks did nothing while the demon sat there and ate Kaleb, Dawn and the rest of the unconscious knights sprawled across the lakeshore.

I remember I wanted to help. I remember how I looked around for others to help. The demon, Slyce, held Ollie and Marshall at bay. Ollie tried to fight the swordsman. A laggard blur as she leaped and maneuvered around, but the demon laughed at her attempts. Marshall was stuck slowly drawing his claymore, but instead of a blade being pulled from its sheath, black flames spilled out and crawled up Marshall's arm. His face slowly being gripped by pain with each extension of the flames, but he continued to draw his sword anyway. I wanted to urge him not to, but my voice was absent.

I turned to find Nessa and Junah. She buried her face in her hands, weeping, while Junah was held in Bansha's embrace. They were kissing. At least, that is what I thought at first. My face baffled as to why Junah would be kissing that demon witch, but then I realized that Junah's arms and hands quivered and flinched. He wasn't holding her, Bansha had him. Her hands were blackened talons that dug into his neck. As she moved her head in the act of kissing, blood drifted into the air. When I caught a glimpse of her face, her lips were painted red. Her mouth covered in blood. Her eyes were black with golden slits like snakes.

Her toothy smile was full of fangs. She pivots Junah with one hand that held him by his neck. He had no expression. He had no face. Just a gaping hole full of blood that drifted up and lingered in the air around them. Bansha laughed, snickered, hissed. Her face slowly changed; it became darker, more demonic.

"Is this what happened?"

I remembered hearing. The pale world of mist slowed to a crawl. It was only I that had the ability to move. I rose to search for the voice and there he was. Rhodain, fully lit, and very much alive.

"Is this what I sacrificed myself for?"

"Rhodain," I sobbed. His body was lit with warmth, but his face was cold with disappointment. "I tried. I tried to be a king, but I can't. I don't know what you were thinking when you threw me into that seat. When you thrust this responsibility on me."

"You tried?" He panned to the scenes around us. "This is how you try?"

"I failed!" I screamed at him through my watery vision. "You failed! You did this to me, you're the reason they're dead or dying!"

"So that's what you do?" He glared at me. "You run? You cry? What happened to the boy that I met in the tournament? Where's the child that did what he saw necessary to survive and protect his cousin?"

The scene blared. Fire surrounded us and images of the tournament danced in the flames. I saw Sophia standing like a statue, molded by fright. I stand yards before her with my arms spread wide as thugs charged us. I tried to protect her. I turned to a scene of me leaping over crates as I rushed in to distract Roxette. I was securing our odds of survival by risking my own life. I saw the scene where Rhodain was tossed against the castle wall in his fight against Lawrence, Matthews, and Greg.

Even in a memory, Greg stopped to wave at me at the thought of his name. I saw myself rush across the damaged roof, forgetting about the rules of the ring. No. I didn't forget. I just didn't care. Rhodain was my only concern as I thought he was about to die. Then he did. The last image. The scene of his death.

"You died…You were supposed to be king, not me."

"I never wanted to be king!" Rhodain glared at me as he barked, and the flames roared high. "My intentions were selfish. I knew that in the end."

The scene of him stumbling for the throne replayed. I remember *I* wanted him to be king, *I* wanted him to end the tournament so Sophia and I would be safe.

"I would not have been a good king," he walked across the sand as the flames closed around us, forming a circle.

Rhodain guided my attention to the images as there seemed to be a battle. A clash in memories. My images of the tournament versus Rhodain's.

"A good king needs to be more than strong; he needs to be courageous. A good king needs to think not only of himself but of the others around him. He needs to recognize the evil but still see the good. I did none of this. That was all you."

His images faded. My memories filled the flames. Rhodain stands before me. He is still, calm, but his eyes continued to burn into me.

"I died," the flames vanished as we stood in darkness. "But so did you. So did the boy I saw in that tournament who against all odds found his own way to the top of the castle. Not with violence, but with intellect. You showed me what it meant to be king, and how you were right for the role the whole time."

"I am a boy, I can't –"

"Don't," he cut me off. "Don't continue to lie to me. You're just lying to yourself. Don't tell me you tried. Don't tell me you can't. Tell me the truth."

"…I'm afraid," I admitted. "I'm afraid I'll get everyone killed. Just like I killed you."

There was a long pause between us. A frown tugged at his mouth, and he walked over to me.

"Take this as your lesson," he placed his hand on my shoulder. "This is not the game you played for days by yourself. You cannot control people like you controlled those pieces. We listen, but we act on our own accord. I did what I did, and I died for what I believed in and by my own decisions. Understand this, accept this, and move on. There was nothing else you could have done. There was nothing else within your power to change anything that I decided to do. Annoying as you were."

He said this and the darkness began to gradually lift from beneath us. I saw a pale green light fill in from the bottom. In the absence of the nothing around us.

"Stop trying so hard to be a king," Rhodain began to fade with the darkness. "You **are** the king. So be you."

With that, the vision ended. As the darkness had lifted, I opened my eyes.

The pale hue of the morning light fills the forest. I lie next to Ollie. She's curled up at my side. The campfire's embers cling to life and my knights are scattered throughout the site asleep. Alan and Thalia are next to each other, she's sleeping with her arm across his chest. Nessa and Junah embrace each other and she has a faint glow while Junah buries his face into her shoulder. Is this to help him nullify his snoring so that he doesn't emit any Divinity? Marshall rests upright against a log. His head hangs in peace as he looks like he kept watch for as long as he could during his shift before falling asleep.

I carefully get out of my dirty bedroll, making sure not to wake Ollie. Quietly brushing off the soil and leaves, I grab my sword and don my cape that I used for a pillow.

There's a familiar feeling. A pull much like the night I was lead to Ollie's chambers. I take one last look at my knights and walk into the woods.

The path seems to open up for me. The forest or Elkrin or something is guiding me to where I need to go. With each stride, step, and crunch of leaves beneath my feet. I think long and hard about my vision, what Rhodain was trying to tell me. Why I need to stop trying to be the example of the king that he saw in me during the tournament. That was the whole point of the tournament.

To test the participants so that whoever made it to the top, sat in the throne was the right man to be named king. I just didn't notice nor realized that I was participating. I was so focused on getting Sophia to the castle to end the tournament that I didn't realize my actions were what got us there. My decisions led me to become the king and started me on the path that I am on now. I stop walking to glance down at my feet and the trail. Not the literal path I am on currently, but the metaphoric path I've been following since I sat in that throne and those ceremonious alarms rang over the kingdom.

I keep going, I have to keep going. I can't let my men's sacrifices be for nothing. Much like I didn't endure the tournament for my own safety, it was for Sophia's. I will put others before me, I will do what matters most, and I will follow whatever this is that's guiding me beyond these trees.

I stop as the forest ends. Once again, I was so lost in my thoughts that I didn't realize how far I've come. Through the trees, I can see the waking morning light merge with the pale mist and dull overcast. Whatever's out there, I will face it on my own. I take a step forward when I hear something behind me.

"Elkrin?" I turn around.

I'm surprised that I'm wrong and it's an out of breath Ollie.

"How? What…?"

"Assassin's Guild…" Ollie reminds.

"I may have given up a lot of my Divinity, but I'm still fast and stealthy. I thought that was obvious."

"It was," I admit still dumbfounded that Ollie is even here. "But it's me you're talking about."

"That's why…" she says between breaths. "…I'm surprised you didn't turn back."

"You thought I'd run?"

"I thought you'd have the sense to come back for your court," Ollie crosses her arms. "*Alan* thought you'd run."

"Are they here?" I search the trees and the bushes.

"They're coming. I'm faster so I sped ahead."

"Then I need to hurry," I say as I turn to proceed in exiting the woods.

Ollie takes one silent step to catch my arm.

"West," she says, and her soft voice freezes me in place.

"Don't be an idiot. Wait for your knights. I don't care if you are a Hand of Fate, if something's out there you can't face it alone. That's why we're here."

"To die for me?" I ask without looking back.

"I don't want that. I don't want to stand by and watch everyone throw their lives away for me." "But West…"

"But nothing!" I bark and rip my arm away from Ollie.

"I am tired of all this death and sacrifice. This is my path, my task, and my choice to make."

There's a pause. Ollie doesn't say anything in protest, but instead stands beside me.

"Then let's go then."

"What?"

Did she not hear me? I was being perfectly clear.

Ollie rolls her eyes. "Well don't stand there staring, I wasn't able to fix myself up properly after sleeping in the dirt and losing my supplies to the abyss of the lake."

"That's not…"

I really hadn't noticed the lack of glimmer and shine Ollie applies to her face every day. I also hadn't noticed a lot of Ollie's features in the past so that's not saying much. I should be more observant moving forward.

"If it's your decision to be an idiot and tread on without back up, then it's my decision to follow your dumb ass, as I'm your Second Grand Advisor," Ollie says.

"Also, I couldn't face your cousin if something terrible to happened to you."

"She's not even that intimidating, how does she scare you?"

"I'm not scared!" Ollie snaps. "It's a show of respect. It means a lot knowing that after my attempts to kill you she also trusted me to protect you."

"Yeah," I say looking off and scratching my cheek. "Perhaps I'm a bad influence on her?"

"You do have an infuriating aura about you," Ollie agrees, and she gives me a light kiss on the cheek.

I blush madly.

"Shall we? Your *path* isn't going to wait all day."

"Well, if it's just laid out in front of me…"

"West."

Ollie growls and I realize I'm doing that thing that annoys her so much. I laugh, wanting to remind her that this ability of mine got us through the demon swordsman, but think better of it. Together we stride forward and exit the forest.

As the cover of leaves is behind us, we venture into a stretch of land layered in jagged rocks and large boulders. Cold air blows through us as the clouds above churn black and gray. The emptiness around us gives an ominous feeling as I stroke my arm and shiver not from the chill but from nerves. I am familiar with the lands of Eurosia being abandoned after the battles in the Days of Hellsfire. This land is the border between with soil fertilized with the deaths from those battles. I can only imagine the men and women that sacrificed themselves back then, much like how my knights do now.

"Where to next?" Ollie asks squeezing her arms from the bitter air. "This flank seems to stretch endlessly in both directions." "Flank?" I ask taking another look at my surroundings.

She's right, as the mist rolls from view I see the rock faces up ahead. Mountain passes and trails seem to carve their way through the massive wall ahead of us.

"Well, Ivan did say the mountains surrounding his kingdom was his crown."

I study the trail that opens up on the opposite side of the terrain. The distance is a bit far, but with how this unseen force seemed to guide me in this direction, from what little I recall from when I left the campsite, I figure that this has to be the path I need to take.

"Straight ahead."

"How can you be sure?"

"I don't know," I shrug. "Fate?"

"…Please don't make that your go-to excuse."

"But what if that's what Fate wants me to do?" I ask making Ollie irritated.

I chuckle, this is fun.

"What if this is my Fate?"

"Stop or I will change my mind and leave you here."

"Guess we'll just have to let Fate decide."

Ollie growls. "I will strangle you with your *Hands of Fate*."

I finally agree to stop with the jokes. She trusts my judgment and we proceed forward. The further we put the woods behind us, the more I feel like we're being watched. I scan back and forth. There's nowhere around us to hide. I observe the rocky faces ahead of us, looking for caves. Maybe someone is watching us from there? I can tell Ollie is also on guard.

My hand is at my hip, ready to draw my sword if necessary. We keep forward, and then I hear it. A flap and a swoosh. It's coming from above. We both turn to the sky and catch a black blur soar over us and vanish in the overcast. It moves too fast to discern what it is. Then there's another swoosh, and our attention falls ahead. Standing in all black, his coat flapping in the wind as the sinister glare of his one yellow eye meets us.

"*Eli.*"

"Where did he—" Ollie begins, but the sight of his black blade silences her.

It extends like a long talon from a silver gauntlet that appeared from black vapors around his right wrist. That must be the blade that cursed Marshall.

"Fall back," Ollie says, fear thick in her voice.

I've never seen her confidence abandon her so quickly, but with one look of Eli, I don't try to protest.

"If we try to fight him in the open…"

"We'll die?"

"If we use the trees, we might stand a chance."

I don't think we stand a chance in Hellsfire, but I do not relay this to Ollie. My cold sweat is made more chilling with each gust of wind.

Eli hisses as we turn to run. *"You cannot escape."*

Normally I would argue that turning your back on your opponent is a terrible idea, but when that opponent can seemingly fly then all sense goes out the window.

Eli drops down in front of us, cutting us off from the forest. We stand our ground, retreating seems to not be the option here. He can easily get around us faster than we can cover ground. Fighting him seems just as pointless, and I don't think I can talk my way out of this one.

"So," doesn't mean I'm not going to try. "Are you another of those Generals of Hellsfire?"

Eli doesn't answer. His glare only intensifies. I swallow hard and force my hand around the hilt of my sword.

"Because you know, we've beaten all the other chaos demons your king has thrown at us."

Eli hisses and I swear I can hear his voice carry through the wind, into my ear and rest in the back of my head.

"I will not fall as they did. Weaklings. Human at the core. I am nothing like them."

His very voice makes my skin crawl and Ollie is more pale than ever. If she was concerned about how sleeping in the dirt messed up her good looks, I don't want to remind her of how her nervous and panic expression is ruining her complexion.

Eli turns to square off with us. *My intent, is to kill. Your journey ends here.*

"You want to…" I gulp. "Let me grab the Sword of Fate first, so I can at least…"

He doesn't let me finish. The single swipe of his blade frightens the wind away. It becomes dead silent. My legs are locked, my body is frozen. With Eli's next move, Ollie and I will die.

He prepares to rush us. Our jaws clinch simultaneously as we prepare to accept our… Fate. I won't tell Ollie I thought of that one. Though I don't expect I'll have the chance to tell Ollie anything else. Nor did I expect for Eli to stop his pursuit before he starts. A rock flies from the woods and hits Eli so hard that he nearly stumbles. He glares back. He's hard to spot, but I recognize the lime green glow of hair.

Elkrin stands at the forest's edge. "King West, your reinforcements have arrived. Let Fate pave your way."

He places his hand to his left pec and bows his head as he vanishes. In his place, making their way through the woods, are my knights.

Alan steps over a bush and enters the clearing. "Ollie, we told you to stall him, not aimlessly follow his stupid decisions."

He calls *me* stupid? He's the one that willingly walked onto the battlefield. A step behind him follows Thalia. To their left and right, Lieutenant Hayden and my remaining knights step from the woods and fall in line. A single file formation that stands to confront Eli. What they don't know, is that they're facing Death himself.

I yell. "Go back, retreat! You can't win this!"

Alan stabs his Bo staff into the ground and leans towards Thalia.

"He expects us to retreat when he, yet again, put us in this position?"

"I know right?" she says. "Like we have anything better to do right now." "Besides, it's just one guy," Alan says. "How hard can he be?"

"Foolish humans," Eli hisses impatiently. *"You will die for your arrogance."*

"We'll die," Thalia draws her arming sword. "But not today."

Alan whistles. "Smooth."

"Shut up."

Eli points his wicked blade at my knights. *"You'll die with your king."* "I think he's hard of hearing," Thalia mocks as she leans towards Alan.

"Nah, just hardheaded," Alan corrects. "We ain't dying dumbass! Not today, and I am especially not dying for that kid. If I die, it's for the kingdom, and we're a long way from Baronune."

"Then this ground will mark your graves."

Eli proclaims as he slashes the air and drops his arm to his side. Alan and Thalia stare at him.

"Yeah, no, you're right," Alan confirms as he leans back towards Thalia.

"He *is* hard of hearing."

Eli rushes in. *"AH!!!"*

"Knights of Baronune, attack!"

Hayden leads the knights to all rush in to meet Eli. He's outnumbered, my knights have the advantage. We might stand a chance. Then I'm reminded to how easily Rhodain ran through my knights on his own during the tournament, and my doubts immediately return.

Eli meets the blades of three knights at once. They hold him but only for a moment as with sheer force, Eli knocks them back several yards. They almost fly back into the forest. Two more knights flank him from the sides. It's hard to tell exactly with how fast he's moving, but Eli fans them back with either the flap of his coat or a slash from his blade. "His blade…" I remember, gathering my thoughts.

"Don't let him cut you! His blade is cursed, and any wound will leave you disabled!"

"I won't leave a wound!" Eli hisses in protest.

Hayden slashes downward. Eli dodges, jabs upward with an uppercut, causing Hayden to stumble, and stabs his cursed blade through my knight's armor and abdomen.

"I will kill every last one of you."

"Empty promises!"

Alan yells as he launches himself in the air with his staff. He aims at Eli with a dropkick. The man in black prepares his blade to counter.

"Too slow!"

Thalia rushes in from the front. Eli barely had time to block her slash as their blades meet and the sound of metal fills the air. Their struggle is brief as Alan stays on course, coming down with a heavy kick to Eli's face, making him roll several feet across the gravel.

"Keep on the attack!"

Thalia cries and the knights still able to fight rush in again.

Eli is quickly back on his feet, blocking an attack then leaping out of the way to avoid another knight's sword. He deflects his two attackers only to get gashed and bashed by two more attacking from behind. They have him surrounded and rush him all at once. He held three back with ease, but the additional knight seems to make all the difference. Holding off their attacks, he drops to one knee.

I don't think my knights will accept his proposal. I can hear him strain beneath the combined weight of their offense, but he doesn't seem willing to give up. Instead, he goes up, way up. He shoots into the air with... are those wings? Large black leathery wings that resemble bat's shoot from his back as he soars against the pale gray backlight of the sky.

Thalia glares at Alan.

"What?" He's a *bat man*, that still doesn't make him a demon." "It shifts the odds a little bit," Thalia points out.

"How so?" Alan asks.

Eli swoops in with such speed that he runs his blade through one of my knights, and carries him into the air like a vulture taking off with its prey.

Thalia glares back at Alan.

"You know I don't know odds."

"You think that makes us even?"

Even? *Oh*... I am naive, they were courting each other...I think. I'll clarify later, if there is a later.

With Eli taking to the air, he has the advantage again and with my knights decreasing I look to the forest. I don't know if I want Marshall, Nessa, and Junah to join or not. Whatever they're doing, it might be best that they stay away from this bloodshed.

"AH!"

I hear another knight scream as he gets carried into the sky.

"GAH!"

He's too fast. Another knight groans as Eli dives in and stabs him too. He's going to continue to pick off my knights one by one.

"Gather!" Thalia calls.

My remaining two knights fall in on her as they form a tight circle, well, triangle at this point. Alan seems to have vanished while my attention was focused on Eli. Did he run back into the woods? Maybe he went to fetch Marshall and Nessa.

"I'm going to try and slow him down!" Ollie announces, and before I can say anything, she rushes off.

From within the sleeves of her hakama, Ollie flings silver scalpels as Eli swoops at my knights. A few of her blades pierce his wings, but they don't seem to do enough damage to ground him.

"Ollie!" Thalia cries and Ollie's attention falls on her. "Stay with the king!"

Ollie nods and with two great leaps backwards she's at my side. Eli looks annoyed at Ollie's attempt but seems more focused on my knights. They're the easier target as they remain huddled together. He lifts his bladeless hand to his mouth, then his expression turns fierce as he opens his maw to summon black fire that he flings at the formation. With Thalia's speed, she uses the Mirrogold side of her sword and cuts clean through Eli's corrupted fireball.

Enraged, Eli dives for a direct attack.

"KNEEL!" Thalia screams and all the knights drop.

Alan emerges from the center of the formation and whirls his Bo staff overhead. They set a trap that Eli flew straight into it. Alan slams his Bo staff into Eli's face and bats the *bat man* away. I hate myself for thinking that.

Eli rolls across the rocks and gravel again but is quick to get back to his feet. He retracts his wings and rushes in. This time, Thalia matches his speed, rushing to meet him with a metal dance of blades. The pings of their weapons echo through the air as they circle around the terrain in wellexecuted parries, strikes, and slashes. They showcase their swordsmanship well, though Thalia seems to lose steam.

Their blades meet once more, and her legs look ready to buckle. Alan rushes in, Thalia presses forward once more, and Eli pushes back in protest. She uses this momentum to leap back and leave distance between them.

Meanwhile, Alan gets close enough to jab at Eli with his staff.

The one eye, one blade, two-winged man in black blocks the flurry of attacks, then rolls inward. Not good, Alan fights better at a distance, and Eli's trick blade is not something to test your luck against in a close-range confrontation.

Eli slashes. Alan defends. Eli swings back around for another attack. Alan blocks again, but his expression screams panic. Eli is far too fast for Alan at this range. With his free hand, Eli grabs the Bo staff. Alan tries to hold him off and keep him at a distance, but it's useless. Eli tosses the staff aside and follows through with another stab of his blade. Alan cries, but only in reflex as he narrowly manages to avoid being pierced, but the blade still cuts into his armor. Alan locks Eli's arm under his own, holding him in place.

"Got you," Alan struggles as Eli fights to get free.

Eli hisses and black flames leak from the corners of his mouth. *"Fool!"* In this moment, Alan sees his mistakes and recognizes his demise.

"No!"

Thalia cries, rushing in. Eli notices that he's left himself open and spreads his wings to fly again. Alan releases him, not wanting to be airborne as Eli soars into the air, circling the two knights that remained in their previous formation. My last two knights aside from Alan, Thalia and Marshall. He spits black fire, and their tortured screams break the silence.

"Gods…" Ollie gasps as she tries to cover her mouth.

Her hand is shaking in violent protest.

"There are no Gods to help you here," Eli proclaims as he lands with his black flames dancing endlessly at his back.

A reminder of what the Days of Hellsfire must have resembled as I can still hear their screams amongst the crackling fire. A history lesson I didn't intend to sit through today. Where's that Divinity? Where's the power Elkrin said I possess? I struggle to force something, *anything* out of my body.

"This is your fate. This is my promise. I will leave all that you know in my endless flame."

Just then I hear a faint *"No!"* from a woman, and next thing I see is Junah darting out of the forest.

In the seconds it takes for my brain to process the next turn of events, I am unable to react in time. Junah screams, Sound Divinity carrying across the terrain with enough force to crack boulders and turn rubble to dust. Striking Eli with the full force of the soundwaves, he howls in pain.

"Ah!"

The force of Junah's voice pushes against Eli's might as he fights to remain in place. The black flames are finally extinguished, revealing the charred corpses of my former knights. Neither survived.

We all cover our ears as Junah pushes Eli back. His feet dig into gravel for leverage, but he doesn't find it as he falls to his knees. His one eye rolls back as he fights for consciousness. I see tears stream down Junah's face as he grimaces and grabs at his tearing vocal cords.

His screech breaks as his voice finally gives out. Blood begins to run like red rivers from his ears, eyes, and nose. Dropping to his knees, Junah falls forward.

"You—insolent—FOOL!"

Eli roars as he rushes at Junah. Everyone else stumbles, still suffering from the soundwaves as well. As Eli staggers to stab at Junah, a brilliant light flies from the forest, crashing in between them. Nessa, she makes it just in time to shield Junah.

Eli snarls. *"What is this?"*

"Please…" she pants, as the shield shatters.

Eli slaps her across the face, sending her rolling several feet across the gravel.

"No!"

I cry and try to move. My body vibrates and I fall. My muscles have turned to mush. Junah's efforts to help have hindered us this time. How is Eli this strong? How is he unaffected? What kind of demon is he?

Chapter Eighteen

For Honor and Pride

Eli turns his attention back to Junah, vengeance burning in his one eye. He readies his raised blade.

"I'll silence you now!"

A voice calls from the forest.

"ELI!"

I'm still having difficulties distinguishing sounds, but I know there's only one other person left.

Marshall marches from the woods. "You dare strike a man when he's down? Have you no respect. No honor?"

"Do you?" Eli drops his blade and steps away from Junah's exhausted body.

"I thought I severed your honor when I cut that arm."

"You should have taken the whole arm if you wanted to truly leave me scarred."

"I wanted to kill you," Eli points his blade at Marshall. *"But your father held me back. Your father is why you live today."*

"One as strong as you, why do you bow to a man like my father?"

"I have my orders," Eli hisses in disgust. *"You're lucky I serve my master and obey his wishes. You all are."*

Marshall reaches for his claymore. "You'll wish you had finished me off, Eli."

"Your father isn't here," Eli says. *"There's no one to save you this time. You will die."*

"Maybe," Marshall eyes me from across the terrain. "I leave that for the Gods to decide, not you, demon."

"You sound as foolish as these dead men behind me."

"Chalk that up to the Baronooner in me."

"Then you will die with them!"

Eli slashes through the air and a wave of black vapors ripples from him and spreads throughout the plain until dissipating.

"For them," Marshall grips his sword and doesn't wince.

"For my king, I will give my arm… For my kingdom, I will give my heart. But for my honor and pride…"

Marshall draws his massive claymore from its sheath with indents in the blade that gives it the appearance of an hourglass. With two hands he grasps tight to the hilt and holds it with ease. It's the plains that quivers under the weight of the sword as an intense pressure shakes everything around us.

Marshall is not as fast as Thalia. He's not even as nimble as Alan. He takes long stallion-like strides as he advances on the murderous fiend eagerly awaiting his attack. With the distance closed, Marshall swings his mighty sword downward. Eli meets with ease but is visibly surprised by the overwhelming weight of the attack. The force carries through the steel, Eli's body, and into the ground.

Eli buckles and drops to one knee.

"…I will give your soul."

The pressure from Marshall's sword clashing against Eli's blade hits us. Who knew Marshall possessed this much power? How is he able to do this now? Isn't this risky to his already damaged arm? With a long grinding screech, Eli slides from under Marshall's sword and glides back.

He soars across the rocky terrain to slash at Marshall. My Grandier is calm and ready, seemingly anticipating his next attack. As the black blur closes the distance, Eli raises his blade to pierce through Marshall and in that moment, Marshall leaps back then slashes across Eli's chest and shoulder. Such strength should have cleaved him in two, but the sword seems to slide off Eli's clothing.

What kind of material is that? It's far tougher than the Eel Worm silk that makes up our capes and under armor. Regardless, Eli is knocked upward and topples through the air until his black wings spread wide to halt him. His one eye glares down on Marshall, studying him.

"I'd forgotten how strong you were, but how much longer can you last? How long can that arm hold up before you grow weary again?" Eli asks.

Marshall answers with an intense glare.

"You're against Time. I can feel my corrupted mark itching its way through whatever healing spell you placed to bind it. Your arm will fail, and you will die."

I glance over to Nessa. She's out cold and Junah's no better off. How long can Marshall hang on without her healing touch? I glance at Thalia. She's slowly inching around the circumference of the battle. Where did Alan go?

I scan the terrain and find him darting off somewhere. I know he's no coward… His staff! Eli threw his weapon away. He must be looking to retrieve it, but Eli is no fool. He sees everything with that one eye but remains focused on Marshall. Though, maybe he doesn't see *everything* if he doesn't consider Thalia and Alan to be a threat. I hope that will cost him, they're the only knights I have left.

Eli raises his hand to his mouth and spits out another black fireball at Marshall. Dodging, Eli spews a stream of black flames down on my Grandier. Even after jumping away once more, Eli's changes the fires direction to chase him behind a cluster of boulders.

The intense heat begins melting away the stones and the wall of boulders smolders down to a single rock. Eli ceases fire. Marshall casually walks from what's left of his defense.

He raises his sword in a stance.

"Really, Eli? You expect me to believe you would be satisfied killing me with your tricks? Or wouldn't you rather kill me with your bare hands?" *"I can do as I wish,"* Eli admits as he gradually lands and closes his wings into… wherever they go.

They just seem to disappear and reappear out of thin air on Eli's command.

"But yes. It would be more satisfying to watch what little light is left leave your eyes."

Marshall smirks. "Let's not compare visions."

"…Because yours will end here!"

Marshall raises his sword to defend Eli's strikes that push him across the terrain. Eli then leaps back. He lands in a squat and springs across the terrain. He slashes as he passes Marshall, his blade scraping off the steel of the massive claymore. Eli keeps this up, darting in from different directions. He's either trying to catch Marshall off guard or make him so wayward of his surroundings to where he can't defend anymore.

Marshall spins and dances until he's back against the wall of the mountains behind us. Ollie and I keep our distance so that we're not caught in their volley of attacks. Eli rushes in and keeps Marshall pinned to the wall. He swipes viciously as Marshall does his best to keep Eli's blade from cutting him. Sparks fly from each slash. Marshall winces and flinches as he's unable to break Eli's ongoing assault.

"Come on, Son of Ivan" Eli hisses between swipes. *"Where's all that vigor? Where's that pride you hold so dear?"*

He spins in time to avoid Eli's blade as the tip pierces the mountain behind them. He tries to remove his blade to follow up on his attack, but the blade is stuck. Eli struggles to free himself. Marshall doesn't give him the opportunity. With great strength, Marshall swings. His sword digs into the mountain wall and cuts clean through the rocky face as it follows the path Marshall intended and strikes Eli in his exposed ribs.

Much like before the blade seems to slide off Eli's coat, but the weight of the blow carries the one eye fiend and frees him from his rock embedment. Eli bounces and skips for yards on yards until he finally stops. Marshall digs his sword's tip into the gravel as he uses it for a brace.

"That's two…" Marshall groans. "One strike left. Damn it, what is he made of?"

"You better make your next move count!" Eli roars as he takes off in a sprint. *"Because I'm going to kill you where you stand!"*

Eli soars like a disturbing black projectile across the terrain at Marshall. He rolls out of the way, abandoning his sword, and the demon flies straight into the mountain. The rock wall shakes on impact. More rocks tumble below. Marshall sits on one knee as he struggles to breathe. His right arm looks limp. He's in bad shape and getting worse.

Eli flies out of the crumbling mountainside. His wings spread wide as he hovers before Marshall then comes down with a strike. Marshall manages to duck under each attack, but his old body is slowing down. Eli swings and Marshall steps in. He takes the blunt force of Eli's arm as it bashes into his shoulder. Marshall takes this moment to grapple and lock Eli's arm under his. Much like Alan as he tries to rid Eli of his cursed blade. He struggles to slide the gauntlet off his wrist, but the blade is as stubborn as my body. It refuses to budge. Eli struggles against Marshall's raw strength.-

He also looks ready to spit fire again, but Marshall elbows his jaw shut. Eli spreads his wings to fly, and Marshall stomps his foot and grounds him instead. He tries using his wings to knock Marshall off, but he tucks under the bladed arm and jabs the demon in the gut.

The first punch does nothing yet strike after strike the demon grows tired of Marshall's efforts. He opens his maw again and Marshall slams his fist into Eli's chin to shut him up. The sound of breaking bones in his fist carry along with the force that lifts Eli high off his feet. His wings spread wide once more and he dives on Marshall who drops. He kicks Eli in the gut launching the winged man head over heels where he rolls across the terrain. Marshall rolls back to his feet and takes off towards his sword. Eli recovers and launches at Marshall, who grabs the hilt and rolls into a kick that sends the demon rolling like an accelerated tumbleweed across the gravel. Marshall takes up his claymore. Eli continues to roll, and Marshall takes up a quickened stride. Eli rolls on to his back and Marshall leaps. As the one-eyed man takes in the sight of the sky, all he sees is Marshall coming down with his great sword.

"Three!" Marshall screams.

He digs his claymore straight into Eli's chest, letting the weight of the sword, the force of his might, and the fall from the sky converge into his final impact. The strike is heavy with such vigor that a small pocket of the terrain sinks in under the pressure.

Eli roars and Marshall hollers. A gust of wind kicks up from the source of Marshall's strike and carries throughout the terrain in a massive spiraling vortex. Alan and Thalia stand their ground. Ollie and I cover our eyes to shield them from debris. I can barely see Marshall's head sticking out of the indent he made in the ground. Ollie and I dart to inspect the center of the pit.

We get there in time to find Marshall breathing raggedly as he pins Eli down at the bottom of the crater beneath his sword. Then, black vapor emerges from beneath Eli as he growls and struggles under the sword's weight. Marshall has done it, the demon is defeated as he evaporates taking the darkness with him. Marshall collapses, his left-hand resting on the hilt of the claymore that buries deep into the ground. Marshall is on his knees as something drips from his right arm. I'd call it blood but it's too dark.

"Marshall…" I begin, then Ollie grabs me.

"West!"

She cries and spins me. Standing only a few yards away is Eli. The black vapor rolling off his shoulders. The darkness from before must have been some sort of way to travel from one space to another. Worst of all, he's not even injured. Marshall's last strike was for nothing.

"W-what… are you?"

"I…" Eli swipes his blade across, and the vapors dissipate. *"Am tired of these games. I believe I have entertained you enough."*

Eli rushes us. Ollie and I flinch, unable to find it in us to defend ourselves. It all happens so fast. Eli slashes. The sound of steel meeting steel. I open my eyes to witness Alan and Thalia crossing their weapons as they intersect. They stand shoulder to shoulder in front of us, holding Eli back.

"Ollie!" Thalia calls back. "Get the king out of here. We'll hold him off!"

"What?" I ask, coming out of my daze.

"Her words," Alan protests.

"No…" I step forward. "I can fight…"

"You can die trying," Eli hisses, pushing back against my two remaining knights.

Alan struggles. "Just get out of here, kid! There's nothing you can do."

This is playing out too familiar. Watching them risk their lives for me, my mind returns to Rhodain. I shake my head in protest, but instead of moving forward, I'm being pulled away. Ollie has me by the arm but I rip myself free.

"No! We have to do something…"

"King West," Marshall calls from the pit.

I turn to find him crawling his way back into the fight, his sword acting as a cane as he pulls himself up.

"Go. Use the mountain pass for cover as we hold him off. You might be able to lose him in there in case we…"

"NO! Marshall you're in no condition and you only have one arm."

"I meant what I said."

His right arm dangles. His hand unable to close. Pain and sweat cloak his face. His body hangs in exhaustion. He switches his grip on his sword so that he may swing it when necessary.

"I gave my arm, but I still have my heart. I will fight until its last beat." "Don't be a fool!"

"Neither should you," Ollie says with a pained face. "This is what they swore to do. They are Grandier Knights, they will fight for you. They will fight for their king."

"Your words!" Alan grunts as he and Thalia thrust in unison and force Eli back.

He stumbles a little but remains on his feet. Alan takes up his Bo staff.

"I fight for myself, but I'll die for my kingdom."

"If that's the case," Thalia steps beside him and raises her arming sword. "I fight for my kingdom, but I'll die for my comrades."

"And I..." Marshall lifts his claymore, but it slams immediately back down as his one arm is not strong enough to support the weight. "...Will fight with my comrades but will die for my king. For honor!" *"For honor!"* Alan and Thalia cry in unison and they charge Eli.

Their weapons collide as the demon takes a step back from the weight of their combined assault. Together, Alan and Thalia slash, jab, and stab as Eli parries and defends against them. I don't want to leave, but Ollie pulls me. Marshall meets my eyes and pleads for me to go.

I hear familiar words echo in my head, *"Get out of the way, kid."*

With that, I take off with Ollie at my side and the wind at our tails as we escape into one of the many passageways ahead.

Chapter Nineteen

The Fate of the King

I can hear the battle raging on behind us. The cries of metal against metal as Ollie leads me away. We don't look back. Ollie and I head straight into the pass, kicking up pebbles as we tear and turn through the rocky trails until sure we are safe.

Ollie pants harder than me, and I punch the rock wall beside us, leaving a perfect indent to mark my rage, and disappointment.

"We shouldn't have run! We should have stayed and fought!"

"West…" Ollie pants. "He tore through all of your knights. What more could you have done? You would have died."

"Then we would have died together!" I roar as I spin towards her, my cape whipping around behind me.

"We could have gone out fighting."

"And what good would that have done?" Ollie asks standing upright. "We'd be dead and then what would stop King Richards from taking Baronune? Or did you forget that's why he's been trying to kill you?"

A small rock in the path is much easier to glare at than to face Ollie and the truth.

"This isn't about you, West," she says.

I'm not sure if this is more painful for her to admit or me to hear. "There's something about our kingdom that has piqued his interest. It was probably just coincidence that we came to him with the idea of uniting the kingdoms rather than coming to us with a full-scale attack."

There's something to that. My rage simmers as my thoughts sharpen. Ivan may have wanted Baronune, but he waited until we addressed our issues to him first before attacking. He could have ambushed us earlier if it was just about killing me. He needed something else.

"WHOOOMPFF!"

A massive explosion shakes the mountain pass. I turn to the sky and see the pale gray clouds fuse with black and red smoke.

"What's happening back there?"

Ollie takes my hand. "I don't know, but we can't go back. We have to keep forward. Maybe we can find a cave or something in case Eli tries searching overhead."

I had almost forgotten the demon could fly. Demon. Fiend. What is he? He's not human that's for sure, but he's far stronger than anyone I've seen thus far. Marshall hit him with everything he had, but Eli shook it off like it was nothing. As if it really was me that was fighting him. I glance down at my fist and then back at the rock wall I punched. I have grown, just not enough for it to matter.

We hurry off down the path of the rocky canyon, but don't find a cave. Of course, when I want to run and hide, Fate denies me the opportunity. Instead, the mountain pass shakes from another epic explosion from the battle we left behind. The trail finally spits us out into an open plain. There is nothing for miles except for a large pile of rocks a few hundred yards away, and at the top of the formation is…

"Is that a stick?" I ask and Ollie punches me in the head. *"Ow!"*

"Sword," Ollie growls. "We have been out here looking for a sword and the first thing that comes to your mind is a stick?"

I rub the back of my head. "Well… I was imagining like, I don't know. Something more like this."

I hold up my long sword and compare it to the tiny shape in the distance. Ollie holds up one of her scalpels and compares it too.

"It's a trick of perception. From this distance, it looks small, but once we get closer, I'm sure it will be something magnificent."

"I hope you're right…"

We advance on the rock formation, keeping a constant eye out for Eli. Ollie scans the sky, I survey the ground and we periodically switch. As we get closer, I glare at Ollie.

"It's a stick."

"It's not a stick!" She roars in return. "It's a… Gunto?"

I study the sword sitting on top of the rock formation. Going off the hours of studying in the castle's library and comparing it to the weapons that Slyce used, it does share a resemblance, but it's different. It looks ancient. The sheathe the blade resides in appears worn and ragged strands of cloth hanging from its hilt drift in the wind.

"Looks old."

"What do you expect?" Ollie asks. "Who knows how many others wielded this before King Xi, of course the sword looks old. West, we found it. *You* found it."

"*Hooray…*" I say unenthusiastically. "It looks *so* worth the lives lost to get it."

"Just get the damn sword."

"And do what?" I shout, throwing my hands up in protest.

"My knights are dead. Everyone that's been with us on the task to unite the kingdoms has died, and I'm looking at an antique like that's supposed to prove or solve anything!"

"West…" Ollie looks like it's taking everything in her Divinity to restrain from attacking me.

"If you don't get up there and claim that sword, I'm going to take my scalpel and…"

I don't let her finish. I keep my opinions to myself and begin to climb the rock formation. It's just hundreds and hundreds of gray oval stones stacked on top of each other. I have a bit of trouble climbing because every other step sends more and more rocks sliding back down to greet Ollie's feet.

"Be careful," she warns, more for me than herself.

"I'm trying…"

I struggle as my efforts to answer her make me lose my footing again and I slide back a few feet. Maybe if I knock over the rock formation, I can just pick up the sword from the rubble… Never mind. Knowing my luck, I'd bury the sword and Ollie will have me dig it out next.

It takes a few attempts, but I reach the top of the rocks. The sword is as long as my leg and looks even less impressive up close. I let out a sigh and grasp the hilt. All this trouble, all these sacrifices for…

"…West?"

As I pull the sword from the stones, a brisk breeze picks up, and it crumbles to dust. Only a few grains of sand remain in my hand. My jaw struggles to open as my rage makes my body quake.

"*AAAAAAAAH!*" I scream. "Are you kidding me? It's fake? It's fucking fake!?"

"West?"

Ollie's voice full of sorrow and regret. Then there's laughter. Someone's laughing, and it's not Ollie. I spin so quickly that the rocks shift under my feet and the formation gives out.

I slide as the rocks crumble and Ollie gasps. As the dust settles, I'm left partially covered in oval stones. Coughing as the debris gets into my mouth. Ollie tries her best to hurry to me, and whoever was laughing before is laughing harder now.

"West," Ollie takes my hand and lifts me to my feet. "Are you…?"

"Alright? Yes. Pissed off? Also, yes."

We climb down from what was once a rock formation and stand on the solid ground of the open plains. As the wind blow away the dust, standing at a distance, laughing outrageously to himself, is Ivan.

"Oh, bless the Gods that was priceless! I am so glad I got here in time to see the look on your face when the sword… Oh, *Gods*, when it turned to dust!"

"*You!*" I cry and he stops laughing long enough to regard my fury.

"You lied!"

"Wrong!" He suddenly becomes serious. "I didn't lie. There was, in fact, a sword waiting here for you. I just never thought you'd actually make it. Everyone else I've sent on this quest died in the lake. How did you make it through that?"

"I—"

He waves his own question away. "It doesn't matter, that was simply priceless!"

I take a step but Ollie stops me.

"Hold on," she says as she puts her hand to my chest.

Her attention is on the king.

"What was all this really about, Ivan? Why'd you send us out here if there was no sword?"

"Didn't one of those demons fill you in?" Ivan stops laughing long enough to answer. "I want you dead, boy. I want the Kingdom of Baronune for myself."

"Why?" I ask, stepping around Ollie.

"Why go through all this trouble? If you want my kingdom, why not attack us? Why not ambush us before we got to Woodsforge?"

"You want answers?" Ivan raises an eye. "So did I. Seriously how are you a king if you don't know the first thing of war? You must understand your enemy if you want an advantage. It's not like I was able to spy on the goings-on in Baronune…Baron – uuuuuune? How do you even pronounce that damn kingdom? It's such a tongue tie!"

He flicks his tongue and it reminds me of how a lizard tastes the air.

"No bother," Ivan gives up. "I'll change the name once I take over."

"You still haven't answered my question," I growl. "Why do you want Baronune?"

"Straight to the point with you, huh?" Ivan lifts one hand from beneath his massive king's cloak. Perhaps had you learned to take your time to assess the situation as I did, your knights would still be alive."

"I seem to count that you're a few demons short!" Ollie barks.

"Foolish…boy, girl. What the hell are you anyway?" He asks in return, and Ollie restrains from answering.

"Whatever, you'll be dead soon enough. But for those demons, *tch*, they'll be back. They'll return to Hellsfire and be back in my court in no time."

This doesn't make me feel any better. The vision, the nightmare I had last night creeps back into my mind. I could do without seeing any of those demons again for a lifetime, especially the jester.

Ivan claps. "Don't think I'm not impressed, I didn't think you make it past the lake let alone the demon duo of Mongo and Slyce…" Ollie growls, and I place my hand on my hilt.

He may be a king, but he's not Eli. He's just a man. In the words of Alan, he's no demon. Between Ollie and I, we should be able to take this old man. With every shift of his body, laugh, and raise of his hand I have studied him and analyzed his movements. He has no weapon, no way to defend himself.

"Oh wait," Ivan holds out his hand to stop us.

He looks concerned, as if he knows we're about to attack.

"Before you dash at me with whatever fancy moves you have, let me finish. You asked me a question, and it would be rude if I didn't get to the answer before we fight…Well, really before you die."

My hand grips tight around my sword. I want nothing more than to cut his throat and make him stop talking, but I also want to know why he's been obsessed with Baronune.

"Get on with it Ivan," I growl. "No more funny business."

"Ha!" He points at me. "You *do* have a sense of humor! Let me explain. You see, I got myself into a bit of a bind." "…Go on," I say, withdrawing my blade.

"You know your history, right? I'm sure you're well aware of the… Days of Hellsfire and the Black Dragon." He says much like he's giving a lesson.

We continue to stare at him intently. The longer he prolongs this, the more I'm eager to attack.

"Is that a yes or a no because neither one of you is easy to read…"

"Get on with it, Ivan!" Ollie snaps, and the king quivers and looks ready to run.

"Okay, okay, you win! You don't have to beat it out of me," he whimpers.

I don't blame her. If she didn't snap, I would have.

"Okay, so you know how the Black Dragon scorched everything across Eurosia and Arcasia, leaving Baronune, Woodsforge, and Dragon's Guard as the only pieces of civilization left in the world?"

"In the world?" I ask, regretting my reply immediately.

"The world, King Westley! The Continent of Imica was already ruined by the battle between the Phoenix and the Beast of the Abyss. Sprinkle some demons across the land and boom! No more Imica. That's why people fled to find other continents, other faraway lands to escape the battles. I lost Crystal's mother in the evacuation. To protect all I had left, I brought my family here, only to find out that it was not better off."

This tracks to what Marshall had told me last night. How their family fled to Arcasia in hopes to survive but the Dragon of Hellsfire was here too.

"But you defeated the dragon…" I say. "…didn't you?"

"Depends on what you mean by …*defeat*," he answers, and Ollie and I weigh heavy in disbelief.

"Did we stop the dragon and rebuilt Arcasia into what it is today? Yes. Did we kill the dragon…?"

"…You didn't kill the dragon," I assume, and Ivan looks at me as if to apologize.

"Not even close," he admits and tries to laugh it off.

"Have you ever tried to slay a dragon? It's not like how they wrote them in those old bedtime stories. The Dragon of Hellsfire was ruthless. August could withstand his flames, but he couldn't damage it. Bruno was skilled in his Martial Arts, but it wasn't enough. I even sacrificed my teeth and ate a Gorgon's Heart to try and get an edge on the beast, but I got nothing. A far more disappointing feat than you pulling that sword from the stones and…"

He starts laughing again. Ollie and I look to each other as if to ask which of us gets the first attempt to kill him.

"King Ivan!" I call and he stops laughing. "What does that have to do with Baronune? Why do you want me dead?"

"Oh, right, the point. Seriously, King Westley, you had potential to become a good king."

His mood darkens and his smile fades. I suddenly feel the need to draw my sword.

"You see, what truly happened the day the black dragon was, *defeated.* August had exhausted himself warding off the dragon's flames that will burn you even into life after. And Bruno, oh, he was a fool to think mere hand to hand combat would be enough to defeat it. That was his sword you pulled from the rocks, and you saw what was left of it. *Ashes.*

It came down to me, and though I was a knight, I was also well… a coward. I only returned because I was wrongfully assured that I had gained the advantage we needed to turn the tides on the dragon. I would have died that day if I hadn't used the one thing the Black Dragon couldn't overpower…"

"Your terrible jokes?" I ask and he gives me a slight smirk.

"No, you foolish child…" He lifts his hand and points to his head. "My *mind*, no brawn could topple such a beast. So I looked that demon in the eye, and I made a deal."

Crystal had mentioned that her father made a deal, but I had thought it to be the summoning of the demon generals to aid him in his conquest to take over Baronune. The way his words hang heavy when he says, *"Deal,"* makes me think there's something more than requesting a few demons to kill one small boy and a bunch of knights.

"…What did you do?" I ask as my hand slides from my sword.

"I wagered the souls of a few for the lives of the many."

A cold chill blows through us as the wind pick up across the plains.

"You see, it's not easy being king. You have to put others before yourself and be strong enough to make the hard decisions. I was… none of those things. That's why I ran when we assembled to confront the

Hellsfire Dragon. A creature on this continent as dangerous if not more deadly than the beast we just fled from. I only thought of what was important. Me. Then I thought about what mattered to me. My family. I couldn't abandon them again.

What kind of father would I be if I didn't do absolutely everything to make for a better world for them? I took the responsibility of sacrificing souls to Hellsfire to spare the lives residing in Arcasia. He took the deal, and our people were spared. The Black Dragon retreated back to Hellsfire, and I was named a hero—as were August and Bruno, but that's just because they were there. They had no idea of the sacrifices I made. What I did to survive."

"So…" I shake my head finding this difficult to follow. "Then why Baronune? Why try and kill me? If you only had to sacrifice a few souls…"

"Oh Gods, you are so young," King Ivan rubs his head as if I'm the irritating one on the field right now. "You, boy, girl… *Greenie*! How do you deal with him?"

Ollie smiles. "He grows on you, I find his impudence adorable when he's not giving me a headache."

"…Thanks?"

Was that supposed to be a compliment? Maybe in Ollie's world, that's probably the kindest thing she could say about me.

"Well, it's been frustrating me for days. Seriously, how hard is it to kill a teenager?" He asks gesturing frantically with his hands.

"I'm starting to get how you survived that stupid tournament of that dead king now."

"*Hey…*" I say feeling offended for both me and King Sorenson. "I thought he was your friend?"

"He was!" Ivan exclaims "But he was just as hardheaded if not worse than you."

"I find that hard to believe," Ollie admits, and I scold her.

"You didn't know him," King Ivan responds looking stricken with disappointment.

"And you don't know anything about me!" I protest and Ivan laughs but not as hysterically as before.

"Oh, I'll give you spunk but that's not going to be enough to save you, Kid King," he gives me a sadistic toothless grin that makes my skin crawl under my under armor. "You see, if you had lived long enough to be an adult, you'd understand a little more about greed. When you offer someone powerful one thing, then they push your limits and ask for more. I gave that demon some souls, and he came back and asked for more. Two became four. Four became Four Hundred! Do you have four hundred or more souls in your pocket…? I didn't think so!"

He didn't give me time to answer. Of course, I didn't, but I would have liked to have been allowed my voice in the matter.

Ivan begins stomping back and forth. He pivots sharply with each turn.

"You see, I could give him my people, but they have become my people. I have appreciated being the King of Woodsforge. I simply can't just turn away the respect I've gained… I mean, I can, and will, if necessary, but why should I when the stubborn fuck that refused to unite his kingdom with me just keeled over, and his replacement is a five-year-old idiot?"

"You just said I was a teen…"

"I know what I said!" Ivan snaps and he seems to have snapped elsewhere.

He's lost it. His eyes are manic and he breathes heavily.

"You don't get it. You're too young to understand what's at stake. If I don't keep up my end of the deal, it's back to those dark days. Arcasia is as good as gone, and your efforts to be king wouldn't have mattered anyway. Just give me your kingdom, and I'll let you live… maybe."

"No deal, just because you couldn't find a way to defeat the Black Dragon, doesn't mean there isn't away. If we just…"

"*We?* What we? I just butchered your knights. You have no *we!*" Ivan exclaims loud enough to make Ollie and I flinch.

"There is only me. Only I can satisfy this beast's hunger, and if you won't cooperate… Then I'll just have to move forward with my plan and take your life. Then there will be no one left in power to refuse me. Baronune will be mine, and I will sacrifice your people to Hellsfire!"

"Over my dead body!" I exclaim as I draw my sword.

King Ivan had been advancing on me, but stops and stares at me blankly.

"I mean… yeah, that's kind of the point, kid."

"You'll have to go through me!"

Ollie yells as she jumps in my path and flings her silver drying needles at King Ivan.

With Ollie's speed and precision, Ivan is as good as dead. Or at least he would be if he too didn't have something else up his sleeve.

With a single wave of his arm, he deflects Ollie's blades and gives his toothless grin.

"Is that the best you can do?"

Ollie growls as in one second she's in Ivan's face. I forget how fast she moves, but this isn't enough. She swipes at him with her scalpel, but Ivan blocks it. How? What is he using? What did he say not too long ago? That he ate someone's heart? Ollie swipes again and the same happens. This time I hear a sound similar to when my knights were fighting the Mountain Golems. The sound of metal scraping across solid rock.

Ollie keeps up her attack. Slash after slash, she's at least pushing Ivan back, but the king uses his forearms to block each time. Ollie uses her speed to dash off to Ivan's right and rounds a blinding kick to his face. The king catches it without budging and tosses Ollie aside. She moves. Becoming a pearly white blur with green as she darts back to Ivan's frontside and slashes at his face. Ivan deflects Ollie's attack again, turning her into a spinning blur as she leaps to gain distance.

"Extend!"

Ollie yells as she slashes the air, and her green blade of Divinity reaches across the gap between them. I see it. Ivan raises his right arm to defend, and I catch his hand change. It shines and mimics the reflectiveness of my armor. *Mirrogold.* His right arm has become

Mirrogold, and he blocks Ollie's attack with ease. Ollie is left in astonishment, as am I.

"I see you've trained with the assassins of Dragon's Guard. Very good, but you forget. I was there when they were reassembled. I am aware of their speed, power, and techniques."

His hand returns to normal.

"Though the magic is a nice touch. Nice way to make up for your lack of strength. There's no weight behind any of those blows. It's as if you're not whole. Not quite complete. Just somewhere, in between."

"I'll show you…!" Ollie yells and blink, she's gone. "…Not to underestimate me!"

With her *Quick-Step*, she's immediately in Ivan's face. She's glowing. Her Divinity lining her body with a faint aura.

She slashes at Ivan's throat. So fast, so direct, but so ineffective. Ivan's body immediately becomes Mirrogold, shattering Ollie's scalpels.

"Fast, but too fragile."

Ivan grabs Ollie by the arm, his grip leaves her screaming.

He pulls Ollie in and clutches a fist. I'm taken back five months to when Ollie faced Alan, and her weakness was exposed. Ivan throws a sharp punch that embeds itself into Ollie's chest.

My heart stops as Ollie's screams cease.

The wind falls silent across the plains. All I hear are cracking bones. Ollie's body flies towards me, and I fumble to catch her. Blood seeps from the corner of her mouth as her beautiful eyes that I felt so embarrassed being mesmerized by, stare absently.

"N-NOOOOOOOOOOOOO!"

I scream with Ollie in my arms. My eyes flood as my legs abandon me. I drop to my knees and her head hangs. My tears drop on her face. It feels like hours. It's only been minutes. I stare at Ollie expecting this to be some kind of joke. Some long-awaited retorque to get me back for all my nonsense she's endured for the last five months. This is no joke. This is real, yet someone is howling. I don't regard him, but I can see Ivan laughing his brains out.

"That was about as priceless as the Sword of Fate bullshit!" He laughs.

"Don't underestimate me, I'm an *assassin*! It doesn't matter what you are now, you're dead and I couldn't have delivered that punchline better if I had planned it! Oh wait, I *did*!"

He continues to chortle. I continue to stare into the soulless vessel that is Ollie. Why does this keep happening? Why do people I care about die? My mother... Rhodain... my knights... and now...

I lay Ollie's body down, as my endless tears rain down on her face, chin, and lips. I stare into her eyes. It's almost as if she had something else to say, something else to tell me. Even Rhodain managed that much. This... This... I feel robbed.

"Oh Gods, what are you going to do?" Ivan chuckles as he takes me in his sights.

"Are you going to waste your breath trying to bring Green Hair back? Learn to let go, the *person* is dead..."

"Ollie..."

I manage her name, but it comes out weak and in whimpers. Another loss. Another needless sacrifice, but for what? For why? I am not worth dying for. So why do people keep doing it?

"Oh, get up," Ivan says. "There's nothing you can do. I felt those ribs crack when I punctured her heart, there's no coming back from that."

I wipe away my tears and stumble back to my feet. The wind sweeps across the plains again. I watch Ollie's lavish hair whiff, and I remember her words. How she wondered how long my body would take to react, to respond, to finally break the wall I hide behind cowardly. Well no more.

I feel the air shiver through my armor and meet my skin. My fists squeeze and I feel my strength ignite as my mental wall crumbles. I see Ivan quiver, but he's a blur. Divinity acts as a screen for my vision. An orb of teal light roars around me in a fiery aura. My cape flaps in my personal funnel of wind, and my body and mind could not be more in sync.

"What…?" I hear Ivan squeal in his panic tongue.

He looks ready to retreat.

"What is this? What kind of magic is this?"

"It's not magic… it's Divinity…"

I remember what Ollie was trying to tell me all those months ago. Reminding me to free my mind and accept the Divinity around me. You're right Ollie, we choose our own fate, our decisions are what make us different, our weaknesses can become our strength. With this strength, this Divinity, I will open that door.

I will show the world just who I am. I am not a fraud or a coward. I am a thirteen-year-old boy. I am young, inexperienced, and naïve, but that is nothing to be ashamed of. It's what makes me who I am and separates me from Ivan, Susan… and Rhodain. I am King Westly Jameson of Baronune and…

"…I am a Hand of Fate!" I bark.

The wind, aura, and Divinity all collapse into one central point drawn into my fist. I want to hit him. *Reach him*, my mind and body speak in unison as I throw a vicious punch. The sharp wind and Divinity spiral into a singular beam of light that Ivan is not prepared to block. I nail him dead in the gut and my divine punch carries him several yards across the empty plains.

Nothing fatal, but I still hurt him. He hugs his stomach and gets to his feet while I guard Ollie's body.

"You think you've won?" He gasps. "You think this is over? This isn't over, King Jameson. This is war!"

"Then bring it," I glare, and the wind dies down.

My Divine aura continues to blaze around me. I've become my own beacon of strength.

"Rally your demons, call upon your forces. I will meet your army with mine if that's what you want Ivan, but as my best friend said, you will not underestimate me. We will settle this as kings… if you even know what that word means."

"K-Kendra…"

He struggles as his stomach seems to ache more and more. My mind flashes back to when Elkrin threw that stone through the trees. Looks like I did more harm than either one of us expected.

From behind Ivan appears another black hole. Dark vapors seep across him as his Black Knights steps forward to grab and pull him into a void that they disappear into. The black hole closes behind him, and I am left all alone. My strength leaves me. My aura fades, and I drop back to my knees, lingering over Ollie's body as the wind returns.

Chapter Twenty

On the Path to War

I remember the cold, though I don't know how long I stayed there watching over Ollie. There was a golden flash, a gentle hand, and then I was pulled away into a blinding light much like what I saw the night of the jester's attack.

I lay in my bed staring up at my chamber's ceiling back in Baronune. The return was brief considering it was Avery who transported me. He has some kind of Divinity over light. Returning to my castle, I immediately ordered Avery to retrieve Ollie's body. My maidens rushed me off to rest. I don't know if he went back. I don't even know how he knew where I was to begin with. I glance at my hand. I had somehow tapped into my Divinity, the abilities gifted to me from becoming a Hand of Fate. I used it to strike Ivan where it hurt, but I don't know if I did enough. I do know he got away like the coward he is. He wants to start a war between our kingdoms.

He killed Ollie, my best friend. Regardless of where things go from here, regardless of the state of our kingdoms after. He will pay.

I'm not sure how much time has passed since my return. Once my maidens laid me in my bed I didn't move. I still wear my armor. At best, my sword sits by my side. I've been stewing in my rage all day. I should have known from the start that I couldn't trust Ivan. He had lied and played tricks on me from the jump. I was so focused on the needs of my kingdom, so blinded by my goals that I didn't see the demon before me, and I'm not talking about Eli. I recognized his murderous aura but opted to ignore it for my task. The two of them, Ivan and Eli, the two monsters that I couldn't overcome. The two beings that took everything from me, my friend, my knights, my honor. How can I face my people now? How can I continue to be the king? I failed. I utterly failed and lost everything that is important to me. Next, I'll lose the kingdom.

I roll over facing the door, my wardrobe, and my sword. Maybe I should hand over Baronune? I'm not fit to rule. I never wanted this; I didn't ask to be king. I roll back over on my back and stare up at the ceiling. I can't do that either. If I give up, if I run away from this, I'll be no better than Ivan. It's because of his fears that he's in the situation he's in. He didn't save anyone, just temporarily halted it.

He's a fraud, a coward, and it makes sense what that jester was saying to Crystal that night. I thought he was talking about me, but he was referring to Ivan the whole time. Now he wants to take my kingdom to continue masquerading as a hero. I can't help but let out a joyless laugh. Once the truth is out there, no one will follow him.

I sit up and roll my feet over the edge of my bed. I can't give up, someone must stop Ivan, or he'll sacrifice every soul in Arcasia. I have to face him. I can't guarantee that I can beat him, but I can't sit here and let him continue to rule under false pretenses.

There's a knock at my door.

"My king," one of my maidens calls to me. "Are you alright?" "I am…" I answer weakly.

I haven't spoken since my order of Avery to retrieve Ollie's body.

"Is Avery back? Did he do what I told him to do?"

"Yes, my king," she replies. "He returned and we placed Ollie's body in the medical chambers to keep him on ice until the… until the burial." "…Thank you," I say letting the thought of burying Ollie sink in.

"I'll be down in a moment to help."

"Well, my king, that's why I am here. You are requested in the Meeting Chamber."

She didn't say it, but I knew what she meant. I am wanted by Terry to discuss the next step as we prepare for war.

I grab my sword and strap it back to my waist then exit my chambers and follow my maiden to the Meeting Chamber. She opens the door and my eyes widen at my surprise to see who all sits at the table. They immediately fall on Alan and Thalia, they're *alive*. Alan's head is heavily bandaged and his left arm is secured in a brace. Aside from that, he's fine. Angry, annoyed, but fine.

Thalia isn't as banged up, but she winces whenever she moves. Marshall is here too? He's looked better, but his right arm is strung up to a wooden device that limits his movement and use.

Beside him are Nessa and Junah. They look in the best shape, probably due to their lack of fighting. Junah's ears are covered with bandage muffs, but he's alive. Nessa looks the most uncomfortable. It must be hard on her, being a nurse and a fairy with the gift to heal, and yet, her comrades are all in such a poor state. I'm glad that they're alive though. Surprised that they made it out of their battle with Eli, but glad.

Before I can take in the rest of the chamber, someone rushes me from around the table and hugs me. Sophia nearly tackles me out the door, but I find my footing.

"Oh Gods, thank you!" she screams. "You're alive!"

"Sophia?" I ask getting a chance to take in the rest of the chamber as I hug her.

One long room with a single wooden table to fill it. No windows. Just cold stone walls surround us and ruby red pennants with the Baronune symbol, the outline of a Baron Yak's face and horns stitched in gold, hang from the ceiling. Next to my chair at the head of the table stand Terry and my Aunt Janis.

"What are you…?"

"Your family was adamant about seeing you after they heard everyone returned from Woodsforge abruptly," Terry explains.

"Everyone?" I ask letting Sophia go.

She doesn't release me as easily. "Everyone that survived."

Alan groans and glares at me with his one good eye. I accept his harshness. I know who he's referring to. When we set off on the task to unite the kingdoms there were twenty-two of us in total. Only six returned alive. I nod and remove Sophia from her embrace of me. I walk around the table to my aunt, she reminds me of my mother. I hug her.

"I swear," she hugs me tighter. "Every time I let you out of my sight, you nearly die."

"Well…" She's not wrong, but I don't tell her that and I definitely don't want to mention this to my uncle.

"None of us could have predicted this."

"I apologize, my king," Terry bows. "I should have been there beside you… I could have—"

"What could you have done?" Alan asks. "King Richards has an odd assortment of demons in his ranks. We were outmatched through and through. It's a miracle we made it out alive."

"You're welcome," a little voice calls out from the corner of the chamber I completely overlooked because Sophia distracted me.

Standing off to the side of the entrance were two knights in bulky armor that conceals their faces and other features, but I recognize them and that voice to belong to Nova. The taller knight is Avery.

"And the only miracle is that Avery convinced me to go along and help. We had no business being there, but he had this odd feeling that you were about to get yourselves killed."

"Honestly," Avery shifts uncomfortably. "It was my doubts that the king would survive that had me worried. We already had to save him once, I felt we'd have to do it again. And I was *right*."

He practically sings that last word. I fight from my aunt's embrace.

"Thank you, Nova and Avery," I bow to them. "Your services are most appreciated. If not for you—"

"We'd be dead," Alan interrupts. "Can we get on with it? What are we going to do about King Richards?"

"Alan…"

Thalia puts her hand on his wrist, but he quickly moves it away. They both wince from their efforts and pain.

"What he means is, what's our next move?"

"Before we get to that," I turn to my aunt. "Where's Uncle Lester?"

"Your Uncle is on the way, my king," Terry stands proper with his hands cupped before his waist.

"It will be a few more hours before he arrives, but your aunt was adamant that he be fetched to see you safe."

"Thank you," I smile slightly. "Aunt Janis, everything will be alright now. I'm home, I'm safe, but I have to fulfill my duties and speak with my court."

"Right, king stuff. I swear I'll never get used to that."

"I appreciate you being here, but I'll come see you and Sophia after we're done and catch you all up once Uncle Lester arrives."

"Okay,"

She agrees and hugs me once more then bids me farewell with Sophia. I take my seat at the head of the table, tapping my finger as I take in my court with the addition of Nova and Avery. I don't know why they're staying, but I'm not going to ask them to leave. I owe them my life and the lives of everyone present.

"I want to open with properly thanking Nova and Avery for saving us."

"You're welcome," Avery says, and I can almost see his smile beam through his helmet.

"Just don't go making it a habit," Nova growls.

I can sense the relation she has to Rhodain as she crosses her arms.

"My king," Marshall struggles to speak.

It's as if everything is pain for him. Nessa goes to put her hand on his arm but hesitates, reading that the device he's strung up to is a reminder of *'do not touch.'*

"What happened after you left? Why is the Second Grand Advisor…"

I take a long sigh and relay everything that took place after Ollie and I parted from the battlefield with Eli, how we navigated through the winding pass and found where the Sword of Fate resided.

When I revealed that the sword was fake, Nova laughed. Everyone turned to her, but she didn't apologize. I continue to explain how it was all a set up by Ivan to have me killed along the way, but when I reveal Ivan's motives…

"Are you fucking serious?" Alan slams his hand on the table.

He winces in pain, as does Thalia as she jumps, startled.

He points at Marshall. "Your dad is an asshole!"

Marshall sighs. "You don't have to tell me."

"Yeah, but you could have told *us.*"

Thalia tries to calm him down but it doesn't work.

"No, no, no, we almost died for this asshole," he points to me, and then back to Marshall.

"Because his old man decided to go make a deal with some demon dragon thing to what exactly? Spare us or just wait until our souls were ripe enough to reap?"

"I didn't know the exact details of my father's deal," Marshall's voice rises to meet Alan since he can't physically get up himself.

"I just knew that he wanted to unite with Baronune for… some nefarious reason, that's why I couldn't support him anymore."

"You shouldn't have supported him *period,*" Alan sits back down.

"What was that last-minute hoorah you did? Where was that strength the entire time we were fighting those demons? You could have saved us a lot of time and knights! Or are we forgetting those that we lost while you were, what? Waiting for your moment to shine?"

"That's partially me to blame," Nessa timidly raises her hand. Marshall tries to argue but as he attempts to turn to her, his body rejects every ounce of his movement, and he remains in place.

"I had no idea about Marshall's previous injury. I used a lot of my Divinity to reverse that cursed scar. Even Elkrin's forest only gave me so much strength. Had I known sooner, I could have been working on healing him from the start."

"That's not your fault, Nessa," Marshall argues.

"I chose to keep this to myself. I didn't tell anyone about my cursed scar. Once I discovered Nessa's secret, she worked diligently to heal my arm. Had we more time…"

"But you couldn't have mentioned the demons in your father's court?" Alan growls through his teeth and Marshall meets his eye with a glare.

"I didn't know his allegiance to the demons. I was just as lost as you were. My father is a liar and a trickster. He fooled me, he fooled us, and he's been fooling all of Arcasia for years. He is not to be underestimated."

"That's for damn sure," Alan sits back. "So does anyone else have any tricks that they're not telling us? Fairy Girl? Loudmouth? Our Royal Hand of Fate? What even is that?"

He asks, looking at me to respond, but I remain silent.

Thalia speaks up. "That's not what's important right now, we need to focus on what we do next. King Richards wants our kingdom so he can sacrifice our people to feed souls to the… the Black Dragon. How do we beat *that*? How do we beat a man with demons in his ranks?"

"Well for one, my father doesn't have that many in his ranks to back," Marshall admits.

"This is probably why he's using the demons to begin with. Two, our forces are limited, stretched too thin providing security throughout the kingdom. We manage the few we had on this task and lost all of them. With the rest in the dungeons for conspiring with the former Queen, we're shorthanded. If King Richards attacked, we'd be outmatched. He'll take Baronune easily."

"No, I doubt that." Nova speaks up and our attention falls on her.

"When Avery and I arrived and saved you all. You're welcome, no need to thank us again. We got a taste of what we're up against. Eli wasn't using his full strength. I don't know why, but it didn't take much for us to match him. So that leaves me to believe that he wasn't expecting us…"

"That's because you weren't there at the beginning," Terry interjects. "That first test with the Mountain Golems was King Ivan's way to size up his opponent and recognize the threat they provided. Seeing how little they faired against those monsters and how two knights were lost already, he didn't see the need to go all out against the forces King Westley had for protection. While he surely wasn't expecting you to squeak by the other demons, Eli surely didn't see you guys on his level.

Even Marshall on his best day probably wouldn't have been a match. When Nova and Avery arrived with their mastery in the Mystic Arts, the scale tipped into their favor. When King Westley single-handedly knocked King Ivan back, they knew they had to regroup. That may take some time, it may take no time at all, but next time… They'll be ready for us."

"So, we need to tip the scale again," Alan admits having calmed down. "Any suggestions?"

"How about Dragon's Guard?" Nessa asks.

"Any suggestions that are feasible?" Alan says and Nessa makes a disapproving noise.

"I'm serious, I lived there. We lived there," She gestures between herself, Avery, and Nova.

"Dragon's Guard has more than enough forces to back us if Woodsforge attacks."

"They're not going to attack us here," Terry says. "King Ivan needs to be sure Baronune stays intact so he has souls to offer up once he takes it…" All eyes fall on Terry and he becomes uncomfortable.

"…*If.* If he takes it. He won't risk the people being caught up in the battle, but Nessa has a point."

The mood shifts, and Nessa sits a little more proudly.

"Our plan to unite with Woodsforge was because we eliminated Dragon's Guard as an option knowing King Westley would look more respectable having successfully united with King Richards. Now, with all that we know, we stand a better chance of having King Xi open his gates and uniting with us. Plus, King Westley is owed an audience with him, so that will at least get us through."

"Yeah, but once we're there we're back at square one," Alan says. "Asking another kingdom for help because our king is an incompetent child."

Alan glances at me again but still I do not respond.

"So, we try our hand at uniting with Dragon's Guard," Thalia says. "Okay, does anyone know the way? Without an invite, we'll never get through those woods. The Guardian Forest is supposed to be enchanted as a line of defense against intruders."

"We'll extend an invitation," Terry says.

"You risk that getting intercepted by King Richards," says Marshall.

"Then we go on foot," Nessa says. "We'll have to hope that the forest won't reject us and treat us as enemies."

"Can't you get us in?" Alan asks. "You're a fairy, right? Don't you get a special passage?"

"No…" Nessa lets her head hang from her shoulders. "Since I gave up my wings, my Divinity won't be enough to get us through the forest."

The room falls silent with this. I admit. I was hoping that Dragon's Guard would hold the answer. I thought all their stories of magic and enchantments were just that, stories, but with everything that's transpired over the past five months. I'm willing to believe anything.

"Fine…" Nova speaks, and everyone turns to her and Avery. "We'll lead you through the forest."

"You can do that?" I ask.

"Avery can," she points back to him. "He's fumbled his way around that forest for years. I'm confident he'll find a way."

"Wow Nova," Avery leans in. "I didn't know you had that much confidence in me."

"I don't," she replies coldly.

"I said you could find *a* way, whether or not that will be a direct path or some long roundabout way that gets us lost is more prominent."

"Fine," I say speaking up and everyone's attention turns to me as my voice is firm, strong, and blaring with authority.

"Then that's our next course of action. We'll divert our plans to unite with Woodsforge to unite with Dragon's Guard instead. Nova and Avery will lead the way. Together we will earn an audience with King Xi and explain the situation at hand. Ivan wants our kingdom; he'll have to pry it from our cold dead hands. I for one am not willing to give up without a fight. If anything has been made clear is that King Richards is not a king to admire, Ivan is not a man but a coward. Still, he is a threat. He is *our* threat, and he has thus become the fool in the end. He has made us his enemy rather than an ally. We will show him how wrong of a decision that is. We will unite our forces, we'll face his demons, and we'll take every bit of laughter from that liar's face. If Ivan wants a war. He's got one."

Everyone remains silent. No one protests. No one calls me out for portraying false confidence. They believe me, and most importantly, I believe myself. Everyone shifts to sit more formally. They sit as if in the presence of a true king.

"Alright then. Let's go kick his ass," Nova nods in my approval and everyone looks to her.

There's a long pause. We continue to stare at her expectantly and I get the sense we're making her uncomfortable. "What?"

"Well," Alan clears his throat.

You'd think I had given him goosebumps or something.

"After that speech and you stepping up there. Kind of was expecting a great reveal or something as you took off your helmet."

"Why would I take off my helmet?"

"To reveal your face or whatever," Thalia says. "It's not like we don't know what you look like, we just haven't seen you in a few months." "We were exiled," Nova says.

"Well, you're not anymore," I admit, growing curious. "I've never seen your face."

"*And?* Was that supposed to be an order or an invitation?" She asks, and I honestly can't find the words to respond.

"I don't even know you, I certainly don't owe anything to the rest of your court. If I want to show myself, I'll do it when I'm ready, so take the hint."

"I don't see how it would hurt..." Avery says.

"I've listened to you enough for today," Nova snaps and it seems to be getting more and more heated in here. "I'm leaving it on…" "What about me?" Avery asks.

"You too!" Nova says.

Terry speaks after our united silence during Nova's little outburst.

"Then I'll go ahead and get preparations in order. There are procedures and such that will take some time to get ready if we are going to war."

"The people are not going to like that after we left to unite with Woodsforge, we came back at war with them," Marshall says.

"They'll grow to understand," I admit and scoot back from the table.

I stand and everyone, but Marshall, stands with me.

"With that, I call this council to adjourn."

My court bows to me and takes their leave. Nessa and Junah help Marshall maneuver with his new medical attachments, while Nova and Avery remain.

I feel them take me in their sights as if studying me, and then after a few awkward seconds they take their leave too. I am the last to. I walk out and find Terry waiting in the hall. He looks to me as if to ask something but decides not. He gives me a nod and then parts ways down the corridor. I head in a different direction. I imagine that my Aunt Janis and Sophia will be waiting for me in the dining hall, but I do not go there. I follow a different path and take the familiar hall that leads into the dungeon and make my way through the rows and rows of cells.

"Still alive?"

I turn to Susan, the once glorious picture of the former king is shredded. She stands limp. The darkness falling on her enough to cloak her face and mask her features, but I can see her mangled blond hair drape down in a pair of bangs that remind me of wet noodles.

Her voice is strained. "Word travels fast… the mentions of your meeting with Woodsforge. I knew you'd fail. I said that you would get us all killed…"

Though I hate her. I don't have time for her today. I am not *here* for her today. I walk by her cell and into darkness. It's cold, but I know I'm in the forge. A flame spurs as Sassarus steps to me from the shadows.

"King Westley?" He asks as his smoggy hands wipe down something small and silver with a cloth.

"You've returned. Is everything alright?"

My body shudders as the memories all come flooding back at once. Tears break free from my face and meet the sand-covered floor. I say nothing as I fall into a brief run and my body sinks into his. My arms latch on to him and I bury my face into his shoulder.

I can't wait until Uncle Lester arrives, and I can't hold these emotions in anymore. No longer can I fake my strength and hide this pain. As I tell Sassarus all that's happened, I'm reminded how, with all his blacksmith skills, he has always made time for me. He has always been there to listen to me. As I bring up the loss of my knights, of Ollie, I realize it. Despite all I've loss, I still have someone. I still have him.

"There, there," Sassarus pats my back as he holds me. "There, there, Little Sparrow."